TWISTED
THREAD

TWISTED THREAD

EMMY GRAY-WINTER

Riverside Publishing Solutions

Emmy Gray-Winter asserts her moral right to be
identified as the author of this book.

Published by Emmy Gray-Winter with Riverside Publishing Solutions
www.riversidepublishingsolutions.com

Copyright © 2019 Emmy Gray-Winter

ISBN: 978-1-913012-20-5 (Paperback)

For permission requests, write to the publisher, addressed
"Attention: Permissions Coordinator," at
contact@riversidepublishingsolutions.com

Printed and bound in the UK.

To all those dyslexics who dare to dream.
"Live for today, because tomorrow
will be your yesterday."

Emmy Gray-Winter

CONTENTS

ABOUT THE AUTHOR

Emmy grew up in the home counties in the 1970's. She trained to be a nurse, midwife and health visitor in Reading. She moved with her young family to Wiltshire in 2005, to escape the rat race of life. Emmy currently works for the NHS as a clinical practice educator.

Emmy was diagnosed with dyslexia at the age of 40, having struggled for many years with the challenges of being undiagnosed, and periods of depression. It was over 10 years ago, during a period of ill health that she came up with the idea for her debut novel. With the encouragement of family, friends and colleagues, Emmy decided to take the plunge putting pen to paper, to write the novel which had been burning inside her. Thus creating her debut novel a "Twisted Thread."

CHAPTER 1

GIRL ON A BENCH

It was New Year's Day January 1994 – a day of new beginnings, resolutions and new promises, hopefulness filled the air. The previous year had been left behind, the inevitable repentance and apologies for the past year's misdemeanours now forgotten. The sky was a soft, pale blue with a crisp, bright nip in the breeze. The ground was covered with white, sparkling, icy gems glistening in the sunlight. The leaves lay, apologetic for not resisting the frost which had enveloped the frozen branches. Cars, park railings, lamp posts and trees stood clothed in the previous night's dusting of snow.

It all looked so perfect, so beautiful. But it wasn't...

A publican walked his two Jack Russells through the streets and on into the park in the early morning. He was thinking about the work he needed to do back at the pub, clearing up after last night's party; more New Year well-wishers would be coming in later. He had a lot to do. But all of that disappeared from his mind when his dogs barked at the body lying frozen on the park bench.

He dialled 999, his hands shaking.

"Emergency. Which service do you require?"

"Police."

He wondered whether he should have said ambulance, but she looked dead, so there wasn't much point, and he wasn't about to touch her to find out.

"Police. What's your emergency?"

"There's a body in the park. A woman."

"Is she breathing?"

"No mate, I don't think so. She's covered in snow. Must have been here all night."

"Are there any signs of foul play?"

He looked at her, even though he didn't want to.

"Dunno. She's got a big coat on. Mind you, she hasn't got any shoes on. That's a bit weird, ain't it?"

"Okay. Stand by, please. I'm sending a car. Can you confirm the address of the park, please?"

He told the operator the location and stood waiting in the cold, trying to keep his dogs under control. They wanted to carry on with their walk, but he didn't feel right, leaving the poor woman there on her own.

What he hadn't said on the phone was that he recognised her. She'd been in his pub last night. But should he tell the police or not?

The stillness of the early morning air was broken by the screaming of a siren. Moments later, two plain-clothed police officers, a man and a woman, approached, and crouched down to examine the body.

She lay shrouded in a coarse duffel coat, curled in a foetal position on the park bench. Her bare feet blue with cold, poked out from the bottom of her coat. She appeared motionless, tangled hair covered her face; gloveless hands gripped the hood around her head to keep out the bitter chill. The publican stood by the bench with his two dogs who were barking at the newcomers.

The male officer gently rocked the body, noticing how cold and frozen the coat felt through his black leather gloves.

"Hello, can I help you?" he said. He looked up at his partner. "She's really cold..."

He leant forwards and listened for breathing.

"I can hear breathing, it's really shallow but she's alive," he smiled.

The police woman then approached the girl.

"Come on, sweetheart, you've gotta get up, you can't stay here." She gently stroked the girl's face. She could smell alcohol on her breath. "Did you have one too many last night?" she asked jokingly. She surveyed the area. "Where's your handbag and shoes?"

"She had them last night at the pub, I'm sure of it." said the man with the dogs.

"Do you know her?"

"No. I just saw her in the pub last night."

"Did you see her leave the pub?" the female officer asked.

"No, sorry love, it was so busy." He rubbed his stubbly grey chin.

The male officer kept trying to gain a response from the girl.

"Can you open your eyes?" he asked her.

"I think she's in a really bad way, Phil," said his colleague. "We'd better call an ambulance. I'll go back to the car and get a blanket."

"Alright, good idea, be quick."

The men stood watching as she spoke into her two-way radio, while walking briskly back to the police car.

"Control, this is DC Andrea Doyle, can we have an ambulance to Brockwell Park Gardens, Trinity Rise entrance, please?"

The radio crackled as the control room operator responded. "What's the situation, Andrea?"

"We have a white female, approximately 30 years old, collapsed on a park bench. She's unconscious, very shallow breathing, possibly suffering from hypothermia."

She unlocked the car and grabbed a survival blanket from the boot.

"Does the casualty have any injuries?"

"Any injuries, Phil?" she called out, as she jogged back from the car with the blanket.

Phil took off his gloves and did a quick survey of the girl. He moved the hood of her coat aside and saw the congealed blood on the back of her head.

"Looks like a head injury," he replied.

"Hello, operator, it looks like the casualty has a head injury, she's in a pretty bad way."

"Thank you. ETA of the ambulance is approximately 6 minutes."

"They're on their way, Phil," she said as she reached them. "Should be six minutes."

"Super; right, let's get you wrapped up until the ambulance arrives," he said to the unconscious girl. He wrapped the survival blanket around her.

The casualty was now incredibly pale and had started to shiver uncontrollably. Her breathing was still very slow and shallow. Phil checked her pulse.

"It's barely there...She's really bad. I hope they hurry up."

Andrea looked at Phil, raising her eyebrows as if to tell him to shut up. He stood up, tucking the blanket around the girl more securely.

As he turned to address the witness who'd called in, he recognised him. "Trevor Arnold!" he exclaimed.

"Phil? Sorry, mate, I didn't recognise you out of uniform."

"I don't suppose you would, Trev, but I'm a DS now."

Trevor, the publican, nodded approvingly, looking Phil up and down in his dark trench coat.

"Mr Arnold runs The Prince Regent, Andrea."

She nodded as she started to make notes.

"So, what can you tell me, Trev?" asked Phil.

"Like I said, she came in last night, but I'd never seen her before then. I found her here on the bench when I brought the dogs out this morning. I thought she was dead. I'd have called an ambulance otherwise."

"No, well thanks for calling it in. We'll take it from here. I'll be in touch about taking your statement, probably later today."

"Right you are, Phil." Trevor turned back up the path towards the direction of the pub. The two dogs pulled him into the park, but Trevor snatched at their leads forcing them to take another route. The dogs dropped their ears disappointed, muzzles down as they reluctantly returned to the pub.

By now, more people were in the park walking their dogs, all getting a load of what was going on. Judgemental looks were thrown in the direction of the prone woman, assuming that she was yet another drunk who'd gone out the night before and got wasted.

Andrea shook her head. "It's incredible the human mind, isn't it?" she muttered to Phil. "They're all so high and mighty when everything's going right in their lives. But they can't possibly choose to walk in the shoes of someone else. It really riles me." She felt incredibly protective towards the injured woman and tried to shield her from intrusive glances.

"There's nothing to see here, ladies and gentlemen. Unless any of you know the casualty or are medically trained, please move on."

This was why Andrea had become a police officer – to care for the most vulnerable in society.

Whilst the two officers cared for the girl awaiting the arrival of the ambulance, the world bustled by them. Men in heavy overcoats and thick woolly hats; their gloved hands holding onto their loved ones. Women walked by, chatting and laughing on their phones, sharing New Year's greetings. Children rode by on their Christmas gifts, weaving in and out of pedestrians. Dads could be seen holding onto the backs of their seats, hesitant about whether to release the bike on its first unstabilised journey.

It all seemed so idyllic, but it really wasn't as here lay a young woman, alone and completely broken. It was such a sad scene when the only two people in this whole world who cared about her were the two police officers attending to her. What had led her to this point?

CHAPTER 2

KINGS COLLEGE HOSPITAL

Detective Sergeant Phil Lewis and Detective Constable Andrea Doyle watched the paramedics as they loaded the girl into the back of the ambulance. The heavy doors slammed as they climbed into the awaiting black BMW.

"Control, this is DS Lewis at Brockwell Gardens, Brixton, can you show that DS Lewis and DC Andrea Doyle are attending Kings College Hospital regarding the women who was found this morning. The woman has a head injury, we couldn't find her shoes or handbag, so we suspect that it's an assault." The two way radio crackled, and a women operator's voice replied.

"Do you require a scene of crime officer at the park DS Lewis?"

"There isn't much point, as there doesn't appear to have been a struggle. It's been snowing overnight and lots of people have been in the park. I think there will be too much disturbance and the whole area will be contaminated."

"So, you are not requiring SOCO at the present, is that correct?"

"Yes, I can confirm that SOCO is not required."

"DC Doyle and myself are accompanying the ambulance to Kings."

The ambulance arrived at Kings College Hospital accident and emergency department. The doors clattered open and the trolley holding the casualty was wheeled through the sliding entrance doors. The crew took her immediately to the resuscitation area, where a team had been awaiting her arrival.

The paramedic handed over her care to the A&E staff.

"We have an unconscious female, approximately 30 years old, found in a park in Brixton by a local resident. She may have been there all night. She has a Glasgow coma scale of six. There's an injury to the back of her head with a small laceration which we've cleaned and dressed. She is maintaining her own airway; pupils are equal and reactive. There's no ID on her. The police are attending and will want to speak to you as soon as possible."

"Thank you. We'll take it from here," replied the small, balding doctor.

An oxygen saturation probe was placed on the patient's finger, and the team began to record their observations.

"I think it's quite possible she will be severely dehydrated. Let's face it she has been outside all night. And had a skin full last night that wouldn't have helped. I would suggest that we put in a drip of 1000mls saline and do some bloods to see what we're up against? What are her obs like?"

"Definite Hypothermia, temp of thirty-four degrees," replied the nurse. "Pulse, forty beats a minute and slow, shallow breathing."

"Okay, let's warm her up slowly and then get an X-ray of her skull and see what injuries she has sustained." He squeezed her hand, tapping the veins.

One of the receptionists approached the cubicle where they were working. "The police are here; they want to know whether you think she's been attacked".

"The police will have to wait," the doctor snapped. "Our priority is to get her stable."

"Okay, I'll let them know," the receptionist replied.

"I'll speak to the police once she is stable," he called after her as he inserted the cannula into the back of the patient's hand and took some samples of blood.

"Let's get a drug and alcohol screen, full blood count, U and Es, etc, etc..." He handed the nurse the samples and connected up the drip.

"So, she has no ID. What else do we know that will help the police with who she is?"

"Well, she was found in a park by a local, she's well-dressed in a warm coat, her fingernails are cut and recently polished, and she's all dressed up for an evening out in her little black dress. Her stockings are snagged, make-up smudged. Her hair's a bit matted from the trauma to her head but she obviously cares for herself. Definitely not a homeless person." He checked over her body, looking up and down her arms.

"Shall, we get these wet clothes off her, as that won't help the hypothermia."

"Yes, okay...on your count. 1...2...3..."

The nurses rolled her onto her side and the doctor undid the long metallic zip that ran the length of her dress, making it flop forward.

"Oh!" The nurse gasped, as she saw the girl's chest.

"What?"

"Oh dear, look, there are some nasty marks on her chest."

They rolled the patient onto her back.

"Oh, they do look nasty!"

"What are they?"

The doctor looked closer, touching the marks with his gloved fingers. He looked at his colleagues, eyebrows furrowed.

"They're bite marks. Look, they're all over her collarbone. It appears someone has been abusing her."

The nurse removed the dress sliding in over her slim hips to expose her laddered tights.

He then continued to examine her body for any other clues as to what had happened to the girl.

"There are no signs of intravenous drug use, no wedding ring, no shoes, no handbag. She has a head injury and she's unconscious."

He took a deep breath and looked at the nurse "Of course we need to examine her for evidence of rape." They lowered her tights and removed them putting them into a bag, followed by her knickers. "Going by the bruising on the inside of her thighs, it looks as though her legs have been forced apart. It isn't new, maybe a week old. I would like the crime scene photographer to come and take photographs and the police doctor to be informed. Can we get onto that?"

"Of course, straight away."

"What else have we got to help us?" He scanned the woman.

The nurse looked at the clothes discarded on the dressing trolley and picked up the dark coat.

"Well, only her clothes, doctor, including this coat; which looks too big for her."

"Is there anything in her coat pockets that could help us find out who she is?"

The nurse picked up the black duffel coat and rummaged through the pockets.

"There's nothing in here, apart from this old receipt. It's dated May. That's..." she paused, counting up in her head "...eight months ago."

"Where's the receipt from?"

The nurse looked hard at the printed receipt" Hmm, it's not clear, but it's – oh, I'm not sure!" She took it over to a light to examine it more closely. "It looks like it's in French. It's quite faded". She paused looking more closely. "Yes, I can make it out now; it's from a boulangerie in Paris."

"Right, so, do we think the girl is French, then?"

"Well, maybe. Or she could have gone on holiday to France?"

"But May would have been the wrong time of year to wear a thick coat in Paris," he pointed out.

"You're right, Dr Scott, you wouldn't." The nurse took the coat and looked at it "and come to think of it, it's not really a ladies' coat" she checked the label. "It's a large, made by someone called APC, Paris".

"I've never heard of them, but it certainly looks expensive. But it would be if it's from Paris." Dr Scott remarked.

"So, she's wearing a man's coat, not her husband's, as she's hasn't got a ring – but maybe a boyfriend's coat?"

"Either that, or it's from a charity shop," he suggested.

"You wouldn't buy an oversize men's coat from a charity shop. Perhaps it's a French couple living here."

"But where is he?"

"No idea!" She thought for a moment. "Perhaps the police could use the coat to find him."

"And…?"

"We'd find out who she is."

"You don't truly think that the police will be able to find the boyfriend through a coat."

"Why not? They're pretty good at that sort of thing."

"Really?" He rolled his eyes. "Well, right now, Miss Marple, we need to get on with our jobs and leave the police work for the police".

"Well, I think we should give it to the police. I'm sure they could use it as evidence."

The receptionist came back into the resuscitation room with a hospital porter.

"They're ready for you in X-ray," she said, "the porter is here to take her round."

***

DS Phil Lewis and DC Andrea Doyle waited at the hospital to speak to Dr Scott. A few moments later the door opened and the nurse left with the porter who was wheeling the girl on the trolley, the doctor followed them out.

"Thank you for waiting." He guided them both back into the room and closed the door behind them. "I have sent her for a head X-ray to ascertain the extent of the injury. It appears there have been signs of abuse. I'd like you to contact your police doctor and crime scene photographer to establish whether she's been raped."

"We can certainly do that for you right away. DC Doyle, could you contact the station and ask for the duty police surgeon and photographer? They need to come as soon as possible as we need to collect evidence of an alleged assault."

"Certainly Sarge, anything else?" DC Doyle looked from the doctor to DS Lewis.

"No that will be all for the moment."

***

DC Doyle left the hospital and returned to the BMW sat in the forecourt of A&E. She pressed the button on the two-way radio. It crackled and hissed.

"Bloody thing," she muttered hitting it hard. She turned the knob. Surely it wasn't dead.? She sighed and rummaged around in the car trying to find the back up, but to no avail.

"Oh, sod it" she put her hand inside her jacket pocket and took out her Nokia mobile phone. She looked at the screen; at least it had a signal and a battery. She pressed in the number purposefully.

"01...71" she muttered, punching in the remaining numbers. "Hi, its Andrea here, is DI Jeffordson about?"

"Hello Sir, I'm currently still at Kings College with DS Lewis, the doctor in A&E is requesting a police surgeon and a CSI photographer. This is for the girl who was found in the park. He suspects sexual assault." DC Doyle paused, listening intently to her superior officer.

"Is the girl conscious yet?"

"No sir,"

"Well, you won't be able to take any samples without her consent. But you can bag all her clothes, and have the photographs taken. Contact me as soon as she wakes up and we can have a police surgeon straight out to you."

"Thank you, Sir."

"I'll contact the duty desk and let them know that the police surgeon will be required at some point. In the meantime, CSI will be with you shortly. Anything else they can tell us?" DI Jeffordson queried.

"She's just gone for a scan. That's all I know."

"Well, I think the best thing you can do is to stay there with her and wait for her to wake up. Understand."

"Yes Sir."

DC Doyle returned to the department back through the glass doors, in time to see the girl returning through the corridor on the metal hospital trolley, clattering its way along the shiny tiled floor.

DS Lewis, was sitting in the waiting area, thumbing through a battered 'Women's Weekly.'

"Anything interesting?" DC Doyle nodded towards the magazine.

"Just the odd knitting pattern and a recipe for mushroom risotto."

"Fancy! You didn't strike me as a Women's Weekly kind of guy, Serge."

"I'm not." He slung down the magazine, his cheeks flushing as he did. "So, what did Jeffordson say?"

"He's sending the police surgeon when she wakes up, in the meantime CSI are heading over, I have to remain here until she wakes up."

"Well, good luck with that then." DS Lewis got up from his seat.

"You are not going, are you?" she grumbled.

"Yep" he chuckled, "I'm not sitting around here waiting for her to wake up. There are lots of other things I can be getting on with to push this investigation forward. Doyle, you are not a newly qualified green horn, you can handle this. Call me as soon as she wakes up?" He grabbed her shoulder and gave it a squeeze, "Okay?"

DC Doyle felt that she had no choice. Yes, she was experienced, but there was always something unsettling about waiting for a patient to regain consciousness. What would happen if she didn't? DC Doyle took a deep gulp.

"Okay Sarge, but you'll need to give me your radio, mine's broken". DS Lewis unclipped his radio and handed it over.

"Thanks, Sarge,"

CHAPTER 3

TRAUMA WARD

DC Doyle woke up with a start. She looked around the waiting room, had she really been asleep? She wiped the side of her mouth as she felt the wet drool. Oh god, she felt sick, as the pit of her stomach rumbled. She looked at her wrist watch. It was 11.30pm. Christ alive, she must have been asleep an hour! If the Guvnor had caught her, she would have been in trouble. Quickly she got up and straightened her crumpled shirt and re-adjusted her ponytail. She paced up and down the corridor trying to pull herself together.

"You alright love?" a northern voiced asked her.

DC Doyle looked around to see a very tall skinny blonde nurse walking towards her.

"Yeah, yeah. I'm fine."

"You look shattered, fancy a tea and a nice slice of Jamaica ginger?"

"Lovely..."

"The girls waking up, you know."

"Is she?" DC Doyle's eyes widened.

"Yes," She smiled "Were not quite ready for you yet. But I'll be getting you that drink and we'll call you when we're ready."

"Okay, thanks" DC Doyle smoothed back her thick dark fringe. "Will she stay here all night?"

"Oh no...We'll transfer her to the trauma ward upstairs when the bed is ready for her, now sit yourself down and I'll bring the tea out."

"Thank you." DC Doyle paced up and down and had the odd furtive look through the slats of the resuscitation area door, but all she could make out was movement. She sat back down in the seat and took out the two-way radio she'd exchanged with DS Lewis. She switched it on and spoke into the mic. DS Lewis picked up the call immediately.

"It's me, Guv, the girl's awake. She's going to be transferred to the trauma ward."

"That's good. Any sign of CSI at all."

"Yes, Sir they've been and gone."

"Okay, I'll call the police surgeon. I think its Dr Bowen on tonight. We'll meet you there."

By the time DS Lewis and Dr Bowen arrived at Kings College the girl had been transferred to the trauma ward. As they approached the ward, he saw DC Doyle waiting outside for him.

"I thought I would wait for you Guv, there is quite a commotion and the staff are dealing with it."

"Anything that we can help with?"

"I don't think so; they seem to be in control."

As the two police officers with the police doctor approached the nurses' station it was clear there was quite an uproar at the other end of the corridor.

DS Lewis and DC Doyle, showed their warrant cards. "We're here with Dr Bowen our Police surgeon in relation to the young woman found this morning with a head injury."

The receptionist nodded, pointing down the ward. "Can you hang on for a few minutes?" she asked. "That's her screaming. They're trying to calm her down."

At the other end of the ward, the nursing staff surrounded the distressed woman's bedside as she thrashed about, trying to get out of the hospital bed.

"Get me out of here, this is the first place they'll look!" she cried in an alarmed French accent. Her staring eyes scanned around the ward. "What's happening to me?"

One of the nurses gently took hold of her arm, trying to reassure her and get her to lie down; she resisted, pushing her away.

"You don't understand! She'll find me here."

"Who will?" the nurse asked.

The patient looked around, pointing at one of the other nurses. "She will."

"She's not going to hurt you. We're here to help you, dear. Come on, let's get you settled. You've had a nasty bang to your head."

"Listen to moi!" she spat angrily pointing at her own chest. "She did it before, she'll do it again."

"A woman attacked you?" the nurse asked.

The girl scanned the room, pulling at the nurse's uniform. She was clearly muddled.

"I don't know. I can't remember," she brought her hands up to her face, wiping away the tears that ran down her face. "What happened?"

Other patients on the ward were now watching the girl as she sat sobbing, clearly confused and bewildered. The nursing staff quickly drew the curtains around the bed to prevent prying eyes.

"Can you page the on-call doctor – I think it's Dr Scott today – and tell him the girl from the park is very distressed," said the senior nurse.

"I think the best thing we can do now she's awake and stable is to move her into a side room. It will offer her more privacy and away from the rest of the ward. Can you move Mrs Parker out of her side room? She won't like it, but it's about time she got out of that room after her hip replacement. Once she's been moved, the police are here to see her. They're waiting at the nurses' station."

The other nurses immediately set to work rearranging the ward while the senior nurse reassured the girl.

Dr Scott arrived on the ward and met the waiting group from the Police.

"Anthony Bowen, Police Surgeon". Dr Bowen extended his thin hand to Dr Scott. "The officers were telling me that you saw her in A&E, and made the initial assessment of her, is that correct?"

"Pleased to meet you, Doctor" he said responding with a firm hand shake. "Sleeping Beauty is causing a scene, isn't she?" He turned to the nurse at the desk, who was busy writing.

Dr Bowen looked at the officers raising his fair eyebrows and then back to Dr Scott.

"Yes, Doctor," she replied. "She's quite upset. We could hear her screaming from here. She's convinced someone is going to attack her."

"I'm not surprised. According to her toxicity screen, she's loaded with drugs and alcohol. I'm amazed she's woken up at all. These levels could've killed her."

"So, she was seriously under the influence of drugs and alcohol?" asked DS Phil Lewis.

"Not unusual for New Year's Eve, let's face it." Dr Scott chided.

"Do you think she just got too drunk and fell over?" DS Lewis questioned.

"It's quite possible, although that doesn't explain the head injury – the head injury location is not consistent with a fall. It looks like someone hit her. Thankfully it's not serious, just a flesh wound."

"Well, that's a blessing," said DC Andrea Doyle.

"You mentioned that you believe that there may have been a sexual assault." Dr Bowen asked.

"Yes, that's correct, bruising and bite marks really."

"Okay, so DS Doyle and I'll question her and obtain what samples we can with her consent."

"Great, in view of the tox screen results, I'd like to get the psych team to assess her later after you have seen her. This isn't just a typical girl sleeping rough, who got a bit drunk and had a few drugs. It just doesn't add up. She was dressed up to go out. I believe that she was out for New Year and got attacked. But why that level of drugs?"

***

The girl sat in her hospital bed; the sheet wrapped up tightly around her as her body shook. She looked out at the snow-loaded sky, bewildered at how she'd ended up as a patient in a hospital bed. It was all vaguely familiar, the smell of the disinfectant, the noises from outside as the trolleys and wheelchairs scuttled past. She could hear the call bells ringing and the anxious voices calling for nurses. The hairs on her skin bristled and she shuddered.

She had no idea what had happened. Her feet were cold and sore. She looked down at them, noticing that they had small cuts. As she lay back against the pillows, she realised for the first time that she had an injury to her head. Her fingers threaded their way through her matted hair where she found a soft dressing.

There was a knock at the door and one of the nurses entered followed by two men and a woman that she didn't recognise. The woman seemed really pleased to see her.

"Hello, you won't know us, but we were with you at the park," said the woman. "I'm Detective Constable Andrea Doyle and this is Detective Sergeant Phil Lewis."

"No, no I don't remember," said the girl, looking confused.

"And I'm Anthony Bowen, the police doctor". Dr Bowen, took the seat in the corner of the room.

"We've come to see if you can answer some questions for us."

"I don't remember anything." The girl was bewildered.

"The doctor said you might be a bit confused. It's understandable, but there maybe a few things you might recall that could help us to build a picture of what happened to you," suggested Andrea.

"Let's try some simple things," suggested Phil. "Can you tell me your name?"

"No," she shook her head.

"Do you know when your birthday is?"

"No!"

"Where do you live?"

"I don't know."

"Do you know what you're doing in London?"

The girl shrugged her shoulders and muttered something.

"Sorry? Did you say something?" asked Andrea.

The girl frowned. "No," she said.

"You don't sound like a Londoner. Have you come from another country? Are you here on holiday?" he asked. "Or do you work here?"

"I told you, I don't know! I can't remember anything," she spat, getting angry.

"It's no good, Guv. She hasn't got any idea" said Andrea. Then, turning to the woman, she added. "Maybe it'll come back to you when you've had a rest."

The girl looked blankly around the room, trying to retrieve the information from her mind.

"I'm very sorry," she said slowly, shrugging. "But I cannot remember anything at all."

"It's okay, in the meantime, Dr Bowen would like to ask you a few questions and we would like to obtain some samples, for forensic testing".

DS Lewis, who was standing waiting patiently, gestured towards the doctor. The slight man in his fifties stepped forward.

"Yes, we need your consent to take some samples, to see if we can discover who assaulted you."

"Assaulted me!" She looked from one officer to another. "Really!?"

"Yes, maybe a sexual assault" Dr Bowen offered. "Would you be happy for us to take samples from you?"

The girl's face dropped and the tears rolled down her face, she sobbed silently. Her shoulders shuddered. Slowly she looked up at him.

"Yes, that's fine," she muttered almost inaudibly.

The doctor nodded to the two officers to indicate she'd agreed.

"Okay, so we'll get everything ready, Andrea will stay with you. Is that okay for you?"

"Yes," she replied softly.

DS Lewis and the nurse left the room and made their way back to the nurses' station.

"Do we suspect foul play?" the nurse asked Phil as they walked back down the corridor.

"Well, she's got huge levels of drugs and alcohol in her system. As they said before, going by her size, I'm surprised she's still alive."

"What sort of drugs?"

"I don't know, but I'm sure Dr Scott can enlighten us."

***

Dr Scott sat at the desk, flicking through the recent path lab reports.

"Anything?" Phil asked.

"There's no sign of IV abuse, but she has been taking a concoction of drugs – amphetamines being the main type. Going by her liver function test, it's been going on for a long time alongside alcohol abuse. She's in a bad way. We're getting her a psych referral. I believe she's really vulnerable and someone took advantage of her. She was hit from behind, probably by whoever stole her handbag. Did you find her shoes?"

"No, no sign of them."

The doctor nodded. "Maybe if you find the bag, you'll find the shoes as well. Judging by the marks on her body, I would say she's in an abusive relationship."

"That's what it looks like."

"You've got all the clothing?"

"Yes, DC Doyle has it. They're just collecting samples now."

***

DS Phil Lewis and DC Andrea Doyle headed back to Brixton to find their superior officer. Detective Inspector

Mike Jeffordson was a small, portly man with thick, grey hair parted on one side and a bushy moustache. He wore his trademark shirt, tie and jumper as he sifted through the latest files.

"Morning," he smiled brightly as the two officers entered his office, which was strewn with opened files and old half-drunk mugs of tea.

"Morning, Guv. We're trying to put the pieces together on the girl in Brixton," said Phil, opening his small, black, well-used notebook.

"What have we got so far?" DI Jeffordson inquired, folding his arms and leaning back in his chair.

Phil looked at his notebook. "We've got a female, late twenties to early thirties, found on a park bench with a head injury. She has no tattoos or distinguishing features. She is approximately 5 foot 5 inches tall, dark brown hair, green eyes, petit build. Dressed for an evening out in a black party dress. Her shoes and handbag are missing. She's suffering from amnesia. Her tox screen is back and she's full of drugs. The doc says it also looks like she has been abused."

"Any distinctive clothing?"

"She was wearing a man's coat that we've bagged with her clothes. The coat had a receipt in it from a boulangerie in France. She seems to have a connection there, but I don't know what."

"Anything else?"

"Not really, Sir." Phil looked bemused.

"She's conscious Sir, but she's really confused." Andrea added.

DI Jeffordson frowned. "No clues to who she is?" he asked.

"No, Sir. But she does sound a bit foreign," Andrea replied. "It's a real puzzle."

"Okay. Well, the first place we should go to is the Missing Persons Bureau and see if anyone has reported a woman of her description missing. The other thing we've got to think about is the media – particularly local newspapers, radio and television. The general public usually come up trumps for us. Phil, can you get hold of the Communications team so we can create a press release?"

"Yes, Sir."

"We need to arrange police protection; in case her attacker returns. Andrea can you get uniform to the hospital to stay with her. If you go back yourself, you may get some more information, she may give us a lead."

"Okay, Sir," Andrea replied as she left the office.

"Phil, have you got that coat?"

Phil handed over the grey hospital bag and DI Jeffordson took out the dark duffel coat and looked inside it. "I agree it looks like a man's coat." He rummaged around in the pocket and pulled out the receipt. He looked at it, trying to decipher the writing.

"Take this to DS Celine Clement," said the DI. "See if she can get any details on the bakery in France. In the meantime, I'll contact Missing Persons to see what they have."

"Will do, Guv. Then I'll head down to The Prince Regent and see what Trevor Arnold has to say for himself."

"Trevor Arnold? What's he up to then?"

"He's the publican who found our mystery woman on the bench."

"Did he now?" the DI replied. "We've had dealings with him before, haven't we? The name rings a bell."

He scratched his head. "Oh yes, I know Mr Arnold. I'm surprised he got a licence to run that pub. Dodgy character, not known for attacking women, though."

"No, Guv," Phil's baby-blue eyes twinkled, as he grabbed his coat. "I'll see what Trev has to say for himself."

CHAPTER 4

THE PUBLICAN'S EVIDENCE

The Prince Regent pub took up the corner plot of a row of Victorian terraces. Its red brick exterior was dull and lacked any curb appeal. It really was a local boozer, a real working-men's pub – a right spit-and-sawdust kind of place. It certainly wasn't a place a nice girl would go.

When DS Phil Lewis arrived, it was approaching lunchtime. He entered the pub and could see the regulars having a fag inside the saloon bar, putting the world to rights. He looked around for Trevor Arnold. He walked into the empty main bar, but could hear music coming from the back of the pub. He opened the door to a smoke-filled room as the afternoon's aged entertainment wiggled and giggled, stripping to her drunken punters.

"Go on, love, show us a bit more," one bloke called out as he took another long drag of his cigarette, dropping the ash onto his sheepskin coat.

The others laughed as she pranced around flirtatiously twirling her nipple tassels.

Phil was stunned by the scene unfolding in front of him. The woman was old enough to be his own mother. He picked up a coat lying across a chair and threw it at the wrinkled woman.

"Get dressed," he demanded.

"Says who?" a grumpy punter slung him a look.

"The Police! Now hop it!" Phil pulled himself up to his full 5'11" height and the punter withered into a corner.

Trevor Arnold stood up, a fag hanging out of his mouth. "Oh, come on! Can't you see we are just having a bit of light entertainment? Surely, you're not here about this, Officer?"

"No, I'm not. But you need to clean up your act if you want to keep your licence Trevor, I thought you'd stopped all this."

He shrugged. "The lads like it."

"Trev, it doesn't matter what your customers want, you can't do it. You're playing with fire, mate. Your licence doesn't cover you for live entertainment. You need to get rid of the girls," he looked over to the older woman, slipping on her jeans and sweater. "If you can call them that."

The stripper glared at him. Trev shrugged and muttered to his punters that it was time to go.

"Where's me money?" asked the woman, holding out her hand.

"I'll see you later," he said, looking sideways at the officer.

"Well, make sure you do," she snapped, picking her up bag and coat and stalking out.

The show over, the disappointed punters dispersed.

"So, now you've ruined my business for the day, what you here for, Phil?"

"It's about that girl you found on the park bench."

"Is she okay? She ain't dead is she?"

"No. She's still alive," said Phil, his eyes narrowing. "She wasn't one of yours, was she?"

"No, nothing like that!"

"What was it like, then?"

"Like I said, I never seen her before New Year's Eve."

"Never?"

"Never."

He looked down, stubbing his fag out onto the wooden floor scuffing his foot over the butt.

"So, on New Year's Eve you didn't notice anything out of the ordinary? She just came in on her own, had a drink and left?"

"That's right."

"And then you found her in the park the next morning?"

"That about sums it up."

"Well, here's the thing I just can't get my head round Trev," he paused for effect. "She's dressed for a party, but she's drinking on her own in your pub. So, how did she end up with a head injury only a quarter of a mile down the road from here, with no bag and no shoes?"

"I don't know, it's very odd," he replied unconvincingly.

"I can't help wondering, what's a nice girl like that, doing here on New Year's Eve? This isn't the sort of place you'd dress up for, is it, Trev?"

The publican looked offended. "Isn't it?"

"No. So, I'm going to ask you again. What was she doing here, and with who?"

"I have no idea!"

"So, you're saying she came here by herself on New Year's Eve, all dressed up, by herself and didn't even meet anyone here? It really isn't the place for a woman to come to on her own, is it? Let's be honest."

"It's not that bad!"

They both surveyed the tatty-looking pub – the threadbare burgundy stools, scratched mahogany tables, rickety chairs, worn wooden floor. The air had a stench of sour beer and stale fags.

"Really?" Phil raised his eyebrows. "No, Trevor, this is exactly the sort of place you wouldn't bring your girlfriend. You would only come here, if you needed to come for some other reason."

"What other reason would you need to come to a fine establishment like this?"

"Yeah, right," Phil laughed. Trevor was clearly delusional. "I believe she came with someone, maybe for a meeting with a dealer. One that you know about."

"Honestly, Phil. I know nothing!"

"Well, remember, Trevor. Let me know when you do know something or I will be back. I'll be keeping an eye on you. And get rid of those dancing girls, you need to clean up your act! Got it?"

With that, Phil left the pub.

CHAPTER 5

PRESS CONFERENCE

DS Lewis made his way back to the station through the busy London traffic. He found DI Jeffordson preening himself in front of the mirror, combing his hair and smoothing out his thick moustache.

"Anything from Trevor?" He gave Phil a sideways glance as he pulled at a stray grey eyebrow hair.

"Not really, Gov." Phil looked bemused.

"The usual bullshit?" He flinched as the hair came out in his fingers.

"Yes, Gov, that about sums it up. He's got a stripper in again. The woman was old enough to be my mother." Phil paused.

"What?"

"I'm sure he knows something, but he's keeping his cards close to his chest."

"What do you think he's up to?"

"Could be anything, but I reckon she went to meet someone there. Would she go there by herself? But then again it's not the sort of place you'd take a girlfriend on a date either."

"Do you think that she was a nice girl" Andrea indicated with inverted air commas, "With the levels of drugs and alcohol in her system, how do we know that she isn't a dealer. Just cos she's dressed up, doesn't mean she's a nice girl."

"She could be a Tom?" DI Jeffordson frowned.

"Well, Trev denies that she's one of his dancers, but as DC Doyle said she could be a dealer."

"I think you're right. We need to keep digging around on that. If we can find out why she was there, we might be able to work out who she was meeting."

"So, that's all we've got to go on – a French coat and a grotty pub – is it?"

"No, we've got the tox screen; she had high levels of amphetamines. Someone supplied them to her. Who was it?"

"If we can find the dealer, we'd find out."

"Well let's hope the press conference will help shed some more light on the situation."

***

DI Jeffordson walked down the long corridor to the main seminar room where they were holding the press conference. In the room a podium had been erected at the front with Brixton police station as a backdrop. The local press and the TV news reporters had set up in the room, ready for the appeal.

"Good afternoon. I'm Detective Inspector Mike Jeffordson and I'm leading this investigation. At approximately 8.30am on the first of January, a young woman was found in Brockwell Park, Brixton. She was unconscious, suffering with head injuries after what appears to have been a vicious attack. We are appealing to you, the members of the public, to come forward if you have any information, to please contact us. This is a serious situation and we would advise all women not to walk through the park alone late at night. In addition to this, we are asking for your help in the identification of the victim. She is in her late twenties to early thirties. She has green eyes, dark brown hair, is approximately five feet five inches tall with a slim build". He showed a photograph of her face.

"Please, if anyone has any information about the attack, or the identity of the victim, contact myself or my team in the incident room on the number we'll give you at the end of this conference. Thank you."

The cameras flashed as Jeffordson answered questions from the waiting reporters.

"Can you tell us anything about the girl? Will she recover?" a journalist shoved a microphone in his face.

"ITV News. Do you think she was robbed?" another reporter pushed his microphone forward.

"Can you tell us if the girl's awake?" The first journalist persisted with his interview.

"All I can tell you is that we have an unidentified young woman, who has been found in Brixton and we are trying to find out who she is. We are also appealing to members of the public to keep a look out for her missing shoes and handbag. If anyone has any information, please come forward and as I said, please stay vigilant and don't walk through the park alone. Once we have more information, we will let you know. Thank you and goodnight." DI Jeffordson turned on his heel and left the conference room.

"Well done, Sir, you handled that well," Phil said to his boss.

"They're a bunch of vultures, Phil, and we must always be mindful of that. They're not here to help the police or the victim, they're here to sell papers," he said, rubbing his fingers together, indicating loads of money.

"Yes, Guv."

"Don't tell them anything more than I did. Got that Phil?"

"Yes, Sir, I've got it."

"Let's hope that someone will recognise her and come forward. Right now, unless our victim remembers who she is and what happened, the general public are our only hope!" He walked through the hall with Phil. "Are the phone lines ready?"

"Yes, we're all systems go."

"Excellent."

CHAPTER 6

WHIPPS CROSS HOSPITAL

In the Incident room the following morning, DI Mike Jeffordson was heading up the investigation. The team were all assembled.

"Right lads and lassies," he said. "We put out an appeal through the media. It would appear that we've had several reports saying they know who the victim is. We've had our usual nutters of course, claiming that she's their ex-girlfriend, sister, lover, etc. Obviously, we need to follow all the leads".

There was a groan from the officers sitting in the room.

"Yes, as tedious and laborious as it is, we still have to follow every lead," he emphasised every syllable. "We need to find out who she is."

"But we know some of our regular nutters won't know her." DS Lewis interjected.

"But how do you know that, Lewis?" Jeffordson challenged.

"We don't, Sir," said Andrea Doyle.

"That's right, Detective Constable. I'd like to remind you all that we have a young lady currently in hospital, with a head injury. She was drunk and drugged up; she looks like she's been through the mill. It's our job to find out who she is and what happened to her. We currently have no next of kin, no ID. This is not a joke and I expect everybody and I mean everybody, to do their utmost," he said, looking directly at Phil.

"Yes, Guv," he said.

"I want no stone left unturned," continued Jeffordson. "This girl is the victim of a serious attack and someone knows something. We do, however, have one promising lead. A Sister Oliver from the maternity unit at Whipps Cross Hospital believes she recognises the girl. She believes that she's a lady called Aline Deniaud. I have arranged to see Sister Oliver this morning."

The team of officers looked at one another, nodding with approval.

"In the meantime, Lewis, I want you to go back to the publican and see what else he remembers about that night. Someone must know something and I suspect it was some lightweight from the pub who thought they could take advantage of her. Andrea, you're to head up the investigation on the telephone leads. I know it's painful, but it's got to be done. The rest of you – I need you to go out into the community and make door to door inquiries.

As I said, leave no stone unturned. We are lucky we're not running a murder investigation. But if this girl doesn't pull through, that'll be exactly what we've got."

"Yes, Chief," they chimed.

"Come on, set to it, time waits for no man!" and with that DI Jeffordson picked up his coat and hat and left the room.

***

He arrived at Whipps Cross Hospital. It was no more than twenty minutes from the station on a good run. But today it was the usual London traffic – bumper to bumper with vehicles.

"Bloody traffic," he swore as he got out of his dark blue Ford Sierra Sapphire. It was his pride and joy. He closed the door carefully, checking and double checking he had locked it properly. He looked across the car park, and strutted towards the main hospital, checking for the maternity unit.

As he walked, he tried to work out the link between the maternity unit and the girl currently lying in a bed at Kings College Hospital. Had the lady just had a baby? This wasn't a scenario DI Jeffordson had thought of at all. The doctors treating her didn't mention anything about a recent pregnancy.

He found Sister Oliver sitting in her office on the labour ward. She was a lady in her late fifties with short, pixie-style grey hair. She sat at her desk bolt upright, writing notes, looking incredibly serious. DI Jeffordson knocked at the open door. She looked up immediately.

"I'm Detective Inspector Jeffordson," he said, walking cautiously through the door. The sister looked blankly at him. "From the station, you called about the appeal for information about an attack victim," he prompted her.

"Oh, yes, Detective Inspector...I'm so sorry, I was a million miles away!"

"Anywhere nice?" he joked.

"No..., nowhere nice," she softened. "Come in, Inspector, do take a seat."

"Thank you." He sat down on the hard NHS grey plastic chair with its heavy steel frame.

"So, Inspector, how can I help you?"

"Mike, please call me Mike..."

"Thank you, but I prefer to stick to your proper title."

"Righto," he said taking out his pad, and looking down at it. "You phoned this morning and reported that you recognised the girl found in the park at Brixton, is that correct?"

"Yes, I did."

"You gave the name Aline Deniaud, is that also correct?"

"Yes."

"Can you tell me how you came into contact with Aline?" He got out a pen from his anorak pocket and poised, ready to write on his notepad. "Was she a patient – a mum who'd just had a baby?" he gestured with his pen to the maternity unit. "A child protection case? Anything like that?"

"No, it was nothing like that at all".

"So, what was it like?"

Sister Oliver seemed hesitant and got up from her desk. She walked to her office door, closing it firmly. She paused and took a deep breath; her hands shook slightly as she sat down.

"How is she?"

"She's in a stable condition." He smiled gently rubbing his top finger with his lip.

"Do you think she will recover?"

"I'm sorry, but I can't give you that information."

"Yes, yes. I'm sorry."

"So, you know her?" he prompted. "A child protection case?" he repeated gently.

"Yes, I know her and it wasn't a child protection case or anything like that at all." Her composure faltered. "It's all our fault this has happened to her!"

"Why, what makes you say that?" said DI Jeffordson, clearly puzzled by the remark.

"She was..." She cleared her throat. "She's a midwife; she worked here on the unit."

"Well, I didn't see that coming," he said.

"I know." She looked decidedly uncomfortable.

"Come on, tell me all about it".

"Okay," Sister Oliver took a deep breath. "Aline came to us at the beginning of September." She opened her drawer, pulled out a manila file and flicked through the pages, looking at her records. "Yes, that's right. She trained in France, at the Université Paris if I'm correct. Her English was excellent she was very knowledgeable and we offered her a post instantly. Aline was arranging for all her certificates to be sent by her mother. We were very happy with her; she worked hard and got on well with the other members of the team. I believe she settled well into the nurse's accommodation on site."

"However...?" he said urging her to continue.

"Well," Sister Oliver wavered. "She was quite a secretive girl, never staying at the accommodation on her days off. Her colleagues started to suspect something was going on."

"Like what?"

"Well, they couldn't put a finger on it. But Aline never talked about what she did on her days off."

"But surely that's not unusual?"

"No, of course, usually the nurses return back to work with a spring in their step, refreshed. But not Aline, she always came back excessively tired, I would say, and she never discussed anything she'd been doing at all."

"That is odd."

"One of the girls said they would often see her leaving with an overnight bag, generally dressed up as if she was partying."

"Perhaps she had a friend and they liked nightclubbing?"

"It's possible, but it didn't ring true," she paused, thinking.

"Go on."

"One of the nurses thought perhaps Aline was working in the city," she hesitated. "You know – as a working girl. I wasn't so sure. But when Aline came on duty smelling of alcohol, I knew we had a problem. When I questioned her, she got really nasty, saying who did I think I was? Her 'fucking mother?'" Sister Oliver emphasised this with her fingers drawing speech marks in the air.

"She was very aggressive. I knew this was the alcohol talking so I told her she wasn't fit for duty and she needed to go back to the accommodation and sober up. I said that I wanted to see her the following day to discuss this".

"Did she return?"

"Yes, she did, but she still smelt of alcohol. I told her that she was still unfit for work and we couldn't have her on duty in that state. That was then I noticed a bite mark on her collarbone. I could see it as she had her uniform on but it was very loose, I believe she'd lost a lot of weight. I asked her about the mark, but she covered it with her hand straight away, saying it was nothing, that a friend had been mucking around. I said to Aline I was worried that someone was hurting her. She denied this and asked to leave; I told her that I was really worried by what I was seeing, but Aline told me to forget about it. She said it was all good." Sister Oliver took a deep breath. "Anyway, she came into work the next few weeks sober; she got on and did her work, I thought she'd turned over a new leaf and our little chat had changed things. But then she started to be distracted at times and bang – it all kicked off."

"Why, what happened?"

"She came on duty one day, absolutely paralytic. We caught her in one of the delivery rooms inhaling the Entonox".

"Did she have a patient to care for?"

"No, thank goodness."

"Good God! That could have been catastrophic!"

"Exactly…" She shook her head. "She was as high as a kite. She'd seriously overstepped the mark this time. I asked her to leave the building immediately. Security were called and she was escorted off the hospital property. I believe someone in the security team knew her and took her back to her room. They agreed to do this, as she apparently had a reputation in the nurse's home."

"A reputation for what?"

"Oh, drinking heavily. What do you think?" she raised her narrow grey eyebrows. "So, unfortunately, she had to go. Gross misconduct. We did try to get to the bottom of what was happening, but sadly, she saw us as the enemy. She left us and the accommodation within a few days."

"Had you seen her again since then?"

"No. Not until I saw the press conference. I recognised her in the photograph. She looked ghastly and I feel awful to think she might have been sleeping rough. She was a very talented midwife, but..." she faltered. "We simply couldn't have her here, drunk. It was dangerous."

"We understand that. You mustn't feel guilty. You did what was right at the time for the mothers and babies in your care."

Sister Oliver sighed. "I know you're right, but it's so very sad, poor Aline."

"Did you ever find out who she was meeting?" asked Jeffordson, "was it a girlfriend, or did she have a boyfriend in the city?"

"I've no idea. No one had a clue what she was doing on her days off. But whatever it was, it was screwing her up."

"It was all a bit dicey, wasn't it?"

"Yes, she was perfectly fine when she started. It all just turned ugly over the last few months."

"Did you ever manage to contact her parents?"

"I tried, but I only had names and a telephone number."

"And what were they called?"

"Jacques and Johanna...But I don't know exactly where they lived."

"Did you ever try their number?"

"Well, yes. But my French is appalling and I couldn't make myself understood."

"Have you still got the number?"

"Of course, let me see..." She looked through her file. "Ah, yes, here it is, and passed him the note with the number on, "I'm so sorry I didn't manage to speak to them."

"Not to worry, we have people who can contact them."

"Oh, good," she smiled. "I did think about going to the French Embassy, but then thought it was better coming to you first."

"Okay, thanks. You've been a great help." DI Jeffordson stood up and extended his hand to her.

"Is there anything else you need to know?" Sister Oliver asked, shaking his hand.

"No, I think that's about it for the moment," he said, looking at the number. "I'll see what else we can find out about Miss Deniaud".

"If you hear anything, please let me know."

"Thank you once again, Sister Oliver." He smiled putting on his beige anorak, placing the tweed trilby hat on his head. "Hope you have a good shift."

"And you too, DI Jeffordson."

***

He left the maternity unit with the telephone number in his hand. He was bemused by it all. Where was Aline from and what had happened to her? The first thing to do was to contact her parents in France. If he wasn't mistaken that was a Paris number. He recognised it from when he and the missus had spent their silver wedding anniversary there several years earlier. He called through to the station on his radio and spoke to Phil.

"Morning, Lewis. I've got a number in Paris for a Jacques and Johanna Deniaud. I believe they might be the girl's parents. We're looking for any information you can find on an Aline Deniaud. She's a midwife who trained in Paris and came to work in the UK around September last year. See what you can find out on her."

"Yes, Guv."

"Oh, and can you give the phone number to Celine? She can work her magic with the parents and find out some more info."

"Right, Guv, is this for the girl from the park bench?"

"Yes, Lewis. Who else do you think I'm talking about?"

"Sorry, Guv, just asking."

"Sorry Guv, just asking," he mimicked. "Come on, lad, wake up! Too many late nights again, eh?"

"No, Sir."

"Well, come on, get to it. Give the number to Celine, she'll need to talk to the parents, to tell them their daughter's in hospital. Make sure it gets done as soon as possible. Capiche?"

"I think you'll find that's Italian, Sir!"

"Oh, shut it, Lewis!" he snapped. "Anything else?".

"Shall we tell them about her loss of memory and the circumstances?"

"No, not at the moment, let's just get them here."

"Righto, Guv."

"Great. I'm off to the French Embassy."

"Speak soon."

"Roger that."

Mike Jeffordson opened his car door and slung his hat onto the seat beside him.

"Come on, old girl, we're off to the Embassy." He turned over the ignition key and the dark blue Sierra fired into action.

CHAPTER 7

REVEREND HILLIER

The incident room was a hive of activity; police officers were on the phones following up reports of recent sightings. DI Jeffordson found Andrea back at her desk, typing up the recent report to keep the file updated.

"Morning, Andrea, can I have a word? I've received a phone call from a vicar at St Peters Church, West London. He says he's had contact with the young lady from the park. Apparently, he recognised her photograph in the Evening Standard. He's identified her not as Aline Deniaud, but as a young lady called Mary Daniels. He saw her coming into church on several occasions. I'd be really interested in finding out what the Reverend has to say about her. Could you go and have a chat with him?" he urged "Obviously, finish what you're doing first."

"Not a problem, Sir. What's the Vicar's name?"

He looked down at his note pad. "Um, he's the Reverend Graham Hillier."

"Right, Sir. I'll head over straight away...I'm just finished." Andrea shut down her computer. "All done."

She grabbed her notebook and radio and set off for the church on the other side of the city.

***

The Reverend Graham Hillier was sitting in the vestry with a pile of books, preparing for the Sunday service.

"Good afternoon, Reverend. I'm Detective Constable Andrea Doyle. I've come to see you concerning the phone call you made to the station about one of your congregation."

The Reverend lifted up his sandy, balding head from the books. He closed the book he was reading and placed it on the desk.

"About whom?" he looked over the top of his glasses, glaring at her.

Andrea took a sharp intake of breath, her hands trembled slightly.

"Umm..." She looked down at her note pad. "Well um..." she started, "A young lady called Mary Daniels, I believe?"

His pale blue eyes stared at her from across the table. "Ah, yes, thank you for coming to visit me, Detective." He swung around in his seat, opened a huge oak door and shouted loudly to his wife.

"Margo dearest? Get us some tea, will you?" He turned to Andrea, "Do you take milk and sugar?"

"Umm, yes, that would be lovely, thank you." Andrea felt overcome by his forthrightness.

"Milk and sugar," he called. "And don't forget the biscuits this time!"

A small, thin woman shuffled through the door a few minutes later with a heavily-laden tray. She served them each a cup a tea, offering a plate of chocolate digestives, a bowl of square sugar lumps and a small jug of milk.

Andrea was always on a diet, and so hesitated to reach for one. The Reverend immediately took the plate and thrust the biscuits under Andrea's nose.

"Have one, I insist." He took four biscuits for himself, still holding the plate at her.

She really didn't want one but felt that she had no choice in the matter.

"Oh, all right then."

"One won't hurt," he smiled.

Andrea took the biscuit, subconsciously sucking in her stomach as she took it off the plate. She took a sip of the hot, sweet tea.

"Can you tell me about the girl?"

"Well, I met the young lady last October. I believe she came in after a hard day at work. She was wearing a nurse's uniform and said that her name was Mary Daniels, but I wasn't so sure."

"Why was that?"

"Oh, you know," he brushed off some biscuit crumbs. "Her name was Mary Daniels with a French accent. I mean, really?" he scoffed.

"But that could have been the truth," Andrea challenged.

He shrugged. "Anyway, I wasn't in a position to question who she really was. People have many reasons to conceal their identity. Who am I to judge?"

He rolled his eyes, shoving a second biscuit into his mouth.

"Anyway," he continued with his mouth full, "people runaway for all sorts of reasons. Sometimes, they're running from abusers, an unhappy home, bullying, or even coming out. We hope to be a safe haven for all kinds of people. We don't judge, we don't ask questions," he responded in a pompous tone. "We simply hope that we can help people when they come to us with whatever is troubling them. We're not into 'Bible-bashing.' What we do is out of love."

Andrea felt that he was quite disingenuous. She wondered why he had really contacted them. He didn't really appear to care for the young woman who'd called herself Mary. His attitude was high and mighty.

"Mary, did she attend here regularly?"

"Sadly not, she came to one or two services I believe. I think it was all too much for her. We honestly tried to reach out to her but, alas, she was a lost soul."

"Can you tell me anything about her?"

"She never opened up to me to tell me what was troubling her. However, she then started arriving at our soup kitchen, maybe once a week. I noticed as the time went on she became more dishevelled and unkempt. I had no idea where she lived, or whether she was still working. I suspected she'd lost her job but things are not always what they seem. I had no way of knowing what was happening to her, as she didn't offer that information. One day I came into work and found her sleeping in the doorway of the church hall – it's a warm and sheltered spot."

"Oh, and when was that?"

"About a week before Christmas; that time, she was completely out of it. I suspected she'd been taking drugs, she looked really rough. She also looked like someone had beaten her up. I wanted to call an ambulance but she refused. I suggested calling the police, but she said they wouldn't be interested. She said a bunch of homeless men set upon her as she'd managed to get her hands on some drugs. I didn't want to go into the details.

I took her back to my own house; she had a hot bath and changed into some of my wife's clothes while Margo put hers through the wash. Mary had a sleep in the spare room. We called our local GP to come and assess her but when he arrived, she was gone. The upsetting thing was that she'd taken money out of my wife's purse and later we found some jewellery missing."

"Didn't you think to call the police about the jewellery and money?"

"No, no, my wife insisted we didn't call you." He frowned; his pale eyes stared at Andrea. "If we'd called you, this would have been sorted and Margo may have got her jewellery back."

Andrea hesitated; the chances of finding a drug user with stolen goods were slim.

So, was this why he had contacted the police? Was his motivation to get his wife's jewellery back?

"Have you seen her since?"

"No...We did look for her but she'd disappeared. She could have been anywhere – in a squat, a hostel or sleeping rough. London is a big city."

"So, she never came back?"

"No, I'm afraid that's all I can tell you."

Andrea wasn't surprised that Mary hadn't returned to the church again, but she doubted it was anything to do with the missing jewellery.

"Are you able to tell me anything about the discussions she'd with you?"

"Well, there isn't anything to tell you, as I said, she didn't open up to me at all," he shrugged his shoulders in puzzlement. "I can't understand why."

Andrea watched him. There was nothing about him that she liked. No wonder this Mary hadn't spoken to him. He was a fake and a phoney. He clearly liked the position he held but didn't like the work that went along with the role. He was a minister in name only. She had met his type before.

"Did you ever get a full name for her? Or where she worked?" Andrea questioned him.

"As I told them when I called, she said she was Mary Daniels. I believe she was a nurse, but I don't know where she worked."

"Okay, well, if you think of anything else, no matter how insignificant, please contact us. It may just hold the key to unlocking the mystery."

"Yes, my dear, that could be a sermon in itself," the minister chuckled. He leant back in his seat, folding his arms. "Yes, I'll contact you, don't you worry. I'd like to get Margo's jewellery back."

"Don't you think that you should formally report this crime?"

"Why would I want to do that?"

"Well, if you want to make an insurance claim, you will need a crime number."

Reverend Hillier scoffed at her comment. "My dear," he looked down his glasses "my wife's jewellery wasn't insured." His voice rose.

"Oh!"

"We don't require insurance, not with the Almighty God to protect us."

CHAPTER 8

COLIN'S EVIDENCE

Phil Lewis got out of the Vauxhall Astra with Metropolitan Police livery on the side. He saw a young barman in his twenties with a blonde quiff at the side of the Prince Regent, placing empties into the crates ready for collection by the brewery. The clattering of the bottles was so loud that the lad hadn't even heard the car arrive. Phil made his way through to the main bar where he found Trevor mopping the floors with a strong bleach mix. He looked up as Phil approached.

"Alright Phil? Any news on the girl?"

"Not a lot really, Trevor, that's why I'm back. Just wondered if you've got any other leads for me."

The landlord shrugged and carried on mopping the floor.

At that moment the young lad with the blonde quiff came in to stock up the crisps and soft drinks. He caught the end of the conversation.

"Is that the girl from the park you're on about?"

"Yes, yes, it is, do you know anything?"

"Is she okay?"

"Why are you asking?"

"When she left here, I saw her arguing with that bloke," he pointed to one of the empty tables in the bar.

"I think you're mistaken, Colin, you didn't work New Year's Eve," Trevor interrupted.

"No honestly, Trev, I was working."

"No Colin, you weren't," he said through gritted teeth.

"I'm sorry, mate, but I was. Look!" He pointed to the Calendar on the wall behind the bar. "See, you, me and Melissa were on that night. I was definitely here."

"Then you must be mistaken, Colin. She didn't leave with anyone!"

Colin and Trevor exchanged a look with each other. Trevor stared at Colin, his eyes holding his, Trevor's lips tightening. Colin straightened his shoulders and looked Phil in the eyes, ignoring Trevor's menacing stare.

"She did. I was taking out the rubbish and I saw her with the bloke she'd been drinking with and they were having a right old ding dong," Colin told Phil.

"Do you know the man she was with, Colin?" he asked.

"I've seen him here before. He don't stay here long – maybe has the odd drink."

"Really?" asked Trevor with mock surprise. "Have you? I can't say I've seen him before."

Colin looked at Trevor with disbelief.

"Yes, he's well known." Colin blurted out; ignoring the evil eye Trevor was giving him. "He does a few deals here."

"What deals exactly?" Phil questioned.

Trevor blushed, his ears were shining scarlet.

"Drugs," Colin replied calmly.

"And is she involved in all of that?" he asked, looking from Colin to Trevor.

"No," they replied in unison.

"He's a nasty piece of work by all accounts," Colin added.

"Local lad?".

"No, he's always very smartly dressed – seems like a proper gent – unlike the low-lifes that normally frequent this shit-hole."

"Oi," objected Trevor.

"Where's he from?"

"He works in some hotel up town by all accounts."

Phil raised his eyebrows. "Can you narrow it down, Colin? There're loads of hotels in London."

Colin thought for a minute. "He's working up West, one of the Cadeau Hotels, I think."

"A description of him would help."

"Well, he's foreign – French. He's about five foot nine, slim, dark brown hair, and smart-looking."

"Anything else? A name?"

Colin thought for a moment. "He does have a nickname, but I don't know his real name. People call him Lammy."

"Have you seen this Lammy since?"

"No, not since New Year's Eve."

"Thanks, Colin, you've been a great help." Phil turned to leave and then looked back.

"I'll need you to make a statement. Can you pop down the station after work?"

"Today?"

"Yes today, straight after work" he then looked at Trevor, "I'd like you to come to the station too, as there are things you aren't telling us. You're clearly withholding information. Do you really want the drug squad poking around the pub?"

Phil's heart flipped as he left the pub. Had Colin not been working today, he wouldn't have had this good lead on what had happened on New Year's Eve. What was Trevor covering up? Clearly there were some dodgy dealings with drugs going on in his pub. Was Trevor at the centre of all this? Phil couldn't quite believe that Trev was involved in the attack. He was a shady character, with his lap dancers. But Phil didn't think he was stupid enough to be peddling drugs.

He got into the car and radioed through to the station. He was put through to the Guvnor.

"Okay, Sir, we've got something from the night in question. The landlord, Trevor Arnold is clearly trying to cover up something. But one of his barmen, Colin, gave the game away."

"How's that?"

"There appears to be drug dealing going on there. A lad called Lammy is at the centre of it all. Apparently, the victim is mixed up with him. The barman saw them arguing outside the pub that night when he took out the crates."

"Do we know where we can find him?"

"Colin believes he's working at one of the Cadeau Hotels in West London."

"Got a description of this scrote?"

"He's about five foot nine, slim build, dark hair, possibly French."

"French? Did you say French?"

"Yes, Sir. Looks like that's the connection with the victim."

"Any CCTV at the pub?"

"No idea."

"It would be a good idea to see if Trev has got the recordings of the night."

"I'm on to it, Sir."

"Good. Let's also get down to the Cadeau Hotel and see if we can find this Lammy character."

"Okay, Sir. I'll be back at the station shortly."

***

DI Jeffordson and Phil climbed into the shiny blue Sierra Sapphire; Mike started the engine and the car revved into action, heading for the first Cadeau Hotel.

"Right, Phil, this maybe like looking for needle in a haystack. We've got about four or more Cadeau Hotels in the West End alone. But if we start with the one at Paddington, maybe they'll be able to point us in the right direction."

"Do you know how many French waiters are currently working in London?"

"There must be thousands, but we've got to start somewhere, Phil. We've got to nail down what's going on."

The Sierra made its way through the packed London streets as commuters made their way through the city. The two police officers were determined to find justice for the girl. They both hoped this would be found in the Cadeau Hotel and so uncover exactly what had happened to her on New Year's Eve.

CHAPTER 9

COUNSELLOR

Mike Jeffordson felt as though they were no nearer to discovering what had happened to the girl. He gathered his team around to assess the situation. The coat the victim had worn hung in the office. Photographs of the girl and the pub were stuck on the whiteboard, alongside the names of witnesses; Trevor Arnold, Sister Oliver and Colin Walker – and the possible names of the victim – Aline Deniaud and Mary Daniels.

"Let's see where we're at, shall we?" he said as he walked around the room with his arms folded. "We have a girl who speaks with a French accent." He paused stroking his moustache. "We have a positive sighting of her at The Prince Regent on New Year's Eve from Trevor Arnold and Colin Walker." he took a breath. "They reported that she'd an argument with a dealer who we believe is called Lammy. They claim that he is French and works in a Cadeau Hotel up West. Lammy is yet to be found. This is our French connection and I'll bet my bottom dollar the coat belongs to him." He pointed to the garment, directing their attention to it. "If he's as smart and well-turned-out as Colin described him, this is our man. We've also contacted the Missing Persons Bureau. Unfortunately, nobody of this woman's description has been reported missing. I've also been onto the French Embassy; we're still waiting for them to come back to us with information on Aline and her parents, Jacques and Johanna Deniaud. We've a receipt found in the coat pocket which Celine is looking into. Is there anything else?"

He looked around the room, smoothing down his moustache as he did so.

"We're getting CCTV from the pub, to see if we can get a picture of the man Aline was arguing with, Sir," Phil reported.

"Good work, Phil and when do we expect to have it?"

"By the end of the day, Sir."

"Sweet!" DI Jeffordson looked around the room. "Anything else?"

"I have appealed again for witness who might have seen the victim anytime on New Year's Eve." Said Phil.

"Great, thanks."

"We've sent off samples from the clothing and samples from her for tests, to see if it brings up anyone on the criminal records," Andrea added.

"Lovely," he smiled. "Now we're talking."

"Has anyone looked to see if there was any blood found at the pub, Phil?" Andrea asked.

"No, I had a scout around, but I couldn't find anything. But we've had several rainy days since then."

"Yes, it's unfortunate, we'll just have to go with what we've got."

DI Jeffordson looked around the group of officers.

"Celine, could you chase up the French Embassy and see if they've got anything for us?"

She nodded.

"The rest of you, we need to find out who this Lammy is. I want some of you in Brixton, asking around. We've got some snitches down there; someone must know him. Then we need to go back to the Cadeau Hotels personnel department, checking for possible suspects. We'll have to wait a while for forensics and CCTV video tape to be viewed. Can you get onto the CCTV viewing right away Phil.?"

"Can we get onto the national database and see what links we can make for assaults taking place in Brixton, particularly women being attacked in the park. Also, can you look into the dealers in the area? Is there anyone in the area matching the description?"

"Yes, Guv."

The shrill phone rang on the main desk in the incident room; DS Lewis answered the phone to a gentleman with a softly-spoken voice.

"Hello, can I talk to someone about the television programme last week?"

"The police appeal?" Phil asked.

"Yes, yes that's the one," he said quietly.

"I'm sorry, but you are going to have to speak up. I can't hear you very well."

"Oh. Oh, I'm s-s-sorry," the man stammered, raising his voice a little. "Yes, it's about the girl found in the park."

"Have you got some information about the girl?"

"Well, yes."

"And your name and details?"

"I'm Simon Thomas. I'm a counsellor."

"You work for local government?"

"Err...n-no. The NHS."

"Oh, okay, I've got you, a counsellor. So, is that how you know her?"

"Well, that's how I used to know her. She was a client of mine. When I saw your appeal on the television, I had to call you. I haven't seen her for a little while."

"When was the last time you saw her?"

"She had several sessions with me and then she didn't turn up for her last appointment and I never saw her again."

"And when was that?" Phil repeated

"Oh um...now let me see." There was silence, and then the soft voice came back. "Oh, yes that was it. The last time I saw her was August last year."

"Why was that?"

"Why was what?"

"Sorry, that wasn't clear was it? Why was that the last time you saw her?"

"Well that's the question, I've been asking myself. It was really odd, to be perfectly honest. I-I've been quite worried about her and-and then I saw the appeal."

"So, why didn't you call last week?"

"Well, I wasn't a hundred per cent sure it was her. She just looks so different. Normally she wore her hair up, but in the photograph it's down and much darker. Also she has lost a lot of weight so I didn't know whether it was due to that or whether it was the black and white photograph. That's why I held back, but it was really bothering me. I told my partner and he said that I should contact you. You see, she's a lovely girl, but quite a complex character. The more I think about it, the more I'm certain it's her."

"Are you able to give me the young lady's name?"

"E-E-Eve McDonnell," he stuttered.

"Eve...McDonald?" DS Lewis repeated back.

"No! McDonnell – M, small C, D-O-N-N-E-L-L," he spelt out.

"Ah, okay, I've got it. McDonnell."

"Yes. Her date of birth is the first of February,1968."

"Can you give me a description of her?"

"Well, she's not very tall. Blonde hair, long and wavy. Quite a small build."

"How tall would you say?"

"Oh, It's hard to say, but not that tall."

"Where was she living at the time?"

"Eve was living in Reading" Simon responded quickly "Addington Road, Reading."

"What were her relationships like?"

"She had some friends who she lived with."

"Any significant others?"

"She had a boyfriend."

"Where is he?"

"He's gone."

DS Lewis typed the information on his personal computer.

"So, her boyfriend isn't about."

"That's correct."

"Thank you, Mr Thomas. That has been most helpful. I think my boss, Detective Inspector Jeffordson, would like to interview you, if at all possible. Could you come to the station?"

CHAPTER 10

FRUSTRATION

The next morning, a wiry man with cropped ginger hair, stubble and thick glasses arrived at Brixton Police Station. He stood patiently at the raised Formica duty desk. The desk sergeant was making notes and he looked up to acknowledge the man.

"I'll be with you in two ticks, Sir," he said, finishing off his records.

The visitor walked around the entrance hall, reading the wallpaper of posters taped to the flaky walls.

"Right you are," said the Sergeant, putting down his pen. "How may I help you?"

"Hmm, y-yes," the man stammered, "I'm here to see Detective Inspector Jeffords," he said, pushing his glasses up his nose nervously.

"DI Jeffordson?"

"Oh, yes! That's the one."

"And your name?"

"Ah, Simon Thomas."

The sergeant looked down his diary running his finger down the page.

"Ah, yes, Mr Thomas to see DI Jeffordson at midday. Please take a seat. I'll let him know you're here." He picked up the phone and made an internal call.

"DI Jeffordson, your 12.15 is here." he paused, listening. "Yep...yep, great. I'll take him down to the interview room." He put down the phone and got up. "I'll take you down to interview room two, where DI Jeffordson will meet you. In the meantime, can I get you a tea?"

"Oh, yes, lovely, thanks. Milk and two sugars please."

The officer released the internal door and led Simon along the clinical corridor to the interview room where he left him.

Looking around, it wasn't how he imagined it would be from watching crime dramas. No, it didn't have any two-way mirrors or a tape recorder in a desk in the centre of the room. It was quite cheerful, with venetian blinds, bright green seats and a small sofa.

A few minutes later, Mike Jeffordson pushed the door open with his shoulder as he carried in two mugs of tea. Simon immediately got up and held the door for him.

"Cheers," he said as he handed him a mug and gestured to the seats for them both to sit down. "Thank you so much for coming in today, Mr Thomas. Has it been a long journey?"

"No, not really. My partner and I came on public transport from Berkshire. We thought we'd make a long weekend of it..." he explained.

"Ah, what part of Berkshire is that?"

"Oh, um, we're near Reading. We live at Sonning Common as the practice is in Reading."

"It's a nice part of the world. Is the Mill at Sonning still there?" asked Mike.

"Oh yes, we go there a lot. D'you know it?"

"Yes, my sister used to live in a small town outside of Reading," he rubbed his chin. "Let me think – it began with a T."

"Theale? Thatcham?"

"Tilehurst, that's it. We used to go to the Mill for a meal and a show."

"Lovely..." Simon relaxed a bit.

Mike could see that Simon appeared to be a bit calmer and felt sure he would be ready for questioning. He took a sip of his tea.

"I believe you were telling my Detective Sergeant that you recognise the girl found in the park. Is that correct?"

"Well yes, b-but as I said to your officer, without seeing her face to face, I can't be one hundred per cent certain. But from the picture I saw, she definitely looks like one of my patients."

"So, you say."

"Yes," he rubbed his palms together.

"Can you give me any details?"

Simon mumbled and wrung his hands. "I'm so sorry; I'm not used to this."

"It's perfectly all right, Mr Thomas. Take your time," Mike reassured him.

"The woman – my client – I saw her on quite a number of occasions. I thought it was over a period of a few weeks but when I checked, it appears to be much longer. I have my records here." He pointed to a black lever-arch file he'd brought with him.

"It was considerably longer than I initially thought. In fact, I saw her first as an NHS patient, and of course funding inevitably ran out. But I continued to see her as a private patient. We met once a month for a long time. But then she just stopped coming."

"Oh?"

"I don't think simple counselling was ever going to help her and I told her this. But she wasn't prepared to take that next step."

"Why do you say that?"

"She was in complete denial of what was going on."

"What do you mean?"

"Well, she'd had referrals to other services, but she never attended her appointments and was unable to undertake the simplest strategies in order to move forwards. She was non-compliant with her medication and was often detached from what was happening around her. I believe that she'd a deep mental health problems, but she was reticent to do anything about it. In all honesty, she really needed a psychiatric referral but she wouldn't consent to it. Her family challenged her about this, but she felt that they were overbearing and interfering in her life."

"Could that be true?"

"Well, yes, of course. There is always an element of that, although I had no contact with the family, so I couldn't say to what extent it was true. But even if she did have an overbearing family, this girl also has mental health problems."

"What do you think she's suffering with?"

"I'm not a psychiatrist. But if this is who I think it is, you are going to need a psychiatrist to review her."

"Depression?"

He nodded. "Or something much more complex; have you managed to talk to her?"

"Not personally. Why, what has happened to her?"

"Well, I don't know how much I can tell you, as I'm not certain that this is my client that has been found. You know, confidentiality laws. But what I can tell you, if this is Eve, she will require specialist help."

"So, Eve McDonnell is a young lady from Reading?"

"That's correct."

"Is the young lady British?"

"Oh yes, I believe she was born and bred in Reading."

"Thank you for your time, Mr Thomas. That will be all."

"So, th-that's it?"

"It is, for now," he puffed out, gulping back his frustration.

"Please, take a transcript of my notes."

"So, what happened to patient confidentiality? What if it's not her?" DI Jeffordson raised his eyebrows.

"I'm sure if it is her, you'll understand. If I'm wrong, you can shred the file."

DI Jeffordson reluctantly took the file from him.

"Thank you, Mr Thomas," he said as he raised his eyebrows at the weight of the file.

***

Mike reflected upon the three identifications they'd had for this young woman. He was feeling disappointed – he thought he was about to make real progress with the case but now it just had caused him to have more questions. He slung the file Simon Thomas had brought in onto the coffee table in disgust. He hadn't even looked at it.

"What have you got there, Sir?" asked Andrea as she heard the thud of the file hitting the table.

"A bloody file! Look at the size of it! What is it, War and Peace?"

Andrea walked over to the table and picked it up.

"So, who's this from, Sir?" She started to flick through the pages "Eve McDonnell, I don't recognise the girl's name. Who's brought it in?" She looked up from the file.

"Simon Thomas, he runs a counselling service in Reading. He believes our victim is one of his clients — someone called Eve McDonnell."

"Oh?"

"Yes, So, we have a Sister Oliver swearing she's Aline Deniaud from France, Reverend Hillier convinced that she's a nurse called Mary Daniels, and now this from Mr Thomas, who says that the girl he used to see was a British girl, born and bred in Reading, with no mention at all of a French accent at all! So, all these accounts, and none of them are watertight. I just don't like it." Mike scratched his head.

Andrea looked sympathetically at the Guvnor. He certainly was looking his age today.

"What's wrong, Sir? You look shattered."

He looked thoroughly fed up.

"I just can't make head nor tail of it. It's one of my last cases before I retire, and I thought we were getting somewhere but we're back where we started!"

"No, we're not, Sir. We've made so much progress; don't let it get to you. Perhaps you're over-thinking it. Maybe you need to just go with the flow, Sir."

"Yes, yes. Perhaps you're right."

"Can I get you anything?"

"I wouldn't mind a whisky!"

"I can get you a coffee," she chuckled.

"Yes, I suppose so. But make it a tea, milk, no sugar. And can you see if we've got some chocolaty biscuits?"

"Sir, you know you—"

"I know, I know. My Type 2 won't like it. Look, if I can't have the whisky, just find me some biscuits, alright?" he snapped. He paused. "Look, I'm sorry. I'm just pissed off!"

"It's okay Sir."

Andrea returned with the tea and some mint Viscount biscuits; all shiny in their green wrappers on a plate. She placed them on the coffee table.

"There you go, Sir."

"Andi you're a star!" He picked up a biscuit and peeled the wrapper off slowly as though he was opening a very precious gift.

Andrea sat down, picking up the notes and flicking through the pages looking at the closely typed page. She licked her finger to get a grip of the thin pages.

"There's a lot here," she said.

He raised his eyebrows. "Yes, it's going to be a challenge."

"I'm sure it won't be that bad," she exclaimed.

She closed the notes and looked up at him as he stuffed another chocolate biscuit into his mouth and slugged a mouthful of tea.

Mike took a deep breath. "So, we have three members of the public identifying her. One person has identified her as Aline Deniaud, another one said she is Eve McDonnell and then we have someone saying she is Mary Daniels. All have responsible positions claiming to know our victim. But only one of them is going to be right. So, who is it?" He paused, starting to list the witnesses on his fingers "Sister Oliver says she was working with Aline at Whipps Cross Hospital. She is the most recent professional to have been in contact with her. Simon Thomas has had contact with Eve McDonnell, but hasn't seen her for several months, whereas the Reverend Hillier's account is positively sketchy, and I would speculate that he is just trying to get his wife's jewellery back."

"What point are you making, Sir?"

"I'm inclined to follow up the line of enquiry that this is Aline. She's recently been employed by the hospital and they identified her straight away. In addition to this Sister Oliver is the only one to have told us that the girl is French. Our girl has a French accent.

Simon Thomas took over a week to contact us. However, we shouldn't rule out this line of enquiry and should still look into the possibility of this being Eve McDonnell, too. Whereas Reverend Hillier's account is limited and I can't help thinking he's just trying to get on the bandwagon as a caring clergyman whose kindness was repaid with robbery. I'm sorry to say I wouldn't follow up the lead on Mary Daniels at present. I suspect Sister Oliver's account seems more plausible and for the time being it's her evidence we'll run with."

"So, we're sticking with the Aline theory at present, Guv?"

"Correct. Let's look at all the lines of enquiry for Aline Deniaud."

"And what are we doing with Simon Thomas' notes?" Andrea held up the folder. "We'll have to read them. There's no harm in that," she suggested.

"No, you're right," he sighed. "We should at least look through them." He took the file from Andrea. "That'll be a job for me, then," he said, nodding his head.

CHAPTER 11

AMNESIA

The police officers were now following DI Jeffordson's theory that the girl on the park bench was a French midwife called Aline Deniaud who had worked at Whipps Cross Hospital. Andrea caught up with the consultant Dr Scott as he completed his ward round.

"When you've got a minute, we've some information on the girl," she said.

The consultant and one of the nurses caring for the girl headed towards the office, followed by the ward sister pushing the notes trolley. They all went into the small, glass-fronted office in the centre of the ward. Everybody sat down, waiting impatiently for Andrea to inform the staff of the latest news.

"Detective Inspector Mike Jeffordson has been up to Whipps Cross Hospital where one of the midwifery sisters has identified our attack victim. She believes she's a former member of her team."

"What? She's a nurse?" exclaimed one of the ward staff.

"In fact, she's a midwife," Andrea replied.

The shock spread around the room.

"What happened to her? is she a former member of staff?" the doctor asked.

"I don't have all the details, but we believe she's called Aline Deniaud and she worked at Whipps Cross. I have her details from the hospital and we're currently trying to locate her parents, in France. Apparently, she's from Paris and trained at a University there," Andrea confirmed.

"Ah, that would explain the French accent."

"Well, at least we have a name for her now and she's not just the girl on the park bench anymore." Dr Scott remarked.

"Obviously, we're doing all we can to find out more information on her. My DI is currently at the French Embassy and another officer is trying to call her parents".

"Thanks, Officer. It feels like you've made real progress in such a short space of time." Dr Scott seemed quite genuine for once. "Her English is clearly very good if she can work in the UK. But I wonder whether she would be less distressed if we were able to speak to her in her mother tongue? Anyone here able to speak French?"

"I can speak a small amount of French, but when I've tried, she's shouted at me" the nurse caring for her responded.

"Has she?" Andrea looked alarmed.

"Yes, she shouted, 'Speak English, I must speak English.' So, that's what I've done. I hope that was correct!" She dropped her eyes.

"You did the right thing. I'm sure" Andrea smiled.

***

The girl was now referred to as Aline, as this was the only positive identification they had to go along with. The staff had started calling her Aline, but it was difficult to know whether she noticed as she remained so distressed.

Dr Scott pulled out her notes from the trolley and opened them up, flicking through the pages.

"So where are we with Aline?" He asked the nurse sitting at the desk.

"Aline?" She got up from her desk and looked at the green notes.

"Yes, Aline," he snapped pulling the notes back towards him.

"Ah yes, the French girl...well, she's still unable to recall any of the events of New Year's Eve or how she ended up in hospital." She paused.

"Well that's not surprising, is it?"

"No, not really, but the nursing staff have become increasingly alarmed by her frightened and paranoid state."

"Oh."

"She's begun to have what appear to be hallucinations." She pulled the notes towards herself and pointed to the entry. "See..." she looked him in the eyes. "Aline was clearly distressed, calling out for help but couldn't be reassured by the staff."

"Well that's not necessarily hallucinations, is it?"

"No, it's not but look at this..." Her fingers skimmed the text as she read the entry. "Aline's been seen talking to nobody in her room and batting away insects and objects that aren't there."

"I see; I don't think this is an appropriate setting for Aline. I suggest we ask for her to be seen by the mental health team for an assessment. Can you call the duty psychiatrist?"

"Of course."

***

Dr Dhillon, a small, slender young woman arrived with her long, black hair coiled in a chignon tied with an Indian hand printed silk scarf. She had a confident manner about her and forced a smile at the notoriously miserable Dr Scott.

"Tell me, Dr Scott, what have you got?"

"Well, Dr Dhillon, we have a very disturbed young lady called Aline Deniaud who was brought in on New Year's Day after being attacked. She's suffering with amnesia, hallucinations and paranoia. Her initial tox screen showed high levels of drugs and alcohol. We believe she's been in an abusive relationship. The police officer has given us some information on a possible ID. She's believed to be a French midwife. Here are her notes."

"Was there any trauma, like a head injury?"

"Yes, there was an injury to the back of her skull. She's had concussion and hypothermia."

"So, do we think these other symptoms could be a result of the concussion?"

"It's doubtful. We'd expect them to reduce by now, but they're increasing."

"This is very interesting. Has she any concept of time or space?"

"No, none at all."

"Okay, shall we see what we have?" Dr Dhillon took the file and opened it. "It sounds like a drug and alcohol addiction which has become complicated by a head injury."

"That's what I thought," said Dr Scott.

"Okay, let's see her."

Dr Dhillon was taken into a side room. As they opened the door, they could see Aline standing by the window flicking the edge of the broken blind, watching the traffic in the hospital car park. She was clearly agitated as she watched a red Vauxhall Nova driving around.

"They can't find anywhere to park, what are they going to do?" She was anxious and upset, her eyes were wide open. Her fingers, the nails bitten short, traced the car on the window leaving a greasy trail. Her finger stopped and waited and then moved on, copying the journey of the Nova around the car park as it looked for vacant spot.

"They're not going to get in there," she muttered.

"Who are not going to get in there? What's worrying you now?" Dr Scott asked.

"Hello, Aline," Dr Dhillon interrupted, gently touching her shoulder. "I'm Dr Dhillon; I've come to see how you're doing."

Aline jerked in response to the Doctor's touch and looked at her, startled. Her sunken eyes over hollow cheeks glared at Dr Dhillon who was now backing away towards the bed.

"Come, come and sit with me," she sat and patted the bed beside her. "We'll be fine, Dr Scott," she said, politely dismissing him from the room.

Dr Scott gave a huff and vacated the small room. As he closed the door, he glanced over his shoulder to see Aline sitting next to Dr Dhillon.

"I've come to see if I can help you, is that okay?" Dr Dhillon encouraged in a reassuring tone.

"I don't think you can help me," she replied politely.

"Why's that?"

"Because I don't remember anything. This is what I keep telling them. I'm never going to be alright!"

"Oh, and why is that?" she questioned.

"I don't know what's happening. I keep seeing things but they say they're not there. They will come back and get me and then climb out of the television. I heard them the other day, talking about me."

"Who was talking about you?"

Aline stormed across to the other side of the room, pointing at the television. "Look at them, all of them, laughing at me. Why don't you make them stop?"

The screen was blank.

"We'll try to help it stop for you."

"But you're not!" Her hands grabbed the side of her head. "Please, tell them to stop."

"Aline, we can help you, honestly."

Aline looked up her eyes widened. "I know that name."

"Tell me, what do you know?"

"Aline Deniaud."

"Who is Aline?"

It seemed such a simple question, but Aline looked puzzled.

"Well," she looked down at her hands and picked her fingernails deep in thought. "I believe that..." There was a long pause. She bit the skin around a nail bed. "I'm Aline Deniaud."

"Where is Aline from?"

"Born in Paris in 1968." Aline looked surprised as the words came tumbling out of her mouth.

"Okay, Aline. That's wonderful. And you say you're from Paris?"

"Yes."

"And do you know why you are here, Aline?"

"No, not really."

"Do you remember anything about the day you were brought here, Aline?"

"No, nothing," she shrugged her shoulders. "But I know that I'm in danger," she added.

"Why are you in danger?"

"'Cause they want to get me."

"Who does?"

"I don't know!" Aline was becoming upset. "I'm so sorry, I just don't know! I'm so sorry!"

She paced up and down the room. She stopped and stood looking out across the car park again.

"They've gone; the red car has gone. They're not there, no, nor there, or there..."

Dr Dhillon joined Aline at the window as she searched. The patient became more frustrated that she couldn't find the car.

"Perhaps they've managed to park on the other side and we just can't see them" the doctor reassured her. "It's okay, Aline. We're going to figure all of this out together."

"How will that happen? I can hardly remember my own name."

"It's all going to take time."

"That doctor," Aline glanced towards the closed door. "He's been giving me tablets to make me better."

"That's right. Are they helping?"

"No, not really, I still feel frightened."

"Are you feeling like you're going to hurt yourself, Aline?"

"No. I'm just afraid of her hurting me again. She will come. She knows where I am. She saw me from the television. She will come and get me. I heard her again in the shower, but there wasn't anyone in the shower. She will get me – she's tried it before."

"Who hurt your head?"

She looked blankly and then touched her head, her fingers caught in her matted hair that still had the remains of blood tangled up in it. She felt further down and remembered that she'd a dressing on her head.

"I don't know."

"It's okay, Aline. That's enough for now. I think what we need to do is review what tablets you've been given. Then we'll see if we can get you something to help you feel better."

"Okay."

"I also think it would be best if we moved you to a specialist ward as your head injury has improved.

There, we can help you with how you're feeling and see if we can get that memory back."

"When will I be moved?"

"Not today. It will probably be tomorrow. You should feel more comfortable there. It feels a lot less like a hospital."

"She won't find me there, will she?" she grimaced.

"No, hopefully not." Dr Dhillon held her hands over Aline's. "I'll see you tomorrow on the new ward."

Dr Dhillon left Aline and found Dr Scott, Andrea and the nursing team in the office, writing up their notes.

"Yes, I agree, she's a very disturbed individual. Much of what she can remember is very vague, but she seems quite sure that she was attacked by a woman." Dr Dhillon reported.

"Hi, I'm Detective Constable Andrea Doyle" Andrea stuck out her hand. Dr Dhillon took her hand lightly and gave it a slight shake.

"Pleased to meet you DC Doyle, how can I help?"

"Did Aline tell you who attacked her? Or even give a description of the woman?"

""No, I'm afraid not. I'm sorry."

"Can, I ask you something else?"

"Certainly." she smiled, nodding her head slightly.

"Do you think the way she is now is just due to the high level of alcohol and drugs that were in her system? Is this not just cold turkey?" She looked around at the medical and nursing staff, her eyes darting from one to another.

"No, I think substance abuse is due to her mental health, but I'm sure that we'll know more, once more assessments are carried out. We'll transfer her to the Maudsley Hospital tomorrow as an in-patient on Florence Green Ward. Hopefully, we'll be able to make some in-roads to her recovery. I hope that in due course we'll discover what has happened to this young French girl."

"Will that take long?" Andrea questioned.

"How long, as they say, is a piece of string?"

She shrugged her shoulders and then took a deep sigh.

"In the meantime, if I write up some oral Haloperidol, it may help to settle her. Any problems, page me. I'm on call tonight".

And with that Dr Dhillon left the ward.

CHAPTER 12

FLORENCE GREEN

The rain lashed down as Aline climbed into the back of the white hospital minibus, clutching, a grey plastic bag with "hospital property" marked on it in blue bold letters and containing a few toiletries and clothes donated by the League of Friends. She sat in the minibus looking lost and bewildered by the move.

Aline was positioned next to an old man who wore a heavy green checked dressing gown. A nasal gastric tube was taped to his left nostril, his pale face was unshaven and he wore a vacant expression. He sat clutching a grey paper mâché vomit bowl. She looked him up and down, trying to work out why she was in the minibus with this old man. She noticed he had a leg bag, secured with soft Velcro straps which looked too tight. The bag also looked like it needed emptying, as it was filling with dark concentrated urine. She wondered how she seemed to know so much about it?

The vehicle rattled its way across the city to its new location. When they arrived, the ambulance crew escorted Aline, walking with her along the long white walkway to Florence Green ward.

Charge Nurse Stuart Gibson was at the nurses' station, ready to greet Aline to the ward. He wasn't in uniform like the nursing staff at Kings College. He just looked like a visitor in his stonewashed jeans and black Stone Roses t-shirt.

"Welcome to Florence Green Ward, Aline. I'm Stuart, one of the nurses here," said the softly spoken Scot. "Shall I show you around the ward?"

Aline was still shocked to hear him say her name. He noticed that she jumped as he said it. He touched her arm gently.

"You're going to be safe here, Aline. Come on, let's get you settled and show you the ward". As he gently guided her around the ward, Aline held the grey plastic bag tightly to her chest.

"This was a previously a long corridor-style ward but it has been transformed into more homely accommodation, partitioned into small, cosy rooms. You can see we have a television room with sofas and bookcases."

They then walked through into another room. "Here is the dining room. Most of the patients come here for their meals." He pointed out the small rooms which led off the dining room. "And these are the rooms where we do craft and music. Lots of people enjoy these activities."

The dining room had large French doors, leading out to the courtyard which was a little overgrown. It had benches around the edge, looking towards a stone bird bath in the centre.

Stuart watched Aline as she looked around.

"Do you smoke?"

"Yes" she replied, instantly putting her hands on her chest.

"You remembered something?"

"Yes, I'm a smoker."

"Lots of people smoke here, myself included. It's all part and parcel of a mental health hospital. It's okay."

"I haven't any."

"That's not a problem."

Stuart led her through the courtyard into the corridor that was lined with individual bedrooms. He opened the door, and hesitantly Aline walked over the threshold. The small room had its own sink, wardrobe and bedside cabinet. It was decorated with the standard NHS blue floral curtains and magnolia walls.

Aline walked around, taking in her new surroundings. She looked outside the white metal-framed windows that had been divided into small rectangles. She touched the chipped paintwork, running her fingers over the uneven surface.

"It all feels so familiar," she said, distracted by the scene outside. Stuart watched Aline who's thick, long dark hair hung around her face like a dirty curtain. She looked like a street urchin, clothed in mismatched lost property. To him, she looked completely out of place in her surroundings.

"Does it?" he asked.

He saw her flinch again when he spoke to her.

"I'm sorry; I didn't mean to startle you."

"I forgot you were there!" She looked over to him standing by the door. "I'm so at home with this all but I just don't know why!"

"That's okay, Aline" he encouraged her. "It will all come back to you in time."

"I hope so."

CHAPTER 13

BAD SHIFT

Later that afternoon, Dr Dhillon sat with Aline in her room. She checked her patient's yellow drug chart, assessing whether there was any improvement.

"So, Aline, how are you feeling? Are the tablets helping at all?"

"A little, I think. I just feel so tired and sleepy, but when I go to sleep, I keep having nightmares. Sometimes, when I'm awake, I keep seeing things."

"Can you describe them to me?"

"Well they really don't make much sense at all!"

"That's okay, they often don't make sense," she said. "When do they start?"

"Any time – day or night. I hear a sound and then – boom – it's like a trigger and I see this image in my head!"

"Can you give me an example?"

Aline thought for a moment and then her face darkened. "Yes. This morning, a call bell went off. I could hear it ringing and ringing in the distance. I suddenly felt the hairs on the back of my neck stand on end and my stomach started to churn. Then it happened – I was transported to a dark room and I could hear a crash bell, screaming and shouting. I felt really frightened and could feel impending doom."

"It sounds like a flashback, Aline. Can you remember anything else at all?"

"Well I know I'd had a dreadful day at work, I can still see it all now."

"Tell me about it."

Aline began to recount the bad shift to Dr Dhillon. "I was so exhausted by the events that I couldn't make myself anything to eat. I sat on the edge of my bed and unlaced my shoes, they looked sorry for the day they'd had, with traces of blood over the black leather. I kicked them to the other side of the room, my feet were hot and sore and they smelt! I stepped out of the hospital scrubs, which looked disgusting, and climbed back into my unmade bed, still in my paper undies. I really couldn't be bothered to change. The light streamed through the curtains, bright and ready for the day, I couldn't stand the way it poked and prodded me to stay awake. I just felt so cold and tired. I lay shivering and wrapped the duvet around myself encouraging it to warm up my shattered body. All I wanted to do was drift off to gentle sleep but the night's events kept playing back through my mind. It was as though someone had a remote control and kept pausing and rewinding again. I really didn't need to keep seeing it."

"So, can you tell me about that shift?" Dr Dhillon leant forward, encouraging Aline to continue.

She smiled "The shift had started off with a beautiful water birth in a newly decorated birthing room. The moon and stars had been painted to create an ethereal feel to the room. The mother was semi-submerged under the warm water. The lights had been dimmed and scented candles burnt, and the serene music of Enya was playing on the CD player. The atmosphere was one of complete calm. The time had come for the baby to make its appearance, everything was in place. We could see the head crowning, then the small head emerged from its mother and the other midwife and I were ready. Our arms plunged into the water in slow motion and the baby was lifted to the surface and placed on the mother's belly.

"The peace was broken by a crash bell. I immediately jumped out of my skin, the tranquillity was broken. My colleague told me to go as the mother and new baby were safe. I left the room as quickly as I could to see my midwifery colleagues rushing about at the end of the ward, it was pandemonium.

"Someone said, 'You take the admission. She's bleeding, full-term baby, came in on an ambulance, husband is distraught.' I helped the small Irish mother with jet black hair and bright blue eyes, climb onto the bed. It was her first baby and they'd had many years of fertility treatments. All their hopes were riding on this pregnancy. Without delay, we made her comfortable; placing a white sheet over her legs and doing her observations. Then I had to locate the foetal heart, but this was proving more difficult. I could find the maternal heart rate which I checked with her pulse. But I couldn't find the baby's heartbeat. Things didn't look good at all. A registrar was called to see the expectant mother and her husband. The bleeding had now become heavier, an ultrasound scanner was brought by the hospital porters and by now the mother was having contractions. We could feel the contractions very faintly on her abdomen. The gel was put onto the mother's stomach. We all looked at the screen, willing the baby to still be alive. The registrar sat quietly and calmly as he moved the probe around her abdomen. But there was no heartbeat. The baby had died. The father instantly started to scream and shout, hitting walls, kicking over furniture, knocking over the bedside table and went into a full rage. The anger he was experiencing was like a full force hurricane hitting the room. It was truly frightening – I was totally shocked by the explosive nature of a human being. But I knew all the time that he wouldn't hurt any of us. The porters were so incredibly gentle and took this huge Irish traveller out of the room into the main corridor. Here it was quiet, and he was allowed to scream and cry. We could all still hear him and feel the pain that tore this man apart. The mother sat on the bed crying in disbelief and shock.

"We were all shaken by what had just unfolded in front of us. Sister Jones came in and took my hand and in a softly-spoken voice she said: 'Okay, this is what we're going to do. We're going to take Mrs Slater into room 14 and we'll need to deliver this baby. She can't have a caesarean section as she will be permanently scarred. You are to come with me – you'll be looking after her.'

"We transferred Mr and Mrs Slater to room 14. This room was dark, but it didn't feel tranquil. It felt solemn and tense and was filled with the presence of lost dreams and a mist of tears. Mrs Slater got onto the high delivery bed – not a nice new electric bed all singing and dancing, but this second-hand old thing, unwanted and unloved. To add insult to injury, I was so short that I had to stand on a footstool to reach Mrs Slater. It felt so cruel to now deliver this baby into the world, on a day which should have been the happiest. This day would have made a family, but instead it would produce the saddest day of their lives together. This singular event would never leave them and it would be there in their every waking thought and in their dreams.

"For me there was no time for what ifs, and whys. Sister Jones and I had to get on with our job and ensure that Mrs Slater was delivered and safe by the end of our shift. It was a side of midwifery that was never discussed. People always used to say, 'Oh, a midwife, how lovely. That must be a nice job,' and I just wanted to say: No, it's not. It's stressful, you see horrible things, and you have to deliver stillborn babies or help terminate a foetus with abnormalities. You're constantly worried that the mother or baby will die. You constantly live off your nerves. Never a shift goes by when I don't worry and question could I have done that better? I constantly go home tired, hungry and haven't even managed to go to the toilet. I'm thoroughly exhausted by it. It's the nearest thing to hell on earth. However, the general public don't want to hear that, don't really want to hear the truth; they wouldn't be able to handle it. So, I'd reply: Yes, it's a lovely job."

Aline paused as Dr Dhillon waited. Then she took a deep breath and continued.

"When I was a student midwife, my midwifery sisters taught me that we treat women having a stillbirth just like any other delivery. The word midwife meant 'with women', and this is what we were doing – caring for a mother just like we would anyone else who would have a live baby at the end.

"Mrs Slater progressed throughout the night; the contractions came more regularly and closer together and soon came up to delivery. The head was visible and the delivery position normal. The cord was wrapped around the neck twice, so I slipped the cord off and waited for the baby to settle. Then we were able to deliver the lifeless little girl onto the bed, still pink from the placenta. The cord was clamped and cut and the baby girl was wrapped in a soft hospital towel, her face was wiped clean of blood. The beautiful baby girl was handed to the mother as her silent tears fell onto the baby's pretty face. She kissed her tenderly. The room was filled with silence; the sound of life was absent. The darkness pressed down upon us all, the pain permeated every pore. This was made poignant as cries of laughter and joy slid under the door like unwelcome strangers. A fresh gush of blood was seen as the placenta separated and it was lifted into a metal kidney dish. Suddenly there was an almighty tidal wave that poured from Mrs Slater; it ran the length and width of the bed running over the top pouring into my uniform, soaking my underwear. There was no time to worry about this, as we had a medical emergency. The crash bell was pulled for the second time that night. Sister Jones was drawing up an injection to stop the bleeding, I was rubbing Mrs Slater's abdomen trying to get her floppy uterus to contract. The medical team arrived, and the intravenous infusion was set up to replace the fluid being lost. We couldn't lose her too. The rest is a bit of a blur. Mrs Slater was taken to the operating theatre and I was left with the baby girl. Mr Slater and I washed her and took photographs of her before she discoloured. He and his wife had named her Nancy before she went to theatre.

"Poor Mr Slater." "I'm not going to lose her as well, am I nurse?" His eyes were filled with tears. I told him "no – they will take good care of her. Nancy was dressed in a vest and a baby gro and wrapped in a pink blanket and a small knitted stripy hat was placed on her head. Her father sat there rocking her gently, as he waited for the news of his wife."

Dr Dhillon handed Aline a tissue as she wiped the tears from her face. She took a great big heave and her body shuddered. She blew her nose.

"As the shift ended," she continued "I took myself to the changing room and removed all the bloody clothes and put them into the hospital skip to go to the laundry. My underwear was thrown into the bin and I took a hot shower. I felt completely numb from the evening's events. I changed into paper knickers and hospital scrubs and headed home. I can honestly say it was the shift from Hell. I felt emotionally and physically drained. I didn't know how I would ever return the following day. But I did manage somehow to drag myself out of bed when the alarm clock went off."

Aline seemed to have run out steam. She sat quietly, her shoulders drooping.

"Was this, a one-off event for you?" asked Dr Dhillon.

"No, not at all. I had many bad shifts."

"How did you manage to cope?"

"I don't really know. I don't know what I did. I can't really recollect, it's all such a blur."

"Maybe you'll remember more positive events with time," she reassured her. "Tell me, Aline, did anyone support you after the incident? Did you have any staff counselling?"

"I'm sorry, Dr Dhillon. I really don't remember. I don't even remember where I worked! I'm so sorry, really I am."

"It's okay, Aline. You're doing really well."

The two women sat in silence looking at one another. Dr Dhillon shuffled her papers and Aline adjusted her position in her seat.

"I'm so exhausted; I don't think I can go on? Please can I leave?" Aline got up to go.

"Yes, if you want to. What are you going to do now?"

"Oh, I saw an old box of cassettes and CDs in the day room and I thought I'd look through them."

"That's a nice idea. Do you like music?"

"I think so, but who knows?"

"Who indeed? Well, maybe you'll find out by going through the box."

***

Aline made her way to the day room and found the old, battered cardboard box with a CD and cassettes inside it. She soon became engrossed in sorting them out. Dr Dhillon watched her as she straightened and rearranged them. Aline sat with her back propped against the corduroy sofa. She stooped low, looking through the collection, clearly trying to find songs and humming tunes to herself.

Dr Dhillon returned to the nurses' station.

"Well, Stuart, one thing's for certain. She was a midwife, no doubt about it. She's having flashbacks from a traumatic delivery."

"Okay. So, what has made her so ill? Post-Traumatic Stress Disorder?"

"Definitely something traumatic. But I don't think we've even scraped the surface yet! We're going to have to peel off these layers really slowly to get to the core of the problem."

"What do you think it could be?"

"I think she's suffering from PTSD, but what's caused it, I have no idea right now. I think she might do well in music therapy. She clearly likes songs and this maybe a way of unlocking her mind."

"Great idea, we'll get right onto it. I think we've got a personal CD player. She could use that."

They both watched Aline as she stacked the clear boxes, making herself a collection.

"Have we had any bloods back on her?" Dr Dhillon enquired.

"Yes, she'd raised liver enzymes and she was positive for amphetamines. So, her body hasn't quite got rid of them yet."

"Yes Stuart, this is a chronic condition and one that hasn't happened just overnight." She thought for a moment "You know that there's more to it than a stressful job, I'm sure. I think that's just the tip of the iceberg."

CHAPTER 14

FIRST APPOINTMENT

DI Jeffordson made himself a cup of tea and went into his messy office.

As he sat down swinging back into his seat, he saw Simon Thomas' notes out of the corner of his eye.

"Come on, then, let's see what you're all about." He pulled out the file, which had been covered by other paperwork. Opening it, he took a slug of his tea and placed his feet on the desk. The file was full of what appeared to be transcripts of what the patient had told the counsellor.

***

Eve Marie McDonnell
DOB 1/2/1968
5th July 1991 Interview Number 1

ST: Tell me what brought you here?

EMM: They told me, I needed to come. Well they told me I had to come! I'm not ill, you know. It's just them, running me down.

ST: Oh? I can see you're quite angry...

EMM: Too right I am. I didn't ask to come here. They all said they were worried about me. But it's all bullshit. It's them that needed sorting.

ST: Why do they need sorting?

EMM: Why do they need sorting? They're the ones who're fruit loops."

ST: Who are they?

EMM: Mum, Dad and Annabel, colleagues, work... everyone!

ST: Tell me about your family.

EMM: My mum loved me very much, but my sister Annabel despised me from the day I was born. They said Annabel would love me but when she came to see me that afternoon she screamed and clung to Daddy. She hated me the moment she laid her black eyes on me. She hated me more than anything in the world. Her life at a mere 3 years old had been shattered by my arrival. Annabel was never going to share her daddy with me, and she never did. That was the first time I was rejected, I'd done nothing. I hadn't asked to come into her world, I hadn't entered it to punish or cause her any harm. But she was determined to make my life as miserable as she could. She was prepared to ensure that I was always the underdog. She was so angry and so jealous; she became determined to ruin my life. She was my nemesis. When Mum brought me home, Annabel would pinch me when no one was looking. I would cry and she'd act as though she cared about me, stroking my hair. The scream would be piercing and it would upset me and I would cry uncontrollably. This made my mother angry with her and she would be scolded. Annabel would receive a sharp slap across the back of her legs; she would cry in the corner; she wouldn't get her own way. But I would be the one who would cop it later. Annabel's jealousy consumed her. She couldn't bear to share my mother's love and attention. She manipulated and engineered every opportunity to vent her bitterness. It became a lifelong quest. As I got older, I learned to show her that I could beat her at her own game, and she wouldn't get the better of me.

ST: Did you ever get on with Annabel?

EMM: No, she was horrible. She always got the pretty dresses and being the youngest, I got them when she grew out of them. By the time they got to me they were pretty grotty. I'm sure she did it on purpose to make me look the fool. Mum always said that it was because Annabel was a clumsy clod and fell over things. I think it was because she was just plain mean. One day, she cut my Sindy doll's hair with a pair of scissors. I was so upset. My Sindy wasn't new, but she'd been rescued at a jumble sale. I'd seen her sitting, lonely amongst a lot of old toys. I thought she was beautiful with her blonde flicked-out hair, big blue eyes, painted rosy cheeks and pouting pink lips. I'd even managed to get a classy red satin dress. I took her with me to London Zoo in a little green basket. And now she was ruined. I was broken-hearted. When mum came to call us for tea Annabel said, 'Mummy, look what Eve has done to her doll. Eve said that Sindy wanted to be a skinhead.' I remember protesting that Annabel had done it, but Mum wouldn't believe me. So, we ended up arguing and the next thing I knew, Mum had slapped my bum and I was sent to bed without any tea. My sister thought it was brilliant as she went off to have my favourite of fish fingers, beans and chips and Arctic roll. Annabel had worked out that this was a winning formula. The more destruction she caused, the more I got into trouble. She soon became the child that could do no wrong in my parents' eyes.

ST: Did this go on for long?

EMM: It never stopped. Right through my primary to secondary school! It was unbearable living with the 'Golden Child.' I became more distant from my parents and felt resentful of the relationship they had with Annabel. I felt I had no one to confide in, no one to turn to. Nobody was prepared to listen to me and hear my side of the story. Annabel continued with her antics to make my life a misery. I had to get out of that toxic environment as soon as I could.

ST: So, what did you do to get away from them all?

EMM: I had dreams of studying and going to Uni but I knew I didn't stand a hope of passing my A-Levels. So, I found an escape route. I looked for a job where I lived in, something where my O levels were good enough. I could get into maybe the military or into nursing. I had to escape as quickly as I could. I think the final straw came when Annabel accused me of taking £10 from my mother's purse. Mum had come home from work to find the money missing. I was accused straight away. By this time, Annabel was working in a jeweller's and had her own wages so I was the obvious choice. But I didn't have any reason to take the money and I just flipped – I mean really flipped. I ended up slapping my mother across the face, leaving a red imprint on her face. My hand stung as I hit her with so much force. Oh my God, Dad went mental. He pulled the leather belt from the loops in his trousers and he beat me with it. She allowed him to whip me with the buckle end of the belt. I stood there defiantly, making out that it didn't hurt but his just made him crazier! How I hated them then – her for allowing him to hit me and him for not listening to me. Once again, they were taking Annabel's side.

That was it; I needed to get out of there. Away from them all, to stop them hurting me anymore. I vowed when I packed my bags that I'd never return to that house.

ST: Well done, Eve. That was hard work. I think we'll leave it there for today and maybe pick up from there next week. How does that feel for you?

EMM: No that's fine...I feel utterly exhausted.

ST: It really will take it out of you. Please be kind to yourself. It can take quite some time before you see any progress.

EMM: Okay, I'll try.

SESSION ENDS.

***

DI Jeffordson closed the file. There was nothing in the first transcript to connect her to the victim of the New Year's Eve assault. He looked at the thickness of Simon Thomas' folder and realised there was still a heck of a lot to check through before he could finally dismiss the man's claims.

He knew he should be focussing on the fact that the victim had confirmed that she was Aline Deniaud, but these other identifications bothered him. He needed to check everything, leave no stone unturned. He sighed. More bloody work, but his gut wouldn't let him quit.

CHAPTER 15

SUMMER DAYS

The next day, while the other detectives followed up on their house to house enquiries, Mike Jeffordson got back to Simon Thomas' file. He did think about delegating the job to one of his team, but decided he might as well carry on while he enjoyed a nice cuppa and a couple of those posh Viscount biscuits.

***

Eve McDonnell
28th August 1991
Interview number 2

ST: How have you been, Eve?

EMM: Not so good. Those memories last time upset me. I hadn't thought about them for a long time.

ST: It can be distressing, but it's better to acknowledge them so that you can move on.

EMM: I suppose so.

ST: Tell me, do you have any happier memories of your childhood?

EMM: Funny you should ask. I've been remembering something else; although it's...I don't know. I do recall being happy, but it didn't last.

ST: Can you tell me about it?

EMM: It was one of those warm summer afternoons like we used to have in the 1970s. Me and my friend walked home from school. Dandelion tufts where swirling in the air, the sound of the train above us boomed like a roaring dragon as we entered the cold, dark tunnel. It smelt of dampness, dust and urine. We chatted about how it was so unfair how we were never picked for netball. We couldn't help being two of the smallest in the class or that I couldn't catch a ball. I never could, I hated that. I was always last to be picked and the other girls would sneer with curled up lips and folded arms. "Don't pick Eve; she can't catch a ball. She's Miss Butter Fingers." They would push me about and the teachers never seemed to see. I thought I had it bad from those bullies but I got off lightly compared to my friend, Sunita. She was the only Indian girl in our school. When we first met, she told me that she was Indian. I immediately imagined her dad wearing a huge feather headdress, just like a Red Indian Chief but Sunita soon put me straight. "Don't be silly," she said. "My dad doesn't ride a horse and get chased by cowboys!" She explained that she was born in Coventry and had always lived in England. She even believed in the same God as me. Wow, what a revelation – they were a Christian family, just like us. Well, nearly. My mum had always believed in God, but my dad always said it was the biggest con going. He would then go on to tell me, that when I died, I wouldn't go to Heaven but would just rot away with the worms. How disgusting. So, I would rather believe my Mum's idea, that one day we would all go to Heaven to meet with God. Sunita and I had a lot of discussions about dying and what we would need to do if an atom bomb went off. It was something everyone was talking about, particularly with the women at Greenham Common. We talked about how we could prepare ourselves. Sunita said that if you lay on your back at night and folded your arms across your chest, like a cross, if you did die God would know you were a believer and he would let you into Heaven. Well from that night on I tried my best to sleep with my arms folded across my chest, but it was so difficult to go to sleep like that, I would keep waking up if my arm slipped off my body. I felt very disappointed in my ability to stay in this position and if I woke up again and found I wasn't in that position, I would be so cross with myself. Anyway, as we approached her home, Sunita asked whether I'd like to come in for a drink. I said okay. There was a rusty wrought iron gate set in the middle of a red brick garden wall, the house was set back from a side street in middle-class suburbia. A grey path with steps guided you down to a plain, modern mid-terraced house. The entire garden was lawn and just one tree; it looked really lonely on its own. The front door was a bright, sunny yellow. As Sunita put the key into the door, it was at this point that boring ended and exotic began. As the door swung open, the smell of the house oozed out almost through the letterbox, like a snake slithering out of a woven basket. The intense smells – that I later learned were of garlic, cumin and coriander – hit a part of me that I'd never known before. My senses where overloaded by the aroma. The hall was brightly decorated with soft fabrics and curtains, in warm, earthy tones; reds, oranges and browns. The walls were covered by garish wallpaper of floral kaleidoscopes, multiple colours interlinking with an iridescent sheen. There were no carpets on the floor, just a hard wood base, dull from the constant use of the family. We entered a small kitchen. Sunita immediately set to finding glasses and a bottle of squash. The kitchen didn't look anything like my mother's. Heavy, worn, black-bottomed pans were hung over the cooker, oil stains and splashes were now ingrained upon the brown geometric tiles. The whole kitchen was impregnated with the aroma of curry and cooking oil. A huge skillet was on the stove with the remains of breakfast laying curled up from the exposure to the day's warmth.

"What's that?" I asked

"It's a roti, Indian bread. We have it with curry for breakfast."

"Breakfast?" I remember the shock of having curry for breakfast.

Sunita then let the tap run to cool the water down and made us a long refreshing drink. We sipped the sweet orange, and could feel the cold running down our throats. We smiled and relaxed.

"Do you want to come and see my bedroom?" asked Sunita.

"Oh yes!" I replied excitedly. It would be great to see where my friend slept at night and the trinkets in her room.

A noise came from the front door. Sunita looked startled. Her eyes opened wide and she checked the clock on the kitchen wall.

Sunita stood watching the door open, and a tall boy walked through with a bag slung over his shoulder.

"Hey, anyone home?" he called

"Dilraj, what's he doing home? He's meant to be at college! He'll kill you if he finds you here!" she hissed.

Blind panic hit us. I couldn't understand why he would want to kill me.

"I'm not allowed anyone home, especially a white girl," Sunita explained. "Quick, you've got to get out!" Sunita pushed past me to the back door and unlocked it. "Come," she said, beckoning me.

I just followed. I didn't question her; I just did as I was told as I was too worried to do anything else. We ran out of the house and into the back garden and headed for the garden shed. She opened the door.

"Hide in here," she said, "I'll come and get you later."

So, trusting my best friend Sunita, I went into the unloved, dishevelled, rickety old shed. The next thing I heard was the door closing and Sunita locking me in. I felt frightened; I looked back up to the house through the dirty window, laced with spiders' webs. I could see movement in the kitchen. As I stood there, I looked around at the garden tools. They were all rusty and slung on the floor. There weren't any shelves or benches. Nobody came here; my footprints in the dusty floor were the first for many months.

I felt a little reassured. Perhaps Sunita was right to hide me here – it was obviously a place that was hardly used, so her brother wasn't likely to find me. I was sure I wouldn't be here for long and she would soon get me out.

ST: You must have been very frightened?

EMM: I was petrified; I thought I was never going to get out, particularly when I could see through the window the sun beginning to change colour, from the bright satsuma orange, melting into a rich raspberry ripple. "It won't be long now, she'll get me out" I kept telling myself. But the sun sank further and panic came over me like a tidal wave. I grabbed the door handle and shook it hard. She hadn't really locked me in, had she...? Had she? I questioned myself and shook the door again; it really wasn't going to open. Had she forgotten about me? What about my mum? She would be home from work and beginning to get worried. I wondered if I was going to die there and never see my mum again. She would be really worried by now. I could visualise her going up to school to see if I was there. What had I done? I just wanted to get out and go home.

Up at the house, I saw the kitchen lights go on. Someone was in the kitchen. I peered through the filthy window to see if it was Sunita or her brother, but I couldn't see a damn thing. Then I started to worry. Could they see me? Oh no, what if they could and her brother came and killed me in the shed with his rusty garden tools? Then my mum would never find me. I crouched down on the floor, frightened that they might see me. I had no idea how I was going to get out.

I looked around the shed at the broken panels. There must be a hole I could climb through. I scrabbled about on the floor trying to find a way out but I couldn't. The inside of the shed was getting darker and I was feeling cold. I could see the stars in the sky but inside it was pitch black. I wanted to scream but I was petrified. I opened my mouth but nothing came out. I was trapped. I didn't think there would ever be an end to this. I could imagine how angry my father would be, with my mother crying and my big sister gloating that I had got into trouble. It would be all her birthdays and Christmases rolled into one.

Surely Sunita's mum must be home by now, I thought. I didn't know why she couldn't just come out and let me out of the shed. I needed to go home. I needed my mum. "This isn't funny anymore," I muttered. I began pacing up and down the shed, my arms wrapped around myself hugging myself tightly. Next thing I knew, there was a scratching sound and the sound of the key in the lock.

"This is it," I thought. "If it's Dilraj, I'm dead."

The door was flung open and there stood the tiny figure of Sunita.

"I'm so sorry, Eve," she said. "My brother was cooking so I couldn't go out to the kitchen. Come on, let's go, your Mum will be worried."

So, we ran up the garden path to the house in total darkness, with only the inky black sky to witness my escape from the garden shed. We then ran up the side of the house, past the smelly bins to a high gate which Sunita quickly opened. My legs flew as the path took me out onto the main road. I ran up the hill to home. As I entered the cul-de-sac, I could see the curtains were opened and the lights on in the lounge. I saw my mother's back as she was on the phone. I didn't even pause to take in the scene I just stood on the doorstep ringing the doorbell. It was now that I knew I needed a wee and as my mother opened the door, I could feel the hot urine tipping into my knickers. I ran as fast as I could to use the toilet as I could feel it trickling. The relief was immense; I could feel my whole body shaking as I sat on the toilet. I sank my head onto my lap. My mum came in and could see I was shaking.

"Where have you been?" she asked. "I've been so worried!"

"It's all been so horrible, Mum," I sobbed.

"Whatever is the matter? What happened to you?" she crooned as she put her arm around me. She smelt all warm and of Yardley Freesia – all soapy and clean.

"Well," I began, and told her the whole story. Mum helped me into a warm bath and I was packed off to bed.

I didn't see Dad that night but I heard them shouting downstairs.

"I will, Ursula," he said. "I'll go 'round there and kill those bloody Pakis," he shouted.

"They're not Pakis," I said to myself. "They're Indian."

I could hear Mum trying to calm him down. I was shaking as I held the pink candlewick counterpane around my face. I listened hard to what they were saying but couldn't quite make out what she was saying to him as her gentle voice was muffled.

I dreaded what he was going to say in the morning, the repercussions would be immense and his mood would still be fuelled with anger. Hopefully, Mum would be able to reason with him. I ran my fingers up and down the bedspread, watching the tufts of cotton change colour as they changed direction. I felt safer now I was in my own room with my pillow and big scruffy teddy who took up half the bed. I kissed his cold black button nose and snuggled down. I was still worried that my Dad would go 'round to Sunita's and beat up her parents. He wasn't generally a violent man.

Bigoted and prejudiced maybe, but never a fighter. My Dad would've been the one to come off worse, having had polio as a child. He wasn't a physical man; he didn't take part in any type of sport. But he was good with his hands and had a crushing grip after years of working at the benches in engineering. I believe that this is where his prejudiced views were fuelled, by ignorant co-workers. Who had little or no understanding of the Indian culture – not that I was an expert at those tender years.

It was only six months earlier that I'd discovered how dreadfully prejudiced my parents were. I was truly shocked and simply couldn't believe what I was hearing. It was just before Christmas and my parents asked about me having a birthday party. Back then, parties were few and far between. You didn't celebrate with your friends every year like children do in current times. So, for me it was going to be wonderful. I could choose five friends – although one had to be a friend for my sister Annabel. So, I chose to invite Sunita, Kate, Michelle, and Sara.

To my absolute amazement, my mother, who was such a kind lady, said no to Sunita. I asked her why. She explained that she thought that Indians didn't celebrate birthdays and she wouldn't want to offend her parents. I was shocked and couldn't quite believe what I was hearing.

I told her that they were a Christian family. When my mother continued with another excuse as to why Sunita couldn't come, I could feel myself getting hot. My stomach churned and the anger rose up from the very buckles of my shiny school shoes. How could she be so mean, not to let Sunita come to my party just because she wasn't English? My mother denied that was the reason, but I knew my father was behind it all – that he was the one stopping my friend coming to the party. It was then that I realised that my parents were racist, not that we ever called it that. This was a time when my parents' generation were still calling Indians 'Pakis' and Africans 'nig-nogs'. It was a horrible, degrading time in our British history and one which I'm ashamed to be part of. It still makes me cringe when I think about it all these years later. So, the result of all of this was my party went ahead at home without my best friend Sunita.

The morning after I'd been locked in the shed, when I got up, I was expecting it to be World War Three. And just as I'd suspected, the explosion took place as soon as I entered the dining room. Dad had started to tuck into his full English breakfast. I could just about stomach a slice of toast with Marmite on. He went bonkers. It was just like something out of a tabloid newspaper. Before I knew it, the whole thing was completely blown out of proportion. A curfew was in place and I was no longer able to walk to and from school by myself. I had to wait to be picked up by one of my parents. The only advantage to this was I was able to watch TV at the end of the school day. It was on one afternoon with Miss Curtis that I was able to watch Wimbledon and saw Virginia Wade getting herself into the Women's finals.

This lasted the rest of the summer term, and then my sister Annabel was expected to pick me up on the way through from secondary school. You can imagine that went down like a lead balloon.

ST: Thank you for sharing that, Eve. It sounds like a traumatic time.

EMM: It was.

ST: It's clear that your reaction to your parents' racism has helped to shape the person you are today, which is a positive you can take from this.

EMM: I hadn't thought about it like that.

ST: Well, I hope you can think about that now. You felt helpless then, but it didn't change your opinion about your friendship with Sunita.

EMM: No, it didn't. Their prejudice didn't make sense to me. Sunita was a lovely person.

ST: Are you still in touch?

EMM: No. No, I haven't seen or heard from her for years.

ST: That's a shame. Well, that's our time up now, I'm afraid. See you next time.

EMM: Yes, thank you.

SESSION ENDS.

***

Mike Jeffordson closed the file, rubbing his eyes. Still nothing there to link this Eve with Aline he thought. Interesting stuff though, reminds me of the days when 'Paki-bashing' was almost a national sport. Horrible, bloody times. They never managed to get enough convictions for those attacks.

With a weary sigh he got up and went in search of a fresh cuppa.

CHAPTER 16

REGGIE KICKING OFF

Andrea sat in Brixton police station reading through Simon Thomas' notes.

"You know what, Guv? I was thinking you should take a copy of these notes to Dr Dhillon. I bet they would make more sense to her..." Andrea suggested, handing him the file.

"That's not a bad idea at all." He drummed the table and turned to Phil.

"Phil, I think a visit to Florence Green Ward is in order today. We haven't seen the lovely Dr Dhillon for a few days. I'd like her to see what she makes of Simon Thomas' notes." He nodded to Andrea, acknowledging it was her idea.

"Righto, Guv." Phil got up from his desk, turning to speak to Andrea.

"Now, lad!"

"Yes, Sir!" He grabbed his coat. "I'll talk to you later," he said to her as he followed the DI.

Mike Jeffordson placed his trilby on his head. "Come on, then. We've got more pressing things than your little office romance."

"I don't know what you are talking about, Guv!" His voice scaled an octave.

"Really?" Mike raised his eyebrows.

Phil went red. DI Jeffordson smiled to himself. He knew he was right

They headed to the Maudsley Hospital with the counsellor's file.

***

It was now early Saturday evening and the ward had been kicking off all day with agitated and difficult patients. The staff had joked that it was the full moon. It was a throw-away statement, but the moon was more predictable than the behaviour of some of the patients. The nursing staff were attending to a gentleman in his sixties who had long greasy hair that hung down his face. His dark eyebrows furrowed together, the wrinkles on his face contorted and twisted etching the pain manifesting within him. He had become particularly violent and was smashing up furniture and hurling vases at the nurses. He was threatening to harm himself with the broken glass. This patient was known to go into blind rages but there had not been a flare up for a very long time.

"Come on, Reggie," Stuart reassured him. "Let's get you a nice cuppa, buddy."

"No, I don't want no bloody cup of tea...do you hear me?" He pushed Stuart away. "Get me a fag!"

Stuart nodded. "Yes, Reggie, you can have one outside later, but you need to calm down first and tell me what's going on. Alright, mate?"

"I'm not your bloody mate." He pointed his finger at Stuart. He then pointed at each person in turn. "Or you, or you, or you!"

"Alright, Reg..."

"Get me out of this bloody place."

"We can't do that, Reg. I know you want to get out of this bloody place, but you're not ready yet, mate. Soon, though," Stuart reassured him.

Dr Dhillon arrived just after the nursing staff called her.

"He says he was given the wrong lunch, Doctor. We tried to get him the right one but he's not happy," Stuart told her.

"Okay Reginald," said Dr Dhillon. "I understand your brother is coming to see you today and we don't want him to see you upset, do we?"

She had a remarkable calming effect on the patients within her care. Her words distracted Reggie away from his violent impulses.

"Come on, Reginald, let's go for a walk in the garden and you can tell me what's upset you."

Aline felt frightened by Reggie's outburst and the frenzy taking place in the day room. She could feel her anxiety levels rising. Stuart was aware that Aline had gone and hidden in her room. He found her in there, sitting with her knees up and arms encircled her legs. She was shaking, rocking back and forth.

"Aline..." he said as he opened the door.

"Please keep him away from me," she told him forcibly. "I can't have him anywhere near me!" She started to hyperventilate as the panic started to rise in her body.

"It's okay, Aline, Dr Dhillon is sorting him out. You're safe here, honestly." He sat down next to her on the green candlewick bedspread. "Just calm your breathing down. That's it, slowly in and out, nice and slow. You can do it."

They sat there together as Aline shuddered and slowly calmed her breathing down.

"It's all just so terrifying. I can't cope with it...I can't cope with his violent outbursts. It's all too upsetting." She tightened the grip around her legs, biting hard on her finger nails.

"Shhh, shhh. It's all calming down out there, Aline." Stuart got up and closed the curtains and encouraged her to lie down. "You look shattered, why don't you try and get some sleep?"

"I can't," she replied.

"Why not?"

"It's just...I feel so frightened when the dark comes. It's so suffocating. I lie here at night, wide awake, and there's a terrible pressure. It's right here in the centre," she pointed to the middle of her chest. "It's like someone's kneeling on me. And then the bed covers become really heavy, like someone is holding it over my face, willing me to stop breathing. I fight against it and come up for lungfuls of air. I lie there telling myself that it's all in my mind, that there isn't anyone in the room with me...The other morning, I had a nightmare. I woke up and I just couldn't move. I was sure someone was in the room and I was glued to the bed. I'm not making it up. I was paralysed. I tried to raise my arm to save myself but I simply couldn't. The panic was rising and I wasn't even able to scream! Nobody came to help me. Why didn't you come? Then...then, it ended. Whoever was here had gone. I had to check under the bed and in the wardrobe to make sure nobody was there. Now, I can't sleep. I just can't!"

"That sounds really horrible. I'm sorry we didn't know you needed us Aline. I'll make sure we check on you more often, okay? In the meantime, I think Dr Dhillon should come and chat to you. What do you think?"

"Yes, that would be good."

Stuart left Aline in her darkened room and saw Dr Dhillon coming out of Reggie's.

"I've just spoken to Aline. She was very distressed by Reggie and I suggested she had a rest. But she's worried about going to sleep."

"Is she having nightmares?"

"It's sounds more than a nightmare. Aline's inability to sleep appears quite troublesome. She's clearly very frightened, especially with the feeling that someone is in her room."

The two of them walked back down the corridor, passing other patients milling around. Stuart explained how Aline had gone into great detail about what had been happening.

"It looks like she's having waking sleep paralysis," he said.

"Yes, it's quite common. A lot of people get it, particularly in her age group. I'll go and have a chat with her about it." Dr Dhillon made her way to Aline's room.

Aline was in the grip of another panic attack. Her hands were shaking and she was breathing heavily. She was staring into the distance.

"Don't leave me here to die...don't let them hurt me," she repeated over and over.

"Hey, hey, Aline. Come on, you're safe here," she soothed. "What's going on? Stuart tells me you've had some really nasty episodes of feeling like you're unable to move. Can you tell me about them?"

"She's gonna get me, I keep telling you all," said Aline, ignoring the doctor's question.

"Who? Who is going to get you?"

"Eve!" she replied, curtly. "It's Eve! I keep telling them. Last time I saw her, she said she'd kill me!"

"Why do you think Eve is going to kill you, Aline?"

"You — you have no idea..." Aline replied, stumbling on her words.

"Tell me, Aline."

She shook her head. "I can't."

"I think it would really help you, if you could," she encouraged.

***

DI Jeffordson and DS Lewis arrived on Florence Green ward to find Stuart sweeping up shards of glass into a dustpan.

"Dr Dhillon around?" Mike showed his warrant card.

"She's with a patient. Can I help?" Stuart replied.

"We've come about Aline Deniaud. We're the officers investigating her case." Phil added, looking around the ward for Aline. "She still here?"

"Yes. Dr Dhillon's with her at the moment."

"We wanted to give her these notes."

"Oh!" He looked down at the file, puzzled as the name on it was one he didn't recognise. "Eve McDonnell? Is this something to do with Aline?"

"We're not sure yet," said DI Jeffordson. "I'd like her to take a look, when she has time."

"Rather her than me!" He felt the weight of the hefty file. It was almost like a set of dumb bells.

"I wonder if she could shed some light on the subject," said Mike.

"I'll certainly ask her, but she's very busy."

"I understand, but I would value her expert opinion. I can't make head nor tale of them."

"Where are they from?" Stuart asked.

"We got them from a counsellor in Reading. He thinks the victim is an English woman called Eve but he isn't certain. We're pretty confident that our identification of her as Aline Deniaud is correct, but I'd be grateful if the doctor could have a look at this for me. There might be some connection we've missed."

Stuart looked confused as he examined the name on the records in his hand again.

"Yes, we're confused too," Phil added.

"Well, I expect the doctor will get to it eventually, but don't hold your breath. She is completely snowed under with patients at the moment."

"Do you think that we could have a chat with Aline?"

"Dr Dhillon is with her, can you wait?"

Mike glanced at Phil, "Yes, that will be fine, not a problem."

"I'll tell her your waiting."

Stuart walked off down the corridor. Mike watched him as he knocked on one of the doors. Mike began pacing up and down the plain passageway.

"They're a bit odd" Phil gestured with his head.

"You're not wrong lad."

They looked up the corridor as they heard the door open, Stuart quickly walked towards them both.

"She says that she's happy with you seeing her, but she would like to remain present. "Is that a problem?"

"No, not at all" Mike smiled

"Great, she'll be with you in 10 minutes."

***

Mike and Phil made their way into the small tatty room with a powder blue carpet, stained and burnt from cigarette ash. The room had four low armless chairs, one occupied by Aline and another by Dr Dhillon, who got up as they entered.

"Hello Aline, I'm Detective Inspector Mike Jeffordson and this is DS Phil Lewis, I believe you've met him before?"

"Yes..., yes. I have" she stammered not able to look the men directly in the face.

"We are investigating who assaulted you on New Year's Eve."

"I see." Aline looked from Dr Dhillon to Mike and dropped her head.

"Is there anything, no matter how small that you can remember from that night?"

"Ummm..." she stalled

"It's okay Aline, they're here to help." Dr Dhillon leant forwards to Aline, "Tell them what you told me."

Aline twisted the edge of her top over and over again, and bit her lower lip.

"I was attacked by a girl called Eve."

"Eve you say...?"

Phil and DI Jeffordson exchanged a glance.

"Yes..."

"Do you have any other details about Eve that could help us find her?" Phil added taking out his notepad.

"I don't know..." her knees started to knock together. She held her hands over them, trying to stop the movement. Mike looked at Dr Dhillon to see if she was happy with them to continue.

"Who hurt you Aline?" Mike repeated softly

"Eve" She replied almost inaudibly.

"Did you say Eve?" he repeated.

Aline dropped her face into her hands and cried, her whole body shook.

"Yes..." she cried.

***

Phil and Mike got into the Vauxhall Astra and headed back to Brixton police station. He immediately got onto his radio.

"Andi, I need you to start looking for this Eve McDonnell, I want to know her movements, last home address, everything you can find out about her. Aline has told us that she's our attacker from the park."

"Yes sir, I'll get to work straight away."

"You've got her date of birth and what not from the notes, I want you to find out where she is, got it?"

"Yes sir."

"Phil, I want you to contact Thames Valley Police. Any info, okay?"

"Yes Sir."

CHAPTER 17

THE QUEEN'S SILVER JUBILEE, 1977

DI Mike Jeffordson found himself flicking through the thin, typed papers to the next entry in Simon Thomas' notes. He needed to know more about this Eve character. He found the page for the next session. Eve was recounting the Queen's Silver Jubilee in 1977. As Mike started to read the account it brought back many memories. He remembered it well.

He put down his pen and swung back on his chair, taking a minute to reflect upon that year...It was when he became a Detective Inspector and got his first position here at Brixton nick. He'd been here ever since. The job had changed a lot over the last seventeen years but one thing that never changed was good, old-fashioned policing. He smiled and went back to Simon's notes, reading though the events which were so nostalgic. He skipped through the first couple of short exchanges and went straight to the main part of Eve's account.

***

Eve McDonnell
DOB 1/2/1968

EMM: It was 1977 and street parties were being held all over the country. Our cul-de-sac had been transformed from the boxy, Wimpey-home suburban close, into a vibrant, fun and cheerful street party. Each of the open-plan gardens wore the essential bunting, looping across the close. The bright red, white and blue flags were decorated with the Queen's face from the year of her coronation. Trestle tables had been dragged out of dusty garages, releasing the spiders to find another home. The tables were lined up all down the street, covered with plastic Union Jack tablecloths. They were laden with a variety of sweet and savoury treats – all the classics were there – cheese and pineapple on sticks, stuck into a tin foil covered potato to look like a hedgehog. The oh-so-necessary hula hoops and cocktail sausages, iced gems were piled into brightly coloured paper dishes with wavy edges. Paper cups were stacked up high, all standing to attention, ready and waiting for your favourite fizz. The huge glass bottles of neon Tizer, luminous limeade, cheeky red cherryade and clear cream soda – always such a treat – fizzed and popped.

The Jubilee party was in full swing. Everyone was singing. The boxy, mock wood speakers were blaring out of Mr Dunn's lounge window on his latest Goodman stereo, playing Brotherhood of Man's song, *Angelo*. Everyone – and I mean everyone – came in fancy dress. It felt like a carnival. Mum was in a pink, purple and yellow nylon swirly-patterned, flared cat-suit and a brown curly wig. She really thought she looked like one of the singers from ABBA. She wore huge pink platform shoes, clumping around setting out the afternoon tea. Dad came as a medallion man with a stick-on hairy chest, a blue shirt with massive winged collars, an orange nylon suit and a fake moustache! Oh, he was a sight! Honestly, I was quite embarrassed by the two of them. Once everyone had arrived, the tea party started and the whole street sat and ate together in their ridiculous outfits. Soon, the fancy-dress competition took place. My sister Annabel was dressed as a Nun carrying a bottle of wine. In 1977, there was a popular German wine called Blue Nun. My mother thought it would be fun to dress my sister up. Annabel looked the part, with her dark hair hidden under the white starched wimple which my mother had made from linen serviettes pinned under a white veil. The long, satin dress had been nipped in around the waist with a thick leather belt.

A large wooden cross hung around her neck. She held the wine bottle, which my mum had drawn a beautiful label for. My sister was so proud of mum's handiwork. As for me, I was a drum majorette – very fashionable in the seventies, particularly in America. My costume was made up of my red, white and blue swimsuit with the netted skirt. I had a long, white nylon polo-necked jumper underneath it – you know, the ones that pull over your head so tightly you think that your head might explode before you pop through the opening like a champagne cork? No wonder I've been claustrophobic ever since, I was truly scarred for life. My mum made me a tin foil top hat and a foil covered baton with a covered ping pong ball on the end. She really was a whizz for creativity. The whole outfit was rounded off by the long white knee-high socks and brown sandals. I was the height of fashion! It was a spectacle not to be missed, I can assure you.

ST: It sounds like your mum made a big effort for the party.

EMM: She did, she loved making stuff. You know it really was quite amazing. I can still see them parading around. There was a couple dressed as Queen Elizabeth and Prince Philip, but the twist was the wife was Prince Philip and the husband was the Queen. Needless to say they came first and received a bottle of Mateus Rose. Second was the family dressed as ABBA and my sister came in third. I came nowhere and felt quite miserable...

The parents now had started to crack open the bottles of wine and the music was cranked up. Most of the neighbours joined in, boogying to great tunes like *Waterloo*, and songs by the Jackson 5 and the Bay City Rollers. The kids all piled into Mr Dunn's house, where the music was coming from. We sat about on the floor, eating bowls of crisps and playing the latest simple computer game on his television. I think it was called pong. This was very first time I ever saw Aline.

ST: Who was Aline?

EMM: She was a girl who started at our school, we started out as friends but she made my life a misery.

ST: I see.

EMM: So..., everybody was engrossed in the computer game, sat in a huddle around the big square TV. I was coming down the stairs from having been to the loo and I saw her reflected in the mirror. I'd never seen her before. I sat on the step and watched her. She was looking at something on the wall. It was a small wooden shelf unit made up of small squares holding tiny little items. She took an object off the shelf and was turning it over and over in her hands. She looked around the room to see if anyone had noticed her, then put the object in her pocket. By the time I got to the bottom of the stairs, she was gone. I didn't know what she'd taken. I went over to where she'd been and looked at the ornament shelf. A small clean area was surrounded by dust, where the item had once laid. There was no knowing what had been removed as the shelves contained a multitude of small nick-nacks – everything from a glass dog to a tiny wooden boot with Special Mum painted on one side. Whatever it was, it and the girl were now gone.

The following day, we were at school. It was a bright day and we were getting ready to go out. Sunita and I wanted to continue our game, Blake's Seven, based on the telly programme, you know? Anyway, today was my turn to be Callie and we would go off on our spaceship (the big climbing frame).

Miss Morris had told us to go and get our snacks from the cloakroom. I rummaged around in my brown leather satchel, trying to find my apple. I found a small object wrapped in toilet tissue. I opened it up carefully, afraid of what I might find. There inside the tissue lay a tiny little red clay vase. A small house was painted on it in white and blue and a word that I didn't know: 'Torrevieja'.

My heart sank and I felt sick. I knew where this was from – it was the object from the shelf in Mr Dunn's house. If I took it back, they would never believe that I hadn't taken it. What was I to do? With the logic of a nine-year-old, I did only what any nine-year-old would do – I decided to get rid of it.

So, I stashed the small vase inside my tunic pocket.

"Come on, Eve," Sunita shouted down the corridor. "Come on! We're gonna miss break."

I rushed down the corridor with my hand inside my pocket, frightened that someone would find out what I was up to. Once I caught up with Sunita we ran into the playground and decided who would play which part. Sunita wanted to be Callie and I didn't protest as I needed to get rid of the illicit object. We agreed to hide. I watched her run off across the playground in search of a good hiding place. Today, I wasn't worried about the game.

I looked around the playground quickly. Where could I get rid of the vase? I spied the oil tank near the huts. It had a low-slung fence surrounded by long, lush grass. I climbed over the fence and went around the back of the oil tank. I took the vase out of my pocket and looked at it. I quickly threw it on the concrete slab and smashed it, grinding it with my foot. I then hid the small pieces amongst the grass, scattering the evidence. I felt frightened but very relieved that I had not been seen by anyone...

ST: Did you feel anything else?

EMM: Yes. I felt strangely elated by the whole incident.

ST: Interesting. Thank you, Eve. I think we'll finish there.

SESSION ENDS.

***

Mike Jeffordson tapped the paper in front of him. So, this Eve and Aline go back a very long way. He assumed it would be the same Aline – it wasn't a common name. He wondered what the doctor would make of this bit of information. How did they meet, he wondered, did her parents move from France for work? If so, where were they? Sister Oliver believed that they were in Paris, so had they gone back? Surely if they were in England, they would have seen her picture all over the newspapers. So, why hadn't they come forward? He made a note to speed up his reading of the file before he turned to the pile of other things on his desk that needed his attention.

CHAPTER 18

ALINE HAS A MELTDOWN

Stuart was sitting in the office, writing up notes when he heard shouting coming from the day room.

"Fucking shut up, you stupid bitch!"

One of the patients stood swinging a walking stick at the figure standing on the pine coffee table. The other patients sat around, rocking with hands clasped over their ears.

Stuart recognised Aline's slight figure as she flayed her arms. She leapt off the table and began cavorting around the day room, singing at the top of her voice. It was menacing and manic. Aline jumped from sofa to sofa, throwing out her arms. The other patients cowered away from her.

"Do you hear the people sing?" she shouted at the top of her voice.

One of the female nurses stepped forward. "Aline, you need to stop. You're upsetting everyone."

But she blindly continued. "You know, it's the song..." Her eyes were glazed as she plucked a cloth from one of the tables, holding it over her head, swinging it like a flag. She marched around the room to an imaginary drum beat, trying to rouse the other patients into action. But they all sat around, stunned by the outburst from the petite woman. The nurse approached her trying to calm her down, talking in hushed tones.

"It's OK Aline. Let's get you back to your room, shall we?"

Aline ignored the pleas from the nurse.

Stuart pulled out his phone and dialled. "Dr Dhillon? Hi, it's Stuart. Aline really needs to be reassessed. She's getting increasingly agitated. Right now, she's running around the day room singing at the top of her voice. Can you hear?" He held out the phone. "She's really unsettled and completely unpredictable. It's disturbing the other patients."

"Have you managed to get a urine sample from her, Stuart?"

"No, not yet."

"I suspect she could have an infection. It would be best to check. Can you try that? I'm with another patient in A&E at the moment. I'll be over as soon as I can. In the meantime, it may be worth giving her a light sedative."

"Can I take that as a verbal prescription?"

"Yes."

"Okay, I'm happy to do that. I'll go and draw it up."

"Good, I should be with you in about twenty minutes."

Stuart went back into the office and unlocked the drugs cupboard. He took an ampoule out of its box and flicked the glass vial, broke it carefully with a tissue and drew the liquid up into the syringe. Placing it in a kidney dish, he took it through to the day room. Aline was gone.

He could hear her shouting in her room. As he opened the door, he found Aline with the nurse. The nurse looked over her shoulder as he entered the room.

"Thank God you're here. She's in a really bad way."

Aline was now kneeling at the head end of her bed, her full weight on her arms, ripping the wallpaper off the wall with her fingernails.

"Putain de bâtard!" she screamed, ripping a large chunk off in her hands. She threw the paper across the room, completely disregarding Stuart. "Putain de bâtard!" she repeated as she tossed another piece into the air. She seemed intoxicated by the moment, oblivious to Stuart standing in the room with the syringe.

"Hey, Aline, what's going on?" he asked, his voice soothing as he slowly approached her. He placed the dish away from her on a side table. Aline ignored him.

"Come on, Aline. You've got to stop." He took her hands off the wall. "Your hands are red raw!"

She immediately lashed out at him, trying to scratch his face.

"Get off me! You're not going to hurt me again. Get off!"

"Hey!" Stuart grabbed her hands before they could rip his skin. "I'm not going to hurt you. I've just got something to help you, Aline."

"No, I don't want it! All you ever want to do is control me! And now you want me to shut up! You're a bastard," she spat. "You're all bastards!"

"I'm trying to make things better," he said as he sunk the needle into her thigh.

She screamed, pushing him across the room. "You bastard!"

Stuart landed with a thud, skidding across the floor

The female nurse ran over and scooped him off the floor.

"You alright Stu?"

"Yeah, no harm done, come on, let's go". He turned quickly and they both fled the room.

As he closed the door behind them, he leant his full weight on it, taking a minute to catch his breath. Aline continued screaming obscenities from inside the room.

Dr Dhillon arrived. "A problem?" she asked.

"I'm sorry, Dr D, I'd give her a minute if I was you." Stuart replied looking back at the door.

"What set her off?"

"I have no idea."

CHAPTER 19

SCHOOL DISCO

At the same time Aline was succumbing to the sedative, Mike Jeffordson was reading the next instalment of Simon Thomas' notes.

***

Eve McDonnell
DOB 1/2/1968

ST: Hello, Eve. How have you been?

EMM: Okay, I suppose.

ST: Right Eve, what do you want to talk about today?

EMM: I dunno really.

SILENCE FOR 10 SECONDS.

EMM: This morning as I was getting ready, I heard a song on the radio. I hadn't heard it for a long time.

ST: Which song?

EMM: Dancing Queen.

ST: Abba.

EMM: Yes, it reminded me of that awful school disco.

ST: Why don't you tell me about it?

EMM: Okay so it must have been in the early 80's. I can't be sure. I would have been about 11 or 12; it was the top year of primary school. So, when Dancing Queen came on at the school disco, the dance floor would be filled. I was an avid dancer and never missed an opportunity to get up and dance; but not this year.

ST: Why not?

EMM: I was quite a shy girl. I only had a very small group of friends – Sunita being my main one. She couldn't go as they were going to a family wedding in Coventry. So, reluctantly, I went to the school disco by myself.

Musically, the tide was changing and the New Romantics were taking over the pop scene. All my class were dressing up like Adam and the Ants in frilly shirts, heavy black eye-liner and jeans. Most of my class managed to scrape together something that fitted the trend. But I didn't. Mum had managed to get me a new dress. It was a hand-me-down from one of her colleagues. It was royal blue with a gathered-in waist. The high neck and puffed sleeves were trimmed with broderie anglaise. It was a really 'pretty' little dress, like something out of the Waltons or Little House on the Prairie. Not something you wore in the early 1980s. Everyone else wore shiny trousers, pixie boots and back combed hair, and I was in a dress. I could have died. My mum was so pleased with it; I just couldn't break her heart, so I wore the dress, with my flicked out girly hair and school shoes. I felt hideous.

As I arrived at the school hall, I heard girls giggling. I saw them talking behind their hands, laughing. I felt my face flush and my stomach turnover. I didn't even have Sunita to meet. There was nobody I could hide away with like a wallflower. The girls gathered around me like a pack of wolves.

"Eve, why did you wear that old thing?" Aline taunted me. "Can't your mum afford to buy you clothes?"

"Really love your shoes. Are they your school ones?" Sara laughed.

"Really love that goodie-goodie look. It's so Waltons!" Aline continued.

Sara flicked my dress. "Did it take you long to get ready?"

I didn't know what to say.

"No clearly not!"

Virginia then pulled my dress. "Did you tell your mum you were going to a picnic?"

The girls all laughed and said, "What a square!"

"I'd be so ashamed to go to a disco like that," they muttered.

But then that unmistakable music started. They turned their attention to the DJ. Their taunts and jibes ended as they ran onto the dance floor. Like angels from Heaven, in perfect harmonious voices ABBA sang Dancing Queen.

ST: What did you do?

EMM: I had two choices: I could run away and allow them to make my life a misery or I could stand up to them. But was I really brave enough to do that? I wanted to be free of them all. Then of course Aline decided to chip in again.

ST: What did she say?

EMM: Oh, I can't remember exactly, I just remember that she was vile. You know all I wanted to do was get on the dance floor and show them I wasn't worried about what they thought. However, I visualised myself getting up there in my Laura Ingalls dress; and them all mocking me. I couldn't muster the courage I needed. I was rooted to the spot as the wolves disappeared, strutting their stuff. I hid in the shadows of the hall, watching others dancing. I felt angry with myself for not being brave enough to join in the fun. I was mortified by them all. I watched them dancing in small huddles, pointing their fingers in my direction. Nobody came and talked to me as they didn't want to be seen with the freak. It was all too much and I prayed for the evening to end. But it just seemed to drag on. I eventually went and sat on the back step by myself, waiting to be collected. I didn't tell my parents what happened. It was all best forgotten.

ST: You clearly haven't forgotten, though.

EMM: No. I can forget it most of the time, but when Dancing Queen comes on the radio it all comes flooding back.

ST: What do you do?

EMM: I switch it off.

ST: Maybe you should get up and dance.

EMM: Maybe. Can I go home now?

ST: Okay. See you next time.

SESSION ENDS.

***

Mike Jeffordson sighed and closed the file before he went in search of some lunch.

CHAPTER 20

FRENCH O-LEVEL

Twenty minutes later, a cheese and pickle sandwich in his hand, Mike sat at his desk and opened the file again.

***

Eve McDonnell
DOB 1/2/1968

ST: Hello Eve. What would you like to talk about today?

EMM: I've been thinking about when I was fifteen.

ST: Okay. Tell me about it.

EMM: There was a trip to Brittany planned for the O-Level French class. It was an excursion I was really looking forward to as we would be able to take part in a student exchange. I imagined my exchange student coming to stay in my pretty little bedroom at the front of the house. I wondered what they would think of my life here in England where our house backed onto the train line. At night you could hear the track engineers cleaning and mending the lines, the constant noise of trains going through to London was a rumble which was ever present but we'd got used to it and it didn't intrude on our lives. The high sides of the banked garden and a big fence ensured that we never saw any of the trains passing. But when I stood in the back garden looking at the bridge over the road, you could see the intercity with its yellow nose whizzing past. I wondered what the French student would think of this noisy little spot on the outskirts of London.

Soon we got letters to take home and I was so excited when I thrust it into my mother's hand. I was sure that I'd be able to go as my sister had had the opportunity two years earlier. She had a great time in St Paul de Leon.

When Dad came home from work looking tired, he sat wearily at the dinner table. I picked up the letter and nudged my mother.

"Let him have his tea first, Eve." Mum hushed me.

"What's this?" asked Dad.

"Nothing to concern you at the moment, Brian," she said.

She made me leave the dining room while Dad had his meal. I sat in the lounge on the sofa, waiting to be called back in. I sat chewing on the quick around my nails. I waited fervently for them to say…'Eve you're allowed to go!'

When Dad finished his tea, Mum shoved the letter in front of him.

"A French exchange," he said. "What the bloody hell do you want to do that for?" he questioned me.

"Well, I'm taking O-Level French and it will help me to speak it."

"But you don't want to learn French, do you?" he challenged.

"No, but Annabel went and I thought it would help."

"But Annabel wanted to learn French."

I squirmed in my seat. This wasn't going well and I wasn't making a very good point. "I thought it would help."

He looked at the letter and continued to read. "It says you to have an exchange student. Is that right?"

"Yes!" I said, delighted.

He shook his head. "I'm not having no exchange student here! It's hard enough to feed you all," he told me. "And, I'm not having a Frog in my house!"

"But Dad!" I tried to appeal, but he wasn't listening and he carried on reading.

"One hundred and thirty-nine pounds?" he shouted. "What am I? Made of bloody money? They've got a nerve."

"Oh please, Dad," I tried again.

But he wasn't having any of it. "No, and that's the end of it. Give me a pen, Ursula!" he demanded.

The form clearly stated where to sign it and complete whether you were happy to have an exchange student. So, my Dad signed the form and ticked the box that said, 'We are NOT happy to have an exchange student'. He added, "Eve will NOT be going to Brittany."

"Charity starts at home!" my father banged on. "Who do they think they are? Flipping cheek!"

I felt ashamed and embarrassed by my parents' behaviour. Once again, I would be picked on as the odd one out.

As I was unable to go on the school trip, this meant that whilst all my classmates went off to France for the week, I spent the time in Miss Miller's class instead. I thought of all my friends having a great time trying out new food and sleeping in a new bed in a quaint French bedroom. I imagined the chic French mother producing fresh cuisine for dinner every day. It was all so exciting and I missed it all. It felt like a very long week. It was only David Pearce and me that had to go to Miss Miller's class for French whilst our year was away. For David and me, this was a regular occurrence – being left behind. David was one of five brothers and his parents were quite poor. He was always wearing hand-me-downs, which back then wasn't fashionable and was very much looked down upon.

His mother knitted the boys' school jumpers which looked really itchy. But he appeared proud of her for all the love that she'd invested in them. David was a nice boy, quite quiet with short brown hair, large rotund tummy and a leaning back posture. David walked with a slight limp and had a withered lower leg, like my own Dad. I wondered whether he too had had Polio but I never asked as I thought it was rude. We never ever talked to each other during the week. Conversation wasn't a strong point for either of us but we both sat together in class, content in each other's company, looking out longingly through the rainy window for our classmates' return with their French counterparts. When that coach turned the corner into the school grounds, we both got off our stools and went out with Miss Miller to welcome them back with our umbrellas raised. As the coach doors opened, it was like we'd been hit with a joyous wall of sound. Everyone's faces where bright and cheerful and they were full of stories of the week – the weird goings-on, the terrible smells in the meat market, the stink of garlic and the wonderful taste of dunking croissants in hot chocolate.

Oh, it sounded so wonderful and I suddenly felt so sad that I hadn't be part of it all. The French students were met by the parents who had agreed to have them. I noticed that David's parents were there waiting, which meant that his parents had agreed to host someone. I felt so angry and betrayed by my parents as I was the only pupil not to have an exchange student. The Pearce family were in a worse situation than us, and they had the heart to welcome someone into their home. I felt disgusted by Mum and Dad.

As I walked along, feeling gutted about it all, I ended up talking to Aline.

"Honest to God," I said "If someone dropped down dead in the street, I'm sure my Mum and Dad would step over them and carry on like nothing happened."

"No, that can't be true," she said. "I'm sure they would do something."

"We have a good size house, a nice garden, both my parents work." I told her. "My dad has a car. We aren't poor, compared to a lot of families. We have holidays to Butlin's every year. We always have food on the table, clean clothes and a brand-new uniform and shoes every year. We're lucky, so lucky. But all they can say is 'charity starts at home.'"

The more I expressed my sense of injustice, the angrier it made my parents. The arguments were quite bad. They became a regular occurrence at home and I'd be sent to bed with no tea. I hated the pair of them. She was manipulative and he was handy with his leather belt. He'd often beat me when I'd been sent to bed. My mother made out that she couldn't hear him because she knew that it would be her next if she complained. They never hit my sister.

My parents made out to the whole wide world what wonderful parents they were. They gave the impression that it was me that had all the issues and they told teaching staff that they felt that I needed to see someone, but I resisted. They said that I was behaving unreasonably, becoming argumentative, paranoid and bad-tempered. I told them that it was them who made me angry. I told my teachers that I felt well and I was happy with my life, but they listened to my parents and insisted that I saw a counsellor.

Aline said that she thought perhaps they were right. I was so cross with her; she was supposed to be my friend.

ST: So, what happened to Sunita, I thought she was your best friend?

EMM: She was.

ST: She was? What happened?

EMM: She moved away at the end of primary school.

ST: I bet you were upset.

EMM: Yes, Aline was now my only friend, but she wasn't like Sunita.

ST: Why was that?

EMM: Aline had a nasty streak to her. When she suggested that perhaps I should see someone I felt cross that she was taking sides with my parents. I told her she'd no right to tell me what I should or shouldn't do it was my life. I said, "I'll do what I want, when I want, and you're not going to tell me nor are my parents gonna tell me what to do." She was really shocked by my outburst and aggression. But at that moment in time I really didn't care what Aline thought. I was sick and tired of people bossing me about and pushing me around.

My relationship with my parents and Aline was very strained. I felt isolated from people and couldn't discuss what was really going on at home. Dad continued to control us all financially, emotionally and physically. Mum became distant and was in her own little world, living her own secrets and her dirty little books which would turn up in the ironing basket. It was a guaranteed place to hide anything from dad as he never did women's work.

ST: It sounds like your teens were quite turbulent, Eve.

EMM: Yes. And bloody miserable. I never want to go back to that time of my life.

ST: Well, it's good to acknowledge them and move forwards. I think that's enough for today, don't you?

EMM: Okay. I'm really tired now, anyway.

SESSION ENDS.

***

Mike frowned...Aline? Aline and Eve? It was clear there was a connection. He wanted to find out more. What was the progress on Eve McDonnell, had anyone tracked her down? She might be able to help them solve the mystery around the assault on Aline.

CHAPTER 21

DR DHILLON

Dr Dhillon skimmed through Simon's notes. The account was one she frequently saw. Domestic violence. She felt a shudder go down her spine as this family conflict seemed so familiar to her. Aline had clearly known Eve at primary school. It was evident that their relationship was strained and Eve was the key to what was going on. Perhaps if Detective Inspector Jeffordson was able to locate Eve, she may have some insight into how Aline had become so unwell. She wondered how much Aline would be able to remember of Eve.

Dr Dhillon found Aline in the day room, flicking through a magazine.

"Hi, Aline. Are you okay to have a chat?"

"I'm feeling a bit grotty" she grimaced, running a hand through her greasy hair.

"I've heard from someone who thinks he might be able to help us."

"Oh?"

"Yes. I have an account from a counsellor in Reading."

She was intrigued. "What did they say?"

"Well, interestingly, he has an account of an Aline and a girl called Eve meeting at school."

"Oh!" Aline blinked and shook her head slightly.

"Did you meet an Eve at school, Aline? Can you remember?"

"I don't know, maybe, yes. Yes, I believe I did," she said. "I think the first time I saw her was at the Queen's Silver Jubilee party...I don't think we talked."

"Can you tell me about Eve?" Dr Dhillon asked her. "Do you recall anything from the time you met her?"

"Eve first spoke to me in our French class in primary school. Then we were in the same class at secondary school. She found French a struggle and this wasn't helped by our teacher Mrs Harris who was really very cruel."

"How was she cruel?" Dr Dhillon enquired

"Oh..., she..., well." she paused. "Mrs Harris was one of those women who, you know, liked the power."

Dr Dhillon smiled "Go on."

"She was a small, round woman who wore clothes for a woman clearly ten years younger than herself. 'Mutton' was the only word for it – peroxide blonde, permed hair, highly processed to within an inch of its life. She would look across the room with her superior air. She spotted Eve unpacking her bag. She hated her. She complained about her at every parents evening, things like Eve was 'Always the last to be ready, and always the first to leave.' This was typical of teachers back then, who felt they could say exactly what they liked. It wasn't as though Eve had even chosen to do French. She was forced to do it, and would rather have done three sciences as she wanted to be a nurse. But the school in their wisdom felt that she needed a language. Her parents agreed with the school and wouldn't listen to her. So, there she was, with Mrs Harris, having to endure her spitefulness."

"'Asseyez-vous,' Mrs Harris said, pronouncing impeccably as we stood behind our tables, waiting for the lesson to start. Predictably Mrs Harris singled Eve out. The class all responded with peals of laughter as she stumbled, tongue-tied, over the simplest of phrases. Mrs Harris took great delight in making her look a complete idiot in front of the whole class. She would find fault in every area of Eve's work. That day, her target was homework. Eve was so frustrated with French homework that she'd literally got out a phrase book and translated word for word, with a total disregard for sentence construction or grammar. Mrs Harris practically fell off her chair when Eve handed the homework in. Then it started – a small titter, as Mrs Harris's eyes screwed up reading Eve's work – then a splutter, her face was beginning to go pink and then, before we knew it, she was laughing with a deep, throaty voice. 'Do you actually come to my lessons Eve?' she asked."

"Eve whispered, 'Oui, Madam Harris.' We had to reply in French if possible."

"'You're heading for an F,' she laughed almost uncontrollably...and then blurted out, holding her chest, 'No, I'll make that an ungraded.'"

Eve sat in total disbelief, sinking her head in her hands...I felt so sorry for her.

"'We'll show her,' I said in a soft voice. 'I can help you.'"

"'Sorry?' she said, not daring to look back, in case she got shouted at."

"I spoke softly to her. 'I can help you. We'll show that old battle-axe!'"

"Who's talking?" Mrs Harris shouted, scanning the room with her small, piggy eyes. 'Eve, stop talking now! Clearly, by the standard of your homework, you've got a lot to learn. You'd better start knuckling down, young lady,' Mrs Harris said 'If I hear you speak again, Eve McDonnell, you'll be sitting in detention.'"

"I muttered, 'Tire-toi!' Thankfully, Mrs Harris didn't hear me telling her to get lost."

The doctor nodded. "So, your French classes were the beginning of things for you both?".

"You could say that. It almost became a series of counselling sessions. She would confide in me."

"So, tell me, Aline. How did it make you feel, knowing that Eve was confiding in you?"

"Well, initially, I felt really sorry for her. She was completely powerless to do anything about her parents, who were horrible to her."

"So, what did you do?"

"I suggested she stood up to them."

"How did she react to that?"

"She was shocked. Eve had never stood up to anyone in her life, never had a proper argument with them at all. So, I told her, 'you've got to stand up to them, they're bullies.'"

"And then what?"

"Well, she said she couldn't. Normally, she would storm off to her room, bashing her feet up the stairs as hard as she could. She told me she wasn't allowed to cry, never allowed to sulk, never allowed to answer back or tell anyone how she felt."

"That's very sad."

"She was told never to tell anyone how she felt," Aline repeated. "Eve was not allowed to discuss what went on at home. Everything was secret. She had to walk out the front door like a perfect lady, no emotion, no screaming, no crying, shouting, sulking or angriness. It made her feel like a robot. I know she was incredibly upset, having to bottle up her emotions, not being able to express how she felt."

"Gosh, that's unfair."

"Yes, her parents were really unfair. She was completely controlled by them. Every waking thought was monitored by them. She wasn't allowed to do anything. They restricted who she saw, who she made friends with and if they didn't approve of them, Eve was made to end the friendship."

"How do you know all this?"

"She only told me. I'm the only one she spoke to about this."

"That must have been really hard. How did you feel about it?"

"It like felt a burden and I hated it; you know? Keeping it all hush-hush. I knew that I was a secret, too, 'cause her parents would go mad!"

"Why was that?"

"She said they were racists. If they found out about me, they would go mad that she had a French friend. They would say, 'Why can't you get any English friends? Why are they all bloody foreigners?' I understood why she would want to protect me, so that was okay."

"Are you happy with that?"

Aline thought for a moment. "Not really, but sometimes you have to live like that to protect others. But as time went on, our relationship became quite strained."

"Why was that?" Dr Dhillon asked.

"Eve became a bit of a goody-two-shoes. She was always trying to stay out of trouble, at home and at school. It was her tactic to stay out of the firing line."

"Was that not a clever strategy?"

"Well, I became sick of her sanctimonious ways. She was a proper little Miss Perfect, a blooming teacher's pet. Her homework was always in on time, she kept herself out of trouble, never put a foot wrong," she sighed, looking at her bitten fingernails. "I really started to hate her. She never seemed to ever get into trouble. Apart from with the French teacher who hated her because she was rubbish at it."

"But I thought you two were friends?"

"I know, but after a while I felt I just wanted to sabotage her! I know it doesn't make sense." Aline rubbed her hands over her face and then looked up at Dr Dhillon.

"I really wanted to trip her up, show people what a complete fake and a fraud she was. She made me feel angry and resentful towards her. I knew what was really going on inside her. She rarely let her guard down. Eve didn't allow anyone get close to her."

"But she allowed you in, didn't she?" Dr Dhillon reflected on what Aline had previously said. "Why did you want to sabotage her?"

Aline took a deep sigh, running her fingers through her hair "I honestly don't I know......" Her hands stopped at the top of her head and she looked at Dr Dhillon "Oh my God...I just don't know. That's so pathetic isn't it? But I really resented her!" her eyes widened.

"And what made you resent her?"

"I don't really know." Aline looked blankly at Dr Dhillon. "I suppose...I just couldn't live up to her unblemished character, always being kind and considerate...God it was exhausting!"

"So, you felt you needed to sabotage her?"

"Yes," Aline didn't look at all ashamed by her admission.

"So, the fact she was kind just made you angrier?"

"Yes, because it was all a huge cover for what she was really feeling."

"Are you certain you knew what she was really feeling?"

"Yes, I told you. She told me everything."

"Even when you were horrible to her?"

"Yep!" Aline was smug, positively proud of herself.

"Did you enjoy making her life a misery?"

Aline became quite angry with Dr Dhillon. "She wasn't as good and kind as you first thought. There was a darker side to her, you know!"

"So, is this why Eve wanted to attack you? Was it retaliation for all the years you tormented her?"

Aline got up and threw a chair across the room.

"You have no idea! You haven't the foggiest!" she shouted.

"Aline, please sit down."

"No, I won't. See? None of you understand. You, of all people should know what it's like. Once again Eve wins. Aline is the baddie! And you know what? She's an evil, manipulative bitch under that princess exterior," she hissed, and turning on her heels, stormed out of the room, slamming the door as hard as she could.

CHAPTER 22

BRIXTON POLICE STATION

Dr Dhillon left the consulting room and after a brief discussion with Stuart went into her office to put a call through to the investigating team at Brixton Police Station.

"DI Jeffordson," an efficient voice replied.

"Hello, it's Dr Dhillon from the Maudsley."

"Yes, Doctor. How may I help you?"

"Well, I've just had a very interesting interview with Aline. I don't know how far you've got in Simon Thomas' notes yourself, but it appears that Aline knows Eve McDonnell. They were school friends."

"Yes, I've just discovered that."

"Good. Do you need to find out where she is? Not that I'm one to tell you your job."

"No, of course not."

Dr Dhillon wasn't sure whether he was being polite or sarcastic.

"We'll certainly try to locate her," he went on. "Is Aline well enough to give a statement?"

"Not yet, I'm afraid. She's very volatile at the moment. But her memory seems to be coming back, so maybe soon."

Mike sighed. "Okay, Doctor, thank you. Anything else please let me know."

"I'll call you if we find out more. Goodbye."

***

Andrea walked into Mike's office carrying a tray. She placed a mug of tea and a bacon butty next to him. "I thought you could do with one of these. Brown sauce?" she pushed the bottle towards him.

"Lovely jubbly," he smiled, squirting the sauce between the slices of soft white squidgy bread. He gave her a wink. "The missus is not to know about this," he mumbled, mouth half full.

"Mum's the word." She tapped her nose as she sat down opposite him and started tucking into her own butty. "So, what have you got?"

"Well, Dr Dhillon's confirmed that Aline knows Eve McDonnell."

"What?" Andrea almost dropped her butty on the floor! "The same Aline we have in Florence Green Ward?"

He nodded. "The same. I found her name in the file Simon Thomas gave us, and the doc says Aline confirmed it. They were at school together. She thinks

Eve was her attacker. Trouble is, the doc says she's not fit to give a statement yet."

He handed her the notes, opening the file to the page which had the account he'd just read. He pointed out the reference to Eve talking about Aline.

"Look, here and here she talks about Aline".

"Do you think they knew each other as adults?" asked Andrea.

He nodded again. "I suspect they were in Reading together. So, I think we need to extend our enquiries around Reading and find out what they know about both of these girls."

"What else does it say in the notes?"

"I've no idea; I've only got that far."

"Well, you'd better get cracking, Guv," she joked.

"I really should". He smiled; he had that warm feeling inside. He felt quite excited by this confirmed connection. It meant they were making progress and heading along the right track.

"How are you doing Andi, anything back from forensics?"

"We've had the DNA results back on the coat, Guv. And what did they find? Human hair." she smirked. "Like we need to know that!"

"Okay. Did they provide us with any useful information?"

"One of the hairs is female; obviously Aline. Another came from a male. They've managed to confirm he's of European descent. We've run it through our DNA profiles but there isn't a match to anyone on the Criminal Records Bureau. They've shared the details with our colleagues in France, who likewise haven't come up with a match. So, whoever the man's hair belongs to, he hasn't got a criminal record.

"Thanks Andrea. So, now we have Aline's DNA. Did they check that too?"

"Let me see. Yes, it looks like they did."

"And...?"

"Nothing on record for her, Guv."

"Hmm, that's interesting. So, neither the man or the victim has a criminal record, but she's been a drug user. Is the lack of records because they've never been caught?" he ruminated. "Well, first things first, we need to get onto the Royal Berkshire Hospital. See if Aline or this Eve McDonnell might have worked there."

"Good idea. I'm happy to do that, Sir."

"Great. Can you get straight onto that?" He took another bite of his sandwich, wiping the grease dripping down his chin.

Andrea got up from her chair, leaving her unfinished bacon sarnie on the table.

"Only after you've finished your sandwich."

"Oh, okay!" She smiled and returned to her seat, blushing.

CHAPTER 23

LEAVING HOME

DI Mike Jeffordson arrived at the station in the pouring rain, his trilby pulled over his face; the collar of his coat turned up to keep the water away from his neck. It was 6am. He'd got up early so he could get into work and start reading Simon Thomas' notes before the rowdy bunch arrived. His wife had tried to encourage him to stay in bed a bit longer. She said he looked tired and could do with the rest. But he insisted he wanted to get to the bottom of what was going on in this case. So, she reluctantly agreed for him to leave early for work. Mike however was now wondering whether it was in fact a good idea as he walked through the downpour.

He got into the office and shook out his coat and hat and hung them up. He realised he wasn't alone when Andrea walked through the office with a stack of papers.

"Morning, Guv! You're in bright and early."

"I could say the same about you."

"Oh, you know what they say, 'The early bird catches the worm,'" she smiled brightly. "Cuppa, Guv?" She looked like she'd been up hours, blouse pressed, make-up on, brown hair pulled back into a tight bun.

"Yes please. How long have you been in?"

"Oh, since about five, I think."

"Crikey Andi, couldn't you sleep?"

"No, Sir, too many thoughts going on in my head. I decided I might as well get up and come in."

"What's troubling you?"

"Nothing, Guv!"

"Come on, I know you're not telling me the truth. Is it Phil?"

"No, Guv!" she tutted, alarmed. "Nothing like that!"

"Well then, what?"

"It's all just a bit painful, Guv."

"I'm here for you too, you know. It's my job to look after my team. I'm not here just to solve crimes."

"I know, Guv," she sighed, looking at his sincere face.

"Well?"

Andrea let out a deep sigh. Was it really the time to tell him? She looked around the office to make sure there was no one else in, knowing full well that it was empty.

"It all happened a long time ago." She paused and took a breath. "I had a brother – Liam. He was a bit of a lad, a real risk taker; never saw any danger, even when he was a little boy. Mum would tell him to stop climbing trees and walls. She was so worried he would fall."

"So, what happened?"

"He carried on like that, a bit of a joker. Didn't get any O-Levels and got into trouble with the wrong crowd. He thought he was invincible but he wasn't. They were all into drugs. I could see it but Mum would back him and say he wouldn't be so stupid. He was a right Mummy's boy. He would flick his long blonde fringe and flash his blue eyes at her; she was putty in his hands. Then one day the police arrived to say that he'd been found in a derelict house."

"He was dead?"

"Yeah, a massive overdose."

"Oh, my." Mike shook his head sadly.

"None of his so-called friends were there when the Police arrived. He'd been left to die on his own."

"Oh, Andi, I'm so sorry."

"Me too, he was only nineteen."

"How old were you?"

"Seventeen, I was halfway through my A-Levels. It was then I decided I wanted to be a copper. I had to do something right, for Liam."

Mike stepped forward and put a hand on her shoulder.

"He couldn't be more proud of you, Andrea. You've worked bloody hard and you're one of the best coppers I've ever worked with. One day you'll be a DI."

"I hope so, Guv."

"I know so!" He gave her shoulder a reassuring squeeze. "Thank you for telling me about your brother. It must be really hard at times." He contemplated what she'd told him. "So, what has stirred it all up for you now?"

She shrugged. "I did hope that I'd be able to detach myself a bit better from this case. But Aline just keeps going over and over in my mind. I can't believe that a nurse would've been into drugs. She knows the risks far more than Liam ever did. Is she really that stupid – to get involved with it all? I just can't get my head around a health professional, doing drugs. It doesn't seem right, does it, Guv?"

"Andrea, there are a lot of bent coppers out there, as you know. Unfortunately, there are also crooked nurses. Our job is to find out the truth. And as unsavoury as it is, if Aline is mixed up in all of this, if she has committed a crime, well she will have to do the time."

"I know, Guv." She looked defeated by it all. "You are so much better than me at this!"

"No, I'm not. I've just had years of experience, with all these to prove it," he pointed at his grey hairs.

Andrea gave his arm a squeeze and went back to her desk. Mike thought about what she'd just shared with him. She had kept it so very private but why had this case stirred something inside her? It wasn't like her to be so sensitive about things. He opened up the notes to see if he could gain further insight and perhaps see what had stirred Andrea's feelings about this case.

CHAPTER 24

NURSE TRAINING

<u>Eve McDonnell</u>
<u>DOB 1/2/1968</u>
<u>27th September 1992</u>

ST: So, how have you been?

EMM: Good.

ST: Shall we continue from where we were last time?

EMM: I can't really recollect where we'd got to.

ST: Shall I recap for you?

EMM: Yes.

ST: You'd just had a fight with your parents and were about to start your nurse training.

EMM: Oh, yes. Well, the day I left, Mum and Dad had a massive row. I could hear them downstairs he was blaming her for letting me go off to do my training. She was screaming at him that he shouldn't have hurt me. She said that he was a selfish, cruel man and he told her that she was a wet blanket. I didn't care. They could say what they liked to one another 'cause where I was going, they wouldn't be able to hurt me anymore.

I piled my bags into the back of Dad's car and they continued to argue all the way to the nurse's accommodation. I felt completely cold and bitter towards them. Everyone else arrived with their parents, who helped them in with their bags, whereas mine watched me struggle. I should have been excited to be starting my training but instead I knew I was running away, the only legitimate way of doing it, with no questions asked. They still continued to argue as I unpacked my bags.

"I don't know why she has to stay here," he said. "Why can't she live at home?"

"Because she hasn't got a car and will be working shifts," Mum said defensively. I knew she was looking after herself, not me. She was placating him, to protect herself as she would get it in the neck when they got home. You could feel the atmosphere coming from my room, the bitterness swept under the door like a smoke cloud. I'd had enough of them and willed them to leave, wanting them out of my life. I was pig sick of being made a scapegoat for their own issues. They both eventually left after an awkward goodbye. I watched them go down the drive in their blue Mark II Ford Escort, I followed the square tail lights as it left the hospital grounds. This was freedom and I could feel the relief as the car disappeared up the road. They were gone...hopefully for good.

Soon after that, there was a knock at the door from two girls, who were also starting their training that day. They'd both been unpacking their bags and setting up their rooms. I'm sure they must've heard my parents arguing, as they both looked slightly embarrassed as they stood there.

They told me they were called Verity and Sue, both were really friendly. We agreed to all meet in Verity's room to celebrate the start of training. Verity had brought herself a huge bottle of Pernod. Sue had a bottle of wine which her parents had given her. I didn't have anything to offer. It hadn't even occurred to me to take any alcohol. We all sat in Verity's room, getting to know one another. It was just what the doctor ordered. Both girls had been at a convent school together in Thatcham and had then gone on to do a pre-nursing course together. They really were a pair of party girls and a good laugh. We spent the evening playing drinking games. I had a real tinge of guilt for behaving like this. I was surprised that the girls with a Catholic upbringing would behave like this. But Verity assured me that convent girls were the worst and poured me another drink. As the evening went on, I managed to block out what had happened earlier that day. I became more and more drunk as the evening progressed. I could hardly stand up! The next thing I could remember is hugging the big white telephone and being violently sick. I filled the bowl with purple stained vomit! God, I was rough…the smell of aniseed haunts me even today.

ST: Did the relationship continue with Verity and Sue?

EMM: Yes, pretty much…Verity was a party girl, and Sue was more of a real steady eddy – completely reliable. Someone you could go to in a crisis.

ST: So, nothing significant happened between you all in your relationship with the girls?

EMM: No, not really. Sue met a guy in our third year and she was really keen on him. She'd only come out with us occasionally after that. She was so dedicated to Ollie; they were a right pair of love birds.

ST: Did that affect your relationship with Sue?

EMM: Ollie? No, not at all. He was what Sue needed. Ollie was lovely, a real sweetheart. We used to say he was one of the girls. [EMM laughs]

ST: And how about you? Did you have a boyfriend?

EMM: I wasn't ready for any of that, I wanted to get on with my studies and get qualified.

ST: So, did you settle down into your training?

EMM: Yes, I think I did. I was so busy, studying, working and then clubbing. I don't think I really had time to really stop and think.

ST: It all sounds very hectic.

EMM: Oh, it was. I really don't know how we all did it!

ST: I can feel a 'however' coming.

EMM: Well...It was all going so well, but it was about this time I saw Aline again. I'd not seen her for years. Not since secondary school. She became part of my life again towards the end of my training. I didn't really

want her back, as she really enjoyed pulling me down.
But she was able to fill a hole. A loneliness hole.

ST: Why were you lonely? What about Verity and Sue?

EMM: I don't know why. It's as though something was
missing. But with working hard and playing hard, it
squashed those feelings deep down. I always had the
girls around. They were a good laugh and I could talk
to them about how I was feeling. But sometimes it all
felt so superficial. So, I confided in Aline, just like old
times. It was crazy, I know.

ST: So, did you still remain friends with the other girls?

EMM: Oh, yes, if I needed pepping up, we'd all go clubbing.
I didn't drink much initially. I simply couldn't afford it.

ST: Initially?

EMM: After a while, we got quite clever. We'd drink
before we went clubbing and then, in the clubs, guys
would buy us drinks. I didn't much care. Most of the
time we'd never see them again. Don't get me wrong,
I didn't sleep around. There was no way I wanted
to end up pregnant, because that would have been
all I needed, to have been chucked out of training

and sent back home! I had a few boyfriends but nothing lasted. I preferred going out with the girls and having fun, no strings attached. The drinking continued throughout the whole of my training. But it was always very well controlled. It helped me sleep after a bad shift. I got shocking headaches though, as the alcohol was really cheap and nasty. One evening I did go out with a boyfriend and we got thoroughly drunk on Hooch. We were so ill in the morning. It put me off for quite some time.

ST: So, do you think that your drinking calmed down then?

EMM: Yep, absolutely. My training was too important and I pulled myself together.

ST: Again, I can feel a hesitation.

EMM: Well the head stuff never stops.

ST: What do you mean?

EMM: The depression kept on creeping up on me. It felt like a big black cloud at times. I didn't want to admit I was depressed back then. Nurses don't get depressed, do they? Or so I thought. You know, sometimes I felt that it would never be a sunny day again!

ST: And?

EMM: And then the sun would come out again.

ST: How would the sun come out? How did you get over these episodes of depression?

EMM: Oh, going dancing was always the highlight of my week. But I know I was just escaping. That's what we all do, isn't it? Just hide away from our real feelings and create a façade.

ST: Put on a front?

EMM: Yes, exactly. I think I became so good at it, so wrapped up in work, clubbing and drinking, that I wasn't able to own my feelings any more. Does that make sense?

ST: Perfectly. And what about your parents, did you still see them?

EMM: I tried to avoid them as much as possible. Mum and Annabel said that I was a nut case and said that I should go and see someone.

ST: That wasn't very nice.

EMM: No, but they were right, weren't they? Mum kept on saying I looked low. I always felt low when I saw them both; they just knew how to upset me.

ST: And your Dad? Where was he?

EMM: Oh, didn't I say? Dad died at the beginning of my training.

ST: Goodness. That wasn't worth mentioning?

EMM: No not really.

ST: Why's that?

EMM: Well...He wasn't part of my life when I was alive.

ST: That sounds quite stark. Do you think you've grieved properly for your father?

EMM: I don't think I need to. As far as I'm concerned, he died many years ago in my eyes. He was just so cruel and I had no respect for him at all.

ST: Okay. [Silence for one minute] So, tell me Eve. This loneliness and depression that you feel – is it possible that it's a father-shaped hole? You're shaking your head. Do you have any significant men in your life, Eve? Father, uncle, grandfather, brother, male cousins, boyfriend or any paternal figure? Even God?

EMM: No, I don't, Nobody at all...In fact, men scare me, to be honest.

ST: No male role models in your life, no protective force, nobody to show you the true nature of men. Nobody at all?

EMM: [crying] No! I have had no significant men in my life. I hadn't realised that until now and I'm in a female-dominated profession!

ST: Yes, you are. Would you say you are straight, Eve? Or do you find yourself more attracted to women than men?

EMM: No, not at all. I've had plenty of crushes on guys, I can assure you. I'm not a virgin if that's what you asking?

ST: So, do you have a sex life, is there anyone at present?

EMM: No, as I said. I'm no good in those situations, like asking people out. I don't have a good track record of that sort of thing!

ST: So, you're not sexually active at present?

EMM: No, I'm not and I don't think it's any of your business either, what's that got to do with how I'm feeling?

ST: I want to understand why you don't have anyone in your life. Can you tell me why that is?

EMM: I told you, men scare me.

ST: They do?

EMM: Yes, I just don't know what to say or do. It's like they're from another planet.

ST: We're very simple souls really. I think you may generally over-think situations. Just try being yourself. I'm sure that they'll like you.

EMM: You think that is the solution, not to over-think it?

ST: I think that's exactly what you should do. Well, I think we should finish here.

EMM: Okay.

SESSION ENDS.

***

Mike licked his fingers and flicked through the pages in Simon's notes to the entry that had been made several weeks later.

CHAPTER 25

HAMMERSMITH PALAIS

Eve McDonnell
DOB 1/2/1968

ST: Hello, Eve. How are you?

EMM: I need to tell you about Laurent.

ST: Laurent? You've not mentioned him before.

EMM: No. I haven't.

ST: Why's that.

EMM: I have only just met him, soon after our last session. I listened to what you said.

ST: You did.

EMM: Yes, he is quite an amazing guy.

ST: Okay. Tell me about Laurent.

EMM: Well my life has changed completely since last November. The girls and I did our usual trip into London after a late shift. Aline tagged along too, even though I really didn't want her to come.

ST: Why didn't you want her to come.

EMM: Well, she was a bit of a bossy cow. Telling me what to do. I much preferred it if she just didn't make an appearance. So, that night our hair was curled and crimped, armpits and legs shaved, dancing shoes on. We were ready to go out on the town. Little did I know who I'd meet that night and how much they'd all change my life.

ST: Go on

EMM: Well, the excitement was palpable as we all piled into the car and headed up to West London to a nightclub. There was never any parking nearby, so we ended up dumping the car in a residential parking area and shoving a 'midwife on call' sign on the front dashboard. We quickly rushed through the dark roads and ran to the club. Neon lights surrounded the entrance to Hammersmith Palais. The bouncers wore dinner jackets and dickie bows. A long line of excited clubbers queued outside, wrapped up against the bitter cold. Girls drew on their cigarettes, sucking the life out of their Silk Cut, blowing out the blue mist. We were all heavily mascaraed, our lips pouting over our turned-up collars. Our hair was heavily back-combed and sprayed rock solid to ensure it wouldn't droop in the damp hot environment of the club. We slid in through the door two by two, like animals entering the ark. But this was a different breed of animal than those Noah welcomed.

The music was loud, the club was dark, the carpets sticky. The beat pulsated through your whole being, taking over every cell. It was exciting, awakening and launched you forward into this crazy world. The atmosphere was electric, with strobe-lights picking out the pillars, platforms, dance floor and bar in fleeting seconds. I headed straight to the dance floor, with no inhibitions whatsoever. I placed my bag in the corner and started dancing, forgetting about work and all the horrors it brought to mind. I was lost in an almost trance-like state. The adrenaline started, the heat coursed through my veins and I could feel the euphoria building as I danced faster and faster. The music, cranked up to full volume, pumped across the floor. The thumping beat released my inner diva. I bared my soul, my creativity and passion. Faster and faster, my heart would race. The excitement would fill my soul, and joy would overflow from my toes to the hair on my head. The sweat would run down my back, creating beads soaking into my clothes.

I scanned the scene and then I saw him – in the distance at first – a tall, elegant figure. He didn't look English somehow; he had real grace and style. Then he disappeared. I carried on dancing, turning on the dance floor to see if I could locate him. Then felt a hand on my back. I turned and there he stood, close to me. His dark hair was slicked back off his olive skin, his trim waist nipped in his crisp white shirt. To say he was drop-dead gorgeous was an understatement. Why would he want to talk to me? I couldn't quite believe it.

"Can I join you?" he asked.

I smiled and nodded, slightly embarrassed.

"Your friends," he said, pointing at Verity and Sue at the bar. "They say you've been dancing ever since you arrived."

"I have," I agreed, continuing to dance. His cognac-brown eyes followed me as I moved. He stepped into my space.

"You like dancing?" he asked me.

"I love it," I told him.

He danced with me, mimicking my moves, mirroring rhythm and pace. We weaved in and out of each other, it was exhilarating and mesmerising. He took my hand. We twisted and moved in time with the electric beat and boom of the heavy base. One song rolled into another. It was as if we had the whole dance floor to ourselves. I twirled in my black leggings and short Ra-Ra dress. My soft, frilled hem spun out. His eyes smiled as we danced together, throwing ourselves into the music. He clearly loved it, too. He moved forward, holding my hips. I could smell him as he leant in, I could feel the heat radiating from his body. There was passion – we could both feel it in the air. I felt breathless as I inhaled him.

"Would you like – ?" he said into my ear.

"I'm sorry, I can't hear a thing," I said shrugging. The music was deafening.

"A drink?" he pointed at the bar and I shrugged.

He grabbed my hand and led me off the dance floor. His hand was firm and warm, reassuring like a father taking a small child to a place of safety. I smiled as we arrived at the bar and with great chivalry he bowed.

"A drink? What would you like?"

"I don't want anything, thank you," I told him. "I'm just happy dancing." The attention of this gorgeous man made me feel shy. I was now completely out of my comfort zone and really didn't know what to do. Luckily, he had a good sense of humour.

"Oh, my money's not good enough for you, eh?" he joked, smiling.

I smiled, feeling uncomfortable with my emotions and not knowing what to do.

"That would be lovely, thank you," I replied in a controlled manner.

He obviously sensed my apprehension and took my hand "It's okay," he said. "I'm just buying you a drink."

"Thank you. A diet coke would be great," I smiled shyly.

"Are you sure? Just a coke?" he asked.

I nodded. "I'm sure. I'm just thirsty."

I looked at his kind, heart-shaped face, his strong Gallic nose, his olive complexion. His hair was thick and dark and slicked back to perfection. He took pride in his appearance and was incredibly refined. He was completely out of my league. He got us our drinks and then we approached a table of guys, seated around the table.

"These are my colleagues." He introduced them. "Fabian, Pierre and Thierry, this is...excusez-moi," he smiled at me. "You are?"

"I'm Eve," I extended my hand. "As in Adam and Eve." Then I felt really stupid.

ST: Why did you feel stupid?

EMM: It just came tumbling out; I wasn't used to this kind of attention.

ST: Did he indicate that he thought you were stupid?

EMM: No, he was too much of a gentleman to do that.

ST: So, what happened next?

EMM: He introduced himself and his colleagues. I can still see him now smiling and then he took my hand. "So, lovely to meet you Eve. I'm Laurent."

I know I blushed as Laurent and his friends all kissed me on both cheeks. We then had a conversation about how I infuriated my friends as I liked to dance and they liked to be on "the pull".

He didn't seem to understand that. It was clear from his accent that he appeared to be French.

"They like meeting guys," I explained. "They get drunk and you know..." I trailed off.

"I don't know, tell me," he teased, brushing his top lip.

I knew he was teasing me. "You know..." I squirmed.

He laughed. "Yes, I know. I have met many girls like that, who just screw around!" He was so direct. It surprised me.

I looked over to Verity and Sue, who were now chatting up a bunch of lads at the bar. Verity had clearly had too many already. She was sitting on a high bar stool, flirting with some bloke.

"Are you from London?" asked Laurent, diverting me from watching Verity and the bloke.

I told him that we were midwives from Reading but we liked coming into London as they had the best nightclubs. I asked if they were on holiday and he then told me that they were working in one of the hotels, but they were all from France. We chatted for a while and I took his hand and led him to the dance floor. Here was my home, the place I wanted to be...I felt at ease, confident of what I could do with my body and knew how to express myself. I'd always found it hard to say what I felt. But here I could play the part. I knew my role and the rules of the game. Laurent was happy to play this game with me and we laughed and danced. Maybe I should have been a dancer and not a nurse... communicating through this art form rather than with words. There was no language barrier between us once we were dancing. I didn't want it to stop. My heart was filled with joy. I felt as though I would burst. We danced long into the night, both of us sweaty and smiling.

Then the pace of the music slowed. We found ourselves leaning on one another in an embrace. I rested my head on his chest, his shirt was damp and I knew I was soaking wet too. We were shattered. He smelt delicious – of Giorgio Armani – I recognised the fresh tones; it was so heady, mixed into his natural musk. And the sweet melody of Luther Vandross, his deep, rich voice smothered us in a blanket of warmth and comfort. I cuddled into Laurent, drifting off, enjoying this moment with him as the melody swept over us. I could feel the heat of his body and his firm hold around my waist. I hoped that it would be a long song to enjoy this snippet of time with him. Would I ever have such a soulful encounter with another living person again? I didn't know...

But all too soon, the song came to an end and it was over. The moment had been lost. I could feel my heart sinking, but he continued to hold onto me, slowly dancing in the silence.

"Come. Let's go," he suggested. "The club's closing." And sure enough, the lights were being switched on. The girls were waiting for me.

"Are we off then, Eve?" Verity asked, motioning to the door.

I hesitated.

"Eve, come on," called Sue. "We've got to head home!"

"You and your friends can come back with us, if you'd like?" Laurent suggested.

Verity smiled at him. "Well, it depends" she flirted. "Have you got any drink?"

I was embarrassed by her forthrightness.

"Come on, I'm never one to miss an opportunity." Aline hissed in whispered tones.

After a short debate, we agreed to go back to their place; Sue couldn't have driven back anyway without sobering up first.

The lads grabbed their coats, shoving their cigarettes and lighters in their coat pockets and we left the club. Boy, did that cold night air hit us! Like someone had opened the door to the mortuary! We scuttled our way down the side roads like ants running from a fire. Heading out on the dark glassy roads, Laurent hailed a cab and took us to their flat. We all climbed the stone staircase grabbing the iron handrail to support the gaggle of clubbers. We kept on laughing and then the odd person would hush the noise with a finger to their lips. This just provoked more laughter. The door was opened to the flat, and we were greeted by a tortoiseshell cat who sat swishing her tail, as though she'd been checking her watch!

"What time do you call this?" she meowed.

"Yes, yes, Bella," Laurent laughed at the cat. "We are very sorry." She followed him proudly with her tail held high, mewing insistently, wanting to be fed.

"Come on," Laurent waved us through into the flat and slung his coat over the brown sofa. "What's your poison?"

"What ya got?" Verity pushed her way to the front.

Laurent offered her wine or absinthe.

"That sounds exotic," she flirted, flicking her dark curls.

He warned her it was very strong.

"Great!" said Verity, grabbing a glass from the cupboard.

Laurent mixed up several glasses with a little water, and the concoction turned milky white. We all helped ourselves to a glass and watched each other as we all tentatively took a sip.

"Oh, that's lovely. Really warms you up," smiled Verity. She loved the aniseed taste.

Sue immediately spat hers out. "Oh my God," she said. "It's like sucking on a battery! I'm sorry, but that is vile! Can I have wine instead?"

Laurent looked hurt. "Hey, Thierry," he said. "Open the wine."

"Oui, Chef!" Thierry joked, saluting.

Fabian was rummaging around in the corner getting out a small square tin of tobacco, and started rolling up some cigarettes, breaking into it a dry sweet-smelling resin. Soon, the atmosphere was filled with a heady smoke, standers became sitters, watchers became participants. Bottles and glasses passed around; self-consciousness was being lost as we become entwined with our French cousins. Verity was all over Thierry, or was it Thierry was all over Verity? There were no surprises there. Wherever we went, Verity with her dark curls and huge cats' eyes was always the first to pull. She was a larger than life character – bold, assertive and to hell with the consequences. Sue, on the other hand was more reserved and had been engaged to Ollie since the end of our training. Verity pooh-poohed Sue's moral values and couldn't understand how she could resist temptation when there was so much out there to offer. Why settle down now? She'd ask. Me, well, I'd never found the right guy. I was always too shy to make that first move. What if they said no? But Verity would say, "There's no harm in trying, Eve. You're a big girl now, and it's time to grow up!" With a twinkle in her eye, she'd be off with another one. I'd have something inside me, holding me back. Now I sat on the sofa, watching Laurent pouring the drinks into the glasses with the confidence and skill of a waiter. I watched him laughing with Fabian as they shared a joint together. I so wanted to be with him, but I couldn't.

"Go on then, what are you waiting for?" Aline asked.

"He's not interested in me," I replied.

"But he is. He's been watching you."

I didn't believe her.

She got angry with me. "Eve, for crying out loud," she said. "You've got to start learning to read the clues. Did you not see the way he was when he was dancing with you? He's so into you. Now, why don't you get off your fat arse and do something?" she sneered.

This didn't help at all. In fact, I felt like I wanted to withdraw into my shell even further.

"You're not going to get anywhere with him, if you don't do anything about it!" she continued. "Look at Verity, she's got stuck in!"

I looked at Verity, who was now heavily into snogging Thierry. I admit I felt a pang of jealousy. How did she have so much confidence?

Aline kept on at me. "Why don't you get another drink inside you? Or try what they're smoking? Look – even Sue's joining in!" I looked over at Sue and she was smoking a joint with Pierre, snogging him. Yes, snogging him! What the hell was happening with Sue? What about her boyfriend, Ollie?

And still, Aline went on. "Well, Eve, it looks like its last man standing," she smirked. 'Either you go for it or I will.'

I asked her what she meant. She told me to wake up and make a decision.

"The choice is simple," she said. "It's either Lovely Laurent or Fab Fabian." She paused "Or maybe I'll try them both?"

I felt sick, she was so coarse and it was unnecessary. Yes, I was interested in Laurent but I couldn't cope with being rejected again. But perhaps I would lose my opportunity tonight and that would be it. All the girls paired off...even flipping Sue.

I got up and slowly, and as cautiously as a cat stalking its prey, I made my way to the kitchen. I could feel myself shaking inside. This was so difficult. I would rather have delivered a baby than expose myself. So, meekly I stood there with my empty glass, feeling awkward, not knowing what to say. How had I got this far, still unable to talk to guys?

Laurent looked down at my empty glass. "You'd like another?" he asked. I nodded and he poured red wine into my glass.

"Lovely," I said, unable to take my hands off the glass as I was shaking. He placed his hand over mine to steady the wobbling glass.

Laurent looked at me as he put the bottle down. "My sister is also very shy. She really doesn't like being with a lot of new people. It drives my parents crazy. My mother she's a wonderful cook and always makes far too much. So, she invites many people to eat. My father has a very big...hmm, how do you say?...character! He has his own vineyard so we have many visitors, for business and pleasure. It drives my sister Appoline mad. She would rather sit in her room, reading. But this makes my father very cross. My mother tries to tell him that you cannot change Appoline and we must love her for who she is. You are very much like Appoline. I really like that you don't follow your friends." He looked around the room at the girls, who were now drunk, stoned and half-naked playing strip poker in a group. "Do you want to join them?" he gestured with his wine glass.

"No." I felt embarrassed for my friends, but also for myself. I simply couldn't do it.

"Let's go somewhere else," he suggested.

So, we made our way to his bedroom. It was decorated in a typically French style, plain and chic. The antique white bed sat in the centre of the room which was occupied by the cat, curled up in a ball, softly snoring. You could see her chest wall rising and lowering. She turned and looked at us with her tired, squashed eyes.

"It's okay, Bella, go back to sleep" he soothed her, stroking her mottled fur. Laurent was gentle and I could see how kind he was towards Bella.

We sat on his bed and we talked about our families and what they were like. He clearly loved his family and had had a very happy life in France. His parents supported him coming to London even as a lowly waiter. At some point, he would return to Bordeaux. He was surprised that my family weren't nearly as supportive as his.

Laurent's grandparents, auntie and uncles were a big part of his life and the well-rounded characters were good role models for him as he grew up. Whereas I was lucky to see my grandparents four times a year, and my aunts and uncles twice a year. Family arguments, feuds and isolation formed the basis of my upbringing. I didn't have the experiences that Laurent and his peers had received and it was something I wanted my own family to have. Our lives were complete opposites; he was able to recollect wonderful camping holidays with his extended family. It seemed idyllic. I had never had a holiday with any of my aunts or uncles, I really didn't realise what I had missed until I heard about his wonderful family. His mother still phoned his grandmother every single day to chat...I found it incredible.

"What do they have to chat about every day?" I asked.

"Oh, you know," he said. "The weather, the news and whether the cat's been sick."

This made me laugh. I said, "You must miss them very much."

As we exchanged stories of growing up, it was evident that we were from very different worlds. Yet we seemed to connect with one another. He told me about previous nightmare girlfriends and how they borrowed money and never paid him back. Apparently, the final straw was when he walked into a bar in Paris to find his girlfriend kissing another bloke. That ended their relationship and it was the catalyst for him coming to England. He told me he'd left his job in Paris and got a job in London. I said I hadn't really had a lot of boyfriends because of my lack of confidence after all the horrible bullying I'd had at school. I told him I'd had the odd kiss at a nightclub, but they'd never come to anything. It was really my fault as I just couldn't relax or let go. This got me the nickname of the Snow Maiden. It was really hurtful.

He poured another glass of wine and lit his cigarette. He put on some gentle music. He smiled. "I thought of this just now," he looked slightly bashful as he came and sat next to me. He kissed me on my forehead. It was a song I'd heard only once before. It was a ballad; the husky female voice sang.

He told me how he had come to London after a break up with his girlfriend Marianne, he had arrived broken hearted and homesick. He hadn't had a relationship with anyone at all since arriving here. But then he saw me. Something had changed and he wanted to get to know me. Well, you can imagine I was flattered and so shocked I nearly fell off the bed. This gorgeous Frenchman was completely delusional, clearly the drink was talking. He would feel different in the morning, I was sure. However, I decided to relish this moment with this attractive man.

"It's the truth…" He slurred his words and slowly closed his eyes, resting his head back on his pillow. I took the full glass of red wine from his hand as it slowly tipped. I placed it onto the bedside cabinet. I stole a kiss from his lips as he went off to sleep, gently snoring. As I had suspected, he'd had far too much to drink. I watched his face relax, his dark hair framing his handsome face. His long, dark eyelashes lay against his warm skin. I pulled the blanket up and snuggled into him; listening to the remainder of his tape as I slipped off to sleep.

The night soon became day and London was slowly waking up. I was absolutely freezing cold in my little skimpy Ra Ra dress, curled up on top of Laurent's bed under just a blanket. Laurent lay asleep, still fully dressed, his crisp white shirt now crumpled. His chin now had a bluish sheen, his hair almost in the same position as it had been the previous night. Bella lay next to him, contented. I didn't want to just leave him and walk out of the door, as that would be the end. Should I leave a note? Or should I wake him?

I moved off the bed, looking for my handbag. I'd decided to write a note and ask him to call me. It was a bold move for me. The trouble was I couldn't find my bag. Had I brought it with me? Then I saw the strap sticking out from under the covers. I grabbed it and opened the stiff clasp, which made a horrendous noise. I looked up to see if I'd woken him, but he remained asleep. Rummaging inside the bag, I couldn't find a pen!

"Great," I muttered, looking for something to write with. I noticed he had a pen on his side table, so I went to get it and managed to trip over a pair of shoes, making a huge clunk! Laurent opened his cognac-brown eyes with a start.

"Oops, I'm so sorry," I said. "I was just getting a pen to leave you a note."

"You're leaving?" he asked.

I told him I had to get back for work. I shivered at the thought.

"Shall we meet again?" he asked.

I told him I would like that very much.

ST: Did you do want to see him again?

EMM: Yes, absolutely. I gave him the number for our nursing accommodation. We kissed and then I left for work.

The girls hadn't managed to get up. Verity was still asleep with Thierry in his bed. Sue was nowhere to be found. I realised she'd made her way back to Reading in her car. This was alarming because surely, she would have been over the legal limit for alcohol. I wondered whether she was so ashamed of her behaviour with Pierre that she simply had to leave the whole sordid event. Whatever happened between them was none of my business, but she'd left us all stranded in London.

Aline had been furious. "Flipping great," she said, "I can't believe she'd leave us here and not even find out whether we wanted to head home!"

"I didn't want to go, though," I reflected. "I'd had a nice evening dancing and chatting with Laurent."

"But she left us here!" Aline shouted. "How could she do that?"

I said I expected she was upset.

"That's no excuse!" she said. "I'll give her a piece of my mind when I get hold of her."

"No, don't", I said. "She'll be upset as it is. She doesn't need to get it from us as well."

"That's her problem Eve," Aline argued. "She was the one who got herself in trouble. I didn't see you ripping your knickers off for the nearest Frenchman, did you?"

I admitted I didn't know why she'd done it. Ollie would be so angry if he found out.

"Good," said Aline. "So, he should. I have a good mind to tell him what she's done." I told Aline it's not worth it. But she told me I was too soft. She said Ollie deserved to know, especially if they were going to get married.

I knew she was right, but said it wasn't our place to tell on her. She needed to work it out herself.

It wasn't till I left that I realised he hadn't given me his number or details. All I knew was his first name. I really had no idea where I was in London. But this time I felt confident that this handsome, French waiter would call me. My journey back to Reading was quite surreal. Aline was still rattling on about Sue and her behaviour but I tried not to let it get to me and concentrated on building the image of Laurent in my head. I didn't take much notice of my surroundings but had managed to negotiate my way across London and to Paddington

Station, finding the correct platform and train in time to get back for a late shift. How that happened, with my mind completely elsewhere, I don't know. The rush and hubbub of the station passed me by and I kept on getting the same images of the previous night returning.

My memory would flicker and I would try hard to concentrate on him, but it would be lost. I opened my eyes and closed them again trying to recreate his image, but it was gone. I felt upset that I wasn't allowed to access that part of my brain. I then became worried about whether I'd recognise him if I were to meet him again.

"Why are you upset?" Aline asked.

I told her. "Will I recognise Laurent if I see him again?"

She sneered at me. "Of course you will, you complete loon!"

I wasn't so sure.

She sighed. "I'm sure you'll be able to recognise him, I'm certain."

It was most unlike Aline to be reassuring. She was generally the first person to criticise me. But here she was, genuinely reassuring. Had Aline changed her ways? Was this the start of her becoming nice to me? I hoped so, but I doubted it.

ST: Well, Eve, I'm afraid our time is up. Thank you for sharing with me. It looks like meeting Laurent was important to you.

EMM: It was. It means everything to me.

SESSION ENDS.

**

Mike Jeffordson put the file down on his desk, his expression thoughtful. So, Eve McDonnell had a connection to both Aline and a Frenchman, and the coat Aline had been found in appeared to be a man's coat bought in France.

He needed to get to the bottom of these connections. His gut was telling him he was getting close. If only the doc would let them speak to Aline, she might be able to fill in the gaps.

CHAPTER 26

THE LIST

Detective Sergeant Phil Lewis arrived in the office with a sheet of paper, which he waved in front of Andrea.

"I've got it!"

"What?" Andrea asked.

"A list of all the French waiting staff working in the London Cadeau Hotels group, complete with all their duty rotas," he smiled. "Not only that, there's a good few who could be nicknamed, Lammy."

"How have you done that?" asked Andrea.

Phil nodded his head and tapped his nose. "That's for me to know, Missy," he laughed.

"Have you heard, Guv?" Andrea asked as Mike entered the room, clearly lost in his own thoughts. "Phil's got the list from the Cadeau Hotels."

Mike gave Phil a slap on the back. "Well done, Phil. Good work, now did I hear someone put the kettle on?"

Andrea rolled her eyes. "Yes Sir, of course."

"You see, Phil? She'll go far, I'm telling you." He gave Andrea a wink as he sat down with Phil at his desk.

"So, what have we got?"

"One of the operations managers was able to draw up a list of all the French waiters who work in the London Cadeau Hotels group." Phil showed him the long list of names. "From these, he broke it down into all those who could possibly be called Lammy."

"So, did he not know anyone with that nickname at all?"

"No, Guv."

Andrea returned with three mugs of tea. She sat down with the two men.

Mike slurped loudly and gasped, "Lovely drop of rosie, thanks, Andi."

He was the only one who ever called her Andi and the only one who could get away with it. He took off his anorak and slung it on the seat.

"Right, let's have a butchers' at these then."

Phil gave him the list. He read it out.

"Pierre Lamont, Gabriel Lamond, Thomas Lamb, Ludovic Lambard, Hugo Lamar, Fabian Lambert, Simon Lammas, Laurence La Torre, Thierry Lamarche, Alain Lamberg, Victor Lamprecht. Okay, so if we can establish the whereabouts of these lads on New Year's Eve, we can eliminate the waiters who were on duty. Let's see which ones went home to France for the holidays. Then we can discover who was at The Prince Regent on New Year's Eve. Excellent work." He handed him back the list and turned to Andrea. "Phil if you can focus on Pierre, Thierry, Fabian and Laurence as they're the ones mentioned in the account and they're also on this list. Can you get onto that for me straight away?"

"Have you spoken to anyone at The Royal Berkshire Hospital in Reading, Andi?"

"I'm waiting for one of the midwifery sisters to get back to me, Sir."

"Can you chase them up, please? I'm going to see what else is in these notes, as we need to find out more about these girls."

"Yes, Sir, I'll give the hospital another ring."

CHAPTER 27

THE PRINCE REGENT

Dr Dhillon sat with Aline in the courtyard. Aline lit a cigarette and exhaled the smoke into the air. She was looking a little distant, watching the smoke coiling and swirling into the air. Her whole body was turned away from Dr Dhillon.

"So, Aline, New Year's Eve. Do you think that you can recollect anything from that night?" Dr Dhillon watched her as she nervously nibbled around her nails. "It would be good, if you could try and think back to what happened."

Aline grimaced. She was flustered and twisted the hem of her dress, picking at the seam.

"The thing is, if I say anything, Eve will come back and get me, I know she will. She tried to kill me before."

"You're quite safe here, I assure you. When did you last see Eve?" Dr Dhillon asked, calmly.

"I really don't know."

"She was there on the night of the attack, Aline? Can you remember, you told me that?"

"I...I think so."

"Where were you?"

"I was outside a pub."

"Here in London?"

"I think so."

"So, can you remember anything from that night? From New Year's Eve? When you were attacked outside the pub?"

"Oh, I don't know! The thing is, it doesn't make sense!" Aline replied as she pulled a long thread from the hem and coiled it around her finger.

"Why not tell me and we can see if we can make sense of it?"

"It's a real jumble sale of ideas!"

"Don't we all love a good jumble sale?" the doctor smiled. "There are often lots of treasures to be found among all the rubbish, there could be a real gem in there!"

"Okay, so what I remember is...I was sitting in the pub...I'd had too much to drink...I was feeling sick and I was mentally trying to work out how much I'd had. I drank two glasses of wine before Fabian came home; then we'd had half a bottle of wine at the pub."

"Who's Fabian? You've not mentioned him before."

"Fabian..." She paused, "No, no I haven't, have I...? He's um, a guy I know."

"Is he your boyfriend?"

"I don't know, it doesn't feel like it. It's more like we just put up with each other."

"Because of what?"

"I don't know, I just remember being angry with him"

"Okay, tell me, what else you remember?"

"I just remember being pretty cross with Fabian, he'd said to dress up for a New Year's Eve party. I stupidly thought we'd go to the Cadeau Hotel. But no, we ended up in that dump in Brixton. He couldn't miss the opportunity to deal drugs and this made my blood boil. He couldn't take a night off. 'Always trying to keep his customers happy' was his excuse. I, on the other hand, felt like a spare part. There was a nice bartender – a young guy who chatted to me a few times."

"I was so fed up I just accepted more drinks from the other punters. It was all so dull, with dirty old men ogling me. I appeared to be the only female under the age of fifty. I didn't need this unwanted attention, so without much thought, I kept on drinking. The nice bartender suggested I should slow down as he thought that I'd had too much already. It was true; I was all over the place and then continued with Fabian's acquaintances plying me with even more booze. One of his mates had some drugs. I was pretty up for anything, so later we popped the pills into our mouths. The world started to spin around and I slumped onto the table. That was the last I remember. I was awoken by a banging."

"Bang, bang, bang! I opened my eyes slowly; a strong feeling of nausea was welling up in my chest. Someone was hammering on the table."

"Someone yelled, 'Get up, you bitch!' in my ear. I looked around the pub, dazed and disorientated. I was slumped over the table on my arms, sliding through the spilt drinks. The banging had stopped. There wasn't anyone there. I must have been dreaming. I closed my eyes again, placing my face on the cold, wet, wooden table. And then it started again. Bang, bang, bang, as someone rapped their knuckles again."

"'Get up, you lazy bitch.' It was a woman's voice and she was seriously angry. She said, 'So help me, God, I'm gonna kill you when I get my hands on you. Get up!' She screamed. This really wasn't a dream, it was happening. I looked up and saw Eve standing in front of me. I felt drunk, like a boxer. My legs felt unsteady. I was sick with drugs and drink."

"'So, this is where you are,' she said. 'You're unbelievable. Look at the state of you. You're a disgrace.'"

"I was confused, looking around the smoky room. 'I'm not a disgrace' I said. I couldn't believe Eve was here. How had she managed to find me?"

"You are," she said. "You're completely smashed! You've been taking drugs again, haven't you?" She shook me, angrily. "What the fuck are you playing at, Aline?"

"I've had a lot on my mind," I said, running my fingers through my hair. "I can't believe you'd drop me in it," she continued accusingly.

"Why? What have I done?" I asked.

"What have you done?" She was astonished by my reply, flicking her hair behind her ear. "I'm in big trouble because of you."

"I was completely flabbergasted by Eve, how dare she start having a go at me?"

"I didn't know what she was talking about."

"I'm gonna lose my job and it will be your fault."

"I shook my head and said, 'I've done nothing."

"You told them about the drugs and now there's codeine missing. Did you take it, Aline? Tell me the truth!" she demanded.

"I said, 'I can assure you that it wasn't me, Eve."

Eve grabbed hold of the shoulder of the coat. "It must have been you," she screamed. "Aline, stop lying! Get up! We're going outside. I can't talk to you with all these people in here."

"As we got to the pub door, she shoved me outside into the cold. She called me a fucking bitch. 'Look at the state of you,' she said. 'You're drugged up again!

Can't you control yourself for one evening? My God, you're an embarrassment!' She grabbed my coat tightly around my throat. I thought she was going to strangle me. Then she let go, taking a swing at me."

"My anger rose, I could feel it writhing through my body, my fist clenched and I could feel my fingernails digging into the palms of my hands. I was ready to launch myself at her but she grabbed my hair and before I knew it, she was pulling it forcing my head down towards the ground.

She called me an evil, manipulative bitch. She said I always had been and always will be. I found the strength to break away from her. I screamed, pushing her in the centre of her chest.

She lunged at me, grabbing a beer bottle from a crate. The next thing I knew she was attacking me in a frenzy, chasing me down the road, swinging a bottle above her head. I was screaming at her to get off and leave me alone."

"The pain to the back of my head was sharp; I saw a flash of light, then lightning, and then the biggest floodlight I'd ever seen in a stadium. Then the image became scrambled, like someone trying to tune the TV in...And that's the last thing I remember. I've got no idea how the hell I ended up here in hospital."

Tears welled up in Aline's eyes.

***

Dr Dhillon returned to the nurses' station and rang Mike Jeffordson.

"Hi Mike, it's Dr Dhillon here. I've just had a very interesting conversation with Aline. She had a boyfriend called Fabian; he sounds like a drug dealer; he was there the night she was attacked by Eve."

"Interesting, we're already trying to find her. Did she say where the attack happened?"

"She thinks it happened outside a pub."

"Will she be fit to make a statement soon, do you think?"

"Yes, soon. Give it another day or so."

They talked a bit longer before the doctor needed to attend to her next patient.

"Thanks, Dr Dhillon," said Mike. "That's fan-blooming-tastic."

Mike came off the phone and looked up, puzzled. "What do you make of this?" he said to Andrea and Phil. "That was Dr Dhillon on the blower and it's a bit strange. Apparently, Aline says she was attacked by Eve McDonnell outside a pub. They were arguing about drugs taken from a hospital."

"So, she was involved!" Andrea replied, looking downhearted.

"Well, it certainly looks like Aline and Lammy were up to something."

"Well, Colin the barman reported seeing her with Lammy that night," said Phil. "Perhaps that's what they were arguing about."

"And you know what else? Aline's boyfriend appears to be called Fabian."

"There is a Fabian on the list of employees working for Cadeau Hotels."

"Yes, that's true. It would fit." Mike Jeffordson scratched his chin. "But Dr Dhillon says that Aline was arguing with Eve. Have we got anything back on CCTV yet, Phil?"

"Perhaps they were both there?" Andrea suggested.

"Yes, that maybe the case."

"Look what came in this morning," Phil smiled, holding up the video tape.

"Let's get onto it right away."

CHAPTER 28

CCTV

They took the CCTV tape into the viewing room, and pushed the tape into the VHS video player.

"Trevor was making it hard for me to get this but I got it in the end," he said.

"Well done, Phil," said Andrea. "He's a slippery one."

"I hope this isn't a wild goose chase and Trevor has given us the wrong tape."

"Or he's recorded over it."

"Oh, don't say that. That would be typical of him to do that!"

The screen in front of them flickered, and then in an instant, images revealed a couple outside The Prince Regent, arguing. The man looked like he was in his late twenties, dark hair, smartly dressed, just as Colin Walker had described him. However, all they could see was the back of his head. The girl was petite with long, dark, straight hair, dressed in the coat in which she was found in the park. Her face was quite clear as she faced the camera. It confirmed that it was indeed the face of Aline. Nobody else was with them. They moved away from the camera, around the corner of the pub.

"Where have they gone? We've lost the image. Quick Andrea, forward it. We must have hit a blind spot," said Phil. "Keep going, stop – right there!"

The next image they saw was Aline clutching the back of her head.

"Well that certainly looks like our girl, Aline," Phil stated, pointing to the frozen image. He ran the video back and forth, trying to see who had hit her.

Andrea leant forward. "Look, Phil. She has her shoes and handbag with her. Hold it just there and let me just take down some details. Okay, so I can't make out the colour of the bag as the film's black and white. But I'd say she had black stilettos on, with a dark, shiny handbag, most likely patent leather." She wrote the details down on her notepad. "Okay, you can continue. Look! It looks like Aline's running towards the park where we found her. And he's following her."

"Look!" exclaimed Phil excitedly, freezing the image. "There's our Lammy!" The man had turned around and given them a great shot of his whole face.

"Can we zoom in on that image?" she asked.

"Certainly" Phil managed to zoom in and cropped it to gain a better picture.

"Brilliant! Let's print off this image and we can use it to ID him."

"Is there another woman at all in the footage?"

Phil peered closely at the screen. "I don't think so. I didn't see anyone."

"Let's run back through the tape to see if we can see any images of anyone else. Aline claims that Eve struck her. I'm just a bit concerned that if we don't look carefully, we'll miss her."

Phil and Andrea ran the CCTV tape backwards and forwards, stopping at regular intervals, looking for Eve.

"Nothing; that was disappointing. I was hoping that she would be there. She must have been hiding in that black spot."

"Well, at least we have got the image of Lammy. We could take it to the Maudsley hospital and see if Aline recognises him," Phil suggested, sending the still shots to the printer. "Then, if we can find him, he might be able to lead us to Eve. He must have seen the attack."

***

Mike Jeffordson strode into the viewing room as Andrea and Phil were collecting the images from the printer.

"So, what have we got guys?"

"We've got some footage of the night in question, Guv, and look, I reckon this is Lammy, the lad we're looking for."

Mike took the photos and examined the first one. "It certainly looks like Aline, that's for sure." He scanned through the pictures. "Any pictures of the attack?"

"No, none."

"Any images of Eve at all?"

"None, I'm afraid," Andrea added, "I very much doubt that Eve was even there. I suspect that the attack was by Lammy".

"I think you are correct; it really does look like it was just Aline and Lammy at the Prince Regent. I think we should concentrate our efforts in that direction."

"Yes Sir, anything from Cadeau Hotels?"

"I've just been onto Mr Cole, one of the managers, we talked about anyone whose movements couldn't be accounted for and we've come up with a name. He gave us Fabian Lambert. Dr Dhillon has told us that Aline said that she was with Fabian on New Year's Eve. From Simon Thomas' sessions with Eve, she also mentions Fabian. I'd therefore surmise that Fabian is our Lammy; but Mr Cole can't confirm that that's his nickname. But it seems that Fabian wasn't working at the Cadeau Hotel on New Year's Eve. All the others have been able to confirm their whereabouts on the evening. It's only Fabian Lambert who hasn't got an alibi for that night.

"Well, that sounds pretty conclusive to me!"

"It certainly does...Have we got that address yet for Eve McDonnell? We need to track her down."

"Last known address appears to be the nurse accommodation in Addington Road, Reading."

"I think we need to make a little trip to the Cadeau Hotel to see this young Mr Lambert. And then a trip out to Reading."

"I couldn't agree more," said Andrea.

"We were also going to take the stills from the CCTV to Florence Green ward to see if Aline could also identify the man as Lammy," Phil suggested, "And then see if we can get Aline to make a statement."

"Great idea," said the DI.

***

When DI Jeffordson and DC Doyle arrived at the Cadeau Hotel, London Bridge they found the manager in charge, who took them into an office behind the kitchen. The office was windowless and hot, the smell of bacon fat wafted in from the kitchens.

"Ooh, lovely," said Mike, breathing in the aroma. "You can't beat an English breakfast: double eggs, sausage, bacon. Oh, and a nice bit of fried bread!"

"Can I get you both something? I'm sure the chef won't mind whipping something up," the manager offered.

"No, no, you're alright. We won't be long. We've just come to see Fabian Lambert."

"Ah yes. I'll find someone to get him. He's working in the main restaurant at the moment. Breakfast service is nearly over."

A few minutes later, a smartly dressed young man in his later twenties, with short, dark, cropped hair arrived at the door of the office.

"Fabian, we have two officers here who have come to ask you some questions." The manager directed Fabian to a chair.

"Bonjour," said Fabian, shaking hands with both officers.

"Good morning, Sir. I'm so sorry to disturb you. I'm Detective Inspector Mike Jeffordson and this is Detective Constable Andrea Doyle," said Mike, pointing at Andrea.

"Good morning," he replied, looking bemused. "How can I help you?"

"We need some help with an investigation."

"Okay," he pouted, shrugging his shoulders.

"Can you tell us where you were on New Year's Eve?"

"The one just gone?"

"Yes."

"Umm," he looked around the room. "I cannot recollect."

"Come on, it was New Year's Eve! Surely you remember?" DI Jeffordson pressed him.

Fabian thought. The manager shuffled in his seat.

"I was out with friends. That's right. I was with my friends, drinking. I remember now."

"Where were you drinking?" Mike pressured him.

"In London."

"We gather that much," Mike raised his eyebrows. "I'm not a fool, Mr Lambert, so please don't take me for one. Do you understand?"

Fabian nodded.

"I'm going to ask you again. Where were you?"

"I went to a pub."

"Which pub? There are a lot in London."

"That's the problem. We went from pub to pub!"

"So, you did go with a girlfriend, then?"

"No!" He looked shocked by the suggestion. "I don't have a girlfriend."

"So, who were you with? Who did you meet?"

Fabian started to look flustered. "Just some friends."

"Some friends, eh?" Mike twisted his moustache and started pacing around the room, trying to size up this cocky French waiter.

"Do you have any connections with an Aline Deniaud?"

"No. I have never heard of her." He looked at the manager, seemingly offended by this.

"What about Eve McDonnell? Have you ever heard of her?"

"No, why are you asking me these questions? I don't know either of these girls."

"So, you don't know anything about the attack in Brixton on New Year's Eve? It was at The Prince Regent pub. Aline Deniaud sustained a head injury." Andrea stood with her hands on her hips.

"I have said, I never heard of this girl, Aline," he protested.

"Well, Sir," said Mike Jeffordson. "We have reason to believe that you have had contact with her recently."

"Have I? I don't understand."

"Yes," Andrea glared at Fabian, trying to stare him out.

Fabian's face twitched.

"Shall I refresh your memory, Mr Lambert?" DI Jeffordson took the photograph out of his pocket. He placed the CCTV picture of Aline and a man onto the table. "You see, I think this looks like you, Fabian Lambert!"

CHAPTER 29

FLORENCE GREEN WARD

DS Phil Lewis arrived on Florence Green Ward and found Stuart Gibson coming down the corridor with the medicine trolley.

"I've come to see Aline briefly, if at all possible. I'm one of the officers who've been looking after her case," he showed his warrant card.

"She's in her room, come with me."

They found Aline looking a little better than when Phil had last seen her at Kings College Emergency department.

"Aline, I've brought you some medicine," said Stuart. "And I've brought a police officer to see you, hen."

Phil walked tentatively into the room and took the photograph out to show her.

"Hello, Aline. I have a photograph of the night you were injured and wondered if you could identify the person in the picture."

He sat on the seat opposite Aline and handed her the print.

"Do you recognise this man?"

She looked down at the photograph, her eyes widened and then she blinked and started to rub her sore eyes. Phil pursed his lips together and took out another photograph.

"This is a photograph of the girl a few moments later. She's holding her head, do you see?"

Aline instantly put her hand to her head.

"This is me?" she asked.

Phil and Stuart exchanged looks.

"It certainly looks like you, "Phil took the photograph and handed it to Stuart.

"It really does look like you, Aline," Stuart commented. "Have you any idea who the man is? It could really help the police find out who hurt you."

Aline took the photo back and looked at it again. Her hands trembled as she held the photograph.

"He's vaguely familiar...but I don't know why!"

"Does the name Lammy mean anything?" asked Phil.

"Lammy?" she questioned.

"What about Fabian Lambert?" Phil replied.

Aline's face grimaced, she gulped swallowing down the bile in her throat. "Yes, I know that name."

"You do...?"

"Yes."

"And is this him?

"Yes, yes, it is"

"Do you have any idea why you were both the pub that night?"

"I was there because it was New Year's Eve."

"Do you know why you had an argument with him?"

"Like I said to the doctor, it was Eve I had the argument with not Fabian." She shook her head. "I was cross with him."

"Why were you cross with him?"

"'cause he was dealing."

"So, the assault wasn't by Fabian?"

"No, like I said already it was Eve."

"Okay, we'll leave it today. We may pop back again another day," Phil reassured her, getting up to leave. "If you remember anything else, please tell the doctor and get her to call us, okay?"

She nodded as they left the room.

Outside, he handed the pictures to Stuart. "Perhaps you'd like to give these to Dr Dhillon. They may be helpful at some point."

***

That evening, when Dr Dhillon arrived on Florence Green Ward, Aline was pacing up and down, scratching at her arms, distracted by her own thoughts. She was dressed in a long winceyette nightie with a high, frilled collar and long sleeves, and tiny pink flowers on it. The nightie was something a grandmother would wear, not a young woman. On her feet she wore a pair of slippers from lost property. They were several sizes too big. One of the nurses had helped Aline to have a bath and wash her hair, its dark, rich glossy appearance shone for the first time.

"How is she?" Dr Dhillon asked Stuart.

"Oh, she's doing okay. But she's been a bit agitated ever since she had the visit from the policeman earlier. She was shown some pictures from the CCTV camera of herself and a man."

"Have you got the pictures?"

"Yes, they left them with me. Since then she's been pacing up and down. It was a real trigger for her. Then she had a bit of a problem with one of the regulars wanting to turn the telly on," he explained in his soft Edinburgh accent as he handed over the pictures.

"Goodness me," said the doctor, wincing at the image of Aline holding her injured head. "Have the police any idea what happened to her?"

"They're still trying to piece it together but they believe that perhaps the attack was by the man in the photo, not by Eve. She's nowhere to be seen on the CCTV tape, just Aline and the man. Oh, and they're still trying to contact her parents in France but they haven't found them yet."

"Okay, so maybe the attacker wasn't Eve."

Stuart and Dr Dhillon made their way over to Aline who continued to pace up and down the lounge, her gaze fixed on the floor.

"Aline," said Stuart. "Dr Dhillon is here to see you, hen!"

Aline kept on pacing.

"Hello, Aline," said the doctor. "Stuart tells me that you had a visit from the police and that they showed you a picture."

Aline halted and started to scratch her arms.

"Did the pictures make you feel anxious?"

"NO!" she denied, rubbing her arms. "I do feel a bit better, honestly. It's my skin, it's so itchy," she said, scratching at them again.

"Talk to me" Dr Dhillon said soothingly, leading her to the sofa.

"I just feel a bit upset...They want to keep turning the television on." She looked around the room, her legs jiggled as she talked.

"Just people putting the television on, is that correct? Nothing else has made you upset?"

"You know how it upsets me, particularly when I know I'm safe here. When they switch it on, I know she'll be able to find me!"

"Yes, yes Aline...I know that you think that 'she' will be able to see you, but I promise you, she can't,"

"But I can see them on there, why can't they see me?"

"Well, it's a special camera...a bit like taking a photograph. You can see the image of the person printed out," explained Dr Dhillon. "But they can't see you. Do you understand?"

"I know a photo can't see me. It's not alive," she spat out, irritated. "I'm not mad you know!"

"We know that."

Immediately, Aline pointed at the television. "But it is... Look at it. They're all moving. How can they not see me?"

"Because it's not a window, Aline," Dr Dhillon reassured.

"It doesn't make sense." Aline started to scratch at her arms again.

"Your arms look sore, Aline. This is a side-effect of the sedative you are on, I think we should give you something to help. Your scratching is making it worse." She turned to Stuart. "I suggest we half the dose for a couple of weeks and review her. Some antihistamines will help the itching."

"Aline, you are perfectly safe here, nothing is going to happen to you. Try not to worry."

Dr Dhillon and Stuart left the room, they strode up the corridor and headed towards the office. Dr Dhillon indicated for Stuart to come in and close the door behind them.

"She's clearly having hallucinations and I believe that her account of what happened at the pub was also an hallucination. It's probable that Aline's become so obsessed with this woman Eve, that she believes she can see her."

CHAPTER 30

ALL THOSE WHO
ARE WEARY

The following morning, after Aline had had a good night's sleep, and the medicine had now started working, she appeared more comfortable than the previous day. She sat across from Dr Dhillon with Stuart to her side, in the small consulting room off the main corridor. The main light flickered, casting shadows which jumped and jerked. The bulb crackled and hissed. Aline looked up, distracted by the noise.

"I'm sorry, that's really irritating," said Stuart. He got up and turned the light off, putting the room into partial darkness. They sat in the gloom, the rain outside poured down, drumming onto the metal roof.

"Now it's too dark," he exclaimed. "I'll go and find another bulb."

"No, it's fine, honestly," Aline replied meekly. "I quite like it."

"You didn't like the dark when you first came here," Dr Dhillon suggested.

"No, I suppose I didn't." Aline looked out of the window. "This is much like the day I ended up at the church."

"Oh?" Stuart encouraged.

"Yes. I'd had a long day, you see. I was pretty exhausted by life and..." she reflected. "I'd trudged my way through the streets of London with a set of baby scales on my back. The straps cut into my shoulders. Events on my case-load kept going over and over in my mind, leaving me exhausted. Hopping on and off the buses was a regular occurrence, there was no point taking a car out visiting. The congestion, parking and general melee of traffic spewing around the capital through every main artery and the smaller capillaries made the life of a community midwife all the harder. The local buses were used to me now, popping on and off between stops. That day, I'd visited the Jarvis family. It was a pretty desperate case. Social services were involved as the two previous children were now in care for neglect. She had a one-year-old, seen regularly by her health visitor who had grave concerns about her parenting skills. And here we were again, Sally Jarvis was pregnant again. No regular partner, she boasted about how she'd picked up a bloke in the local boozer and brought him back to the flat. The rest is, as they say, history. This was an all-too-familiar story, one that saddened my soul. I reflected upon what future these children would have, how the toddler was sat in its high chair with jam sandwiches for breakfast, lunch and dinner. A bottle of tea thickened with a dissolved rusk was propped on the corner of the child's cot, ready to choke it. All done to make it 'shut up' and 'get through the night' by staving off the hunger. It's easy to be cruel when they have no voice, no voice to say that their cries are ignored; the nappies so heavy that they're hanging around their knees, held on fast with gaffer tape. The Jarvis's weren't unusual; most of the families I visited were dysfunctional. The burden of carrying this took its toll on me. I felt irritated by their feeble excuses – the 'Yeah, I've tried that!'; the rolling eyes and sucking through their teeth. I was exhausted by the parents' disinterest in the future of their children. It had seemed to be such a romantic notion, becoming a midwife. But as time went on I felt increasingly more reflective and despondent. The average family of 2.5 children just didn't exist anymore. It just seemed to be this living hell of child protection cases. No wonder I was finding it harder to sleep at night, constantly thinking and worrying as I lay in bed. I'd started having a glass of wine to help take my mind off the day's events. Honestly, some of them I just wanted to pack up and put them on the next bus out. I would lie there, thinking about them all, running through my case-load one by one, ensuring I had done everything possible, contacted all my fellow professionals to ensure I had done all I could to protect them.

"The bus stopped on the Brompton Road and I staggered off under the weight of the scales. I felt emotionally and physically drained like a chewed piece of string. I smiled to the driver and gave him a small wave as I left and he nodded his head.

"As I left the bus there was a huge billboard in front of me: 'Come to me, all you who are weary and burdened and I will give you rest...Matthew 11:28.' I stood, staring at the board, the bold font on a cream background. It was so simple yet it smacked me in the eyes. I could feel the emotion rising and hot tears running down my face. I was tired, so very, very tired. My eyes followed the sign which flapped against the black metal railings. It had been secured by cable ties. My gaze looked up over the top of the fence and I could see the lights on inside the church. Like a moth to a flame I walked through the gate and along the path, feeling drawn.

"But the feelings of apprehension grew like a weed, wrapping itself around my toes. I felt like the building had cast its net over me, like a fish in the sea. I hadn't been inside a church since I was a teenager. I felt guilty and ashamed for not attending in over fifteen years.

I'd loved going when I was young, being part of a lively Pentecostal church – gospel music just filled your soul. It was young and vibrant. That church was nothing like I'd ever been to before; the congregation were pleased to be alive and enthusiastic in their worship, unlike the boring, dull Church of England. No wonder their numbers were dwindling. It wasn't just about the worship – I felt I could be myself, explore God and ask difficult questions there. No one judged me.

"But it all ended when I started my nurse training. It was very easy not to practice when no one else believed in God. I thought I'd continue on the right path and never leave Him. But it wasn't that easy and before you know it, you've lost your moral compass, arrogantly thinking that you were okay with God, and you don't need him right now. How wrong could I be? So, here I stood in front of the church in West London. Its name rang a bell in my head, St Peters Church. But I just couldn't place it. I took a deep breath and stepped inside. There were others inside chatting, but no one noticed me. I slipped off my coat and the scales and sat at the side of the church. I looked up at the glass windows and felt a darkness overtake me. I was overwhelmed by the sense of doom, a crushing sensation started to push upon my chest, it pressed me into the chair. Pains were shooting down my legs. I felt as though I was having a heart attack with my pulse pounding in my head. The lights around me became blurred, the sound was muffled. I felt incredibly dizzy.

"As I fell off my seat onto the floor, I crashed down onto my knees knocking over the chair in front. The crash reverberated around the church. A very overweight middle-aged man with sandy hair sauntered over and dropped onto his haunches and said, 'Come on, get up.' He grabbed my wrist. I gripped my chest and told him I couldn't breathe.

"He shoved me up against a chair and said, 'You need to sit up.' He was holding onto my hands with a firm grip. He sat in silence, scowling at me. His piercing blue eyes were penetrating. I felt disorientated and unsure of where I was. High above, the chandeliers hung accusingly, emanating a harsh light that made my eyes sting. My tears poured and a flood of pain overtook me. I gulped down hard on the guilt. Rising out of my seat I pushed his hands away. 'I've got to go, I shouldn't be here,' I said."

"You're not in any fit state to go anywhere," he said. "Sit yourself down." He forced me back into the chair. He said his name was the Reverend Graham Hillier and he asked me to tell him what had brought me there. I didn't like him; there was an element of crossness in his manner. I felt like I was taking up his valuable time and I felt embarrassed by my outburst. I wanted to wriggle away, but that's what I felt like I'd always been doing. I'd never been able to talk about what was causing the pain inside, because no one was truly prepared to listen. And if they did, it was only to fulfil their own agenda. I wondered what box this would tick for Reverend Hillier? Another soul saved? Why did he think he was the person I would talk to? I was shocked by what I was thinking; it was all such a muddle. I wanted to tell someone, but who could I trust?

"I looked into his pale blue eyes, searching to see if I could really trust this man. I tried to minimise the sheer enormity of what was going on in my life. I told him I was incredibly tired."

"'You're a nurse?' he asked, nodding at my uniform. I'd forgotten I was still dressed for work. I nodded, smoothing down my uniform. 'It's an admirable vocation,' he said. He told me his sister was a senior nurse too, back home in the north of England, Macclesfield in fact. She was in charge of four wards and all its staff. He looked at the church which we were sitting in. He sat up straight. He was clearly proud of her and her achievements.

"I sat there, deathly quiet, unable to tell him what was going on. He looked like he didn't have a sympathetic bone in his body. I could feel my emotions rising. I was not going to cry...I mustn't cry. I gulped, holding it down, pushing my feelings into my stomach."

"'I'm under the same code as you,' he said. 'Whatever you tell me is in confidence. It's between me, you and

God.'" "He was condescending, clearly trying to wheedle out of me what was going on. But I felt on my guard and I wasn't prepared to tell him. What had just happened was embarrassing enough. The unease of the situation started again and I wanted to run. He sensed that I was uncomfortable. I had to go. This man didn't care. He may have been wearing a dog collar but he was only a man. He released his grip on my hand and said, 'It's okay if you want to go...I'm not keeping you here.'"

"I thanked him and got up from the chair and could feel myself making a bolt for the door. But I tried desperately not to run or to look harassed. He told me to take care and followed me across the church. At the door he asked me my name. I lied and told him it was Mary. I don't know what came over me but I wanted to be anonymous. I didn't want to give my name. I didn't want to come back; I didn't deserve any love and compassion. I left the church swiftly, brushing past other guests in the entrance hall. I had to get out quick...Then I felt a hand on my shoulder. I looked back, shocked. 'I believe you've forgotten something, Mary,' he said, holding up my scales. I took them from him and felt a solitary hot tear run down my cheek."

"'Please, talk to me,' he said. His voice had softened for the first time, and he directed me back to one of the pews. We both sat looking at the stained-glass window. He asked if I'd been in London long. I told him I'd been there about six months. He wanted to know why I'd moved here. I said I needed a fresh start. Then he asked me what did I need a fresh start from and I blurted it out."

"'From Eve,' I said. He asked who she was. 'She's my worst nightmare,' I said. It was true. He didn't know what to say to that. I sat there, looking at a huge stained-glass window. I could feel his eyes fixed on mine. I didn't know what else I should say. I took a gulp and told him, 'She got me into trouble, so I ran. I ran away.' I felt so ashamed.

"He wanted to know what sort of trouble I was in. I told him it was trouble at work. I burst out crying, the pain was just so immense and I could feel my chest tightening again."

"'Can you tell me what happened?' he asked."

"'Well,' I cried, my shoulders shuddering. 'I had to leave as we'd both been suspended.' He wanted to know why we'd been suspended and I just blurted it out. 'For taking controlled drugs.' After I said it, I took a sharp intake of breath. It was out in the open now. I had stolen drugs from the ward. He looked shocked and repulsed by what I'd told him. I knew it! I'd told him too much."

CHAPTER 31

FLORENCE GREEN WARD

DI Jeffordson and DC Doyle made their way down the long corridor towards Florence Green ward. It was all very still, and in the distance, they could hear the odd voice calling out for a nurse. Andrea felt quite uncomfortable being at the Maudsley Hospital. Give her a visit to a prison any day of the week. A trip to a psychiatric unit felt so unpredictable. At least in prison they were locked away in their cells. Mike, however, strode along with a confident air. He could have been doing his weekly shop for all he cared. They found Dr Dhillon in the staff room with the nurses, enjoying a welcome break.

"Afternoon, Doc. How's it all going?"

Dr Dhillon got up and shook Mike's hand.

"Would you like a coffee?" she asked, picking up her empty mug.

"Tea, if possible, please" Mike smiled, giving her a wink.

"And you?" she asked Andrea.

"Yes lovely, tea please." Andrea scanned the ward and shuddered as she watched the patients shuffling around; arms limp by their sides, their expressions vacant.

Dr Dhillon became aware that Andrea was looking decidedly uncomfortable. "It's all quite calm now," she said. "You should have been here earlier. We've had quite an afternoon."

Andrea gave Dr Dhillon a nervous smile.

Mike surveyed the ward; he spotted Aline in the corner with her headphones on, singing to herself.

"She does that a lot. "Dr Dhillon had followed Mike's gaze. "She really loves music."

"Oh, what does she like?" asked Andrea.

"It's pretty varied. Madness, Matt Bianco, bit of Barry Manilow, Michael MacDonald. She plays a few songs over and over."

"All the 'Ms" Mike chuckled. "Next thing, you'll be telling is she likes Mike and the Mechanics – oh – and Madonna!" he laughed.

"Very funny Sir." Andrea rolled her eyes at him.

"Er, no actually. She's partial to Frankie Valle and the Four Seasons too," the doctor said, bemused by their hilarity.

"Please come in, take a seat," she directed them to the tatty NHS chairs as one of the nurses went off to get their drinks.

"What did you think about the Simon Thomas' notes?" asked Mike.

"Well, there's a lot I would like to discuss with you both. Stuart and I had a meeting with Aline earlier. It would appear that she and Eve took drugs from the ward where they were working. She told the Reverend Hillier at St Peters about it."

Mike and Andrea exchanged a look.

"So, you were right, Sir," Andrea remarked.

"Right about what?" Dr Dhillon enquired.

"I said to DC Doyle, I wondered whether Mary Daniels was indeed Aline Deniaud."

"Yes, she's. Aline told me that she changed her name when she met the reverend as she was embarrassed and didn't want to reveal her true identity."

"We thought as much. But why?" asked Mike.

"Actually, Sir, I've met the Reverend Hillier," said Andrea. "Let's say he's not your most compassionate man of the cloth!" She raised her eyebrows and the doctor nodded in agreement.

"I can understand Aline not wanting to tell him her real name."

Dr Dhillon gave them a detailed account of what Aline said about meeting Reverend Hillier.

"And the notes? Anything in there worth mentioning?"

"Well, that's the other really strange thing," Dr Dhillon paused. "Yes I recognise some of the accounts. I need to check a few things before I can say anymore. Is that alright?"

"I suppose it will have to be, but don't leave it too long Doc, I've got a crime to solve!" Mike exclaimed.

CHAPTER 32

REFLECTION

Aline sat on Florence Green ward with a CD player on her lap, flicking backwards and forwards through the tracks. She wondered what the hell she had done and how her life had gone so wrong, to be sitting here in a mental ward. Aline looked at the player and could see her face reflected on the mirrored surface. The earphones blotted out the sounds from the ward.

Everything was so screwed up and she was the biggest screw up of them all. Aline didn't know if her life would ever be normal again. Life never was as it appeared to be, she often walked around feeling one way inside, often hiding behind a mask on the outside.

Why do we hide behind these masks? Aline asked herself. Well, she thought, that in itself is a good question. Is it to protect ourselves or protect others? She often asked herself this question. Was it a bit of both? Often, she couldn't express the pain she felt deep inside herself. This constant pain of being hurt was over-flowing. We all need to be loved and to be wanted, she thought. It's only when we find that true soul-mate that we can be our true selves. But until that day comes, we have to hide behind that mask. It's just too dangerous to expose yourself when you're so vulnerable to being hurt again. Aline believed the safest option was to drop the portcullis and put up defences; stop your heart being invaded by the incoming poisoned arrows. She felt that if she didn't become involved and cut herself off, then she didn't have to take on everyone else's issues and reveal herself. She wondered if that seemed selfish, but you know what? she thought, that's how I'll survive. That way she kept everything bottled up inside her and didn't have to talk to anyone about what's really eating her. So, she supposed that yes, it would eventually find her out. It was doing so now, wasn't it? The pain gnawed at her like a dog chewing a bone. Slowly but surely it was taking its toll in sleepless nights, panic attacks and constant feelings of anxiety.

Aline was paranoid about forming new relationships as she expected to be deceived, torn down and humiliated. It was so easy for him to abuse me, she thought. So easy to be hurt by him. Her emotions were now numb and she felt dead inside. It was like going through the motions. She remembered him on top of her, again and again. Yet, in a strange way, it was the only thing that kept her going. Aline knew it wasn't love or even lust. That emotion had been lost a long time ago. It was the sense of having human contact – the feel of him, the warmth of his bare skin.

She didn't know what would become of her. All too often Aline had worn her heart on her sleeve and been an open book. But after all these years of being exposed, belittled and made to feel like the villain, she'd now closed the book and locked it. Just like those old-fashioned dairies. It would take a very special person to open this book again. Aline would sometimes imagine the one she'd loved in her head – his smile, his kisses and even try to conjure up his smell to block out the hell she was going through. This all seemed as though it was her destiny and she thought she was never going to be redeemed. Yes, they were right; she did need help, but Aline just couldn't see it then and now she was here in a mental ward.

Her thoughts rambled around like windmills in her mind; it was like someone was constantly whispering to her, telling her untruths. The voice called her a worthless piece of shit. She could feel the panic rising in her chest. She had to stop it. She turned up the volume on the CD player, blocking everything else out.

Bright lights switched on inside her, a sense of peace, love and calm. She could smell the scent of a man, her man. She closed her eyes and she could almost see him. But the next track that started stirred unwelcome emotions deep inside of her. Hot tears rolled down upon her face. Why was this all so familiar yet so distant? Why the hell couldn't she remember what had happened to her? Anger grew inside and she just wanted to scream. She picked up the CD player and threw it at the wall.

"Merde!" She screamed. The force of her throw smashed the pieces of the CD player across the floor. Dr Dhillon opened the door to the office, as the CD played was hurled across the room. Mike and Andrea stood in silence as Stuart came running into the room. Aline crumbled to the floor, completely broken.

"Hey, Aline what's happening? What's going on?" He picked up the shards of plastic off the floor.

"It's screwing me up, Stuart! It's all screwing me up!"

"What is?"

"All this! I'm never going to get better."

"You are, Aline, you will get better."

"But I'm broken. I can't remember!" Tears poured down her face.

"Don't you see? The fact that your emotions are getting stirred is good. It means that it's working. Parts of your brain are waking up. You've already remembered a lot."

"Perhaps I don't want it to wake up if it's going to cause this much pain."

"It is going to hurt, but you've got to do it. You owe it to yourself." He put his arm around her. "Come here."

"Goodness" remarked Andrea looking from Dr Dhillon to Mike.

"It's quite normal, I'm afraid."

They stood and watched as Stuart rocked Aline like a small child. He looked over his shoulder towards them.

"Okay?" Dr Dhillon mouthed.

"Yep" he mouthed back; continuing to sooth the heavy sobs coming from Aline's shaking body.

CHAPTER 33

BRIXTON POLICE STATION

Andrea and Mike arrived back at the station with the accounts which Dr Dhillon had given them. Andrea felt alarmed and upset. The anger inside her made her feel hot and sweaty and she made her way to the ladies' toilet. She splashed cold water onto her face and looked at her pale complexion.

"Come on Andi," she looked at her reflection. "Get a grip." She scooped up the running water in her hands and took a drink. Celine came in the ladies just at that moment.

"Andrea, are you okay?" She put her hand reassuringly on her back.

"Yes, I'm quite all right, honestly," she said, trying to sound bright and in control.

Celine wasn't quite so sure. "Certain?"

"Yes, thanks." Andrea left the ladies toilets immediately. She didn't want to go through it with Celine.

She made her way back to the incident room and without thinking, she took a large slice of carrot cake from the desk. She looked around the room furtively as she licked the butter cream icing off her fingers. Right now, she really didn't care. She felt so confused by Dr Dhillon's account of Aline. She questioned herself again. Was Aline mixed up with drugs? Was she an innocent victim or had she been involved in something more sinister?

She rifled back through her notebook again, trying to recollect exactly what she'd said. She took herself to a quiet corner to read through what she'd written.

Mike noticed she looked upset. "You alright, Andi? You look like you've seen a ghost!"

She took a deep breath. "I'm fine, Sir!" she said, looking back at her notepad, trying to ignore his attention.

"You sure?"

"Yes, Sir, I was just about to start going through my notes again."

"So, let's recap." He nodded in the direction of the pad. "What did the good doctor tell us?"

"It does look like Aline is mixed up in drugs; she was suspended from her previous position with a girl called Eve. I would suspect that this does all tie in with Lammy."

"Yes, Andrea. I think you're right," he said.

"I don't know what to think about Aline, but it would appear that she'd nicked controlled drugs from a hospital ward. And yes, I think she and this Lammy and Eve were all working together. That about sums it up."

"Yes, Sir."

"From Whipps Cross Hospital, do we think?"

"No, Sir. It would appear that is was from the hospital she worked at prior to Whipps Cross."

"She didn't give any indication of where she worked before Whipps Cross?"

"No, Guv."

"Are we sure?"

"One hundred per cent."

"We need to find out where she was."

"Yes, Sir."

"Use my office. It's quieter in there. See what you can find out. Contact Sister Oliver to see where she worked previously."

"Thanks." Andrea got up from her seat, appreciative that he'd noticed she needed the space. She headed to his messy excuse for an office. She closed the door, relaxing on his chair. She felt exhausted and took a minute to reflect before she started to read through what she'd written. Andrea sat dazed by the account Dr Dhillon had just given them, she felt quite sick. Had they thought all this time that they were looking after an innocent victim, when really, they were investigating a drug addict masquerading as a wholesome professional? Was Aline really a criminal, or had she been coerced by an abuser? And looking at all the signs of abuse on her body, what was really going on?

Andrea really didn't know what to think. She picked up the receiver and punched in the numbers for Whipps Cross Hospital.

"Hello switchboard, could I have Sister Oliver in maternity. This is DC Andrea Doyle."

"Certainly, just putting you through."

"Hello DC Doyle here, could you give me the details of Aline Deniuad's previous employer?"

CHAPTER 34

LUTON V MILLWALL

DI Jeffordson was still in his pyjamas, sitting downstairs in his small kitchen. He had come down in the middle of the night, thinking about Eve's account. He flicked through to the next entry in Simon Thomas's notes. There was one thing for certain – Simon Thomas certainly was very good at keeping records.

"What are you doing, Mike?" His wife, Shirley, opened the glass-panelled door. She stood there in her nightie. Her hair was curled up in rollers, covered by a blue hairnet. "It's God knows what time in the morning," she said.

"I know, I just couldn't help myself. I keep getting up at the crack of a sparrow's fart. It's just this girl," he waved the folder at her. "She's really got to me!"

"Mike, you always promised you wouldn't bring work home with you," she tailed off, knowing he wasn't listening.

His focus was already back on the file.

"Now, where was I?" he muttered, flicking through, trying to find his place.

"I'd better make you some breakfast then, if you're making an early start," she sighed.

"Yes, lovely," he replied, engrossed in what he was reading.

"Worms and custard do?" she asked, knowing he wasn't listening.

"Yes, yes, lovely, whatever you think."

She rolled her eyes, getting the bacon out of the fridge.

Mike found the entry he wanted. It was dated November 1992. He skipped over the usual stuff at the beginning of the session and moved straight into Eve's account.

EMM: I was feeling on cloud nine that day as I arrived at work. I'd had a wonderful evening in London and I couldn't wait for the shift to be over to see whether Laurent would call me. Nothing could dampen my mood. It was a bright and sunny Saturday. The day started like any other day on the labour ward.

Verity found me in the stock room, filling up empty cartons. She asked if I'd had a good night with Laurence. I jumped when she spoke, I was miles away.

I told her he was called Laurent and that I was hoping that he'd call me that night after work. "What about

Thierry?" I asked her. She blushed and looked at her feet before she confessed she'd slept with him.

"Verity Matthews you're a little strumpet!" I joked.

She agreed. But when I asked her if she was going to see him again, she said, "Who knows?"

"But he's gorgeous!" I said.

Verity got even redder. She walked forward and started to put a syringe, needle and cotton wool into a kidney dish. "I don't like to get tied down," she flashed her big amber eyes at me. "You know me," she said. "I'm not the type! Anyway, enough of me, what about you?"

"Well," I said, looking around. "He said that he'd call me. If he did, I'd be so delighted!"

Verity laughed at that. She took the mickey out of me. "Oh, Eve," she said. "You're so funny." "If he calls me, I'd be so delighted."

I asked her to stop it. I didn't like it.

"Eve," she said, shaking her head, "take a look at yourself – you're one of the most beautiful girls here. I don't know who filled your brain with so much crap. I wish you could see how goddamn sexy you are! He'd be mad not to call you. I wish you'd believe that and take that huge chip off your shoulder!"

"I just can't help it," I said.

"Well, you better believe it," she said. "He's besotted with you. He couldn't take his eyes off you the whole time!" She gave me a hug. "Just don't blow it!"

I asked her how I would do that.

She shrugged, "Oh, by just being Eve! You know, by emotionally closing him out. Just be who you really are. You can do it for your patients. Do it for him. Be kind to yourself – just like you are to everyone else. Let him into your life."

ST: So, how did that make you feel when Verity told you that you shouldn't shut him out?

EMM: It was odd, as I didn't think that I was like that.

ST: And are you?

EMM: Yes totally, I know that now.

ST: And did you shut him out?

EMM: No, no I didn't.

ST: Why was that?

EMM: Something happened that shift, which made me think about what Verity had said.

ST: Can you describe what happened?

EMM: Well...The silence was broken by the sound of the admissions bell, I broke away from Verity and said I'd better go and see what was happening.

Mrs Dawes arrived on the labour ward alone. She was quiet, calm and quite serene. You'd hardly believe that such a small slip of a thing was in labour. In the delivery room, I asked whether she had anyone to be with her. She explained that her husband was at work. I asked her what he did.

She told me he was a policeman. He was on duty at the match between Luton and Millwall. She said he was a Luton fan, had been since he was a kid. She said he loved being there, the whole atmosphere.

I told her I've never been into football.

"Don't tell Martin," she laughed. "He lives, eats and drinks football. He'll be fed-up, being called away from the match. Mind you," she said thoughtfully. "He gets a bit frustrated, having to watch the crowd!"

This made me laugh. I'd never thought of it from the policeman's point of view. How annoying it must be, to not even be able to watch the game you love so much. We both had a chuckle. Poor old Martin. Over the coming few hours, Tracy filled me in on how they met and all about their honeymoon in the south of France. As her labour progressed, Tracy became quieter and more insular. Her sister arrived to stay with her and help her breathe through the contractions. These were now coming thick and fast, giving Tracy very little respite. Every now and then she would look up and say, "Where's Martin?" She was becoming more and more desperate for him to be there with her.

As she entered the final stages of labour, she became more distressed about the whereabouts of her husband. Her sister reassured her that the station had been called and he would be here as soon as possible. We reassured her. Maybe the traffic was holding him up. She dragged on the Entonox inhaler, angrily inflating her lungs with the analgesia.

This once calm, serene woman had changed out of all recognition.

"Where the bloody hell are you, Martin?" she screamed at the top of her lungs.

Keeping Tracy calm appeared to be an impossible job, but with the help of her sister, Tracy gave birth to a baby girl. The child entered the world still in her bag of water. This was known as being born in a caul – an old sailors' tale, that it would bring the baby good luck, and would never drown at sea. However, this baby was born grey and lifeless. She lay limp on the bed and then the greeny-yellow liquid like mushy peas came rushing out behind her. I knew straight away that this meant the baby had had its bowels open and she'd have breathed it in at birth. The cord was cut and clamped as quickly as possible. The crash bell was rung as I sucked liquid out of the baby's mouth. Instantly, the team arrived to assist with the emergency. Soon the baby girl began to splutter and her colour began to change to pink. The paediatrician checked that no meconium had gone into her lungs and she was fine. She was given to Tracy for a cuddle, who had now returned to herself again.

The labour ward sister asked why I hadn't informed the team prior to delivery that the baby had had its bowels open as in those circumstances the neonatal team should have been present at the delivery. I explained that everything had been normal and clear throughout the labour, and the first sign of a problem was at delivery. About ten minutes later, I was called into the office by the senior sister, and asked to bring my notes with me. This was unbelievable, was I really going to get into trouble over all this? I gathered my notes together, and checked Tracy and her new baby were well before I left them. As I approached the sister's office, I was feeling very nervous and apprehensive about what was about to happen.

Looking through the gap in the doorjamb, I saw two other figures in the room. As I went in, I was faced with two police officers wearing very grave expressions.

Oh no, I thought. Surely, it's not gone that far that they needed to call the police!

"Can I confirm that you're looking after a Mrs Tracy Dawes?" the ward sister asked.

I said, "yes, I was."

The police officer asked me to check her address, which I did from the notes. I started to feel confused and worried.

The tallest police officer asked me to sit down. He asked about Tracy's baby. I told him it was a girl.

The two police officers looked at each other. "Is the baby well?" one asked. "Yes, the baby's fine," I said, feeling incredibly shaky. My palms were sweating and my stomach churned.

The other policemen stepped forward and said, "I'm afraid that PC Martin Dawes was killed this afternoon during the riots which took place at the Kenilworth Road Stadium."

I just couldn't process the information. It all kept going around in my head. Martin Dawes was dead. Tracy, who has just had a baby girl, had now lost her husband! It just didn't make sense. That's not how the story goes – people meet, they fall in love, get married, have their children and then grow old together. Parents don't die on the day their baby is born. And here came the clanger – the ward sister said to me, "As you've formed a relationship with this mother, we think it would be best for you to tell her." I kid you not! I looked at the police officers and then at the ward sister. I've heard of passing the buck, but quite frankly this really did take the biscuit. And so, I had the unenviable task of having to break the news to Tracy and her sister that Martin hadn't arrived to see his daughter being born because he had died in a riot in Luton. How I did it, I'll never know.

ST: Goodness me, how do you feel about that?

EMM: I hated those police officers and my manager for not having the courage to tell her themselves. Why was it my job?

ST: And did you tell her?

EMM: Yes, it was awful. The worst thing I've had to do in my whole career. Tracy was incredibly calm, I expected her to start wailing and crying. But she didn't. A lone tear rolled down her face. "This was supposed to be the happiest day of our lives," she said very quietly. She and her sister decided to name the baby Martina in Martin's memory.

That evening when I got home, the riot between Luton and Millwall was all over the news. There were images of hooligans ripping up stadium chairs and throwing them. I just had to turn it off; I couldn't bear to watch it. And all of a sudden, it came – a wave of emotions. I cried and cried and cried. I cried because of the pain that Tracy was experiencing and the lost future she'd with Martin. But mainly I cried because Martina had no daddy, all because of some violent thugs at a football match.

I thought about what Verity had said to me that morning. This made me realise that I had to seize the day – Carpe Dieum! None of us knew what was around the corner. If I had been given this moment to experience love with this man I'd just met, then I needed to seize it. I would be foolish not to take this opportunity. Look at Tracy and Martin – it was all over for them.

***

DI Jeffordson felt quite shaken. He really didn't expect to read about the Luton and Millwall riots. He'd been on duty himself that day when PC Martin Dawes had been killed. He had been on the team that had been called to investigate the scene. The whole police force had been affected by his death and he'd been awarded a posthumous honourable service award. A guard of honour was formed by officers in uniform, lining the route for the funeral procession. Mike remembered the fallen officer's wife and young baby at the funeral.

He took a deep breath and reflected on the fact he was reading the notes from the midwife who delivered his dead colleague's baby girl, Martina. How was this possible? He sat in his chair and looked out of the window, thinking about the horror of that day. He thought about what Eve said so eloquently – that Martina's life wasn't meant to start without her father. Mike and his wife, Shirley had never been able to have children. It was something that he would have always loved to have been a father and take a little lad fishing or fly a kite. But children never came and after many invasive investigations, Mike and Shirley agreed to remain as they were. He always had that gap in his heart which he knew could be filled by a child. He would have been a good dad, he knew that. So, the force became his child, and he nurtured all the younger officers as they came out of Hendon training college. He was proud to be a father figure for them.

He could understand why, after this event, Eve would want to seize this opportunity with the new man in her life.

Before he got back to Simon Thomas's notes, he went upstairs to shower and shave. He'd take the file into the office and read some more when he had a spare five minutes.

CHAPTER 35

FIRST DATE

It was whole day before Mike Jeffordson got back to the file. He cleared his other reports and team admin, then settled down once again to see what Simon Thomas had got from his patient.

***

Eve McDonnell
DOB 1/2/1968
4th December 1992

ST: Hello Eve, how are you doing?

EMM: I think I am doing really well.

ST: What do you want to talk about today?

EMM: I don't know. My life really is improving so much.

ST: I think that could be due to a certain man, Is that correct Eve?

EMM: Yes.

ST: I can see by the smile on your face, that he contacted you. Can you tell me a bit more about Laurent?

EMM: Yes, he did. I didn't think he would. I was anxious when I got home from work. Had I missed his call? Had someone answered and not taken a message? Or had he not phoned as he'd decided that he wasn't interested? Had he tried to call and got no answer?

I was like a cat on a hot tin roof, pacing up and down my room. My ears pricked up every time the phone rang and I ran down the corridor to answer it. But someone always got there first. They sat on the carpeted step, chatting, wrapping the cable around their fingers. It was going to be an impossibly long evening. I'd almost resigned myself to the fact that he wasn't going to call. But at half past eleven, as I crawled into bed, there was a knock at my door and someone shouted, "Eve, phone!"

I jumped out of bed and rushed down the corridor, and found the receiver spinning around and around from the long dangling cable.

I tried to sound cool, but I was out of breath so I must have sounded a bit weird. But it was him, Laurent, and he apologised for calling so late. He'd been busy at work. I told him I'd had a manic day too, although I didn't tell him how horrible it had been. I didn't want to sound like I was a whiner. Anyway, we talked for a bit about how I'd got back after I left him at the flat and what the others were up to. He sounded so warm and friendly and then he asked to see me again. I was thrilled but also, I was gob-smacked. I even asked him if he really meant me, Eve, and not Verity. He laughed at that. He said he and Verity wouldn't get on at all, they'd argue and it would end in tears. No, he wanted to see me. I was so pleased I did a little dance right there in the hallway! We agreed to meet at 5pm the following afternoon. I was determined I was going to grab this chance with both hands, just like Verity told me to.

I couldn't believe this was happening to me, Eve McDonnell, the quiet, shy girl. You better believe it though, 'cause in less than twenty-four hours I was meeting a handsome French waiter back in London. We'd arranged to meet just outside the station. I worried about what to wear but considering how cold it was there was no choice in my limited range of clothes. I pulled out my Miss Selfridge camel woolly tunic dress and leopard print leggings with a pair of suede pixie boots. Hair washed and blow-dried, favourite Anais Anais perfume sprayed on liberally to mask the lingering smell of the nurses' accommodation. Make-up applied immaculately. I was ready.

He was sat outside on a bench looking relaxed feeding the pigeons with old crusts.

"Where to?" I asked.

"Come, let's go to South Kensington it's Little France, but in London." His warm smile radiated across his face, and eyes danced with excitement.

So, we jumped onto the tube to South Kensington, where he took my hand and practically dragged me into a small French café. The strong smell of coffee and baking filled the room. The hiss of the coffee machine sang as the barista made frothy coffee in tall, conical glasses. The room was with filled with a hotchpotch of scrubbed, clean, rustic wooden benches. The walls were adorned with monochrome pictures showing views of France both in the town and the countryside. Dried flowers, wheat and grasses filled battered milk churns. The people around us chattered away in their mother tongue.

"Welcome to my little bit of home," he said.

I told him it was wonderful. He asked me what I'd like. Everything – the pastries and crepes looked delicious. We decided on hot chocolates and pastries, which Laurent said would be "super."

The plated pastries and drinks arrived. The flaky, buttery, shiny delicacies crunched as soon as you bit into them. The taste coated your mouth as the chocolate centre oozed out. The steaming hot chocolate was covered in thick, whipped cream and dusted with chocolate powder.

"I'm going in," I announced, taking a sip from the edge. Wow, it certainly packed a punch. It was rich, dark, and thick – it was utterly magnificent. Nothing like the poor excuse we Brits were used to, with dried powder floating on muddy milk. No, this was the King of all hot chocolates. Completely decadent. I had never understood how French children could survive on just a croissant and a hot chocolate before school. And on that day it all was revealed – the mystery had been solved! I told Laurent it was the most sensational chocolate I'd ever had and he smiled at me with cream on his top lip. I wanted to lick it off him but I settled for commenting on how bad these drinks must be for the waistline. He told me I didn't need to worry about that.

He truly was a charmer – not in the wrong way of someone who was a womaniser. No, he had a real special quality to him; he wasn't a letch like so many of the men I'd met before. He was unique, head and shoulders above anyone else I'd ever met before. I know this was only our second meeting, but sometimes you just know!

We left the café, and chatted about places to visit in London, while walking past the famous landmarks and across the city to the embankment. We passed theatres, cinemas, restaurants and bars, all with their boards outside, trying to entice the passing trade. However, we had hardly any money between us, so we just kept walking and talking, stopping occasionally to take in the atmosphere.

We were entertained on the embankment by a busker. A regular with his accordion, and battered and bruised face from years of hard labour, each mark telling a story of times once forgotten in his fuzzy head.

We stood looking over the Thames, watching the lights on boats travelling up and down the river. He took my gloved hand and squeezed it hard.

He said, "It reminds me of my home. You can take a trip along the Seine and have dinner and see the illuminations. You know, it is called the City of Lights. It is very magical and very romantic." He leant forward and kissed me tenderly on the lips. I responded to his warmth as he embraced me. We separated and he looked at me with his dark eyes which sparkled.

He told me he'd been wanting to do that ever since he first saw me.

"Me too." I said. I was surprised by my own response and how quickly I'd fallen for this man. He told me I was very beautiful, but you know what. I found it really hard to believe him.

ST: Why didn't you believe him?

EMM: Because nobody had ever told me that before.

ST: Nobody?

EMM: No…nobody, none of them ever…my friends, my family. No one.

ST: So, what did you do?

EMM: Well it was obvious to him that I was embarrassed by what he had said. I tried to explain that I was always made to feel ugly. But he said that they were all wrong. It was lovely really. He immediately jumped to my defence. I cannot remember anyone doing that, other than Verity.

ST: Did you manage to take on what he had said to you?

EMM: Not really, it hard when it's drummed into you. I really don't think that I was good enough for him. I knew deep down in my heart that it would all be over. So, I thought I would make the most of the evening.

ST: So, what happened next?

EMM: Well, the mood did feel a little sombre, he and I hugged on the side of the Thames, I felt sad. Laurent had stirred up a lot of unwanted emotions, memories I didn't want to look at. He suggested that we returned to his flat for dinner and get out of this bitter English weather. I loved the way he said "bitter weather..." it was as though some of the letters were missing. So..., we took a bus across the city.

We arrived back to the flat and Thierry and Pierre had already returned from work, they all greeted one another in French. Laurent spoke to them and I could tell he was talking about me. He then politely introduced me again to them.

"Bonsoir Eve." They kissed me on both cheeks. They then grabbed their coats and left us alone.

He opened the oven and took out a large red earthenware pot, which he put onto the table. The smell was delicious of rosemary and garlic. He lifted the lid to reveal the sausages and cannelloni beans...it looked scrumptious.

"C'est formidable!" I tried in my world's worst French accent.

He chuckled. It truly was awful. Mrs Harris would have cringed.

ST: Do you think she would have cringed?

EMM: Yes, definitely.

ST: Did he cringe?

EMM: No, he said it was pronounced beautifully, it was odd to hear it with an English accent.

Once dinner was over, he grabbed the bottle of red wine and slumped into the sofa. He wrapped his arms around me and we sat cuddled together. I leant my head up against the cosy cable knitted jumper, his hands lightly smoothed my hair, nothing was said between us there was complete silence. Very softly he started to sing in French, it made me smile as I didn't have a clue what he was singing. But the tune was so familiar, however he was really out of tune and quite flat! It was charming, almost endearing that he appeared completely tone deaf.

I asked him what he was singing; trying to work out what it was from his duff notes.

ST: What was he singing?

EMM: A song by Edith Piaf, not Je Ne Regrette Rien... the other one about a rose...Oh what is it called?

La Vie En Rose! He said it was for his English rose and as we sat he lifted the hair out of my face and curled it behind my ear, he then reached forward and picked up his cigarettes and lighter, shook the packet forcing a cigarette over the edge, and offered me one which I took. He then went on to describe what the song was about.

ST: What was La Vie En Rose about; I haven't heard of it at all?

EMM: It's a story of love, finding love and all those feelings that you have. I remember watching his face as he drew deeply on his cigarette and blew the smoke into the air. He told me that it's a beautiful song, even though it is very old. It's about hope, love and those first moments together. He touched my face, stroking my cheek. "It was written after the first or second world war, about the soldiers and them viewing life through a rose-coloured lens."

"OKAY, so we would say in England 'looking at life through with rose coloured spectacles.'" "Exactly, I know the phrase."

I asked him to sing it again. "For sure". He laid his cigarette in the ashtray, sat up straight and with a mock cough, cleared his throat and flung out his arms like he was on stage. This made me laugh; he was so funny and had such a sense of humour. He then broke into song, putting on a great performance, singing from his very soul...In complete incomprehensible French. Then he stopped abruptly.

It was so funny and we just laughed. I told him not to give up his day job, teasing him. He took it well.

He called me his 'Petit Chou', my sweet bun...I liked it, it's the nicest thing anyone has ever said. I told him that I really was the ugly duckling from Hans Christian Anderson. He was so sharp, and replied.

"But Eve, now you have become the beautiful swan, do you not see?"

ST: Good, I'm glad he told you the truth.

EMM: The truth?

ST: Yes, Eve the truth! That you are beautiful, inside and out. I know that seems hard to accept, but this is a man who loved you for being you. You weren't that ugly duckling that they called you. Or more importantly, what you called yourself. Do you see that?

EMM: I do but, its accepting it that's hard.

ST: You need to do that Eve, because you are damaging yourself by not accepting this truth. So, how did you respond to him?

EMM: Well, we drank wine, smoked, kissed and we talked a bit more. It was delicious listening to him. I watched him so animated as he chatted away to me, gesticulating with his hands. I touched his face, kissing his hands and fingers. I loved listening to him; he spoke with great speed and I could pick up the odd word as he slipped back into his native French. Then he stopped, adjusting his jumper pushing up his sleeve, ready to start his next monologue. I put my finger on his lips to stop him. I told him to stop. Then I took my finger away and kissed his soft warm lips. We held onto one another, as though our lives depended on it.

ST: So, what happened next?

EMM: The mood was broken by the bloody cat! She had jumped onto the sofa and wouldn't leave us alone. So, we ended up washing up in the kitchen. Before I knew it, we started kissing again. The washing up was left and well...I ended up in his bed and wrapped ourselves around each other. The love in that room was unmistakeable. Had this really taken less than 24hrs for the two of us to become so consumed by each other's passion. But we just lay there kissing, that was all.

ST: Eve, I'm not here to judge you. You are a grown woman. If you made love that's fine.

EMM: But we didn't, we just laid looking at one another, not wanting to go any further. Almost as though it would have ruined it.

ST: Ruined it?

EMM: That moment, you know when you feel you connect. He lay there kissing my fingertips so tenderly. He asked me about what I had said down by the river, he said that he knew I'd been hurt. He suggested that it was still hurting me. I denied it as I didn't want to go over old ground. He told me that if I told him, it would be over. I couldn't believe that it was that easy to remove the pain like that.

ST: Did you trust him; did you feel like you could tell him?

EMM: Yes, I did trust him, but I wasn't quite ready to face those skeletons.

***

Mike scratched his chin, placing the notes onto his desk, he picked up the mug of tea and took a sip. He spat it out and wiped his mouth.

"Yuk. I hate cold tea." He glanced up to see if Andrea was about to make him a cuppa.

CHAPTER 36

UGLY DUCKLING

Mike returned from the kitchen with a hot mug of tea and lump of cake wrapped in a paper napkin. He wandered back through the offices. Where was everyone? He looked at the empty desks as he made his way back to the desk. Sitting back in his chair he took a bite of the Victoria sponge, and before he even swallowed, he washed it down with a gulp of tea. This one was not going to go cold. He opened Simon's file.

ST: So, did you tell him?

EMM: Yes.

ST: Can you tell me what you told Laurent?

EMM: I told him about my school days and my first crush. It started after school one day. Me, Smiffy and

Aline would walk home along London Road, passing the small newsagent. It was called the Tuck Shop and was sat back from the main road, only five minutes from school. On these journeys home, Smiffy would always talk to me. He was tall with a mop of bleached blonde hair, black eyebrows and piercing blue eyes. He had a gorgeous smile and a real glow about him. His real name was Ian Smith and he was a real cheeky chappy. He could charm the birds out of the trees and he knew it. He always used this to his advantage with me, always asking if I had any spare change for the Tuck Shop. I always did as I never spent all my dinner money. I would rummage around in my bag for the odd twenty pence piece and I'd hand him the coin and off he'd go, smiling.

Aline told me I was stupid for giving him the money. I knew that I was, but I fancied him. I watched him as he walked on ahead of me with his long legs in his tight grey Farah school trousers.

"He won't ask you out," she sneered at me "you're not one of the IN girls."

I felt hurt but knew deep down inside that she was telling the truth. You see, I was one of the swotty girls. I studied hard and didn't get into trouble. But I just liked him. Aline just scoffed at me. "You're a fool," she told me. "He'll never ask you out. You're too much of a goody-two-shoes for him."

She was right. He was one of the cool kids. He was tall, handsome and sporty with his broad shoulders and that swagger. His school bag was slung over his shoulder. He was graceful and elegant. I had a total crush on him, but I just couldn't tell him. One year I sent him a Valentine's card anonymously. I didn't tell a soul, other than Aline – it was my little secret, otherwise I would've been crucified. To say my school was rough was an understatement, so I certainly didn't want anyone else to know. I swore Aline to secrecy.

Anyway, one day she told me that one of the girls was having a party. She suggested that I asked him to go with me.

I thought she was mad. Of course I couldn't ask him! I told her not to be so ridiculous, he was sure to go with one of the IN girls, like Selena or Nicky.

"If you don't ask him, someone will," she insisted.

I said no way. That was the end of the conversation as far as I was concerned. Then Jane came running over, wanting to know about the party.

I said I wanted to go but I'd have to ask my mum if I could.

Jane said she was thinking of asking Paul to go with her. I said she should go for it. She had more chance than me; she'd grown up on the same estate as most of the lads so she found them easy to talk to. She wanted to know if I was asking anyone. I said no, I'd go with the other girls.

Kaye – the girl who was having the party – had wealthy parents. They lived on the edge of the town in a new ultra-modern Swiss-style chalet up on stilts. Her father was a self-made man who had his own engineering company.

My main sticking point was going to be my parents. There was no way they were gonna let me go because her mum and dad were going to be away. God forbid if I was to look at a person of the opposite sex, let alone be in the same room. I would have to think about how I approached the whole situation. Jane got permission to go with Paul, her parents trusted her completely.

ST: What about your other friends?

EMM: The others decided it wasn't for them, so it only left me and Aline.

ST: How did you feel about that? Did you still want to go?

EMM: Yes, but I felt anxious that my parents wouldn't let me go. I knew they'd be afraid I'd get drunk and have sex.

ST: A natural reaction for any parents of a teenage girl.

EMM: But I was sixteen and sensible. I had a good, healthy attitude towards life and my future and I wasn't gonna muck it up.

ST: Okay. What else worried you about the party?

EMM: My biggest anxiety was...what was I going to wear? I know girls say that all the time, but I literally had nothing in my wardrobe suitable for a party. Apart from my school uniform, I had scruffy jeans and t-shirts, school shoes and very little make-up. I would be the laughing stock of the whole party. I couldn't go through the whole school disco experience in my Laura Ingalls dress again.

ST: So, how did you deal with it?

EMM: I decided I just wouldn't go. It would solve two problems: Asking permission and what to wear! It was easier not to go.

ST: That makes sense. How did your friends react?

EMM: I felt a huge pressure to go to the party; they nagged me to ask my parents. I said I would, tried to sound confident. But Aline just sneered and said they'd never let me go. "I know," I mumbled.

"Know what?" asked Jane.

I told her I was sure my mum wouldn't let me go. Kaye offered to ask her for me, but I couldn't see the point. She'd still say no. Like Aline said, she'd be convinced I was going to get sloshed and then have sex!

Jane knew how strict my parents were. She said they'd never trust me again if they found out Kaye's parents were going to be away. She understood my problem. But Aline kept on pushing in.

"But Ian will be there," Aline uttered in a hushed tone. "You love Smiffy!"

ST: How did that make you feel?

EMM: Exposed, vulnerable. I didn't know what to do. Of course I didn't want Ian to meet anyone else. But then again, I didn't stand a cat in hell's chance of getting off with him. And anyway, if I did go, my parents would kill me if anything happened. But they kept on and on. Aline said I was pathetic, that I should stand up to my parents. She said I'd be going to college soon and my mum and dad were bullies. She said I should go and enjoy myself.

ST: So, what happened?

EMM: Kaye asked my mum for me. I don't know how she did it. Jane thought it was a mad idea, she was really worried. Kaye got Mum to agree to let me go, and Jane said she'd lend me some clothes and shoes, and she'd even ask Ian to take me as she was going with his mate and we could all double-date. It was all settled. She'd bring the party clothes to school on the Friday.

ST: It sounds like your friends came through for you.

EMM: Yeah, but I still got the lecture on under-age drinking and the talk on sex before marriage. I had a curfew of when to be home and had to agree to come back at the first sign of trouble. Dad said that if the police came to our house and I had got into trouble with drink and drugs he would disown me. It was all a bitter pill to swallow, just to go to a party.

ST: And what about the boy – Ian?

EMM: That was the next miracle. Jane asked Smiffy whether he'd go to the party with me and he agreed to the double-date idea. I couldn't believe it!

ST: That must have made you very happy.

EMM: Yeah, you'd think so, wouldn't you? Well it didn't last.

ST: Why?

SILENCE 15 SECONDS.

ST: Eve, can you tell me what happened?

EMM: It was a bloody set up. That's what happened! So, Friday arrived and Jane came into school with the clothes she was lending me in a Miss Selfridge bag. Kaye brought in her shoes which were pointed and had a Chinese pagoda shaped heel. They were super dainty. They handed me the bags outside at lunchtime break. I was so chuffed with the items the girls had brought in. I was really excited about the party. Then the boys arrived.

"Got your clothes then?" said Paul, pointing at the Miss Selfridge bag and smirking.

"Yeah," said Ian. "Jane leant you some clothes for Kaye's party, didn't she?" He laughed. I wanted to defend myself, but I couldn't. I felt as though the world had stopped and the spot lights were on me. Everybody waiting outside our classroom was looking at me. I was completely dumbstruck and didn't know what to say.

ST: That must have been tough.

EMM: I was lost for words, I felt betrayed. How could Jane have told Paul and Ian that I needed to borrow her clothes? It was supposed to be our secret!

ST: Go on.

EMM: I couldn't do anything. I just stood there and it got worse.

ST: How?

EMM: Ian laughed. He bloody laughed in my face and said, "Well you better give them back, Eve, 'cause I'm not going to any party with you. Not now, not ever." Everyone just laughed. They were enjoying the spectacle, watching me being destroyed in front of their very eyes. I felt utterly humiliated, but he wasn't finished. He pointed his finger at my chest and prodded it hard. He looked around, playing to his audience. There was quite a crowd by now. "You know why?" he asked. "Because you're just an ugly duckling."

ST: What did you do?

EMM: What could I do? I wanted the ground to open up and swallow me whole. I could feel a ball of fire raging inside me as everyone was laughing and pointing their fingers, echoing what he'd just said. I shouted at Ian. I said "Do you kiss your mother with that mouth?"

ST: How did he react?

EMM: He snarled at me, "No, 'cause I'm not a mother-fucker, you ugly slag!" He told me to go back to my bum chums at the library. Then he and Paul turned on their heels and went into the classroom, followed by the rest of the giggling crowd, leaving me standing there like a fool.

ST: What did you do?

EMM: The hot anger raged inside me. I was so upset by this onslaught of abuse; I turned and looked at Jane and Kaye. They looked at me, absolutely speechless.

I said to Jane, "I can't believe you told them that you lent me some clothes."

She acted all innocent. "Well, I just said to Ian that he'd better not let you down, 'cause I'd lent you some nice clothes." She really didn't see that she'd done anything wrong. "I was only thinking of you," she whined.

I closed my eyes. I didn't know what I was going to do. I knew I couldn't go into Geography now. I couldn't face them all. Aline agreed.

"Go home," she said. "It will be all around the school in no time. You'll be the butt of everybody's jokes! The teachers won't even notice you're not there...Just go home."

ST: And did you?

EMM: Yeah. I threw the Miss Selfridge bag at Jane and just walked away. Kaye tried to get me to stay. She said I'd get into trouble. But I said, "I don't care, I'd rather get detention than face the humiliation in there."

The only one on my side was Aline. "You go girl," she said. "You show them." So, I picked up my school bag and walked away.

ST: Do you think that was the right thing to do?

EMM: I didn't care. It didn't help that Aline continued to have a go at me all weekend though. She kept sticking the knife in, you know? She kept saying, "you really didn't think Ian was actually gonna fancy you, did you? You're so boring – always worrying about what Mummy and Daddy think. I can really see why your so-called friends are sick of you. Did you realise no one has called you? That's 'cause they're all having a great time at the party without you. I bet they're really dragging your name through the dirt. They'll be drinking, smoking and dancing. Why would they want a pathetic loser like you around?"

ST: Do you think she was being cruel to be kind?

EMM: No. She was just telling me like it was, and bloody enjoying it! I wanted to curl up in a hole. I'd lost all dignity. I had no confidence. I felt rejected, betrayed and utterly desperate. I'd been led like a lamb to the slaughter. I was so bloody innocent and naive. The other girls didn't contact me at all. I felt completely ostracised by them all, yet I'd done nothing wrong. Aline said I was a pathetic loser. She said she wouldn't be surprised if no one wanted to be my friend after this.

ST: Did you believe her?

EMM: I didn't want to; they'd been my friends since primary school, but she said they felt sorry for me with my unfashionable clothes and weird family. She said I'd never amount to anything because I wouldn't stand up for myself.

ST: Did you argue with her?

EMM: What was the point? I felt sick inside my stomach; I hated to think they were my friends because they felt sorry for me. Then I started to feel furious. Why was I listening to this onslaught of abuse? I couldn't stand it any longer.

I told Aline to clear off, to get out of my life. I didn't need that shit. I couldn't work out what was worse – the torment from Aline or what I was gonna face at school after the weekend.

ST: That was a positive thing to do. To send Aline away.

EMM: I s'pose so.

ST: So, what happened when you went back to school?

EMM: I didn't want to go. But I had to, it was the first week of exams and I had no choice if I wanted a future. I had to go in. At least I could come home again after the exam.

I expected everyone to be sniggering and laughing at me when I got there but nobody said a thing.

ST: Why was that, do you think?

EMM: I put it down to everybody being nervous. We all traipsed into the school hall. We all took our seats. I could hear a commotion outside, but the invigilator told us to keep our mouths closed and eyes to the front.

The exam ended an hour and three quarters later and the sense of relief was evident by the level of chattering. Through the hall windows we could see two police cars parked outside. A policeman was waiting outside the school hall with our headmaster. They were clearly looking for someone and we tried to see who it was. Miss Handel, the deputy head, joined him and in a loud booming voice told us to get a move on.

ST: Did you find out what it was all about?

EMM: Yes. There was a raid, at Kaye's party. Apparently, the neighbours called the police because it was so noisy. They found loads of underage drinking, kids with drugs, and Kaye in bed with one of her brother's friends. The house was trashed and some stuff was missing. The police were following up on the drugs and stolen goods.

ST: So, the focus of attention was taken off you by all the trouble at the party.

EMM: Yes, everyone had forgotten about what had happened and moved onto the latest bit of gossip.

ST: But you couldn't get over it.

EMM: No. The girls and I never really crossed paths again as we all sat different subjects. In their eyes it was all over. The sad thing was that all that hurt still burnt a hole in me; it was so hard to forget all the painful things they'd said. It was like having a tattoo on your heart and I can't seem to get rid of it. You're only the second person I've told about it.

ST: And the first was Laurent?

EMM: Yes.

ST: How did he react?

EMM: He was so sweet and understanding. When I'd finished, he said, "Eve, that's awful. I'm so sorry, I didn't mean for you to go through that again." He embraced me and I remember him smoothing my hair.

You know, I really tried not to cry but I couldn't help it. He wiped away my tears. He told me I was beautiful, that they were talking rubbish.

ST: How did you feel about that?

EMM: I wanted to believe him, but I couldn't. I told him I'd been a plain, boring nerd at school. He said, "The smart ones are the best girlfriends to have. I would have fancied you."

I still didn't believe him, but he said I was intelligent, enchanting and ravishing! That made me giggle, but he said he was totally serious. He said they were all little shits and he hoped they had all grown up to be really ugly. He said I should forget about them and their lies. They didn't deserve to have me in their lives, whereas he said he was grateful to them all because now he had me in his life. He was deadly serious.

ST: How did that make you feel?

EMM: Amazed! Gob-smacked even. No one had ever talked to me the way he did. We lay on his bed and he said if could he would go back in time and beat them with a stick. But, he said, if it hadn't happened – if I'd gone to the party and fallen in love with Ian – then he might not have met me. He said that would've been a travesty. That's the word he used. He said, even though we'd only known each other a matter of hours, he knew I was special. He called me a "beautiful, wonderful person."

ST: That's nice. What did you say?

EMM: I said, "You don't know me!" But he disagreed. He said, "I do. I'm sure!" It scared me a bit. I told him I was as mad as a box of frogs and wasn't good enough for him. He'd find out soon and want me to go.

ST: And his reaction was?

EMM: He said, "I don't want to hear you ever say that you're not good enough for me again. Do you hear me?" He was quite firm, so I said okay. Just like that: "Okay, Laurent." It might take me a while to believe him, but I wanted to and if he was with me, I thought it might stop haunting me if he was by my side, being so loving and caring.

I felt safe in his arms and tried to block out the images swirling around in my mind. He held my head against his chest and stroked my hair, soothing me. "It's okay," he said. "It will be okay. Trust me."

ST: And did you trust him?

EMM: As we lay together, arms entwined, I was reminded of something I'd once read. It said. "Only trust someone who can see these three things in you; the sorrow behind your smile, the love behind your anger and the reason behind your silence." I asked myself, was this truly the man who was going to be able to look deep inside my soul and stand with me for eternity? I was exhausted by re-living everything I'd told him. He knew that I'd made a huge leap forward, trusting him enough to tell him about my past. But how easy was it going to be, to really exorcise those demons sitting inside my head? I didn't think it was going to be easy at all. But I wanted to try.

ST: Thank you, Eve. You've made great progress today. You must be tired.

EMM: Yes. I'm exhausted. Is it time to go?

ST: Yes. I'll see you next time.

SESSION ENDS.

***

Mike licked his fingers, dabbing the crumbs off the green paper towel, and took the final sip of the last remaining dregs of his tea. He looked up into the main office to see if Phil and Andrea had returned yet. Some of the others were now at their desks writing up notes, making phone calls and following up leads. No sign of Andrea or Phil yet.

CHAPTER 37

HUMANS

Phil and Andrea sat in the Metropolitan Police car amongst the London traffic. Their radio crackled as impatient drivers honked their horns. Cyclists jostled past wearing their protective helmets. Motorbikes weaved in and out of the stationary cars.

Andrea sipped from a bottle of water, watching the London traffic. "It never changes, does it?" she said.

"The traffic?"

"No. Well, yeah, but I meant humans."

"Wow, that's deep for a Monday morning! What are you thinking?"

She sighed. "I feel so disturbed by what's happened to Aline. I don't think I've ever felt so rattled like this before. It's not like me."

"It's okay, Andrea. We're all affected by cases. We're all human after all. D'you remember, last year — that hit and run? It really got to me. It took me back to a time when I was a little lad. One of the boys in my football team was knocked off his bike on his way home. It took us all a long time to get over his death."

"Yes, this case brings back memories of my brother, Liam. He was caught up with drugs. I can't believe a nurse would be so stupid as to get involved in all this."

"I know. I understand."

"Do you?" Her eyes flashed.

"Yes, I do."

"But how can you, Phil? How can you possibly understand?"

"Okay, I don't!" he sighed. "I really have no idea what it must feel like to lose a brother, but I know what it's like to care about a case you're investigating. What I would say is you need to remain as detached as possible," he paused. "I know that you're a brilliant police officer. I know you won't let your feelings cloud your judgement. You've just got to remain objective so that we can get to the bottom of this."

"I know. You're right. It just makes me so cross to think an intelligent girl in a good job would get mixed up with a low-life like Lammy."

"Well, I'll be interested in hearing her excuse."

"I know. I must be more objective and not let my feelings get in the way." She forced a smile, physically pulling herself together. "I must try harder."

"You don't need to try harder at all." He took his hand off the steering wheel and gave her shoulder a squeeze. "Come on. It's going to be okay." He took a deep breath. "So, what have we got?"

"Two dodgy nurses, by the look of it."

"Yeah," said Phil.

They returned to the station to find DI Jeffordson rifling through a grey filing cabinet, chucking out paper files.

"All right, Sir?" Phil looked at Andrea and she shrugged her shoulders.

"Anything new, guys?" asked Mike.

"It looks like the Royal Berks was the last place Aline worked before she came to London."

"Great work, I'll get onto it straight away."

Mike dialled the number and navigated his way through to a Sister Jones on the labour ward. After identifying himself, he said, "I'm so sorry to interrupt you, Sister, but we're making investigations into the identity of a young woman we found badly injured on New Year's Eve. We have reason to believe that she was a midwife working on your unit."

"Oh," she said. "Have you got her name, Inspector?"

"Well, I've got two names, actually. Aline Deniaud and Eve McDonnell, are they familiar?"

"I've worked with Eve McDonnell. But the other name doesn't ring a bell."

"Can you tell me when you last saw Eve?"

"Oh goodness, I would've thought it was towards the end of August last year."

"We have been told that they were suspended a few months ago for taking controlled drugs."

"Yes. I was on duty the day we suspended Eve. She wasn't the only one, Detective Inspector. Several of the staff where suspended for the duration of the investigation."

"Do you know what the findings were?"

"I'm afraid I have no idea. I went on leave to have an operation and have only just returned to work. I believe it was all dealt with by Thames Valley Police."

"Thank you. I'll speak to them. You say that you haven't worked with Aline Deniaud."

"No, but we have many nurses working on the bank or through agencies. She certainly wasn't a permanent member of the team at that time."

"Do you use a lot of bank or agency nurses?"

"Yes, I'm afraid it's the age-old problem in the NHS – we're always so short staffed that we have to use agency nurses. They can be with us several weeks and then they're gone again. I would have to ask my colleagues about this Aline Deniaud for you. I'm only working part-time since my op, so I don't get to know all the girls, particularly if they're agency. I'm sorry I can't be of more help."

"Is there anyone else who could help?"

"Yes, Sister White. I believe she was involved in the whole situation. She's on her days off at the moment but I can get her to contact you as soon as she returns."

"Thanks, that would be marvellous."

***

Mike felt it was time to get the team together to see what they all had and get an update of the progress being made…

"All right, all right settle down," he said, hushing everybody. "We appear to have made quite a bit of progress with this case. I thank you all for your hard work. We've got a few leads which DS Lewis and DC Doyle would like to tell you about."

Phil stood up. He paused for effect, puffing out his chest." Well, after our visit to the Prince Regent in Brixton, Trevor Arnold — our rather tight-lipped publican has now admitted to seeing Aline arguing with a French lad outside the pub. The barman, Colin Walker gave a full description of what the individual looks like. He's believed to be a waiter working for the Cadeau Hotel in the West End. His nickname is Lammy. We have reason to believe that he's a drug dealer. We've been to the Cadeau Hotel and got a list of all the French waiters. Going by Aline's account, we believe that it's a lad called Fabian Lambert."

"We don't think she's caught up with drug dealing, do we?" asked Celine.

"Aline could be caught up in anything, for all we know. A Sister Oliver at Whipps Cross Hospital said that some colleagues thought she was on the game!"

"Okay, thanks Phil," said Mike. "Andi, tell them what you've got."

Andrea got up, and grabbed her notes. "Well, this afternoon, DS Lewis and I met with Dr Dhillon at Florence Green Ward, where our victim is a patient. The doc's a nice lady, very concerned about Aline. Apparently, Aline met a Reverend Hillier at St Peters Church and told him she'd been suspended for taking controlled drugs. It appears that she ran away to London to escape a female called Eve. DS Lewis has been in contact with Reading. We believe the Eve is Eve McDonnell."

"But in Reverend Hillier's statement, he reports that a Mary Daniels visited him, why do we think its Aline?" said Celine.

"That's correct, but Aline told the doctor about how she changed her name"

"Indeed" Mike Jeffordson replied walking around the room with an air of authority. He moved amongst the tables, keeping everybody's attention upon him.

"Thanks for that, Andi. I'll take it from there. So, in view of this, DS Lewis has contacted Royal Berks and spoken to a Sister Jones who remembers Eve, but has no info on Aline. The whole situation is somewhat confusing, I confess. A Sister White who has a better handle on the staffing at Royal Berks is getting back to me in a couple of days. So, we have two lines of inquiry. Firstly, we need more information on Fabian Lambert; he was very evasive when we saw him. We believe he is Lammy, and now Aline has ID'd him from the CCTV. We need some hard evidence about him carrying out the assault so we can bring him back. Secondly, I want more information on Aline and this Eve McDonnell and what happened in Reading. Can you get onto Thames Valley Police as they were investigating the missing controlled drugs at the hospital? The sister I spoke to didn't have any details of the outcome of the investigation."

Mike paced up and down. "Andi did you manage to find out where Aline worked before Whipps Cross?"

"Yes Guv. I contacted Sister Oliver and she confirmed that on her application. Aline came directly from France. Clinique Sainte Thérèse in Paris."

"Hang on, hang on." He held up his hands "Andi, you said that Sister Oliver said her last place of employment was Paris."

"But she told Reverend Hillier that she'd been in Reading!" He looked around the room, "That's a bit odd. Why would she do that?"

"To cover up that she's run away from Reading?"

"Because she really did come from Paris, hence why her name is unfamiliar in Reading?"

He turned to DS Clement. "Celine, can you contact Clinique Sainte Thérèse for me to get the dates when she worked there? I'd also like to know the reason she left. Particularly if it was for taking controlled drugs."

"Of course Sir, not a problem. I'll get onto it straight away."

"Celine, do we have any news from the parents in France?"

"No, Sir. The number Sister Oliver gave us was a bakery in Paris. Nobody there has heard of her. I'm spreading the net wider with her parents' names and rechecking the number, in case it had been written down incorrectly."

"Thanks, Celine. Good work." He looked round the room, stroking his moustache. Everybody was shuffling in their seats, ready to get going. "Is everybody happy with what they're doing?"

"Yes, Guv." they replied.

"Good. Let's crack on and let's be careful out there!"

Phil got up smiling and started to whistle the Hills Street Blues theme tune.

"Go on," Mike laughed. "Get on with it!"

CHAPTER 38

NIGEL KENNEDY

Andrea was heading back to the station; Phil's voice came up on the two-way radio.

"Andrea, we've had a call from Sister White from Royal Berkshire Hospital. She says she has some information for us. Are you heading back to the station?"

"Just in the car now."

"Okay. I'm on my way out to a meeting. Could you contact her?"

"Yes, sure, I'll do it as soon as I get back." Andrea paused, thinking. "D'you know whether Mike has left out Simon Thomas's notes?"

"Yes, why?"

"I just want to cross reference something; I've got a hunch."

"I'll leave them on your desk."

"Thanks, Phil, you're a star."

"Any chance of a drink after work?"

"Yes, that'll be nice. Are we all going?"

"No," he paused. "Just us two."

Andrea was taken back. She blushed. She looked at herself in the car mirror. Was Phil interested in her or was he just being friendly?

"Hello, Andi?"

"That sounds great," she smiled to herself.

"Have you managed to speak to Dr Dhillon today?"

"Yes. Aline's really screwed up by this Eve. They clearly didn't have a good relationship with one another. I'm not surprised that she ran away from Reading – it sounds like a nightmare. It looks like Aline is being made a scapegoat for everything that goes on and she's sure Eve is behind it all."

"According to Aline, don't forget, there are always two sides to every argument."

"I know. That's why I want to look at those notes."

***

Back at the station, Andrea found the file and sat down with a mug of coffee to read it, she had just opened the cover when she closed it again, remembering she had to return Sister White's phone call. She found the number and dialled through to the office in Reading.

"Good afternoon, Sister White speaking how can I help?"

"Afternoon DC Doyle, I'm told you had some information for me."

"Ahh yes…let me see. Aline Deniaud, no record of her being a member of staff here at all. As for Eve yes, she trained and qualified here. I believe that Aline was most likely agency. I can give you a list if that would help. Perhaps they would be able to give you more details."

"Thanks that would be fab."

Sister White proceeded to give Andrea a list of five agencies the hospital used regularly. Andrea put the list on one side; she would deal with those later. She picked up Simon Thomas' notes, skimming through the transcripts that Mike Jeffordson had marked as read until she came to the next entry.

***

<u>Eve McDonnell</u>
<u>February 1993</u>

ST: Good afternoon Eve, how are you since we last met. It's been a little while.

EMM: Yes, I think it has.

ST: So, last time we met; you were telling me about a new man in your life. Laurent, if I remember correctly?

EMM: Yes, that's right, goodness yes that was back in November. Time flies.

ST: It does indeed, so are you still seeing him?

EMM: Yes, I am.

ST: Dare I ask you, but are you happy?

EMM: Yes, deliriously happy.

ST: Gosh, that's quite a change for you.

EMM: Who would have believed it? It's all been really wonderful.

ST: Tell me about it.

EMM: Well only the other night we went to a concert at Crystal Palace.

ST: Wonderful! Who did you go and see?

EMM: Nigel Kennedy the violinist.

ST: Not what I was expecting.

EMM: No, I wanted to take Laurent to see him, so I got tickets for after work. As I got ready, I chatted with Fabian in the lounge. He'd never heard of him and thought that we were going to see football; I soon put him straight. Shortly after, Laurent walked in the front door with his coat on and a messenger bag slung over his shoulder.

"Bonsoir" He called.

"Bonsoir" We called back.

"Tout suite Eve, we must get a move on…we don't want to be late."

I loved it when he spoke French.

I shoved the items back into my make-up bag, and grabbed my handbag and black stilettos. We said our goodbyes and headed out to the tube.

"How long is it gonna take do you think?"

"About an hour I would have thought. Are you going to be okay in your heels?"

"Yes, I'm sure I am." I looked down at my old faithful Dolcis black patent shoes. "I'll be fine."

We made it down to the tube and got onto the next train arriving into the station. I managed to find a seat amongst some businessmen, with their noses stuck in the newspapers. We made a funny face at each other as we mimicked the pompous men ignoring everyone. I opened my beautiful black leather bag and took out the red Lancôme lipstick and applied it to my lips, rubbing the smooth creamy texture over, covering all the edges. Laurent watched as I titivated myself.

As we got off the train and headed to Crystal Palace, he started to tease me, in a jokey way.

ST: What did he tease you about?

EMM: Putting my make up on in the tube.

ST: Oh.

EMM: Yes, he winked at me and said "You know!" and I said completely innocently "No really I don't..." I didn't know what he was getting at. He took my hand and said "Eve, you are so lovely," taking my hand "did you not see all those dirty old men watching you?" You know I was shocked, that people would watch me. I said to him, "Laurent you're the dirty old man!"

"And you Eve McDonnell are a little flirt!" he grabbed my coat, planting a kiss on my newly made up lips and licking his lips as he realised it had transferred across.

"Look who's wearing the lippy now, you old tart" and I ran off down the path in my high heels, not making much pace! It really was very funny. We were both breathless as we were laughing in the park, we held onto each other's coats as we puffed trying to catch our breaths. We stood there giggling.

"Did you see that old couple watching us?" Laurent commented, nodding at them making their way to the bus station.

"I think they thought you were going to send them flying!"

We were both laughing so much now that my sides were hurting. "No, no, you've got to stop, my sides are hurting, please stop...I beg you!"

"OKAY, OKAY we'll stop!" He pulled a serious face and then suddenly a small curl at the edge of his mouth appeared and we were in peals of laughter again. You know when you just can't stop and you have to keep telling each other to stop.

But no matter how hard I tried the laughter kept bubbling over. I had to sit myself on an old wooden park bench to catch my breath. I rocked back and forth trying to stop the giggling and the pain. Laurent came and sat next to me. We were both thoroughly exhausted...And slowly like a wave crashing gently on a beach, the laughter calmed.

Laurent looked down at his watch "Come on you old flirt, we need to get a move on, we're going to be late". He jumped off the bench before I could grab him.

"Right you've had it now" I said rejuvenated.

"Come on then." He gesticulated with his hands for me to chase him.

"No...I'm saving myself!" I joked.

"OKAY" he seemed disappointed.

But I caught him off his guard... "Come on then you dirty old man!" I tottered past him...

"No, no Eve, let's not; it's a silly game."

"OKAY..." I replied, power walking knowing full well that he would catch up with me.

"Come on let's get a cab for the last bit" he called.

"Look we're nearly there look; I can see it"

And sure enough there stood Crystal Palace at the end of the long drive...The concert was being held in the park. We were late; the sweet melody of Vivaldi could be heard throughout the park. The walkways were now lit and we held hands and followed the directions to the main area. We came to a clearing with a dome-shaped stage in the centre where Nigel Kennedy stood, violin in one hand and bow in the other, the legendary maverick taking control of the stage like a true master.

ST: What did Laurent make of the concert do you think?

EMM: He thought it was really magical. I don't know whether you have ever been there for a concert, it's amazing. Wherever you were you could see the orchestra and Nigel Kennedy playing with vigour and pace. He was really funny as well. We both laughed and the audience clapped and cheered at his witty little quips; the Brighton boy had 'done good.'

The music continued throughout the night and people were lighting night torches...It was the first time I had ever seen anyone doing that before. Laurent lit his lighter. It was so atmospheric.

When Nigel Kennedy played the final piece, bright lights shot up into the sky as an explosion of fireworks burst across the vista. Great oohs and aahs could be heard, as they filled the sky with colour. The crowd cheered as the final firework burst, causing a flock of birds to take flight.

ST: It sound like you had a great evening.

EMM: We had a wonderful evening together. It really was the best, so we left the concert and headed home back across the city on the underground. The low rumble and electric whir filled the carriage as it rattled and rocked through the tunnels. I'd never felt so happy in the whole of my life, I looked at him in his dark coat and scarf wrapped around him, and then I gazed down at our hands as we held onto one another tightly. I didn't want to let go of him ever.

ST: I can feel a 'but' coming.

EMM: But, then those seeds of doubts entered my mind once again, haunting me. I could hear Aline "Why would anyone want to be with you!" And then Smiffy and Aline's voices echoed inside my head. "Err is it alive!" Just like they did in the playground all those years earlier.

I felt as though, everyone else in the carriage was looking at us both wondering what he was doing with me. The paranoia kicked in. I'm sure that they thought I really wasn't good enough for him. I could feel the anxiety rise in my chest, and the claustrophobia starting, the carriage felt as though it was getting hotter and hotter and I thought I was going to be sick. Quickly I started to undo my scarf from my neck, as it was suffocating me, and made the nausea worse...and then I undid my coat.

ST: And then?

EMM: Laurent looked up alarmed. And asked if I was okay? I told him I felt sick and needed to get off. I could hear the panic in my own voice. He helped me off with my numerous layers, I demanded cold air. He quickly got up and opened the vent. I just need to get off the carriage, things started to become blurred and I could feel the sense of panic rising again.

ST: What did you do?

EMM: Laurent told me the next stop was 3 minutes and sure enough, the carriage came to a halt. We waited for all the other passengers to leave the train, and we got up retrieving the clothes I had peeled off.

Laurent and I stepped out onto the concrete platform, and the bracing night air was very much welcome. I instantly felt the claustrophobia lifting as we stood there. But the sense of panic was still inside me. I could just hear Aline now having a go..."You'll never be good enough for him and now look at you! Having a panic attack on the train!" I was sure Aline would have something to say on the incident, she always did.

ST: Sounds like you had a massive panic attack on the tube.

EMM: It was dreadful.

ST: But Laurent handled it well.

EMM: Yes, he took me home and tucked me into bed.

ST: And he is still with you?

EMM: Yes.

ST: So, what you believed wasn't the truth?

EMM: No, no it wasn't.

SESSION ENDS.

***

Andrea closed the file. What had happened to Eve? Where were she and Laurent now? They were clearly in love. But what had happened for Eve to now be involved with a drug scandal. None of it made sense. Andrea got up to see if the others had returned.

CHAPTER 39

LES MISÉRABLES

Whilst making herself a cup of tea, Andrea eyed up the leftover buffet in the kitchen but thought better of it. It had been out for hours after the secretaries leaving do. She decided she didn't want a nasty touch of food poisoning, but snaffled a chocolate mini roll before they all went. That should be safe shouldn't it? Andrea returned to the office, opening the wrapper of the small cake. One bite and it was gone. She opened the file to the next entry.

***

Eve McDonnell
10th March 1993

ST: Hello Eve, how are things going for you?

EMM: Good thank you.

ST: So, last time you talked about the trip to Crystal Palace and then the panic attack on the tube. Laurent brought you home, how were you after that?

EMM: Well the following morning. I woke to find that Laurent wasn't in bed. It made me panic slightly. I thought perhaps he'd gone; you know for good. Then I told myself that was ridiculous. I was sitting in his bed.

ST: Okay, that's interesting. So, where had he gone?

EMM: To the bakery.

ST: To the bakery?

EMM: Yes, the morning after the concert Laurent had gone and collected freshly baked croissants and coffee from the French Bakery. He had then been to buy the papers from the local newsagents.

ST: So, he hadn't left you?

EMM: No, I felt such a fool. He was just lovely, asking me how I was after last night. I told him that I was embarrassed. I said that I felt stupid about the whole episode, and you know what? He just said he was worried about me. That was it; he was just so sincere and kind.

ST: Like he really cared about you.

EMM: You know what else. He was so completely open and honest, and could be read like a book. He said that he wore his heart on his sleeve. Just like us English would say. It was then that I saw his vulnerability too. He too had been hurt, but he'd come out the other side.

You know, I truly believed in that moment that he did love me and all those doubts were beginning to be wiped from my mind.

He suggested that we put the incident on the tube behind us, and then he passed me Time Out magazine to read. "You've given me a little culture, maybe I should share something with you. Let's go and see Les Miserables." It didn't sound like a lot of fun; I opened the magazine and there in the centre of the page was a blonde girl with bedraggled hair, wearing a hat. In the background, a French flag. He told me a brief outline of the story and with his typical French flair he created intrigue and suspense. I begged him to tell me more of the plot.

"Non, ma petit chou, you will have to see it for yourself."

"How about 7pm showing tonight?"

"Tonight!?" I remember exclaiming.

ST: So, you got the tickets and you went I assume?

EMM: Yes, it was wonderful. We got the tube to Leicester Square and walked through China Town, under the golden gates and past all the restaurants and supermarkets getting ready for the evening's trade. Lots of tourists were seen ambling along looking at the menus, choosing the place they'd eat tonight. As we turned right the Queen's Theatre stood immediately in front of us. I remember just clutching his hand, looking in wonder at the neon lights that lit up the night sky. People had started arriving all smartly dressed. Ladies in cocktail length dresses and fluffy jackets, all very glam. We looked a right pair of scruff bags in our jeans! Nobody would notice when we got in. The theatre felt huge with a bar on every floor. We found ourselves at the very back by the sound booth and had an obstructed view as the seats overhead dropped forward. The performance was due to start at 7.30pm but nothing was happening, and at 7.45pm there were a lot of people on the stage fiddling with the set. Then, at 8pm the stage manager came out to speak with the audience.

"I'm afraid to say that due to unforeseen circumstance the stage is not working. The winch which drives the barricade is broken and we can't get an engineer here until tomorrow. In these circumstances we shall go to plan B, which is to do the show as a choral."

"This is outrageous, I've come all the way from America to see this," a large American man shouted. "I've paid good money"

"We're terribly sorry, but we can offer all of you tickets to a midweek performance."

"That's no good...I live in Germany; how am I supposed to use it?!" another man protested.

ST: Oh no did the show go ahead?

EMM: Yes, it did, as a choral. Unbelievably, people started getting out of their seats and leaving the theatre. We couldn't believe they would leave, if you've paid good money for the performance!"

I was swept away by the drama, suspense and the beautiful sweet singing. I was truly transformed by this mesmerising musical that took a piece of my heart with it. During the grand finale, I sobbed my heart out and I could see the leading actors also crying too. It simply was the most amazingly emotional moving performance I had ever seen...

"It was beautiful...and so sad, thank you so much for bringing me...I loved it." I sobbed to Laurent.

"I knew you would love it. I saw the film many years ago, but never live."

We left our seats and were met by the manager giving out complimentary tickets to another showing, to be taken by the end of the year. "Your parents could come." I suggested handing him the tickets.

"No, no give them to your parents!?" I then told him quite bluntly about dad dying at the beginning of my training and after then mum later in a car accident. You know, right there, I wanted to leave it in the past. So, I took his hand and practically dragged him out of the theatre. I could tell Laurent was really shocked at how cold-hearted I appeared to be about my parents. We hovered outside several restaurants and found one that took our fancy offering a huge variety of Dim Sum. We were shown to a table laid for two, with chopsticks on a crisp white cloth. He suggested a set menu so we could talk properly. Not like the English, discussing the weather and the time of day.

After pouring the white wine he proposed a toast. "To us!"

"I'll drink to that" and we chinked.

"So, in good French tradition, let's talk."

I felt nervous; he looked at me lovingly and held my hand. I took a sip of my wine and looked at him...

"Okay," he squeezed it, encouraging me. "Please talk to me, tell me what is going on inside that crazy English head of yours."

I took a deep breath. Taking my hands away from Laurent, I clenched them into a fist, bringing them to my face, resting my nose on my knuckle. I could feel the hot breath skimming over the top and smell of lavender handwash.

"So," I started adjusting my seat. "As I said, Dad died from a heart attack at the beginning of my training. I didn't really know what to feel about it. He wasn't a very nice man, so it was really hard to know how to react. So, I bottled it all up. I loved him, but hated him at the same time; it really didn't make sense at all. Soon after his death, mum made it official that her and Mr Van Clair had been having an affair for many years. He left his wife and they set up home together. I knew of course, and I was pleased that she was finally happy. When his divorce came through, they got married the following month, she didn't waste any time. It was beautiful. You could feel that they really were very much in love. The whole atmosphere changed at home with Bruce in her life. But tragedy struck when they were on holiday."

I felt really choked up telling him, but you know Laurent was so lovely, he just commiserated with me, holding my hands...

ST: Is this when the accident happened.

EMM: Yes, they were on holiday in the USA, driving from Miami up to Kissimmee and their car was hit...

SILENCE 10 SECONDS.

They were hit by a truck; the driver was drunk. They were killed outright. It was truly awful.

ST: Here have a tissue.

EMM: Now look what you've done to me.

ST: I'm sorry Eve, that sounds truly awful. Did you manage to tell Laurent the whole story?

EMM: I told him how my family had become so dysfunctional and now I had Bruce's ex-wife on my case. She wanted what was rightfully hers. All I wanted was my mum back. I had this warped image that in France everything was rosy. He soon set me straight "I can assure you it is not all perfect in France, divorces and dysfunctional families still happen, honestly. It's just human nature. It's how we all react to life that is important. I was just one of the lucky ones honestly. Whereas you Eve, were dealt a bad card. But you know what? You rose above it all, and they didn't take away the sense of right and wrong. You have allowed love to fill your soul. You couldn't do the job you do without love."

He was so sensitive, and it was as though he could see straight into my soul, he had been so fortunate to have the love that surrounded him, as he had no problem with sharing it around.

"You were very fortunate to be raised by good people, Laurent." I remember saying to him. He agreed that he had has the most incredible family. It was clear that he missed them a lot. It was then I felt the pang in my heart. This was what would take him away from me, his family.

"You miss them a lot? I asked."

"I do..."

"Then you must return to them all..." I couldn't believe that I had even suggested it.

ST: But you did?

EMM: I know, I couldn't understand why I was so prepared to lose him.

ST: You were, because you loved him and you couldn't bear to see him hurting. How did he react?

EMM: He asked me to return with him?

ST: He did? And what did you say.

EMM: Of course, I said, there's nothing keeping me in Old Blighty. "Not even your sister?" he asked me. I told him that she packed up and left many years ago, to Australia.

Was this my future sitting right here before me? All I ever wanted was to love and be loved in return. This man was offering all of this to me. He was kind and compassionate, never said a bad word about anyone. I knew that he's wasn't a soft touch either, and would be prepared to fight your corner. I was completely suckered in by him and the love he emanated. I loved him to bits, and here we were planning our future together. I knew that I would go to the other end of the world to be with him, I was now completely caught up in all of this. I, Eve McDonnell, was going to have a bright future with Laurent and no one was going to stop me. Not even Aline. And you know what, for the first time in my life I understood what it was like for my mother being swept off her feet by Bruce Van Clair. Did she feel consumed by his love and overpowered by that longing to be with him? Because if she felt half of what I was experiencing at this moment in time, for once in my life I understood her.

ST: That's really awesome Eve, I'm really thrilled for you. So, when are you guys going to pack up and leave ol' blighty?

EMM: As soon as possible.

SESSION ENDS.

***

Andrea looked down at the entry, so what happened? Everything seemed to be going so well for this couple. It looked like her counselling sessions were coming to an end. But Andrea flicked through the pages; there were more sessions together that followed.

CHAPTER 40

THE PLAN

Celine rushed through the corridors, her tight pencil skirt hugging her slim frame. Her long blonde hair framed her petite face and she looked excited when she found DI Jeffordson as he was coming up the stairs. He was a little out of breath as he got to the top.

"Sir, the French Embassy has been in contact this morning," she told him.

"About bloody time! Glad to see they made it a priority," he raised his eyebrows and flicked his head, tutting. "What have they got, Celine?"

She brushed hair out of her face. "Well," she started. "The French authorities haven't got any details of her moving here in the last year."

"Have you got in touch with her parents in France?"

"No, Sir, I'm still checking. I've got the French authorities to help, but it's taking a long time. Everyone's so busy."

"Well we won't hold our breaths."

"No, Sir."

"Have you still got colleagues in the French police that could help you make enquiries? Surely they'd be quicker."

"Yes, I've thought of that. I contacted my old boss, Captain Nicolas Brémont. He's doing some digging around for us. I've given him everything we know. Is that okay, Sir?"

"Of course, Celine, that's fine."

"He said he'll look for them via the Census and also at La Mairie in Paris — it will have a register of residents in Paris. If they've moved to another area, it might be difficult to find them without a location."

"That's fantastic, Celine. Do thank your colleagues in Paris. Please let Andi and Phil know any of the developments if I'm not here."

"Of course, Sir, I'll see what Nicolas has discovered later. Can you let me know if there's anything else we can give him?"

"Of course."

Mike admired Celine as she walked back to her office. She was a real French beauty. She'd moved to England five years earlier, having worked with Interpol in Paris, and ended up working with the Metropolitan Police. She certainly brought a little bit of glamour to the office. If only he was twenty years younger, he mused. He shook his head and dismissed the thought as he walked back to the main office.

***

Mike paced up and down the office twisting his moustache between his fingers, over and over. Andrea and Phil sat watching him as he mulled over the investigation. They exchanged glances. Mike looked up at the pair of them as they waited for him to speak.

"So," he said eventually. "What we're dealing with here is clearly a case of unravelling the past of these two individuals who are entwined within each other's lives. We need to find Eve and why aren't there any records of Aline working at other hospitals. Was she or is she working as a bogus nurse so that she can get access to drugs?" He paced again up and down the room. "Why, if she was a bogus nurse, would she target maternity and not general wards. Surely, they have more available drugs? I'll have to get to the bottom of all of this," he ruminated.

"Don't you think we should be concentrating on finding this Lammy who attacked Aline, Sir? I think we're getting side-tracked by all this back history." Phil felt puzzled by Jeffordson's whole approach to the investigation.

"Ahh, you may think that, young Phil, but as dear old Professor Hawking said: 'The past, like the future, is indefinite and exists only as a spectrum of possibilities.' Therefore, my dear fellow, we must look down every avenue. Hence, why we are trying to untangle this web. I'm determined to get to the bottom of this, even if it kills me!"

"Well, I certainly hope that won't be the case, Sir."

"Oh, get on with it lad! I've got work to do." His eyes twinkled. "We've got to sort it before I blooming well retire!"

Mike returned to his office and opened Simon Thomas's file again.

***

Eve McDonnell
6th August 1993

ST: It's been a few months now Eve.

EMM: Yes, it has, the weeks and months have certainly rolled by. I've been in London pretty much every time I'm off duty and staying overnight in the flat in London with Laurent and his friends from work. Reading had really only become a place of work and I was barely at the nurses' accommodation. Like today, I'm back to work this afternoon after being in London. We hope that eventually we will be in a position to leave London and move to France. I haven't really wanted to tell anyone in Reading what is going on, I knew I'd get people warning me not to do it. Aline as you can imagine was the first to have a go at me. You can just hear her nagging me…"You're mad, you hardly know him, giving up a good job to run away with a French waiter."

"I'm not running away; I'm moving to France and I'm getting another job."

"How do you know you'll get another job?"

"'cause there are always jobs for midwives."

"You're mad, you don't even know French, what if it all goes wrong, and you don't get on, and you fall out with Laurent, what will happen then?"

"I'll learn French, and if it goes wrong I will return."
"I recall almost screaming at her. I was exasperated by her and she didn't stop bitching."

"I'm telling you Eve, it will all end in tears; you hardly know the boy!"

"For Pete's sake Aline, give it a rest! It's my life!"

"Yes, and your gonna ruin it Eve for some French guy you picked up in a club! I suppose you're going to go off and marry him! And then what will happen? You'll go to France and buy a big farmhouse and raise a family," she sneered.

"His name is Laurent!"

"You're not listening to me! This isn't a dream romance, you're not going to marry him, it simply won't happen. Why would he want to be with you for the rest of his life?"

"'cause he loves me!"

"Yeah, yeah, whatever."

"Aline, I'm gonna do this whether you like it or not."

"Don't come running back to me when it all goes ugly."

"I can't help it, if you don't like it! And I'm moving on with my life, you are not going to be part of it any more. Do you hear me Aline? It's about time you moved on and left me alone." I screamed and screamed at her "For the love of God Aline back off!"

ST: And then what happened after the argument with Aline.

EMM: I didn't hear from her. But it still upset me. I told Laurent about the argument. He told me that I didn't need to listen to her. It's your life and it's up to you what you do with it, don't let Aline hurt you.

"But..." I started.

"Shhh" he calmed me "Eve I love you; I'm not going to let anything happen to you, and you are doing it for the right reason, you mustn't let Aline get to you."

"Come on..." he brightened up "I have a surprise for you." He guided me into his bedroom, hanging up on his curtain pole was huge plastic bag, like a suit carrier but bigger. He walked over to it and unzipped the carrier to reveal a black satin ball-gown.

"What's this?"

"It looks like a dress to me!" in his cheeky French accent.

I walked over to it touching the fabric it was soft and supple under my fingers. I could see tiny little black sequins all individually hand stitched on. It was beautiful and I asked what it was for.

"It's for tonight, we have to leave in about an hour and a half, a taxi is coming to collect us!"

Oh my word it was so exciting, I don't think I've ever worn anything so gorgeous before. Slowly, I pulled it out of the covers, hands trembling and undid the zip. I slipped inside the cold dress as the lining slid up over my legs up to my bust. Laurent zipped up the dress at the back. It simply was the most beautiful dress I'd ever seen. "It's amazing".

"You look amazing, but I'm afraid it's not to keep. I hired it for the night. Christina at work helped me choose it for you," a small pang of jealously clutched my heart.

He knew straight away. "Eve, I can read you like a book...You don't have to worry about Christina; she's in her late 40s married with two boys. She's one of the concierges; she's like my mother and really looked after me when I first moved here. She's really looking forward to meeting you tonight!" He put his hand to his mouth, "Whoops, too much information!"

***

The black cab arrived. Laurent looked incredible in his black tie and dinner jacket and he slung his coat over me as we clambered into the cab.

"The Ritz," he said to the cabby, the cab swung round in the street and headed into the opposite direction. I looked down at the dress and Laurent's hand rested on my lap, I took it and held it tightly and we smiled at one another. I could feel myself trembling with excitement and nervousness. I had never been too a posh do with a posh frock on before. We were going to the Ritz; I couldn't believe it! The world whizzed by as we were taken through the streets of London. Shoppers and commuters were heading down the dark streets bustling through the crowds to their destinations after a busy day in the city.

The entrance to The Ritz was as glamorous as ever I could imagine, the name picked out in individual light bulbs, scrolled ironwork under a stone archway, a red carpet rolled out, just like Hollywood. A footman in his top hat and red tails opened the cab door and helped me out of the black taxi as though I was the Princess of Wales. Other cabs and flash cars arrived with chauffeurs and ladies in long frocks and furs. One by one the footman helped them out and welcomed them into The Ritz.

The inside was not what I'd expected. It was incredibly ornate with its baroque style, the huge pillars decorated with sconces and cherubs. In my mind I'd always imagined it to have a 1920s feel, more Art Deco. This certainly was a posh do.

ST: What was the occasion?

EMM: The catering awards, it was very posh. The tables were all laid beautifully and Laurent and I found where we were seated with our names in calligraphy on stiff white cards.

A gentleman in his 50s with a grey goatee beard got up to the podium and talked over the microphone. He made a very grand speech. I was truly overwhelmed by being at such a decadent event.

A buzz filled the air, people chatted excitedly, wine corks popped, glasses clinked, music started. Laurent introduced me to Christina and others from work.

"Are the boys not coming?" I whispered.

"No, just a select few," he replied.

I took a sip of the heavily oaky Chardonnay, so fashionable but really so unpalatable.

"You don't like the Chardonnay, Eve? It's OKAY, it's very of the moment, have something else! How about a nice French wine?" He uncorked the bottle and poured a pale glass of white wine. It was much better.

The live band started to play and I began to tap my feet along to the music.

"Come on Eve, let's get up and dance, I know you want to." His eyes twinkled as he offered his hand. I grabbed my dress and elegantly got out of my seat and we headed to the dance floor. He held me tightly around my waist.

The band started to play, the drum beat picked up... they were playing a classic Frankie Valli and the Four Seasons – *Beggin'*. I loved it.

We outstretched our hands touching each other's palms, almost like jazz hands in slow motion mouthing the words to each other; we stepped back and forth in time with the music. We were the only ones on the floor together, the only ones with the courage to get up and strut our stuff. Laurent knew that I didn't worry about what everyone thought about me, it was everyone else's problem if they needed to drink themselves into a state of confidence, the night would be lost. We shimmed our shoulders, to adoring whoops from his colleagues. He smiled and gave them a sexy little shrug, and wink...

The music changed and Laurent grabbed me around the waist and twirled, picking me off the floor. Mesmerised by the music others had now joined Laurent and I on the dance floor, totally intoxicated by us both. We were both so wrapped up in each other that we hardly noticed the others on the dance floor. I threw back my head as he whirled me round and round, he then gently placed me down and our eyes were fixed upon one another as he raised his arm, I spun and pirouetted under it. He pulled me into his body, singing out of tune to Take That's Barry Manilow classic – Could it be Magic. I was just so happy with him singing flatly, it was all so perfect. We held onto one another so tight, I was almost breathless holding onto him. The music ended and everyone else cheered and whooped. We stood still both breathing heavily, both feeling that the mood had been broken prematurely. I wanted to leave immediately and spend the night with Laurent back at home. We stood looking at each other, holding hands, almost suspended in time.

The evening's master of ceremony arrived at the podium.

"The time has come. It's what you've all been waiting for. It's nice to see some of you enjoying yourselves." He nodded at Laurent and me.

"Come on let's get this over with" whispered Laurent as he led me off the dance floor and back to his adoring colleagues, who shook his hand as we returned.

The MC then continued as we left the floor for the award ceremony. "We have eight categories, the finalists have been selected from the results of nominations from industry experts," whom he nodded at behind him, "and more importantly from you their peers and colleagues."

The audience clapped and cheered as the smart gentleman waited for the noise to subside.

"The first category is for the best chef, followed by best hotel, restaurant manager, best newcomer, menu of the year, marketing campaign, best bar and pub and lifetime achievement award." I could feel it might possibly be a very long evening, but the mood was buoyant and the drinks kept coming. I found myself relaxing into the event. As each category was announced the finalists were introduced to huge roars and cheers; each table anxious to see whether they were winners in their category. Once the winner was announced you could feel the disappointment around you, the heavy sighs and expressions fell. One after another the winners collected their coveted award from the podium and had their photograph taken with the press.

"Oh, will they be in the newspaper tomorrow?"

"No just in the Caterer magazine, they won't go into the national newspapers!" Christina explained. "Nobody is that interested" she looked downhearted "I thought we'd get something tonight."

"What a shame."

"Now we have the finalist for the best restaurant manager."

Christina nudged my arm! I looked at her puzzled.

"Our finalists are..." He opened a stiff white envelope..."From the West Country, Andrew Fullerton, Bowood Hotel, Wiltshire; from the Midlands, Trevor

Wagstaff, Brownsover Hall, Warwickshire; and finally, from London, Laurent Roselle, Cadeau Hotel, Queens Gate, Kensington."

My ears pricked up and I looked at Laurent sitting calmly looking towards the podium, not looking at any of us. Christina and I exchanged glances we all sat in silence; the gentleman on the podium adjusted his glasses, "And the winner is..." we all held our breath. "Laurent Roselle from the Cadeau Hotel, London!" The table exploded everyone was patting him on his back and his colleagues hugged him. He stroked my back as he passed behind the chair to collect his award.

"But he told me he was a waiter!" I exclaimed to Christina.

"I'm not surprised, that's how he started many years ago, but now he's our manager, the Maître D'."

I was completely flabbergasted by how he had kept this so quiet, never one to brag about himself. I watched him glide through the tables to collect his prize. Colleagues from other tables touched him as he walked through. Laurent accepted the award from the judges, "Congratulations Laurent Roselle for winning this year's Restaurant Manager of the year." He handed him the microphone. "Is there anything you'd like to say?"

Laurent cleared his throat.

"Just a few words." He paused, the audience awaiting his response. "This is a wonderful surprise for the whole team...Thank you from us all, as we have worked hard to get better every day. I stand here humbled that the team has been awarded this accolade and if we were all on this stage today, you would see we have become close as colleagues, but closer as a family. Thank you so much for your kind thoughts and well wishes that we have all taken to heart. Merci."

Once he completed his acceptance speech and handed back the microphone, the audience applauded as he stepped off the podium. He stood for the photographers as they took his picture. I was truly flabbergasted by this revelation.

ST: So, you knew nothing about it at all?

EMM: No, not a thing. This is typical of him not to show off. Apparently, all his colleagues knew 1 month earlier. You know when he walked back to the table it was to a sea of applause and cheers. He looked so proud of this achievement; he took my hand and kissed it as he sat down.

"Laurent Roselle, you're a little toad," I exclaimed. "Why didn't you tell me about any of this?"

He rolled his bottom lip over and shrugged his shoulders, "It's nothing!"

"But!" I felt ready to argue with him, that he'd achieved a wonderful thing, that he should be proud of himself. But it dawned on me that this just wasn't him, he was a quiet and humble man, gracious and not one to live on the attention.

"Come on, let's go" he suggested.

"But the evening hasn't finished, don't you want to celebrate with your colleagues."

"No, I see them every day, I'd rather be with you," he stroked my waist. "You're simply stunning in that dress. Did you see everyone watching as you arrived?"

"No, I didn't."

A slight gentleman with a wispy beard interrupted, "Excuse me but can I take your photo for the local newspaper."

"Um yes," Laurent replied slightly shocked.

"We like to have all the latest from all the awards, particularly one as prestigious as this," a short female reporter chipped in "Can I take down your names please Laurent and?"

"Eve" Laurent replied.

"Laurent and Eve Roselle?"

We smiled at one another "Er, no, it's Eve McDonnell" I replied.

"And are you also in the industry Miss McDonnell?"

"No, she's a midwife" Laurent replied.

"Ah lovely, so a chef and a midwife," she looked up. "That must be tough with you both on shifts."

"Well I'm a Maître D' not a chef," corrected Laurent.

"Oh sorry, my mistake!"

The photographer took our pictures, we made our excuses to his friends and we hailed a cab back into the London streets. The rain had now started and the wiper blades were on double time, as we weaved our way back to the flat in Kensington. By the time we arrived the heavens had opened and I pulled the jacket over my head and ran up the steps to get out of the downpour. Laurent opened the door to the flat and we fell in like a pair of bedraggled rats. My long hair was soaked and the long drips splashed onto my bare shoulders and ran down me. Laurent shook his head, but the rain still ran down his long nose. We looked at each other, we looked ridiculous.

"It was a truly wonderful evening…" I smiled.

"It certainly was."

He took my face in his hands and kissed the rain off my forehead and slowly made his way down my face to my lips. His lips were warm and smooth; he kissed me gently, so very gently. A warm glow could be felt right inside my abdomen. I placed my hands around his back and brought him closer to me. The shirt felt wet and cold on his back, where he'd braved the weather.

"Come on, you're soaking!"

"So, are you"

"Let's gets this off" I started to peel off his shirt, and stopped as I came to his bare skin, I felt breathless and giddy.

"Not here Eve, the lads will be back." For once he was the one being coy.

He pushed his door open and no sooner had the door closed the kissing had recommenced. His lips kissed my back and shoulder as he unzipped my dress. Then he slid his hands down, helping me out of the dress. We lay on his unmade bed touching one another and eventually fell asleep after making love. It had been a perfect evening; even the rain hadn't dampened our spirits.

So that morning as I lay in bed, I felt sad, like the grey sky filtering into his bedroom. The light bounced off the pale blue walls. He was sleeping like a baby, his dark lashes resting on his face. His gentle breath moved his chest, slowly rising and falling. He turned slightly over rolling towards me in the big French bed; he flicked the white duvet off himself, exposing his bare chest. The sadness washed over me again, I just knew I didn't want to leave him and go to work. I just wanted stay here, to be suspended in time, you know?

ST: Yes, I know.

EMM: I woke him up; I didn't want him to sleep, knowing that I had to go so soon. "Laurent" I whispered kissing his arm, then moving to the side of his face and then his nose. He opened his eyes looking dazed, and then smiled as he came into focus.

"Evie", he took my hand and kissed the tips of my finger and held it to his chest.

"Laurent I've got to go to work."

"When will you be back?"

"Tomorrow morning, then we can have the whole day."

"Can't you come back tonight?"

"Yes, but it will be very late."

He leant forward and pressed his mouth up against mine, "Eve, I love you so much. Never forget it."

"I love you too Laurent and I always will," I said as I returned his kiss. "I don't know what I would do without you."

"I'm not going anywhere without you and that's a promise."

He leant over and kissed me tenderly on my mouth and I took in his sweet citrus smell, closing my eyes and holding this moment to memory. His hands slowly ran down my body, and I sunk into his bed, pulling the duvet over our heads. I wrapped my legs around him holding him firmly never wanting to release him. We lay there together in each other's arms, kissing one another. The morning ticked away, and all too soon it was time for me to get up and go to work.

"Come on you, you'll be late," he said getting out of bed, his tall naked body walked around the room getting a dressing gown and tying the belt around his waist. "You have a shower and I'll make breakfast."

I climbed out of bed and ran a hot shower, opening the bathroom door so that I could hear the sweet mellow music playing. I smiled to myself as Laurent could be heard cooking and I could hear the clattering of plates and cutlery as he laid the table. He was singing, off key as usual, as he got breakfast ready.

"5 minutes, Mademoiselle" he called.

I climbed out of the shower and wrapped a large towel around my body, and dried myself off. I then secured the towel around my head like a hug marshmallow turban. He gave me a kiss on my forehead as I came into the kitchen...

"Your table awaits Mademoiselle," he teased with a small tea towel over his arm, and pulled out my seat. I giggled as I sat down...He had made a soft omelette with a pot of fresh coffee.

"You know when you get your job here and move to London permanently, we can see about us moving to France..."

"Will I need to do something about a work permit first?"

"Well, your French would need to be fluent and then your professional stuff would need to be sorted, you'd most likely need to do some sort of course."

"OKAY, but what will we do for money."

"We can save here and then stay with my parents. They have a vineyard and a small gite that we can live in. I can either work for Papa or a local restaurant. It's not a problem. We just need a bit of money first."

"OKAY; I'm very excited by all this!"

"So am I, I'm very much looking forward to the time we shall have together here and back home…you will simply love it there…!" he looked down at my plate, "but first you must eat your breakfast and not be late for work!"

The time ticked by so quickly as we ate our breakfast… And sadness loomed over us as we knew that eventually I would need to leave.

I got dressed for work and we said our goodbyes, feeling the love and the bitterness of having to leave him here.

"Until tonight my love," I said.

He whispered returning "A bien tot ma petit chou".

We kissed on the doorstep as I left him in his dressing gown. I looked back and waved, blowing kisses which he returned and slowly he was out of view. I walked further up the road to the underground. As I walked to the tube, I plugged my earphones into my ears and turned on my portable CD player… I felt buoyant as I made my way down the steps to the underground, looking forward to returning that evening.

ST: So, here we are Eve, I think we can safely say that things have work out incredibly well for you.

EMM: They have indeed.

ST: Shall we pencil a date in the diary, for maybe 3 weeks' time. I don't think you will need it but...who knows?

EMM: Yes, I'm happy with that.

SESSION ENDS.

***

Mike rubbed his eye, who was this Laurent Roselle? He hadn't seen his name on the list of staff working for Cadeau Hotels. Had they left him off because he was a manager and they had only asked for waiters? He would need to contact headquarters again and find out where he was, and what he was doing now. Surely, he would know where Eve was.

CHAPTER 41

NEW LIFE

Stuart heard retching coming from the ladies' toilet. He waited outside for the patient to come out.

"Hello, are you okay?" he called.

The door opened and Aline put her head 'round the corner of the door. She looked awful, her face was sweaty and her hair was dripping wet.

"Been sick again?" he asked.

"Yes. I've had a dreadful nightmare again."

"Aww, I'm sorry about that. I'm afraid it's the bug that's going around. You'll feel better soon."

"But this nightmare, it keeps happening. Stuart, was I a midwife once?"

He nodded. "I believe so."

"Can I talk about this nightmare?"

"Of course, where do you want to go?"

"In the courtyard, I like it there, but first, I need my cigarettes."

"I can get them out of the cupboard."

"Don't they trust us to look after our own cigarettes and lighters?" she asked as they walked into the courtyard.

"No, Aline they don't."

It was a cold winter's morning and Aline huddled herself up as she lit her cigarette.

"You?" she offered Stuart the packet.

"No, I'm good, hen, trying to give them up," he smiled, putting up his hand.

"So, tell me about this nightmare. I take it it's a work-related one?"

"Yes, I believe so. It starts every time with a spray of blood hitting the ceiling. Then I see a baby boy shoot out of its mother's body. New life comes into this world with a splash. I hardly have time to get my gloves on and open the delivery pack; I'm in such a rush that I put the gloves on back to front with the thumbs sticking out of the palms of my hands. The mother was pushing for dear life, bearing down, against all my directions to take it slowly. He arrives like a champagne cork, ripping his mother as he enters this world, and I catch him before he lands on the bed. His dark curls are darkened by the blood and his skin is wet and slippery. I wrap him quickly in a towel, clamp and cut the cord, and give him a good rub, as he's a bit shocked by his quick delivery. The mother is elated by the safe arrival of son number four. She takes him in her arms and coos to him. It's happened at such a great speed that the blood has sprayed over the newly painted ceiling, it's travelled in a huge arc and now it's on the walls. The evidence glaring at us; the violent act, over.

"It really strikes me then, maybe for the first time ever, that I had already delivered three babies into the world that day, and I have no idea of their futures – the paths they'll take and the journeys they'll travel. This baby lies there, wrapped in his mother's arms...a little scrap of a thing. This baby is one of the lucky ones; he'll have love for the rest of his life. He has his parents to guide him and teach him, show him right from wrong. They'll be there on his first day at school, help him through those tricky times. Then I realise that some babies will not be so fortunate; they'll face a terrible future. They'll leave the safety of their mothers and then it will start – the hardship, poverty, being unloved, neglected and abused. I think, how could anyone do that? It makes me feel frightened. I think what if I do something wrong? What if I don't spot a problem soon enough and it causes the new born to be disabled? I know that all I would need to do was to make an error and that baby would live with a lifetime of problems and it would be due to me."

"Then I feel the pain inside of me. I worry about the destiny of this small baby. I'll never know what happens to him; if he has a happy life, or one filled with worries and unhappiness. Will he follow a path where he could change others' lives or be the one to destroy the very souls of people? How could something so beautiful become so bad?

"Then I have thoughts of previous families whose babies I'd delivered; they come flashing back into my memory again. The families who just didn't care; who were cruel beyond belief. I start feeling so sick and nauseous. Then I wake up and have the overwhelming desire to vomit."

Aline stubbed her cigarette out, which had now burnt down to the butt.

"It's crazy isn't it?" she said. "Completely crazy."

"No, I don't think it's crazy at all. It's all about love. You loved those babies in your care so deeply, you were fearful for them." He adjusted his glasses and stroked his top lip.

"Love? Really? Do you think that's what this is all about?"

"Yes, yes I do, Aline."

"You know, Stuart, saying you love something is such a throw-away statement. We profess to loving a new pair of shoes or a bar of chocolate. But love is so much deeper than that, isn't it?"

"It certainly is. It gets into every cell of your body."

"Have you ever been in love?"

Stuart blushed. "Yes, I have."

"Are you still in love with her, or him?" she asked "I know I shouldn't be asking, but..."

"It helps? Yes, I know, it helps."

He pondered.

"Well, have you?"

"Yes, with a woman."

"And are you still with her?"

"Yes, I am."

"What's it like – being truly in love?"

"For me, I felt as though," he looked up, over the rooftops of the hospital. "Well," he looked back Aline. "It takes over your thoughts. It eats you up and immerses you into this bubble, away from reality – away from what's happening in the world. It consumes your soul. You can't be without it, it's like the very air you breathe. Yet it leaves you breathless."

He gave a deep sigh as he thought of his love. He looked at Aline as she hung on his every word.

Aline was there in the moment with him, she felt his passion for this woman he loved.

"What do you know about love?" he asked her.

"What do I know about love? I know what it is like to live without love. To feel empty and soulless, because there is no love. It's how I feel right now. Empty and alone. My heart hungers for it, yet I feel that I have been loved, just as I know that I have been abused. How can that be? I simply don't understand it. All I know is, right now, I feel haunted. Haunted by the past that I cannot fully remember. This makes me feel afraid about my future. A life without love is not a life worth living, it's half a life."

"You will find love again, I'm sure of that."

"Will I?"

CHAPTER 42

SHIT HAPPENS

Mike pushed the chair away from his desk, plonked himself into his seat, which squeaked under his weight. He picked up the notes, swung his feet onto the table, crossed his legs at his ankles and flicked his way, through the pages of the next entry.

***

<u>Eve McDonnell</u>
<u>29th August 1993</u>

ST: Hello Eve, how are you?

EMM: Not good. I've got to tell you something – something I haven't talked to anyone about.

ST: Why haven't you talked about it before now?

EMM: It's too painful. My whole life changed that day; the last time I saw you.

ST: So, do you feel strong enough to tell me about it? Sometimes letting it out can help you. Keeping things bottled up makes them seem far worse than they really are.

EMM: NOTHING is worse than this! NOTHING will make it better!

ST: I'm sorry, Eve, I didn't mean to upset you. Can you tell me about it?

SILENCE.

ST: Eve?

EMM: Alright. I'll try.

That day when I left here, I went on duty. It almost feels surreal now. I was walking through the ward, doing the drug round. The radio was on playing *Black Box*. It was the happiest I'd ever been. The music stopped abruptly and a news reporter's voice then broke through. His sober and sombre voice came over the radio.

"An IRA bomb has been detonated at the Cadeau hotel in Kensington, West London, several people have been left with life-threatening injuries, emergency services are still attending the injured. A warning call had been received 1 hour before the attack took place. Unfortunately, the building was not evacuated in time before the explosion took place. The IRA has claimed responsibility for the attack." I can still hear his voice now.

A Cadeau Hotel had been attacked! My heart felt like it had stopped, and someone had hit me in the stomach. As I stood there it was as if time stood still and the newsreader had had a stroke; slurring his words, unable to annunciate what he was trying to report.

Then the voice became crisp and clear again.

"Yes, we can confirm that the attack took place this morning, on the Cadeau Hotel, Queens Gate, Kensington. The whole area is in lock down and Kensington has been evacuated. It's believed that there are many people still trapped inside the Cadeau Hotel and emergency services are working hard to rescue them."

I recollect screaming in sheer terror, Sister Jones came out of the office to find me in pieces. I just remember screaming hysterically "There has been a bomb in London. It's where Laurent and his friends work!" I remember I just thrust the trolley away. "I've got to go!"

"You're not going anywhere..." she ushered me out of the ward and into a staff room.

"She told me that It wasn't safe to go to London!" She gently pushed me into a chair and told me to stay there, then she found Verity to look after me.

ST: Then what happened?

EMM: She said she would find out what was going on. She asked Verity to get me a sweet tea for shock. I pleaded with Verity to go into London, but she told me it wasn't sensible and that sister was right, I needed to stay safe. She then left to make the tea. I remember the staff room was small and airless, no windows, nothing more than a broom cupboard with a few grey armless chairs. I felt claustrophobic and the room appeared to be shrinking and the floor started to move. I felt like I wanted to scream, but I was voiceless, I could feel heat rushing over me and my hands perspiring. Nausea grabbed me round the throat and I launched myself at a small metal waste paper bin. I promptly emptied the contents of my stomach, the tears rolling down my face as I retched and retched. The pain took over my abdomen and I felt like I was going to collapse, my knees buckled and I slumped across the grey chair. All I could think was that he was gone.

"He's gone......" I cried.

"You don't know that" she reassured.

"I know it...I just know..."

"You don't, there is always hope...you just need a little bit of faith, anything could have happened."

"But that's why I need to know" I cried "it can't be happening; we were together last night at the awards ceremony...in London at the Ritz... It can't be happening, I left him in bed!" I rambled "What's happened, what time is it, has he gone to work? Oh Verity, I've got to know if he's safe." I cried "This simply can't be happening...I've got to know; I've got to know! Please find out for me Verity." I remember shaking her so hard, I'm surprised I didn't break her arm. She then left me to see what she could find out. I didn't want her to go either.

I felt utterly exhausted and in a total state of shock. I hunkered down into the chair; my eyes shut tightly. If I could just blot this all out of my head, it was almost as though I was trying to stop time with my thoughts. It was impossible, and I knew that.

The door opened and a cup of tea was placed on the table. I didn't want the tea. Sister Jones returned; she'd no news at all. She asked if she could call anyone, but there was nobody in the world. Nobody I wanted to talk to. It was then I heard a voice, it wasn't that of Sister Jones or Verity.

ST: Did you recognise the voice?

EMM: Yes, yes, I did.

ST: Who's voice was it Eve?

EMM: It was her voice again, with that distinctive French accent.

ST: Aline?

EMM: Yes, Aline.

ST: What did she say?

EMM: She said that my dreams were all over for me and Laurent. She was gloating, saying things like "How are you gonna pick yourself out of this one Eve McDonnell you pathetic creature?" It was awful, the pain inside was tearing me apart and she just continued, "who would have thought it would ever end like this. The love story finishing so abruptly for you Eve."

"Why are you even here Aline?" I asked her, and do you know what she replied?

"Oh, I'm never one to miss a bit of excitement, you know me!" It made me feel sick. Aline was really enjoying herself and she just went on and on, saying things like "how long did you think it would last, you and Laurent?...How long would it be before he got bored with you?" she laughed. "It wouldn't have taken long, he told me that he was gonna dump you!"

I was all so upsetting and I said to her "How do you know that?"

"Cause he loves me...! He didn't love you; he saw you as...um what was it he said, ah yes, his little sister! That's right. He just couldn't imagine being with you the rest of his life; he was just stringing you along!" We ended up just arguing back and forth as I told her it wasn't true.

She told me I was pathetic "You're not the only one that goes to Hammersmith Palais and picks up French waiters you know. You know...I really don't know who I prefer, Laurent or Fabian. They're both pretty good between the sheets."

"What!?" I exclaimed. "You're talking crap. Please just shut up Aline."

"He's not as innocent as you think Eve, why he's quite the cad! Let me enlighten you!...Verity had a great night with Thierry, and Sue jumped into the sack with Pierre. And you were a pathetic looser. I did drugs with Fabian and Laurent and when we were totally stoned, I climbed into bed with Laurent. Boy didn't you just miss the opportunity, with a drop dead gorgeous guy? Eve you're so square! And now he's dead. Well I'm glad I had the opportunity with him!"

"You are lying Aline, 'cause I stayed with Laurent and we talked all night in his room!'"

"Really, did you? You were so smashed I'm surprised you even remember anything! I slept with Laurent."

"That's simply is not true!"

"Why don't you ask him yourself? Oops" she giggled "You can't, 'cause he's dead!" she sneered.

"Oh my God you're so sick, my boyfriend is believed dead and all you can do is rub it in my face that you've had sex with him, no wonder we never stayed friends. You're an evil manipulative bitch!" I was boiling with anger. "You Aline, are making this all up, you never had a fling with Laurent, you certainly didn't do drugs with Fabian. It's all crap... Just go away, I don't need you in my life." I remember just covering my face trying to hide. I dropped my head deep into my cardigan...The aroma was of the stale hospital, an all too familiar smell but strangely comforting. The room hung with silence. The door opened again.

"Eve, it's time to go" said a gentle voice "It's all sorted, the unit's covered and I can run you home." I looked up and saw Sister Jones with her dark curly hair, glancing at me over the chair. "Come on let's take you home. I want you to leave this to the police. Please don't go rushing into London."

***

Sister Jones took me back to my flat and settled me for the evening. She suggested that I took the following day off, but emphasised that I mustn't go into London

"Now you're going to promise me Eve, you're not to go into London tomorrow. I know you're desperate to find out, but you've got to think of your own safety."

As soon as she'd left, I grabbed my things together, getting ready to leave for London as soon as possible.

ST: So, you left for London?

***

Mike knew this day would come; the unravelling of events for Eve and Laurent. He felt that he knew her so well. Mike looked at his watch, crikey he was running late. The misses would be on his back if he didn't get a move on. He picked up the notes and shoved them into his briefcase.

CHAPTER 43

THE AFTERMATH

Mike came in from work and plonked himself down on the sofa, not even telling Shirley that he was home. He took off his jacket, slinging it on the floor and kicked off his shoes. He rifled through his leather briefcase and took out the battered-looking notes.

Shirley came into the lounge, switching on the main light.

"You're home then?"

"Sorry, love," he acknowledged her with a fleeting glance.

"Brought that file home again, I see," she raised her eyebrows. "Your dinner's in the oven. Are you going to be long?"

"Don't know, love. I just want to find out what's happened to this girl. She is the key to all of this. I'm sure of it."

She sighed. "It's alright, Mike. I do understand, honestly. Anyway, I'm off to my book club tonight. I'll be home by about ten."

"Right-o. What was it you're all reading?"

"Oh, it was right up your street," she smiled, waving the book.

"Was it? I doubt that."

"Post-Mortem by Patricia Cornwell."

"Oh, that doesn't sound nice."

"It was a really good read! Gave me some insight into your world."

"Hardly!"

She leant forward and gave him a kiss on his forehead. "Have a good read, love, and don't forget your tea. It's bangers and mash."

"Lovely. I won't forget." His eyes dropped back to the page. "Bye, love, give my love to the ladies."

"I'll see you later." She kissed him again, doubting very much that he would eat his tea.

As soon as he heard the front door close behind her, Mike turned back to the file.

ST: So, you left for London?

EMM: Yes, the following morning. At Reading station, the boards were up to say the network was up and running into London, with only the closure of the underground at Knightsbridge. I watched the commuters around me in their own busy little bubbles, I couldn't get over how incredibly calm everyone looked, as though nothing had happened. There were smart pinstripe suits consulting the morning papers, rustling and flapping their pages. A lady in front of me was engrossed in a book; she never lifted her eyes off the page the whole journey. Totally distracted by the plot, licking her fingers and turning the pages one by one. I couldn't see what she was so absorbed by, was it a thriller, crime or a steamy romance? It was all quite surreal, here I was going into London, to discover the fate of my boyfriend and everyone was carrying on with normal life...I arrived at Paddington Station at the height of the rush hour. I strangely felt safe and reassured with everyone buzzing around. I took the underground as I'd done many times before. However, this time feelings of excitement were absent and were replaced with the fear and dreaded anticipation to discover Laurent's fate. I travelled quickly down the escalator and through the tiled tunnels. Anxiety filled my chest and I rushed through the barrier and headed out to street level. I was in two minds whether to go to the flat first, but my feet automatically turned in the direction of Knightsbridge, taking the short walk to the hotel. As I arrived at Knightsbridge, the atmosphere changed. There was a sombre mood in the air. Walking down the Brompton Road, I could feel the adrenaline kick in. I was wondering what I was going to do. Who would

I speak to? How would I find out where they all were? As I turned the corner of the street, I could see the police tape up, police vehicles and news crews still at the hotel... I approached fearfully. The front of the hotel had a huge gaping hole. Windows in the top had been blown out by the blast. Glass fragments still lay on the pavement and street. Stone urns where upturned and their contents hurled several feet in every direction. There was utter devastation and an eerie quietness to this part of London.

Several policemen stood in the cordoned off area with full bullet-proof vests and firearms. I couldn't get anywhere near the hotel. I spoke to an armed Police officer, but he wouldn't give me any information as I wasn't next of kin. He suggested that I went to their staff accommodation.

I climbed the stone steps as fast as my legs could carry me and hammered on the door. I could feel the tension welling up in my body...It seemed to take forever for anyone to answer. Fabian opened the door, his eyes looked red and sore from crying, his dark hair dishevelled. He wore a crumpled shirt and trousers, clearly those he'd had on the day before.

"Eve," he said. "Thank God you're here. It's been so awful; you have no idea." His eyes were welling up; he ran his hand through his hair.

"Where are they?" I asked urgently, searching the flat. "Are they...?" I couldn't bear to say it.

Fabian looked at me tearfully. "It was so awful, it happened so fast, we were waiting on tables; so many guests were injured by the blast..." he said, shaking his head. It was so completely surreal, it all turned into slow motion.

He told me again there were so many injured, some of them didn't survive. He was mumbling and not very clear. I could feel myself getting really angry.

I said, "Fabian, for crying out loud, what has happened to Laurent? And what about Pierre? And Thierry?"

And then he just said "He died."

He said he had taken the full force of the blast and they couldn't do anything for him.

ST: That must have been a terrible shock.

EMM: Yes. I felt as though I'd been hit by the blast myself. I could feel the aftershock envelope my body. I told him it couldn't be true. Then he said Pierre's parents were travelling from Chantilly to collect his body.

ST: So, it wasn't Laurent he was talking about?

EMM: No. I was so relieved, but then I felt guilty because Pierre was dead, his parents had lost their son. But I couldn't help feeling happy that it wasn't Laurent.

ST: So, where was Laurent?

EMM: Fabian told me he was in the high dependency unit at the Chelsea and Westminster. He was in a bad way. He said he'd take me there.

We arrived at the hospital; a nurse greeted us in the corridor and directed us to a family room. I knew straight away it wasn't good news. Fabian introduced me as Laurent's girlfriend. At first, the nurse said she could only speak to next of kin. I said I understood because I'm a midwife. Then she relented and told us...She told us that Thierry's injuries were so severe that he had died, in the early hours of the morning. Oh God, it was truly awful.

I sat there, numb. Fabian broke down. She offered us tea, but all I wanted to do was see Laurent, to see for myself that he was alive.

Finally, she took us through. She warned us that he was badly injured. She told us he had a drip, catheter and a pump to help with pain. He had burns to his neck, chest and arms, so he was heavily bandaged. The double doors opened into a dark, dimly lit room. It struck me that there were no outside windows. The whole room was lit by artificial lights. I could hear the familiar sounds of syringe drivers, infusion pumps and air mattresses inflating and deflating. It felt like a hostile environment with nurses wearing incredibly serious expressions bustling around, adjusting, rearranging and recording.

She took us to a small bay. I could see an infusion up, a catheter bag. He was lying on his side, facing away from us, covered by a white sheet and a green cotton blanket. I could see the back of his head...his dark brown hair. I tentatively walked over with Fabian, who put his hand on Laurent's shoulder. He spoke very gently in French to him. My heart was in my mouth. Laurent was alive!

I walked around the bed, taking his hand and kissed his warm brown skin. He was as she described – he had heavily-bandaged arms and torso, there were dressings on his neck. Black, sooty stains from the blast were still visible on his forehead and cheeks. His hair was singed at the front and had a distinct chemical smell.

He found it hard to speak as his voice was so croak, but he was pleased to see us both. His main concern was getting back to work. It's odd isn't it?

ST: How do you mean?

EMM: He was worried about getting back to work, yet they'd all been involved in a bombing. That shouldn't have been his priority should it?

ST: Eve, he was in shock. So, what happened next? Thierry and Pierre had died and Laurent is in Hospital in a critical condition, is that right?

EMM: Yes, yes that's right. We told him not to worry; Fabian told him that they would still have work at the hotel, just another building. I told him "he'd be right as rain". And "we'll be all back together again." They both chuckled at the expression "right as rain". They didn't understand it. "It means you'll be better soon, I suppose" doubting my own translation. Quite soon after, the ward sister came and asked us to leave as he was very tired. She suggested that we went and had lunch and returned later that afternoon. She asked where I would be staying. Fabian told her; it would be with him in the flat.

I kissed Laurent again and told him I'd see him later.

"À bien tôt, ma petit chou," he whispered.

Fabian and I left feeling more relieved than when we had arrived. It then hit us as we left the hospital that we had lost Pierre and Thierry and were returning to an empty flat.

Fabian worried that he hadn't asked about their bodies. I tried to reassure him that the authorities would be in touch with their families, but we were both inconsolable. Strangers looked at us both as we stood outside the hospital both crying.

Neither of us wanted to go back to the flat, so we agreed to find somewhere we could have a coffee nearby so that I could get back to Laurent as soon as possible. We agreed that I'd spend the afternoon with him and Fabian would take over in the evening.

We walked into a very smart café. The smell of strong pungent coffee made me feel sick. Ambulance sirens screamed past as we found a table.

ST: This must have felt strange after the stress of trying to find Laurent.

EMM: Yes, it was completely unreal. People just eating their lunch, drinking, discussing where they were going on holiday, or how their children were doing at school. I wanted to get up and scream at them all, I wanted them to stop with the inane conversations of one-upmanship. It was all so trivial. My anxiety levels were rising and I felt like a caged animal. I just wanted to be back by his bedside. Not here, making small talk.

But Fabian insisted I needed to eat something so I could stay strong for Laurent. The waiter brought us a menu, but all I could see was a blur of words that had no meaning. The incessant noise intruded on my thoughts, the constant sound of emergency vehicles heightening my senses and I could feel my skin start to prickle. I felt I was drowning with dizziness and sickness. I had to rest my head in my hands to stop me from falling.

Fabian was concerned. I told him I felt light-headed and asked for some water. He found the waiter, who returned with a jug of water, with ice and with slices of lemon. I poured a glass and drank. I found the lemon flavour eased the nausea. We sat in silence as Fabian read through the menu and I looked at the people around me.

He ordered for both of us, even though I didn't think I'd be able to eat anything. He kept telling me I needed to eat so I could be strong for Laurent.

He was right. I ate and felt a little better.

Once lunch was finished, we went straight back to the hospital. When we arrived, we rang the bell as we'd done before, but no one came to answer it. We waited patiently for a few minutes and then I started to feel alarmed. I imagined a medical emergency on the other side of the locked doors. I could see in my mind's eye the nurse grabbing the resuscitation trolley and the medical staff working on a patient; whose face I couldn't see, but I knew was Laurent.

ST: And was that the case?

EMM: Yes, although Fabian kept saying I shouldn't worry, that he was sure they were just busy with routine work.

ST: So, what happened?

EMM: I could feel the hairs on the back of my neck rise and the colour draining from my face. My anger levels rose immediately and before I knew it, I had gone from zero to angry in seconds. I began banging on the door with both fists, shouting for them to let us in.

My anxiety went through the roof. I just couldn't stop pounding on the door, even though the pain across my knuckles was telling me to stop. Fabian grabbed my shoulders and tried to stop me. People were standing around, watching. In the end two security guards approached us. Fabian explained who we were and asked them to let us in. I was oblivious, pounding on the door.

One of the security officers spoke to someone on his radio, then swiped his ID card on the reader to open the door to let us in. As I had imagined, there was a commotion taking place. Laurent's bed was surrounded by medics. The nursing sister looked over her shoulder and could see us approaching; she immediately came down to head us off.

She told us he'd had a respiratory arrest and they were intubating him. They thought his upper airway had been burnt in the explosion and he needed help to breathe. They were doing that before transferring him to the intensive care unit.

I was angry – surely this should have been done earlier. But they'd missed it in the confusion while their emergency teams had been dealing with so many bomb victims. The sister was kind, she understood how I felt. She said he was sedated but we could see him if we wanted to. Of course, I did. But Fabian looked distressed and wasn't sure if he could take it. Instead he said he would call the Cadeau Hotel to see if they'd managed to contact Laurent's parents.

The sister took me through to his bedside and as she described Laurent had a tube down his throat, there was a mask over his mouth and nose which a doctor was squeezing to get air into Laurent's lungs. A line was giving fluids, and I could see stickers on his chest from where they were monitoring his heart. I felt completely numb. It was as though it wasn't me standing here beside him. It was as though I had left my body. The clinical nurse, Eve, stood there looking at him, assessing him just like another patient. The emotional, loving girlfriend, who completely adored this man lying on the bed, had left the room.

ST: It's quite usual to feel like that, Eve. It's a way of coping.

EMM: Is it?

ST: Yes. Our minds have a way of dealing with things even when we feel completely out of control.

EMM: I suppose so. Even though the anaesthetist told me he was going to be okay, that they'd caught him in time, I had trouble believing him. Laurent looked awful, the colour had drained from his face, his skin looked mottled, and his fingernails were blue. He was completely lifeless and the only movement was that of the artificial respirations the doctor bagged into his body.

This brought me back to my body quite quickly, it was quite sudden. I felt myself land on my own two feet with a plonk. I went over to the bed and held Laurent's cold, clammy hand.

I said, "You're going to be okay, Laurent, do you hear me?" I leant forward and kissed his hand. I felt truly frightened as I did this, I had no way of knowing what the outcome was going to be, and it really didn't look good at this moment. Inside the roll of my stomach twisted and gripped down hard forcing my lunch up into my chest. The burning acid reached my mouth and I gulped down hard, forcing it back with my tears.

Then a nurse came and said they were ready to take him to the Intensive Care Unit. The equipment was unhooked and placed on his bed and immediately the bed was moved into Intensive Care. The hospital bed was wheeled into the bright white room with only five other beds in the unit. Many of them also looked like victims from the bomb. There was a distinct smell of burnt flesh and singed hair. The air was laced with beeps and bings, the constant background noise of ventilation machines bouncing off the walls. The staff attached Laurent to a heart monitor and ventilator. A member of the nursing staff found me a large reclining chair, and positioned it by his bedside.

"Sit with him," she said. "It will be good for him, if he knows you're here." She took his hand and put it into mine. "Hold him," she said, "he needs you." She stroked the back of my hand. I sat down next to him. It was all so awkward. I was a trained nurse but I felt like a fish out of water. I couldn't understand what was happening to me, I loved him so much. But I couldn't express it here in this environment. Was it fear? Was I so consumed by this, so afraid that I was going to lose him, that I suddenly became detached?

ST: Probably. It's okay, Eve. It's what most people do in that sort of situation.

EMM: But it didn't feel right. I had to bring myself back somehow into the present. Oh God it was just so awful…

ST: Here have a tissue. You can take a break if you want to, it's fine.

EMM: No, no…I have to tell you.

ST: Okay, Eve.

EMM: I started to stroke his hand and feel his skin beneath my fingertips, trying to take in the smallest detail to help me connect. I stroked his long, tanned fingers, and encircled his trimmed nails. I brushed the dark hairs on his hands and almost expected him to wake up laughing saying that it tickled or 'Tu me chatouilles!' I lay my head on his hand and pushed my face up against his body as close as I could go. He smelt of hospitals, the smell of disinfectant, dressings and equipment. But if I really concentrated hard, I could just about pick up his lemony scent. I closed my eyes. The more I concentrated, the stronger the smell became. I stayed by his bedside. Nursing staff would go about their duties, doing his observations; I would look up and watch them. As soon as they left, I resumed my position of resting my head by his side. Fabian arrived around ten in the evening to take over from me.

I didn't want to leave Laurent, but Fabian insisted. He said there was a taxi outside waiting for me. He told me that I'd find a baguette and milk and cheese in the fridge. He promised to call me if there was any change, he wouldn't leave Laurent alone but I had to go home to the flat and sleep.

I said I'd see him early in the morning and kissed Laurent before I left. I was exhausted. I didn't want anything to eat and headed straight into Laurent's bedroom, stripped down to my underwear and climbed into his bed. I was instantly hit by the smell of him all over the sheets and pillows. I wrapped myself up in his scent. I closed my eyes, touching the sheets tenderly, resting my head in the dent of his pillow, feeling where he had been before. The image of him smiling came to mind, I could see him propped up on one arm as he read the newspaper, his eyes smiling as I brought him in his early morning coffee before I left for work. I remembered how he would grab the edge of my uniform, pulling me onto the mattress, urging me to give him another kiss. I stopped the thought and rewound that moment again to the second we touched. I sank deeper into the overwhelming pain inside myself and surrendered to the tiredness that crept up through every minute cell, holding him in the forefront of my mind.

The following morning, I returned to Intensive Care to take over from Fabian. He looked tired. Laurent looked the same – still sedated with a tube in his mouth and the machines all taking readings of his vital signs. There had been no change overnight.

Fabian told me Laurent's parents had booked a flight and would be there later that evening. He said he would collect them from the airport.

PAUSE.

ST: How did you feel about that?

EMM: I don't know. Relieved, but also worried. Fabian said they didn't speak much English and my French was rubbish. He promised to be there to interpret for us. But I wanted Laurent to wake up so that he could properly introduce me to his parents. I was also scared they'd take him back to France, away from me.

Anyway, Fabian went to get some rest and the day passed much like before. One of the victims from the bombing was moved out to the high dependency unit as he had made good progress and for several hours his bed area remained empty.

Then an elderly man arrived, escorting his wife who was being ventilated by a machine. He looked very worried and clung onto her as she lay motionless. We didn't talk to each other. Time ticked by slowly, the only measure was the movement of light through the windows and the reflections upon the walls opposite. The light dropped from the sky around 9pm, I could see the whole of London lighting up and I talked to Laurent about what I could see outside the massive windows. It was like being in another world, almost like a spaceship observing the humans on another galaxy. The world kept on turning, the city remained alive and its beating pulse was seen through the movement of the masses. Incidents came and went but it all seemed unaffected by this trauma, it was more resilient than a human body. The city would remain long after we all decayed.

A nurse came over to me, she was on the night shift; I recognised her from the previous evening. She said, "Is Fabian not coming in tonight?"

I told her he was picking up Laurent's parents from the airport. They were due here at about ten. She pointed out it was already gone eleven. I hadn't noticed the time. Their flight from Bordeaux must have been delayed.

She said I looked shattered and should go home for a rest. She promised to stay with Laurent until they arrived. I didn't want to leave him, but when I saw my reflection in the darkened window, I realised what a mess I looked. I wanted to make a good impression on Laurent's parents, so maybe it would be better to get some sleep and meet them in the morning when I'd had a chance to freshen up. I asked her to get Fabian to call me when they arrived.

I leant forward and gave Laurent a kiss and told him I loved him. I whispered into his ear, "I'll be back tomorrow. Don't go anywhere." I felt a tug on my heart as I said it.

I got a cab back to the flat much like I had done on previous evenings. However, this time, I was alone. I poured myself a glass of red wine, ripped off a hunk of French bread and took a chunk of Brie. I found some grapes in the fruit basket and searched around for some cranberry jelly to go with it. I could hear

Laurent laughing at me wanting to put jam with my cheese.

"What is wrong with the cheese that you want to cover it in conserve?" he demanded.

I defended myself – "It's just a bit of chutney."

He'd laughed and called me a Philistine.

I sat in the lounge eating my French tea, with a glass of red wine, trying desperately to relax, waiting for Fabian's call. It didn't come.

ST: It must have been hard, waiting.

EMM: Yes. In the end I drank the whole bottle of wine and fell into Laurent's bed at about 1am. Sometimes I wish I'd never woken up.

ST: Why?

EMM: Fabian arrived at the flat in the middle of the night, he woke me. He was distraught. He told me that Laurent was dead. I didn't believe him, but he told me it was true, it was his heart. There was nothing anyone could do. Fabian wouldn't let me go to the hospital, he said there was no point – Laurent's parents were angry and didn't want anyone coming near. They were taking their son's body home and that was the end of it.

ST: I can see you're really distressed by this memory, Eve. Do you want to stop?

EMM: No! I have to tell you the rest of it. I have to tell you what he did to me!

ST: What did he do Eve?

EMM: He raped me!

ST: He attacked you?

EMM: Um, yes, no. But he did something to me. I know it.

ST: What do you remember, Eve?

EMM: We were so upset, that we both cried and clung to each other. I must have cried myself to sleep. But when I woke the following morning, I was naked and sore, and he was in the bed. Laurent's bed!

Mike got up from his armchair and put the notes to one side. He rubbed the back of his neck. He didn't know what to think. Laurent was now dead, and Fabian had raped Eve. He knew that they suspected Fabian of attacking Aline, but did this lad have a history of assaults on women. This was getting nasty, really nasty. He picked up his home phone and called Phil.

"Sorry to disturb you at home Sarge. But I need you do something for me as a matter of urgency."

"It's not a problem Guv, what can I do?"

"Can you find out whether Fabian Lambert has any history of assaults on women? I'm just reading Eve McDonnell notes; she tells Simon Thomas that he raped her."

"Did she report it?"

"I don't know, I haven't got that far. Could you also ask Celine if she could contact our French colleagues?"

"Will do Guv".

"Let me know if you find anything?"

"Right you are, Guv".

Mike returned to the notes and found the next entry; he sat down with them tracing his finger under each word, trying to take in everything that Eve had reported.

ST: Did you report this to the police, Eve?

EMM: No, I was in such a state I couldn't face it. I just wanted to get away from him, from all the reminders of Laurent around me. He insisted on coming with me to Paddington station. He tried to persuade me to stay. But, when I refused, he got really angry, we had a huge argument and he slapped me around the face. The bastard!

ST: Did anyone witness him slapping you?

EMM: No, it's London. Nobody sees anything, they all walk around with their eyes closed. He left pretty quickly after that. I boarded the train to Reading. I felt completely distraught, in the space of 24hrs I had lost my boyfriend, two friends had died, and now I had been raped by Laurent's best friend Fabian.

I found myself a secluded seat away from other passengers and I opened my bag trying to find some pills – anything to take away this pain. Typically, I found several packets with the foil ripped back, and nothing inside. I found some loose tablets, covered with grit and fluff. I had no idea what they were, but right then I didn't care. I popped them in my mouth and swallowed without a drink. I was exhausted but wasn't able to sleep as I felt too wired by everything that had happened. I couldn't see how I was ever going to recover from this.

ST: Eve, this is so awful for you. I can see how this is hurting you.

PAUSE.

EMM: Yes, it was all just ripped away...All I've got left is my job...Bringing life into this world; when I'm coping with death.

ST: You don't need to go back to work immediately. You can have time off people will understand.

EMM: But don't you see...? It's all I've got.

ST: You need to be kind to yourself.

EMM: Look where 'kind' got me. It got me nowhere! I opened my heart and let Laurent into my life....And now he's gone.

ST: I know. Here, have a tissue.

SESSION ENDS.

***

The telephone broke the silence; Mike went into the hallway and picked up the receiver.

"Hello" Mike answered.

"Guv, it's Phil."

"What have you got?"

"I've got two things; there is a statement from a Miss Alice Berry who worked at the Cadeau Hotel two years ago. She reported Mr Lambert for sexual harassment."

"What exactly?"

"Hmmm, apparently she was a waitress. He put his hand up her skirt and tried to kiss her."

"Okay, and the other report?"

"This one is from a Miss Lucy Robinson, who met him at one of the nightclubs in London."

"What happened?"

"He had sex with her without her consent."

"Were charges ever pressed?"

"Hang on, let me see"

"No sir."

"Why is that, Phil? Can you see...?"

"It looks like Lucy withdrew her statement."

"Why was that?"

"I can't see anything else sir, I'm sorry."

"Thanks Phil, well we need to find these two ladies. Can you find them and get some details from them both about Fabian? Particularly Lucy, I want to know why she withdrew that statement."

"Will do Guv."

"Thanks Phil, I'll see you tomorrow bright and early"

"Yes Guv."

CHAPTER 44

ROYAL BERKS

Andrea picked up the phone; if Addington Road Nurses' accommodation was Eve's last known address, she wondered if they had any information of where she could be now.

"Hello Sister, this is Andrea Doyle, I spoke to you before about Eve McDonnell. We believe that Eve's last known address is Addington Road?"

"Oh, yes, that's right. My colleague said you would be back in touch."

"Do you know where Eve is living at the moment?"

"No, I'm afraid not."

"When did you last see her?"

"The day of her suspension."

"No time after that?"

"Not that I can recall…"

"Okay, can you tell me about that day?"

"Well, I knew Eve fairly well; she was a conscientious midwife, worked really hard here. She had a few really rotten deliveries over a short period of time and found it all a bit tough. And then her boyfriend was killed in the IRA bombing in London at the Cadeau Hotel. When she returned to work she was clearly in a terrible state. She was keen to get back to work, but in hindsight, I don't think she should have been allowed to work.

"Why was that? Why do you think she shouldn't have been at work?"

"She was clearly displaying signs of stress, being forgetful, minor clerical errors like transposing numbers and dates of birth on blood bottles, that sort of thing. She was particularly hard on herself, and when things were pointed out she cried. One error followed another, nothing major at first just silly little things. Then it became more noticeable that she was seriously stressed, she started having the odd palpitations, and small panic attacks. Even writing up notes or looking after a normal delivery was becoming too difficult for her."

"Goodness, did you tell her that she needed to go off sick?"

"I did, I was pretty sure she wasn't sleeping and she was coming in looking dreadful. I suggested that she went to see her GP and get signed off and perhaps go to staff support for counselling. I offered for her to see the psychology services which the hospital could offer to staff. But she refused."

"That sounds serious."

"Indeed. It all came to a head one weekend. Eve had been on a late the previous evening and we did a controlled drug count. The ward had been incredibly busy and tempers were frayed. We did our controlled drug count and found some dihydrocodeine missing also known as DF118. The last person to administer them was Eve, with an unknown signature. We had had a lot of bank staff working and so initially we put it down to a miscount, but now we started to question the patients who were recorded as having it. These women had never received the medicine. That's when we knew that we had a problem and Eve and several others were immediately suspended as no one could identify the other signature. We had to have a full investigation involving Thames Valley Police. It was a very lengthy process as we had to go back to all the agencies to obtain sample signatures. Eve was seen briefly back in the nurses' accommodation by some of her colleagues, but I never saw her again. She just left after the suspension."

"What about the other midwives?"

"Some of them returned, some left. But I never saw Eve again and I don't know whether the other signatory was identified."

"Was it Aline Deniaud's signature?"

"As I said before, she must have been agency staff."

"I see. Did you get a signature back from the agency for Aline?" She thought for a moment making notes on her pad.

"Not to my knowledge?"

"Interesting," she muttered, making further notes. "So, tell me about Eve, did she have any friendships that were significant?"

"Yes. Eve's little group were very close-knit. I believe she did her training with Verity and Sue."

"And do you have their details?"

"Not Sue, I'm afraid; she got married and moved away. But Verity Matthews still works on the unit. I can give you her details. I'm sure she'll help. We were all pretty upset by the attack in London. I'm sure if anyone knows where Eve is, it will be Verity. You know, Detective, it's something you can never ever imagine happening, having your boyfriend killed in an IRA bomb. I wish that we'd done more to support her."

"I agree. It's really a terrible thing to have happened. None of us can imagine what it would have been like for her. You say that she came back to work after the bombing?"

"Yes, pretty soon after. But she was never the same. She worked for a few weeks and then the suspension took place."

"Can you give me a date for that?"

"Hmm...I would have to look it up, but I would say the beginning of September."

"Okay, September, got it. Did Thames Valley Police try and find her?"

"I don't know. But Verity might have more information."

"Thanks Sister, if you could give me Verity's details, I'll try to speak to her."

Andrea replaced the phone.

CHAPTER 45

MISSING DRUGS

Andrea found Mike in his office drinking a coffee and starring into space. She knocked on the door, breaking his train of thought.

"You know Guv, I've just spoken to Sister White and she thinks that if we contact Verity Matthews, she may know where Eve might have gone. I'm going to chase it up."

"Sounds good, you fire away." He looked down at Simon Thomas' notes.

"Whilst you're there Guv, could you see if there are any other clues to where she might have gone?"

"Yes Andi, I'll do just that."

"Thanks Guv"

***

<u>Eve McDonnell</u>
<u>3rd September 1993</u>

ST: Hello, Eve. How are you?

EMM: I don't know.

ST: Last time you talked through some very traumatic events. Can you tell me what happened afterwards, when you got back to your accommodation in Reading? Did you get some help?

EMM: There wasn't anything anyone could do to help. He was dead. I just went back to work.

ST: Did that help?

EMM: Not really.

ST: Can you tell me about it?

EMM: To everybody's shock, I arrived on duty for my early shift the day after I left London. They hadn't expected me to be in. Someone advised me to take compassionate leave. But I just couldn't stay in the nurses' accommodation all day, it was driving me mad, and I had nowhere else to go. I simply had to get back to work; I had nothing else in my life. By now most of the unit had heard about the bomb and many others now knew about Laurent. But I still found myself explaining to colleagues what had happened. Even though it was exhausting going over it again and again, it made them still feel real, just talking about them.

But when Sister White saw the state I was in, she tried to get me to go on leave. She could see...

ST: What could she see, Eve?

EMM: I was a mess – I hadn't ironed my uniform, there were ladders in my tights. I hadn't bothered with make-up and I'd just scraped my hair back into a pony-tail. She told me I shouldn't be there; I wasn't fit for work. But I told her I needed to work; it was all I had left. I wasn't even going to be allowed to go to Laurent's funeral. His family had rejected me, I wasn't good enough, I was English and it was our fault that the IRA had killed their son.

ST: And how did she react to that?

EMM: She was kind, sympathetic. But she still didn't want me to work. She thought I'd make errors, endanger the mothers and babies on the unit. So, she sent me home.

ST: What did you do?

EMM: I dunno, cried...cried lots. I took to my bed, just didn't want to live anymore. What was there to live for? I drank a lot that night and tried to blot it all out. It was really, really bad. And when I woke up the following morning, I felt dreadful.

ST: I'm not surprised; you really had gone through a very traumatic time.

SILENCE 15 SECONDS.

EMM: Several days later I decided that I needed to pull myself together. I got myself ready for work and called the ward. I asked Sister White if I could return. She asked if I had seen my GP. I said I had.

ST: Had you?

EMM: Yes, he gave me some sleeping tablets.

ST: Did he sign you off.

EMM: No, I didn't want him to. I knew I needed to get back to work.

ST: Okay, so you returned to work, how did that feel?

EMM: Initially it was good. but...

ST: But what?

EMM: I kept on making silly little mistakes. You know real silly stuff, every time someone pointed it out, I would end up in tears.

ST: What did they suggest?

EMM: They suggested that I could work a shorter week, have a lighter workload, even work supernumerary.

ST: Supernumerary?

EMM: You're not counted in the number of staff working that shift. So, they had some extra staff help from either bank or agency. Aline was there at this time, trying to help.

ST: That made a change.

EMM: But then things only got worse, I was pulled up for making a drug error. When you administer controlled drugs you always check with another person.

ST: So, what happened?

EMM: It all completely blew up in my face. I was called into the office and I was accused of taking controlled drugs. It was all lies. I'm telling you the truth. I didn't take anything. My job was worth too much to me. I said what about the nurse who countersigned the register with me? Aline? But where was she? She'd gone, disappeared. Poof! Like a puff of smoke.

ST: How did you feel?

EMM: I felt sick; the nausea overtook me in a wave. I felt as though I'd been hit by a hurricane, the full force of the wind would knock me over in a second. I felt afraid to move; the sense of dread came over me like a black cloud. This was it! Aline had played her final card; my career was over. I had no way of proving that I hadn't stolen the tablets. I had no witness, no one to back me up that the final check had happened. I was doomed. I didn't know what to do, I was torn. Who could I speak to? Who would believe me? Where could I go? If I lost my job, I'd lose my home. I had nowhere to hide. I was lost. I wanted to scream in the middle of the ward. I could see my colleagues' eyes watching me. They were behind curtains, through the glass of the cubicles, peering up from the nurses' station. Their eyes accused me, penetrating, stripping me of dignity, completely lacking in compassion or sympathy. I left the ward, ashamed and hopeless. I went down the stark back stairs to the locker room, collected my coat and handbag and changed out of my uniform and back into my jeans and a t-shirt.

I left the building feeling utterly humiliated and shocked by what had happened. I crossed the street almost robotically and entered the nurses' accommodation. In my room, I looked out of the window in utter disbelief, staring at the maternity unit. Its huge grey structure appeared so grand but formidable, looming over our accommodation malevolently.

My future had been stolen by some crazy guy prepared to detonate a bomb. The love of my life had been killed; I now faced a police investigation, and where the hell was Aline, what she'd threatened me with had come true.

I screamed, my knees crumpled and I slumped onto the floor, and wept.

I was so distraught, how could this all be happening, how could I make it stop, how could I get this pain to go away...? I scratched my nails across the paintwork and the varnish peeled off the wall. The anger escalated, heat welled inside and I wanted to break something, but I'd never been allowed to express my feelings. Such crap, I had to hide everything away, put on a brave face...I wanted to let this anger out but I didn't know how. I was like a shaken can of Pepsi about to explode; I could see the brown foaming liquid escaping in slow motion hitting the walls, the release of all that energy.

But I had nowhere to go. I couldn't even express this extreme pain and anger. It was as though someone had taken over my body and ripped away my heart and soul. And now they had turned the tap on to drain away all my empathy and compassion. The love and hope that had kept me alive was draining away down a filthy plug hole and I was falling into it. The final knife had been turned and twisted. My pain and anger were now the conductors of this miserable life. I realised I was in eye of the storm and I was completely trapped. I had nowhere to turn. My life was now of so little value and I couldn't see the point of continuing with it.

ST: What did you do, Eve?

EMM: I searched around my room and found a large bottle of wine and a box of painkiller tablets. I sat on my bedroom floor and drank the wine, taking one paracetamol after another with each glug of wine. I should be dead.

ST: But you're not and that's wonderful.

EMM: Is it...is it really? How would you fucking know? I'm sick of all this shit. I lost everything...Absolutely everything! What's the point of living? I should be dead. Do you hear me!?

ST: There's no need to get angry, Eve. Just sit down.

EMM: I don't want to sit down. I don't want to listen to your platitudes and look into those pitiful eyes. I don't want any of this. I want to go and never come back.

ST: Go where?

EMM: Don't fucking start that! Go where…!?

ST: Okay Eve, I know you're angry.

EMM: Oh, fuck off Simon! I've had it up to here. You know I'd be better off dead.

SESSION ENDS.

***

Mike got up from his chair abruptly,

"Andi," he called. Andrea looked up alarmed by his tone. "Are there any more pages in these notes, none missing?"

"No, Guv, why Guv?" He showed her the final entry.

"Oh, my word, do you think she's done something to herself?"

"Yep, let's get Simon on the blower and you need to get onto Verity too."

"Yes, I'm tracking her down now."

CHAPTER 46

FLORENCE GREEN

Dr Dhillon felt she could see much improvement in Aline. Her mood swings now appeared to have settled. Aline was making progress and able to discuss what had happened to her in the past.

"Aline" she said. "Last time we talked, I asked you about Eve and you got angry. Do you remember?"

"Yes, I do."

"What was that all about? You said she was a witch."

Aline looked up at the ceiling. "God, I'm so sick of going over stuff! Don't you get sucked in by the poor little Eve story, Doctor. She's a nasty piece of work."

"Really? Why?"

"Let's face it; none of us are truly nice; we're all mean." She smiled looking the doctor directly in her eyes "Isn't that the case with all of us? Don't we all suffer with voices inside our heads? Some of us manage the voices very well, but others are swamped by evil,

413

like Eve." Aline was getting riled; she was like a touch paper.

"We all feel frustrated and hear those voices, Aline. It's only human to have these thoughts and it's okay. It's allowed. It's what you do with them; that's more important".

"What do you mean?"

"We all need to have discernment and understand that voice within us, Aline. It's a bit like having two dogs – a good one and a bad one," Dr Dhillon explained. "The one which rules you is the one you keep feeding."

Aline shook her head. "But she rises above it all. No matter how hard I try to make her see sense. And she blindly continues with this ruse of being okay."

"But that's okay. That's how some people cope."

"No! It's lying."

"Is it?"

"Yes. She's a wolf in sheep's clothing. She constantly wears a mask. But I can see through it. If only people knew what she's really like though, they'd be horrified."

"But aren't we all a bit like that, Aline? We all hide what we don't want others to see and put on a good front. The British are world famous for it – keeping a stiff upper lip and not showing our emotions."

"Well, I've never succeeded in exposing her, or convincing anyone what she's really thinking. But life has caught up with her...and I'm glad!"

"That's a strange thing to say."

"Like I said, something had to give and now it has!"

Dr Dhillon shrugged. "That all depends upon whether she can control those two dogs battling inside herself."

Aline frowned. "I don't understand."

"Well, if you allow the bad dog to keep telling you stuff that's untrue and unhelpful, that's all you'll hear. The good dog doesn't get a look in," she smiled. "So, you have to learn to keep the bad dog under control."

"But what do you do when the bad dog is completely toxic?"

"You have to tell it that you've heard its anxieties, but you don't have to take them on board. I'm not telling you it's easy. It takes a lot of practice."

"So, you're saying that she's kept the bad dog under control? I don't believe you. You don't know her. She's vile and bitter. That's why she attacked me." Aline rubbed the back of her head, feeling the slight ridge of her scar under her hair.

"It sounds as though your relationship with Eve has become quite impossible."

"Yes, it is incredibly difficult. We're a big part in each other's lives."

"Maybe you need to deal with those issues around her in order to move on."

"I really don't think I can. There's no hope for me."

"Where there's life, there's always hope," Dr Dhillon suggested. "You need to stop obsessing about Eve. We need address these matters around her, just like we are working on your problems with the alcohol and drugs."

"I'm pig sick of people telling me what I should and shouldn't do!" she sneered. "I haven't had any drugs or alcohol since I've been here! And do you know what? All it does is just make the pain worse. Do you understand that?"

***

Aline was really annoyed that nobody appeared to be listening to her at all. How many times did she have to keep telling them? It was all so exhausting. She regarded this small woman wearing her smart, well-fitted suit, her long brown fingers and well-manicured nails. She noticed that she wore a plain gold band and an engagement ring with a pale blue stone surrounded by diamonds. Life for Dr Dhillon appeared to be sorted. She was clearly married, well-dressed and in a good job. How could this prim Asian doctor have any concept of what her patients were going through? Aline imagined Dr Dhillon going home to her perfect home, her husband waiting with their two, or maybe three children. Once the children had been read to in the subdued lighting of their bedrooms, she would spend the evening with her husband. Aline visualised her getting into bed in a cream silk chemise, slipping under the warm covers with her husband, kissing and touching his brown lips and body. The image stopped immediately when Dr Dhillon pulled Aline back into the present moment.

"Why do you think Eve was going to kill you, Aline?"

"Y–you, have no idea," Aline replied, stumbling over her words, flustered about the image of the doctor that her mind had conjured up.

"Then please tell me, Aline."

"I can't."

"I think it would really help you, if you could," she encouraged. "How about telling me about the suspension from work and how that happened?"

She leant forward to her; her eyes transfixed on Aline's face...willing her to tell her story.

"I can't remember a lot about it." She rubbed her face. "I'd never been in any kind of trouble like this. I just knew Eve was at the bottom of it all."

"What do you mean?"

"She'd been causing me a lot of problems – always trying to get me into trouble, even though I'd been trying to help her."

"Always trying to get you in trouble?" she echoed.

"Yes, you know when she made errors, she blamed it on me."

"So, when you were suspended, what did you think?"

Aline smiled, but it didn't reach her eyes. "I thought, 'Oh my God, what has she done now?'"

"Did you find out what she'd done?"

"Yes, apparently she falsified my name. I was so angry with her. She made sure I would be suspended too, putting my name on the record. I wanted to have it out with her, but she was nowhere to be found."

"So, what happened at the enquiry?"

"It didn't go ahead because Eve had disappeared."

"Was that uncharacteristic of her?"

"It was. She'd changed out of all recognition since the bombing. She was spaced out half the time when I did see her – a right proper 'space cadet'," sniggering at her own joke.

"Which bombing was this?"

"The IRA one, at the Cadeau Hotel."

"Oh! Yes, I remember that. A lot of people were killed in the bombing."

"Yes. Our friends were caught in the blast."

"Were any of them killed?"

"Yes, three of them." Aline delivered her answer in a flat voice, her expression cold and distant.

"Oh, I'm so sorry to hear that, Aline. It sounds like you've both been through a lot."

"Yes, that's why I had to get away!"

"Gosh, so you've got a lot to be angry about – Eve taking things, Eve being the one who took the drugs from the ward, you ending up being suspended from work. And then to top it all the IRA bomb that took the lives of your friends. And I presume that you had to cope with a loss of earnings after the suspension. That must have been really tough for you."

"It's very difficult when I'm the one who is blamed all the time."

"So, what happened next?"

"Well, I had to get away from Reading. There was no reason to stay. I decided to apply for a job in London. I knew I could be fairly anonymous here and I could start again. So, I managed to get myself a job in the maternity department at Whipps Cross Hospital."

"That was a brave step."

"It was, but it was the best thing I could have done."

"But...?"

"Things are still hanging over me; I didn't know if the police would turn up and bring up all the stuff about the missing drugs. I found it hard to make friends. I couldn't trust anyone after Eve."

"Not a soul?"

"No, nobody. You and Stuart are the first people I've spoken to. I tried to talk to Rev Hillier at St Peters, but he was just horrible, he wasn't prepared to listen. He just sat there in judgement of me. You know the look people give you."

Dr Dhillon nodded. "Yes, I know that look."

"That's why I felt so ashamed and I gave him a false name. It's also why I couldn't talk to you at first. I knew nobody in London. My colleagues at Whipps Cross were unfriendly. The only person I knew was Fabian. I was angry with him, so very angry about the way he'd crushed Eve. But somehow, in my weakness, I ended up crashing out at the flat where he lived. I got pissed. I know it wasn't the right thing to do. But you know, what else was left for me? Then the drugs started."

"All of this is not uncommon, Aline. You've been through a horrible episode in your life, you found ways to cope," she reassured. "But now it's time to put this all to bed and forgive yourself."

Aline was silent, considering the suggestion.

"Perhaps it's time to tell me about what happened between you and Fabian," said the doctor.

CHAPTER 47

VODKA AND ICE

Aline shivered at the thought of retelling the story of her relationship with Fabian. She didn't want to talk about what had happened to her.

"You know Aline; I think you need to tell me what happened."

"I know I do." She took a deep breath and breathed out slowly. "Where do I start?"

"Wherever you like...it's your story not mine."

Aline shuffled in her seat and looked into the corner of the room, and then dropped her eyes. Dr Dhillon saw her closing her eyes.

"That's it Aline; that's perfect. Now let's begin."

Aline exhaled "Well..." she started "We were all so shocked by the attack in London. Pierre and Thierry had died and then suddenly we were dealing with Laurent's death as well. All the arrangements were being made for the bodies of Pierre and Thierry to be reunited with their families in France. Laurent's body had been returned with his parents not long after they'd arrived. Fabian was completely swamped by it all. He was distraught over the death of his friends.

"I was angry with him over the way he'd treated Eve. Now she was gone, she'd been destroyed by all of this. She'd lost everything – her lover, her job, her dignity. She'd been crushed. I didn't want her gone! I wanted to have it out with him. Why did he feel that he could do that to her when she was now so vulnerable? I wanted to make him suffer!

When I arrived at the flat, I pushed open the door to find Fabian sitting on the kitchen floor with a large bottle of vodka. He had his lips wrapped around the neck of the bottle, knocking it back.

He was surprised to see me, didn't expect me to return. But I had a score to settle with him over what he'd done to Eve."

"Merde! Why are you here?" He smiled, eyes spinning in his head."

I ran my hands through my dark hair, swirling it and pinning it up. "Did you think I wouldn't be back?"

"Yes, to be perfectly honest."

"Well, I've got a score to settle with you, Fabian," I said.

"I don't understand?"

"You've completely destroyed Eve. I mean, she's totally crushed. She's gone, she's no more! Do you hear me, Fabian?"

"I'm sorry; I don't know what you mean."

"Let me enlighten you." I smiled, running my finger down his nose. "You went too far with her and now you have to answer to me. Do you hear me?" He flinched away.

"You?" he sneered. "Who are you?"

"Yes, me – Aline Deniaud!"

"Okay, Aline, but I'm shocked. I thought that you and Eve..." She placed her finger on his lips.

"Let's say, we go back along way...and I may dislike her, but I don't want her hurt like you hurt her."

"What do you mean?" He asked

Aline ignored him, pointing her index finger into his chest. "Talk to me, Fabian... what is it? Do you like screwing with people?" Aline prodded him hard "Well, what the fuck is it?"

Fabian shrugged and took another slug of the vodka bottle.

"Can I offer you a drink?" he asked.

"Have you heard a word I've said, you bastard?"

"I've heard you, Aline. Will you join me, then?"

He stood up and opened a cupboard and brought out a glass. He half filled it with the clear liquid and added a couple of ice cubes which splashed, crackling as they hit the vodka.

Fabian then got out the wacky baccy and rolled it up in his nimble fingers.

"So, this is what you've been up to, is it?" I demanded.

"What?" He frowned.

"Drowning your sorrows!"

"What is it to you?"

"It'll make you feel worse!" I said.

"It won't...It takes the nightmares away." He poured himself a glass and held it up to me in a mocking toast before drinking it down.

"I should make one of these for you too..."

I hesitated...

"You have got to be joking? I'm not smoking with you, you arsehole!"

"It's okay. It makes you a lover, not a fighter." He lit his joint and the sweet aroma hit the senses.

"You're a sick junkie."

"I can assure you, I'm not," he smiled, half-stoned. "Have a little drag," he handed over the smouldering joint.

"No, I won't, do you hear me?" I pushed it back. Then I watched him preparing a second one. He held the resin in his fingers and crumbling it over the tobacco into the cigarette paper. He lit it and handed it over.

"Come on, it helps to take the pain away."

Something inside of me changed, I don't know what. I so wanted that pain to go away, it was true. So, reluctantly I took the small cigarette from his nimble fingers and placed it to my lips. I took a long slow drag on the white paper joint and felt the room begin to spin. I felt so drunk. I took another lungful, feeling the harshness on the back of my throat.

"Slow down, slow down," Fabian cautioned.

"I will, I feel like I'm floating." I sat down and lay my head back on the sofa.

He took a long drag, blowing the blue smoke in the air. I watched him as I took another, feeling the heat around my mouth and the fire near my fingertips. I could feel colour starting to drain away from my face.

"Oh, I do feel weird," I mumbled. "Really odd."

"It's okay. You're meant to feel like that."

Before too long we were completely stoned. I threw up in the bathroom and lay on the floor. My face on the cold surface made me feel a tad better. Through the open doorway, I spied Fabian slumped on the sofa. Without thinking, I got up and stumbled over to him.

I kissed his lips. I couldn't believe that I had done it. I came to have it out with him. But here I was, snogging him. Fabian didn't bother to stop me. I shoved my hands inside his t-shirt and felt the warm hairs on his chest. What did it matter? Eve was gone and so were the other guys. Nobody gave a shit about us.

"Are you sure?" he asked.

"Yes," I replied, kissing his chest as I lifted up his top. My head was spinning and my vision was going in and out of focus. "Yes," I murmured. "Oh, yes." I unbuttoned the top of his jeans and slowly slipped my hand inside, kissing his tummy...

He responded, smiling at me.

"We can, we can," I insisted even though the voice inside my head was screaming to stop, to get out of there! I just couldn't and I pulled him closer.

"Not here, just not here!" He laughed, taking my hands and trying to stand up. But I couldn't get up. My legs weren't working.

I tried shifting myself off the sofa and onto the floor. I managed to get on my hands and knees, laughing at the ridiculousness of the situation. He grabbed my hands and I managed to get up and we staggered to his bedroom. I slumped down onto his red and grey geometric duvet. He clambered onto the bed like a stranded survivor washed up on a beach. He loomed over me ripping my white t-shirt over my head.

He leant forward, and took off my bra. He then clambered off the bed and leant into his bedside cabinet. He took out a small brown glass bottle and unscrewed the cap.

"Smell it, it will make you relax."

So, I took a sniff and there was a whooshing sensation. My heart beat faster and I felt really hot and relaxed.

"It's good, oui?" he asked, eyes wide.

"Oui." I smiled, feeling a little breathless. I kissed him gently on the lips. They were warm and soft and I began to kiss him hungrily. He reciprocated, caressing my neck.

My head was somewhere else. I felt as though I was watching from above. I could see myself ripping off his clothes. I didn't have time to admire his body, the small freckles, the birthmark on his side, the curly hair on his chest, his toned body and tensed abs, my hands on his skin.

His hands on my body brought me back to reality. His fingers touched my soul, red-hot electricity igniting the fire deep within. The buzzing, swirling, swishing sensations continued. I felt as though I was floating again – I was sitting on his light fittings, I could see his buttocks contracting, the arching of his back and the rhythmic motions of the body below him. She had her legs wrapped around his waist. She was confident and assertive.

When they finished, he let go, collapsing on the bed beside her/me.

"You're a very bad girl," he mumbled into my ear.

"I am!" I suddenly felt sick; this wasn't what I had come here for.

"Stay, stay with me." He said.

"No. I can't. It just won't work." I lay back on the bed, still feeling stoned.

"Wasn't this good?"

"It was, it really was." What the hell was I saying, yes it was good. But did I want to stay?

He leant forward, kissing my naked body. I could do nothing to stop him. I could feel myself melting, don't betray me you evil body.

"I want you" he whispered into my ear me as his musky sent filled my senses and my body arched. I could feel the ache between my legs. My body wanted to be with him even after everything that had happened.

"I know." I replied. We had sex a second time.

Maybe it was the drugs or the alcohol, but for a short while sex had it made me forget how awful my life was. I had nowhere to go, my life was a mess. Was Fabian really offering me an uncomplicated life? Could I, just come to him when the pain inside became intense? Could this be my escape hatch – drink, drugs and sex with no questions asked? I was in such a state right then, I needed to block out the rubbish in my life and he was offering me that.

I had always been teetering on the edge. This would be jumping straight into the abyss and I had a feeling there would be no coming back from this.

"What do you want from me?" I asked.

He ran his fingers gently over my body. I could feel my body being aroused and the surge of blood pumping inside.

"Can't we just make love, do a few drugs, feel relaxed and happy, no strings attached?" asked Fabian in a sultry tone.

"No strings attached?"

"No strings attached," he confirmed.

"No questions asked?"

"None," he whispered.

He kissed me again and I felt intoxicated by him. We had another whiff from his bottle and we were driven into another sexual roller-coaster. I knew that this wasn't good, but then again, I wasn't a saint. I didn't deserve any better.

***

The following morning, I awoke with a cracking headache, alone in the bed. No note was left for me.

I felt unwell and groggy from the night before. What had happened the night before? I rummaged in the bathroom cupboard for some painkillers and at the very back I found a squashed packet of paracetamol. I opened it and popped two pills in my mouth, washing them down with a large glass of water.

Within twenty minutes my headache was gone but my fingers felt strange and tingly. I felt really odd.

My lips were numb. I went back to the edge of the packet. Yes, it was definitely paracetamol. I tried to say it out loud, but my words felts slurred. Yet I felt euphoric. I suddenly felt really hot and faint and thought I was going to collapse. I laid down on the sofa.

The next thing I knew, Fabian was unlocking the door and walking into the flat.

"Hey princess," he cooed. "You've been here all day?"

"Yes," I gasped. "Those paracetamol are really strong."

"Are they?"

"They wiped me out the whole day. But they got rid of my headache."

He smiled and moved the hair out of my face. He kissed my forehead tenderly. "I bet they did, cherie. How do you feel now?"

"Headache's coming back. I'd like some more, please."

"No problem" he replied and went to the bathroom cupboard and returned with the tablets and a glass of water. "Two for you and two for me."

"D'you have a headache as well?"

"Yes, really bad." He smiled. "HUGE!" He smacked his head with the back of his hand dramatically.

This time I was aware of how I would feel and they really were very strong. It was obvious they weren't really paracetamol but rather some narcotic cleverly disguised. But it was too late now. I was past caring.

Fabian started to undo his tie.

"I really did enjoy last night," he said soothingly.

I stroked his face and I began to lose focus. Like before, I could taste his lips and feel his hands sliding up my legs towards my skirt but I couldn't do anything. I felt completely paralytic, I had no idea what was happening to my body, I was all over the place.

"Come," he said, shoving his hands onto my breasts. "Come to me...Yes, just let go."

And I did...I was hot, then cold. Images flashed before my face, the bomb attack, Thierry, Laurent and Pierre – all dead...and the funerals...I flashed back to reality. This was bad, all really bad. I needed to block out this pain I felt. I totally surrendered to him. I blocked out the hurt that was tormenting me, the pain and the guilt were wiped away as he took control over me.

When we finished, I felt completely broken. He had ripped my soul out.

***

Aline looked up at Dr Dhillon, she shuddered. "I feel so ashamed of what I did; getting involved with Fabian. I was such a fool. How could I believe that he would take away the pain?"

"You were at an incredibly low point in your life."

"But it's so bad!" She held her hands over her mouth, "So bad."

"You mustn't judge yourself. I'm not judging you."

Aline screw up her face and pulled at her top! "But it was so bad!" She cried, her finger tearing at her clothes.

"It's okay...it's okay. We all make mistakes." Dr Dhillon offered adjusting her scarf.

"Nothing as big as this, I expect."

Dr Dhillon closed her notepad "I can assure you, it could have been a lot worse."

CHAPTER 48

VERITY

Mike Jeffordson punched the numbers into the telephone keypad.

He said the numbers loudly in pairs, holding the receiver to his ear; the line rang and rang and was eventually picked up by a woman.

"Good Morning, is that Verity Matthews?"

"Yes, it is, who's calling?"

"This is Detective Inspector Mike Jeffordson from the Metropolitan Police."

"Oh."

"I'm investigating an assault case here in London and I wondered if you could help me?"

"Oh, yes. I will if I can...I'm sorry, who are you again?"

"Detective Inspector Mike Jeffordson, I'm based at Brixton Police Station."

"I hope you don't mind, but can I call you back?"

Mike was familiar with this procedure; it was fairly standard to establish the identity of the caller. "Of course, no problem."

A few minutes later Verity rang through the station's main switchboard and was put through to Mike.

"I'm sorry about that," Verity apologised.

"No, it's perfectly fine, I completely understand."

"So, how can I help you, officer?"

"I've been talking to Sister White at the Royal Berkshire Hospital," he said.

"Oh yes, what did that battle-axe have to say for herself?" she sighed.

Mike was surprised by her reply. "We're looking for a colleague in relation to some drugs that went missing from the maternity unit."

"Oh, my God! I can't believe you're dragging all this up again. I spoke to Thames Valley Police about it at the time. Several of us were accused, you know?"

"Does that mean that you were investigated, too?"

"Yes, about four of us were and we were all cleared. Some really good midwives left over it!"

"Including Eve McDonnell?"

"Yes."

"Do you know where she went?"

"No."

"I thought the two of you were friends?"

"We are…"

"So, where is she…?"

"Honestly, I have no idea."

"When did you last see her?"

"On the ward, as a patient."

"Oh, when was that?"

"September time last year, I can't remember the exact date."

"Can I ask you why she was there?"

"She'd taken an overdose, a big one by all accounts. I found her in her room. The paramedic came and she was admitted to the medical ward at the Royal Berks. Immediately people were suspicious and said it was the drugs she'd stolen. But it wasn't, it was the sleeping tablets her GP had prescribed her. I found the packet empty by her bed."

"So, what happened? Did she go home with you after discharge?"

"No…No she didn't"

"Why was that?"

"She had discharged herself."

"Did you find her?"

"No, I didn't. I did manage to contact, her boyfriend's mate in London. He said he hadn't seen anyone since the morning of the bombing. He said he'd contact me if he saw Eve again. He took my phone number but I haven't heard from him since. I've been really worried about Eve."

"Is the lad in London called Fabian Lambert, by any chance?"

"Yes, that's him. They worked at the Cadeau Hotel together."

"Have you got any details for him?"

"Yes. I've got his address and number. He's in Kensington. Hang on. Yes, here we are. It's 73 Lexham Gardens."

"And the phone number?"

She gave it to him and he noted it on his file.

"Inspector if you find Eve please will you give her my number? I really miss her."

"I will."

CHAPTER 49

LAMMY

The tyres screeched as they pulled up outside number 73. The officers jumped out of the cars, flinging the doors open they mounted the stone stairs two at a time.

DI Jeffordson, DS Lewis, DC Doyle and DS Celine Clement stood outside the front door, waiting for Fabian Lambert to answer. There was no reply.

"Bang bloody harder!" Mike insisted.

The four of them stood impatiently. They had him this time...

They heard the security chain sliding across the door and Phil practically pushed the door open. Fabian stood with his arm over his forehead creating a shade for his bleary eyes. He wore nothing but white boxers and seemed stunned by the coppers who came flying through the door.

It was not what Mike had imagined from his initial impression. The flat was a mess. Ashtrays full of cigarette butts overflowed onto the coffee table. Dirty dishes littered the floor. The greeny-blue mould growing over the unwashed plates was a microbiologist's dream. Empty bottles lay discarded around the room. The place stank of dirty bins. It was a mess.

Mike picked up a pile of newspapers and flicked through them. The Guardian, Evening Standard and the French newspaper, La Monde. Fabian was clearly an intelligent man, reading this type of newspaper — there were no tabloids to be seen here.

"Still get French papers, I see," he said as flicked the paper which lay on the work surface next to a black coffee and a slice of toast.

"Yes, it's good to keep up with what is happening back home." Fabian looked at Mike and Andrea suspiciously. "Why are you here? What do you want?"

Mike ignored the questions. "Don't you like tidying up, Mr Lambert?"

"No, not really," He looked around at the disgusting mess.

"Well here's a thing, we're investigating a serious assault and a linked drugs offence and guess what? Your name keeps cropping up, Mr Lambert."

Fabian looked from Mike to Andrea, who was looking around the kitchen, clearly searching for any clues. He turned back to Mike.

"My name?" he answered innocently.

"Yes, Mr Lambert. Or should we be calling you Lammy? That's what they call you at The Regent, isn't it?"

"I have no idea what you're talking about."

"So, you don't go to Brixton selling drugs then, Lammy?"

"What is Brick Stone?"

Fabian was as cool as a cucumber. He was completely calm; he was an incredibly good liar. Mike was astonished by how unflappable the Frenchman was, but his gut was telling him they were on the right track.

"So, you know nothing about a drug dealer in the area who matches your description? Who coincidently has a name similar to yourself Lambert, Lammy? – did you see what I did there?"

"No, I'm sorry but you have got the wrong man. Do I look like a dealer?"

"Going by the state of this place, maybe so," said Mike. "Do you remember we visited you at work a few weeks ago with a CCTV picture of you?"

"It wasn't me."

"I beg to differ. Anyway, since then we have received more information and have reason to believe that you do know both Eve McDonnell and Aline Deniaud."

Fabian looked down at his feet. Mike Jeffordson was like a terrier with a bone, he really wasn't going to let this all go. Fabian was his man; he could sense it.

"Right, I want this place searched!" shouted Mike.

"You cannot come in here and start going through my stuff!" Fabian protested.

"Oh, but we can!" He held up a search warrant.

"What?"

"Look everywhere."

"Yes Guv," they replied in unison.

"Now, Mr Lambert, let's have the truth, now. Do you know Aline Deniaud?"

With a sigh, Fabian nodded.

"Have you seen her recently?"

"No, not since we went clubbing months ago." Fabian looked around the room, unable to hold Mike Jeffordson's stare.

"I'm going to ask you again – do you know Eve McDonnell?"

"Oh yes…come to think of it I do. She was Laurent's girlfriend."

"When did you last see her?"

"After the bombing, she came up to London to see him in the hospital. Then she was gone. I didn't see her again."

Andrea came out of the bedroom which she'd searched, holding a black handbag and a matching pair of stilettos.

"These don't look your size, Fabian," she said sarcastically. She opened the handbag to find a set of keys, a purse with some loose change and a lipstick. She wound up the lipstick. "It's not your colour either."

"I have many visitors," he shrugged.

"How many visitors with a size four shoe?" she asked, peering inside the shoe. "And a love of Lancôme lipstick? A bit expensive for your average Tom, wouldn't you say, Sir?"

"Let's bag them and take them for evidence," said the DI. "The lipstick will reveal its owner."

Fabian looked horrified.

"Oh, and whilst we are at it, we'll also take that half-drunk cup of coffee, and the toast. I think we could match up the teeth imprints with some very nasty bite marks." the DI continued, pointing to the plate on the kitchen counter.

"Sir, look what I've got..." Phil had a kitchen cupboard open and inside a box a Weetabix there was a roll of cash and some small bags containing powder and a small set of scales.

"This is all the makings of a dealer, isn't it Mr Lambert?" Mike smiled. "Right, Fabian, get dressed, you're nicked!"

"This is not mine. It must have been left behind!"

"Read him his rights, Phil."

Phil took out the card from his pocket and read Fabian his rights.

"What am I being arrested for?"

"Let's see. The supply of class A drugs, actual bodily harm, and perverting the course of justice, that should do for starters." DI Jeffordson grabbed Fabian and pushed him firmly back through the flat.

"You can't keep me here! I'm a French citizen and I want to go back to France. I know my rights!" Fabian shouted.

"You will be tried here in a British court and will not be going back to France, Monsieur Lambert. You undertook your crime here in the UK, and as we are under European Law you will be tried here and if found guilty serve your sentence here, too," DC Celine Clement replied.

"No! It's not true!"

"Monsieur Lambert, I would suggest you do exactly what this officer tells you to do."

"You fucking bitch," he spat at her.

The officers cuffed him and led him out of the flat to the waiting cars where he was shoved into the back seat and taken directly to Brixton Station for questioning.

CHAPTER 50

TOXIC

The whole team was assembled in the station's main office for the briefing. Officers sat around the room in neat rows, some in uniform, and others plain-clothed. Mike stood up at the front of the room, pulling himself up to his full height.

"This morning we visited Mr Fabian Lambert in Lexham Gardens, Kensington. There we found what we believe to be the victim's missing shoes and handbag in his bedroom. The lipstick found in the handbag has been sent to forensics. I'm pretty certain it will match the girl's DNA. We're checking Lambert's DNA against what we found on the evidence we took at Kings College."

"Oh, nice one, Guv!" said Phil.

"We've also discovered that Fabian has a bit of a record for assaulting women, sexual harassment of Alice Berry and an assault of Lucy Robinson. Not a nice lad at all. In addition to that, Celine has got some news from France."

Celine sat with her long, elegant legs crossed at the knee. She opened up her file and handed out copies of the fax she'd received from France.

"I have information from Captain Nicolas Bremont, my colleague in France. Fabian has somewhat of a track record in Paris also, and his home town Bordeaux."

"He's a nasty piece of work, by all accounts" Mike scratched his head. "What were the charges in France, Celine?"

"Drunk and disorderly, fighting; apparently he got into a fight with a man over a woman. He had a complaint made against him by a girl in Bordeaux for slapping her in public. Lots of witness, but charges were dropped."

"So, it appears that Mr Lambert has got form. Good job, we've got him in a cell, the little toe-rag."

"About time, by the sound of it" Andrea muttered loudly.

"Anything else Celine? Have we found the whereabouts of Aline's parents?" Mike enquired, twisting his moustache.

"Yes, we've had some results from Nicolas; his team have done an extensive search for Aline and her family on the electoral lists. When that revealed nothing, they spread the search wider. He believes that she must have moved to England over ten years ago. There's no record of her doing her training in France. Sir, you'll see that Nicolas has looked into her employment at Clinique Sainte Thérèse. They had a nurse called Aline Deniaud, but she retired three years ago. She is now 64 years old."

"Okay, so Aline didn't train or work in France."

"No Sir. In relation to her parents, do you remember that I called the telephone number Sister Oliver supplied? Well it was a number for a boulangerie in Paris. They found that it was the same number from the receipt found in the coat pocket." She looked around the room, to see stunned faces.

"Okay, so I spoke to the owners of the bakery in Paris, they have never heard of anyone called Monsieur et Madame Deniaud."

Silence struck the room.

"I believe that this was completely premeditated, Sir," she addressed him directly. "This is not coincidental at all. Aline Deniaud worked it all out and covered her tracks well. What does Sherlock Holmes say?"

"There's no such thing as a coincidence," said Phil.

Celine and Andrea both nodded and rattled off the very famous quote from Sherlock Holmes: "When you've eliminated the impossible, whatever remains, however improbable, must be the truth."

DI Jeffordson's eyes widened. "You know what? That Sherlock Holmes may have been written centuries ago, but he certainly knew a thing or two. He's right. No matter how improbable it seems; Aline has done this all deliberately to deceive."

"Yes Sir," Celine replied.

"Why would she lie about coming here directly from France?" Mike scratched his head.

"Well, obviously to cover up the suspension," said Andrea.

"Yes, yes, that's quite possible. But there's more to it than that, I'm sure of it." He was deep in thought trying to work it out. "There's something going on that we're missing. I just can't put my finger on it!"

"Well, she was running away from something, that's for sure," said Celine.

"Whatever is going on, she's in a lot of trouble."

CHAPTER 51

NO BED OF ROSES

Aline sat in the music room tying to compile another CD after she'd smashed the previous one up against the wall. Dr Dhillon came into the room, closing the door behind her.

"I thought I'd find you here. This has become a bit of habit, hasn't it?"

Aline looked up smiling. "Yes, just a bit."

"What's your favourite?" Dr Dhillon asked flicking through the box of all the CDs.

"Oh, I don't know. They all create different feelings and emotions."

"I do love this one." She picked up an old Carpenters album. "Karen Carpenter's voice is so beautiful. It makes me feel so sad though."

"Why does it make you feel sad?"

"Have you ever listened to 'Rainy days and Mondays'?"

"I can't say I have."

"It makes me think about, well you know. My existence wasn't ideal, staying with Fabian. It had taken on a life of its own – like a rosebush, once beautiful but now it had grown unruly as it had taken us over. I lived in the nurse's accommodation at Whipps Cross but on my days off I'd get a bus back to the flat through the city with a weekend bag.

"Fabian would be waiting for me and I would strip off and climb into bed. Both of us would get pretty high and then get really drunk, and we would use whatever either of us had got hold of...Money was no longer being spent on food.

"We had both sunk into this toxic relationship. It was a terrible situation to be in. We were both pushing down our emotions. Neither of us was prepared to face the pain of bereavement. So now addiction gripped us both. We were fuelled by the next hit."

"How did that change your relationship?"

"The sex changed. Any tenderness had gone...we were both lustful, so we had sex. It wasn't gentle and caring like those first nights. Now he was rough. He was becoming more violent, often forcing himself upon me before I was ready or when I was too drugged up to care. His consideration had been lost and he treated me like I was a sex object or at worse a lump of meat. He enjoyed biting me, on my back, neck and my breasts. This heightened his climax.

"Once he ejaculated in my hair and then left me like trash on the floor. I got up and ran across the room threatening to hit him over the back of his head with a frying pan. He spun round and grabbed my wrist. We screamed at each other, he said that we agreed that we never wanted it to be complicated. He said 'You just wanted sex, Cherie, and that's what you got.' He was angry and bitter with me; he grabbed my face with his hand, forcing his fingers into my cheeks.

'No man in their right mind would ever have you. Look at what you've become, Aline. You're an addict, a junkie! You have no morals, you're lucky to have me, scooping you up from your pit of despair.'

"He ran his finger down my neck and towards my cleavage.

'That's not true,' I sobbed.

'Nobody will have you now, you are worthless.'

'I'm not worthless,' I cried.

'You are Aline; you have screwed with everybody else to get your own way. Look what you did to Eve! Where is she? Eh?'

'I don't know!'

'Lost forever, Aline,' he sneered. 'You and I are more alike than you would think.'

'I'm nothing like you. I'm not a rapist!'

'Nor am I.'

'What are you, then?' I challenged.

'This is not about me, Aline. It's about you. You're the fucking head case.' He was now laughing uncontrollably and released his grip on me.

'What the hell happened to you, Fabian?'

'The same as you, Aline. You and I are into drugs, alcohol and sex...nothing more, nothing less. No strings attached...isn't that what you said?' He was becoming more aggressive. 'I'm just telling you – no, I'm warning you – there are people out there who are willing to screw you over.'

'None of this makes sense...You just forced me to have sex and then said it was my problem.'

'I don't understand you, Aline. You were up for it! In fact, you were begging for it.'

'No, I...I'm so confused by all this. I didn't want it like this. I want it to be different.'

'How will it be different? Tell me,' he gesticulated.

"I stood there blankly...I just didn't know how this would ever change. I realised I couldn't be part of it any more. This wasn't the life I wanted.

I left the room and got my things, 'I'm off, Fabian,' I said very formally. 'I won't be back.'

'I'll see you soon,' he said, looking at me through the reflection in the mirror.

'No Fabian, I won't be seeing you again.'

He leant forward with shaving foam on his face and kissed me on the lips. I could feel the foam transferring onto my face. I didn't respond.

'I'll see you soon,' he replied and held my gaze.

I walked away from him with anger in my heart. He was a mean, malicious bastard and I had no intention of returning to the flat or to Fabian. I grabbed my holdall and picked up my jacket and stormed out of the flat with my head held high, slamming the front door as hard as I possibly could. I could hear something in the flat falling off the shelf and smashing. Fabian was swearing in French. I didn't look back and made my way down the stone staircase and headed away from the flat.

But I didn't know where to go.

The pain and guilt now gripped me. How had I allowed this to happen to me? I walked quickly up the path through the line of trees and out onto the road. I had to go – go anywhere. A bus arrived at the stop and I jumped onto the bus and climbed up the spiral stairs to the top deck. I sat and looked out of the window. I took a deep breath and closed my eyes, trying to calm myself down. What had just happened in there? Why did I feel the need to run? It felt as though I was spending half my life running away. Did I need to be running at all?"

"I think given the circumstances Aline, you did the safest thing, which was to get out of there. So, what did you do next?" Dr Dhillon responded.

"Well, what else could I do, but return to Whipps Cross."

CHAPTER 52

TURNING OVER A NEW LEAF

D r Dhillon and Aline left the music room and walked out to the courtyard, as Aline was in need of a cigarette. Aline lit the match and drew deeply on the skinny cigarette.

"So, you returned to Whipps Cross, how was that?"

Aline raised her eyebrows and took the stray piece of tobacco from her mouth.

"Well my colleagues avoided me and wouldn't make eye contact. I had done nothing wrong. I came into work; I did my job and went home. What more could they ask? Life there was pretty lonely, the nurses kept themselves to themselves in the accommodation.

"One day Sister Oliver asked me into the office. She said she was concerned that she'd had reports of me smelling of alcohol. I wasn't prepared to tell her what was going on. It was none of her business. The isolation and loneliness took over and I missed human contact – any human contact, even with Fabian. But I wasn't prepared to go back to him. I found myself hitting the booze again. Just a little bit at first to help me go to sleep – you know, a little vodka and orange. Then it became a little vodka and orange with my dinner and one before bed. Before I knew it, I was drinking half a bottle of Vodka, starting as soon as I came in through the doors. I just wanted to dull the loneliness. Vodka was my new best friend. It never told me that I was worthless or useless. It never told me that I drank too much. I knew it was becoming a problem, but I needed it and couldn't stop.

"Several weeks later I had really gone over the top, I knew I had. I arrived at work with a cracking headache. I found my way into the labour suite and into a delivery room. I began sucking on the Entonox. It was like pure whiskey. My lips and fingers where tingling. The next thing I knew, two security guards arrived and a melee of people were surrounding me.

"The security guard took my hand off the Entonox tube. 'Enough now Aline; you've had enough.'

"The two men frogmarched me back to my accommodation and I laid down on the bed. They left me alone, as no one wanted to help me.

"The following morning Sister Oliver told me that my contract would be terminated with immediate effect for gross misconduct. I tried to be brave as she gave me the news but tears trickled down my face before I dropped my head in my hands and wept. She suggested that I saw a counsellor for drug and alcohol rehab but I just couldn't absorb what she was saying. That was it, my nursing career was over. She gave me no speech, no long monologue of how I was expected to behave. No withering look or even any signs of compassion. She sat there opposite me, emotionless. Whereas I was an emotional wreck."

"So, that was how it all ended at Whipps Cross?"

"Yes, that's how it all ended." She took a long drag and flicked the ash. "It was over. So, I was left with no choice... I packed my belongings into a small holdall. I got onto a red double decker back to Kensington. I couldn't bear to look back at the hospital. I was filled with sadness. I felt ashamed of my behaviour.

"When I arrived at Fabian's flat, I opened the front door. I was anxious – was he home? What if he was in bed with someone else?

"My hand shook as I stepped inside. The whole place was quiet. Not a soul. I made my way to the kitchen, found a glass and finished off the bottle of vodka I had in my bag. It was a ridiculous thing to do, I know that now. The light was starting to drop and the flat was getting darker and I waited nervously for Fabian to return home, I sat curled up on his sofa with a blanket wrapped around myself peeping over the top. Late into the evening the front door opened and he switched on the hall light. He must have sensed someone was in the flat. He found me curled up in a ball really drunk. I told him what had happened

'I've lost everything – my job, my home, my dignity, my career, my friends. I didn't know what to do or where to go!'

He took my hands. 'I'm glad you came to me. You did the right thing.'

'You hurt me, Fabian, I was scared'.

'I know and I'm sorry. I had too many drugs also. I just couldn't cope with the deaths of my friends. You know I'm finding it really hard and I don't think I'll ever get over it. I shouldn't have got into the drink and drugs. It has changed me. I know for you it was pretty scary and I'm sorry for that. Can we be friends again?'

'Yes, we can. I've been struggling with it all, too. That's why when I left you; I thought it would all be okay. But it just crept up on me like a thief in the night. Before I knew it, the pain became overwhelming. It was eating at me. The only way to get rid of it was to drink. But after a while, the pain wouldn't go away so I needed more and more.'

'I know, I really do know.'

"I want it to stop but it just won't! Make it stop for me, Fabian, please!"

"I would if I could, but I'm not able to."

I sat with my arms around him and cried, just cried. Both of us cried, and you know what. I didn't care what happened. I didn't care. My life was so crap I had nowhere else to go. All I wanted was to get thoroughly drunk."

"So, did anything happen, did he take advantage of you?"

"No, no he didn't, he just left me alone. I went to bed. And then he went off to the Prince Regent."

CHAPTER 53

BETRAYAL

The following morning Dr Dhillon sat in front of Aline with her notes across her lap. Aline wore a new pair of jeans and a bright red sweater. Her hair was tied back into a long ponytail. She looked the best that Dr Dhillon had seen her throughout her whole time on Florence Green Ward.

Today, Dr Dhillon thought that it was time to approach Aline about the assault and the abuse she'd suffered, as Aline appeared to be in a better frame of mind.

"Aline, you know we talked about Fabian last time?"

"Yes,"

"I'd like to know what it was like when you returned to Fabian. Are you happy to talk about it again?"

"I suppose so." Aline chewed the edge of her fingernail. "Well, I think I told you that when I got the sack from Whipps Cross, I returned to Fabian. I didn't want to at first. But I really had no choice. I had no money and I didn't know anyone I could turn to. The days rolled by and before long the old pattern of behaviour returned. We started to drink again – well, I suppose I never stopped – and Fabian began to get a supply of drugs from his friends. He had been into Soho several times now, visiting sex shops, picking up toys. He had definitely got kinkier and this was enhanced by the increased drug-taking. I was pretty much up for anything those days; I was past caring. I lived in a permanent fog and the days were long and lonely. Sometimes I'd wander to the big church near us. Occasionally, I'd go in for a coffee and some cake. It felt safe there. Nobody questioned who I was and what I was doing.

"So, nobody took you under their wing at the church?"

"No, as I said, I was ignored. I was a junkie after all!" She shrugged her shoulders "When I let myself think about it, I felt pretty guilty about the life I was leading. I was hooked on drugs and alcohol and I was with this guy who I didn't really love... We were just together, having sex. We were never in it for the long haul and I knew we had no future together. But I had no idea how this would end. I was oblivious to how bad it was all becoming. I led a bit of a ghostly existence, floating back and forth to the church. Well, on this one day, I went back feeling flat; nobody had spoken to me, only the one who served me soup. Fabian had returned with another of his bags from Soho. He opened up the bag wide... Inside I could see a mixture of leather and studs. It made me feel sick.

"He was as high as a kite and wanted to try bondage. He was like an excited school boy, but I didn't want to have anything to do with it. He wanted to know why. I told him I'd been to church and wanted to get clean. To mend my ways. To get my life back."

"What did he say to that?" asked the doctor.

"He said, 'You know Aline, that God of yours is too busy for the likes of you or me. That's why we are in this shit together.'"

"But you didn't agree?"

"No but he said he was the only one who was there for me. I felt so lonely.

"He told me 'God is not here; he never was and never will be. We have to fight for ourselves in this world. It's dog eat dog.' And he started to touch me. I was torn by what he was telling me. Was God just a big fat lie? Was this life really as cruel and as dark as I feared? Was there no hope for my future? It was all so overwhelming. What was the point of all this? Why was I looking for a brighter future when there clearly was none? My future was here and I felt trapped by it, by him.

"He opened his wallet and took out some small tablets. They looked like something innocent like Piriton or something. But they weren't. He placed a pill on my tongue. I didn't resist, what was the point? What difference would one little pill make?"

***

Aline stopped and got up from the chair..."I can't do this Dr Dhillon, I just can't." She paced up and down biting the edge of her nail.

"It's okay, if you want to stop, we can."

Aline's pace increased as she walked up and down the room. "Oh my God, oh my God," she repeated over and over. She took a deep breath.

"It's okay Aline, he can't hurt you now." She stood up and gently led her back to her seat. Aline wiped a silent tear away from her face. She forced a smile.

"If you want to stop, that's fine."

"No...I want to go on and get this over with."

"In your own time then."

"Well, quite soon after I'd taken the tablet. I felt a swishy sensation and the world changed colours. Fabian led me to his bedroom. He undressed me and secured me to the bed with leather straps, face down. I asked whether they needed to be so tight. He said they did. He got off the bed and went over to his CD player. I could hear him taking a disc out of its case and putting it into the player. He turned off the light. Then it got nasty. The music started. It wasn't romantic or soothing. It was horrible and violent – he said it was a new group called Prodigy. The baseline line vibrated through the room. It was aggressive, a rough voice screamed and wailed and rumbled over me. My skin crawled and the hairs on my arms stood on end, and for the first time in my life I was getting really, really frightened. Fabian chanted as he pushed my face on the bed. I could hear the pulse beating inside my head; I was finding it hard to breath. He prepared himself, putting on a mask and picking up a whip. I was petrified by this madness. I screamed with pain as he hit me repeatedly."

Aline clenched her stomach, gripping down her teeth, she rocked back and forth. She paused trying to find the courage to continue.

"And what happened next Aline?" Dr Dhillon spoke softly.

Aline looked at her and through gritted teeth she replied "He told me that I needed to be punished," Her breath caught.

"Okay."

"It's was then, it all started." She paused wiping a tear away "He hit me. He said I was a fool to go to church, seeking forgiveness. 'God won't forgive you,' he said. My back arched, trying to get away from the whip. But then another pain started. He got on top of me he roughly entered my back passage. I screamed and screamed. It burned like fire. I begged him to stop but he continued to thrust his pelvis. I felt hot and sick and thought I might die as the pain split me in half, but he wouldn't stop." Her breathing rate increased as she spoke more rapidly. "He said I deserved to be punished. He hit me harder across my back. I was so shocked that Fabian was treating me like this. How could he do that to me? It went on for so long. His frenzied assault didn't seem to stop. He was grabbing me and biting me. When he finally came, he got up and wiped himself with a tissue and pulled on his trousers.

"Fabian had changed in the blink of an eye. He'd been so kind to me since my return and now in one moment he became mean and so very cruel...evil! I didn't recognise this man. Who was he? Had I been dancing with the Devil? I was outraged by him. Electricity, anger and rage coursed through my veins. He walked off closing the door behind him, leaving me tied to the bed. I screamed at him to let me go. But he wasn't coming back. He just left me there."

"Goodness me Aline, that's horrendous. What did you do?"

"Then I started to panic, what if he comes back and tries to kill me? We both knew he had gone too far. Even though I was completely drugged up I had enough sense to get the hell out of there. I pulled and pulled at the straps as hard as I could. The cuffs cut into my wrists, but I was determined to get away from this hell. Eventually, the strap broke free from the bed. I got dressed in any old stuff lying around in the room. Blood was running down my legs and the pain was excruciating. I grabbed a coat from the coat hook in the hall and I staggered out of the flat. I had no idea where he had gone but the flat appeared empty. I certainly didn't want to be here when he got home.

"I made my way out into the evening streets and staggered to the church. It was locked up. The streets were dark and felt sinister. I could feel fear pressing down on me and I kept looking back up the street as I stumbled along, expecting him to come chasing after me. Anxiety filled my chest as I turned the corner, thinking I wasn't going to make it. I ran and I found my way to a side entrance to the church, which was a sheltered spot and collapsed.

"I suddenly saw a girl with long black hair standing on the edge of a cliff. In the distance, the sun was setting and it was dropping over the edge of the horizon. The sky was going black. I could feel the apprehension within the girl, the force of it had pinned me to the spot. I wanted to help her but I couldn't move. I could hear the pumping and rushing of blood within my head as I watched the girl run and jump off the cliff. I could hear her screaming, the sound fading as she fell into the great abyss. But it didn't stop. Then I realised the screaming was me...It was then that I blacked out."

"This is simply terrible Aline. We've got to let the police know. Are you happy for me to do that?"

"Yes, I am."

***

"Hello Mike, Dr Dhillon here."

"Good afternoon, Doctor. What's the latest on Aline?"

"Well, she's generally okay and getting stronger every day. But we've just had another session together and it was quite traumatic."

"Why was that?"

"I'm afraid it's become very evident that this man Fabian beat and raped her."

"Oh my, that's truly awful."

"Yes, it's no wonder she's been so reluctant to remember."

"And it was Fabian Lambert?"

"Yes, how did you know?"

"Oh, we've already arrested him on drug offences?"

"Fabian?"

"Yes, he's a dealer."

"And a rapist?"

"Don't worry Doc, we've got this."

CHAPTER 54

MR & MRS DENIAUD

Celine came in to the incident room looking for Mike with a handful of paperwork. She had a broad smile on her face.

"I've been onto my colleague in Paris, and Nicolas tells me Fabian has quite a long history of crime in Paris. He's sending us details."

"Is that what you've got there?"

"Oh, no, this is quite something else," she thrust the papers under his nose.

"What have you got?" Mike asked.

"As you know Nicolas looked for Aline's parents and they can't find them living in Paris. Well, this is the thing – her parents, this Jacques and Johanna Deniaud, they don't even exist!"

"What?" He looked puzzled. "Nobody in the whole of Paris called Jacques and Johanna Deniaud?"

"Nobody in the whole of France was the right age, or had a daughter called Aline!"

"This is impossible!"

"However," Celine added. "There is another possible link my colleagues came up with. There is a couple called Jacques and Johanna."

"And you think they could be Aline's family?" he asked. "Have you contacted them?"

Celine shook her head. "No; the thing is Sir, it would appear that Aline has had us on a wild goose chase."

"Why's that?"

"This Jacques and Johanna are the main characters in a French film called The Big Blue. It has quite a cult following."

"And?"

"They suggest that she may be a fan of the film and has taken her parents' names from it."

"I'm sorry, I don't follow. Are you telling me Aline's parents' names are fictitious characters from a French film?"

"Yes, that sums it up."

"No, this isn't possible." He rubbed his chin.

"I know. Nicolas and his team felt the same. But one of them thought it was the only explanation. Like I said, it had quite a cult following. A lot of criminals tried the same trick. Apparently, Fabian had done the same with his own parents.

"Clearly your colleague is quite a fan," he smirked. "So, if her parents really are fictitious characters in a French film and the phone number is from the boulangerie in Paris, which we found on the receipt, what the heck is Aline playing at?"

"There is only one possible explanation for all of this Sir. We know that she didn't train or work in Paris, she isn't on the board for English trained nurses. I really don't believe that Aline Deniaud even exists."

"But we have positive identifications of her from Sister Oliver and Reverend Hillier."

"But she gave a false name to the reverend and nobody has managed to verify Aline's identification, have they? And nobody has come forward before her move to London a few months ago," she pointed out.

"No, they haven't." Mike Jeffordson frowned. He pushed the papers across his desk. "Bloody hell, Celine. This is a right sodding mess."

CHAPTER 55

PERVERTING THE COURSE OF JUSTICE

Fabian was taken into a bare interview room, accompanied by DS Celine Clement and DS Phil Lewis. He was sat next to the duty solicitor. The two officers took chairs on the opposite side of the table. A tape recorder was turned on.

"The time is 6.15pm. An interview is being held by Detective Sergeant Clement and Detective Sergeant Philip Lewis. Fabian Lambert is accompanied by the duty solicitor, Ms Emily Blake.

"Please will you confirm that you are Fabian Lambert?"

He nodded.

"For the tape, the interviewee has nodded," said Phil. "Mr Lambert, we arrested you at your home, 73 Lexham Gardens, Kensington. Is that correct?"

"Oui," he replied.

"We are charging you with possession and the intent to supply amphetamines and crack cocaine."

Fabian's solicitor sat tight-lipped as Phil rattled his way through the charges.

"Fabian, we know that you're the man known as Lammy who's been dealing drugs at The Regent pub in Brixton. We have witnesses. There's no point denying it," Phil challenged.

Fabian shrugged and folded his arms looking defiantly at the officer. "It's not me," he said.

Phil opened the file on the table. He took out a still photograph of Fabian outside of the Prince Regent, clearly doing a deal with a punter. Fabian looked down on the file. Fabian's confident expression faltered. He gulped and his fingers fidgeted. Phil smiled. He certainly didn't look quite so cocky now.

"You don't have to say anything," his solicitor reminded him.

"So, can you explain this then?" Phil pushed over the second picture of Aline and himself having an argument in the street outside the pub.

"No comment," said Fabian.

"Fabian, you might as well come clean and tell us what's been going on," DC Clement coaxed.

"Nothing, nothing at all." He ran his fingers through his hair. He looked up at the ceiling.

"I'll advise you again, Mr Lambert, that you don't have to say anything," said his solicitor.

"Fuck off!" he swore at her in French. Celine translated for the tape.

"There is no need to swear, Monsieur Lambert," Celine warned him.

"Okay, okay. Yes, I was at The Regent with Aline. She had no idea why we were there. I wasn't dealing but when she saw the drugs, she went crazy. That's why we argued. She stormed off and I stayed. That was it!"

"Fabian," his solicitor appealed.

He shot her a look, his dark eyes glaring at her.

"And what about Eve McDonnell? You said that the last time you saw her was at Paddington Station after the bombing of the Cadeau Hotel. You claim that you never saw her again, but we have information that contradicts that," Phil pressed him.

"Really? I don't know why someone would tell you that."

"Because it's true, isn't it?" said Phil. "I find it odd that you deny it. And who better to supply the drugs, than Fabian?"

The net was tightening around Fabian and he knew he was trapped and the police were not going to let it go.

"Okay, okay! I admit I do know Eve; she stayed with me whilst Laurent was in a critical condition. We both got very drunk and she cried most of the night. I didn't take advantage of her, honestly. We were both upset.

We'd lost both Pierre and Thierry, and Laurent was in a critical condition. He was the love of her life. She was so vulnerable. We got really, really drunk. She climbed into Laurent's bed and hugged his duvet."

"Did you sleep with her?"

"Yes, but non!"

"But 'non' what?" asked Phil.

"Yes, I got into bed with her. But non, we didn't have sex. She was my best friend's girl. I couldn't do that to Laurent."

"So, what happened, Fabian?"

He shrugged. "We were so drunk we went to sleep. I went to work in the morning and when I returned, she wasn't there."

"She went back to work?"

"I don't know. I suppose, yes, she went back to work."

"Are you sure she didn't stay another night?"

"Yes, certain," he looked around the room, avoiding their eyes.

"You're certain about that, because you sexually assaulted her?"

"I didn't assault her." His voice went up an octave.

"You don't sound so sure," Phil challenged.

"Well I told her the news that Laurent had died. He never recovered from his injuries. Eve, as you can imagine, was really devastated and was totally inconsolable when I told her. That night we hit the alcohol and smoked. She was in pieces." He paused.

"Go on," encouraged DS Clement.

"We ended up in bed together. She started it, not me. Honestly. She kissed me. I'm not making this up. I guess she thought I was Laurent," he took a breath. "She kept saying, 'I do love you,' and she ran her fingers through my hair."

"And then what happened?"

"I didn't lead her on at all...really I didn't. We were both so upset with all that was going on."

"And..." Phil encourage him to continue

Fabian shook his head. "We ended up together, I admit. I asked her if she was sure and she said she was. We had sex. The next morning, I left for work. I assumed she'd be there when I got back but I never saw her again."

"So, why didn't you admit this earlier?"

"I just felt so guilty. Laurent was my best friend."

Phil could feel himself getting angry. "Fabian Lambert you are a liar and a cheat! You raped her, she was vulnerable and you raped her. Didn't you?"

Fabian's head went back as though he'd hit him. He then lunged across the table.

Celine reached across the table stopping them both in their tracks.

"Interview suspended at 6.50pm," DS Clement said as she pressed the button on the recorder. "Okay, I think everyone needs to take a breath. Sergeant, may I have a word, please?"

Celine and Phil left the interview room. She turned to him as they closed the door.

"DS Lewis, I think you need to cool it. I know he's a low-life and we want the truth. But this is not the way to do it. This shouldn't be like a TV show where we are playing good cop, bad cop."

"None of this makes sense, Celine. He must be lying. Nobody has any idea where Eve is and we have Aline in hospital after a head injury. He's our link between the two of them and he bloody well knows it!"

"I know, but you cannot return to the room this angry."

Phil rubbed his hands over his face and blew out a frustrated breath. "You're right. I need a coffee and maybe a walk. We'll let him stew for a bit, then go back in."

CHAPTER 56

EVENING STANDARD

Andrea came into the rest room tucking her dark brown hair behind her ear. She could hear the laughter coming down the corridor. She stopped, looking at a bunch of the fellas, laughing about some escapade of Phil's at his expense. She leant up against the door frame watching them all, having a welcome break.

"So, tell me again. You were stark naked and you came out of the bathroom and got into bed with your mate and his wife?" Mike laughed, almost choking on his biscuit.

Phil blushed. "Honest to God, I'm telling you. I was sleepwalking!"

"So, what happened then?"

"She nudges him and says 'Tom, Tom! Phil's just got in bed with us!'"

"And?" egged on by one of the other officers.

"Well, he elbows me, and says, 'Phil, you're in the wrong bed, mate.' That was when I woke up. I dropped and rolled and tried to get out the room. But they'd been decorating and there wasn't any handle on the door. The moon was shining through the window as there weren't any curtains up either. So, the light was shining off my arse."

Andrea shook her head, smiling. Everyone was screaming with laughter.

"So, you're telling me that you had a pee in your sleep?" said Mike.

"Yep," Phil confirmed.

"Bollocks," said one of the lads, tears of mirth running down his face. "You're having a giraffe!"

"No, straight up! Ask Tom when you see him."

Andrea shook her head again, not really understanding what was so amusing about a bloke walking around butt naked.

"There's something else that will put a smile on your face, Guv," she remarked.

"Let me be the judge of that," said Mike, still reeling from Phil's story.

"I have a gentleman downstairs who's asked to see you."

"In relation to what?"

"Eve McDonnell."

"Is that right?" he said, sobering himself up. "Eve McDonnell, eh?"

"Yes. You'll need to speak to him right away, Guv. He says he has some information for us."

Mike straightened his tie, and pulled on his jacket.

"How did he know we were looking for her?" he asked. Before she could answer he turned back to the rest of the team, who were still giggling like schoolboys. "Come on you lot... haven't you got work to do?"

***

Downstairs, Andrea opened the heavy cream door and Mike followed her into the room where a man waited. He was tall, in his early thirties, handsome with thick, dark, collar-length hair and a well-groomed beard. He was stylishly dressed, with his black shirt unbuttoned at the collar under a tailored blazer. He sat drumming his fingers on the table.

"Detective Inspector Jeffordson," said Andrea. "This is Monsieur Roselle."

Mike frowned. The name was a familiar one. "Monsieur Roselle, thank you for coming."

"It's nothing. I just had to see you as soon as possible." He looked anxious.

"I see. So, how can we help you?"

"I'm looking for my girlfriend, Eve McDonnell. She went missing after the IRA bombing in London, but I believe that you know where she is?"

"Your girlfriend?" Mike hesitated. "Are you Laurent?"

Laurent smiled, his face brightening up. "Yes, I am. How do you know?"

"It's rather a long story."

Laurent nodded. "So, you know about Eve and where she is?"

"We know of Eve, but we can't say exactly where she is. Please, tell me about when you last saw her."

"Yes, of course. On the day of the bomb, I was in the main restaurant and I was injured in the blast. I was admitted to the Chelsea and Westminster Hospital after the attack. I had severe burns. Eve came and visited me with Fabian; I think it was the following day, I can't really remember, I had been given some strong stuff to take the pain away. I was in the intensive care unit and ventilated. My parents then took me back to France, as Lyon has one of the best burns units in the world. I can't remember much about it, apart from being taken to the airport by ambulance. That's all I can remember."

"Did you have any contact with Eve at that point?"

"No, nothing at all, she only came into see me that first week and then I never saw her again. After that I had no contact from her at all."

"Don't you think that was strange?"

"Yes, of course. I was really upset; we were planning our future together. I asked Fabian about her and he said that he hadn't seen her. He said she was selfish and only thought about herself and her career. It didn't make sense. I asked him to contact her. He said that he'd told her how bad I was, and that plans were being made for me to be transferred back to France. He said she seemed not to care, that she was on nights and most likely wouldn't be able to get into London. I couldn't believe that Eve would react like this. Fabian wondered whether she couldn't cope with my burns. But this wouldn't be the case because she was a nurse."

"What did Fabian have to say about that?"

"He said you never really know a person until something really bad happens. I felt shocked and so hurt by this, and there was a part of me that simply couldn't believe that Eve would react like that. But I was powerless to do anything in a hospital bed."

"So, then what happened?"

"I stayed in hospital in Lyon for quite a few months. My family visited every day. It was a great relief to be back in my homeland, but I couldn't understand why I didn't hear from Eve. Fabian said he'd told her where I was. When I left hospital, I returned to my parents' home in Bordeaux where my father owns a vineyard. But I couldn't forget Eve and decided to come and find her now that I'm fully recovered."

"And this is the first time you've returned to London?"

"Yes. I want to return to my life in London and to find Eve. I knew something was going on. I tried to contact her in Reading but they said that she'd left. I finally managed to get hold of her friend Verity; she was so shocked to hear from me because she thought I was dead.

She told me about Eve being suspended from work. I didn't believe her when she said Eve had stolen drugs and had taken an overdose soon after hearing about my death."

"When did you speak to Verity?"

"Only a few days ago," he nodded. "It was then it really dawned on me that it was Fabian — that he had told her this lie about my death to Eve. But why? To get Eve out of my life for good? It was too cruel; I was so angry. I simply had to find her. But where could I start? It has been like looking for a needle in a haystack. Nobody seemed to know where she was. I had to go to Fabian, to make him tell me why he'd done this to us — to me, his friend and to Eve, my love."

"So, did you discover her whereabouts?" Mike Jeffordson asked.

"I think so. I went to the flat to confront Fabian but I met a neighbour on the stairs and she said he'd been arrested. I let myself into the flat. It was a wreck. I started to clear up — I couldn't live in that garbage, I had nowhere else to go. That's when I found the newspaper. It was dated several months earlier. I was going to throw it out with the rest of his filth, but then I saw the report of a girl found on a bench in Brixton and the picture. I knew straight away it was her, my Eve."

The officers exchanged looks.

"What? What are you not telling me?" demanded Laurent.

Mike cleared his throat. "I'm very glad you came forward, Monsieur Roselle, we have been trying to figure this out. We have had this lady identified as Aline Deniaud."

"Aline Deniaud, you say?" Laurent looked at Mike Jeffordson, trying to work him out. "The midwife from Reading?"

"Yes, that's correct. Do you know her?"

"I never met her. But Eve used to talk about her a lot."

"Well, I'm afraid that's who we've got," he said. "I'm afraid we're still trying to find Eve McDonnell." He smiled sympathetically.

Laurent shook his head and pulled something out his pocket. He handed Mike the newspaper article containing the appeal for information. The DI didn't bother to look at the all too familiar picture.

"I know this is Eve," he insisted, pointing with his finger at the photograph. "She has changed, her hair is different; she used to be blonde. But it is Eve, I'm sure of it. These are her almond eyes and her petite frame is unmistakable. I know it is her. When they said she was suffering from loss of memory, I thought it had to be her. Who told you it was Aline? They're wrong, believe me."

Mike Jeffordson looked at Laurent sympathetically. "Look, son. I know you're upset and you want to find

Eve, I just don't want you to pin your hopes on some random girl in a park."

"I can assure you that this is not a random girl."

"Mr Roselle, you've been through a traumatic time yourself after the bombing and then having all the surgery and treatment in France. I'm truly sorry. I just don't want you to be let down…"

"Are you listening to me? You asked the public to come forward to identify a woman you found on a park bench. You're the ones calling her Aline Deniaud; I'm here to tell you this is Eve McDonnell. This isn't rocket science. She's unwell and unable to say who she is. I'm here to tell you who she is."

Laurent got up angrily, thumping the table with his fist.

"Look, you have my coat, they wrote about it here," he pointed at the article again. "The one that she was wearing; it's by a designer called APC. That wasn't in the newspaper, was it?" He leant on the table with both hands firmly rooted to the spot.

Andrea and Mike exchanged glances.

"You have my coat, because she was wearing it in the park. She must have gone back to the flat and taken it," he continued. "There aren't many people in England with that coat I can assure you… There could be no explanation for Aline having my coat, as I've never met her."

Mike opened the file. Laurent was right about the designer label. "Yes, that's the description of the coat that was found."

"So, you believe me?"

"I'm sorry, Mr Roselle. But we get a lot of nut cases claiming to know people." He sighed heavily his brushy grey eyebrows furrowing together. "You're at least the eighth chap to turn up claiming you know her; I'm just doing my job."

At that moment Andrea got up. "Sorry to interrupt Sir, but I think we could all do with a quick break."

Mike looked up, puzzled by the interruption.

"Would you like a coffee, Sir?" she asked Laurent.

"Yes, thank you." Laurent looked worn out.

"If you've got a minute, Guv," she gestured to the door for Mike Jeffordson to come out of the interview room.

"What's up, Andi?" he asked as they closed the door behind them.

"I'm not one to tell you how to conduct an investigation, Sir. But I've had an idea." Andrea paused, knowing she was on to something. "This Laurent is French, right?"

"Yes, so?" He looked at Andrea quizzically.

"Guv, don't you see?" She sighed, pointing back at the interview room. "Until now we've never found the owner of the coat and we haven't had anyone come forward who fits the description of Eve's boyfriend."

"No, that's true." DI Jeffordson starred at Andrea. "But what has one got to do with the other?"

"Sir, I'm pretty sure this is Eve's boyfriend."

"What are you suggesting?"

"Nobody can find any background information on Aline – she just doesn't exist, does she? Celine can't find any evidence of an Aline Deniaud in France, and we have no account of her at Reading, or even any evidence of her training here in the UK. What if..." she stalled. "Well, what if Aline really doesn't exist?"

"What are you trying to get at, Andrea?"

"Remember you thought perhaps Aline was a bogus nurse?"

"Yes, that's right."

"Well, what if Eve is Aline, like he says? Nobody can find Eve, even Laurent. So, perhaps, just perhaps, the reason we can't find Eve is because she's currently sitting in the Maudsley Hospital? Let's face it, we haven't found anyone claiming to be Eve, have we? Perhaps Eve changed her identity to Aline."

"Andrea, you could be right! It all fits! But why would she do that? And if so, the only person who says he has ever spent time with both women is Fabian, so he's looking more sinister and unreliable with every minute!"

Andrea shrugged. "Considering what she's been through, maybe she couldn't face being Eve anymore."

He glanced back at the room where Laurent sat. "Let's get the coffee and see what else young Mr Roselle has to say for himself."

Andrea and DI Jeffordson returned to the interview room with Laurent's coffee and placed it down on the table.

"Merci."

"You're welcome. Now, I have to tell you, Monsieur Roselle, the girl you believe to be Eve claims to be an Aline Deniaud, born in France but living here in London."

"I don't know why, but I don't think that's right. I'm sure it's Eve."

"Your girl Eve, can you describe her?"

"Yes. Her name is Eve McDonnell. She's a midwife from Reading. She's in her early thirties, about 165 cm tall, emerald green eyes. Petite frame, blonde long wavy hair. But of course, judging by the picture, she's changed that."

"But this girl we have is from London, not Reading."

"I think that you are mistaken about the identity of the girl. Anyway, Eve said that Aline lived in Reading also."

"Did you ever meet Aline?"

"No never. But Eve used to talk about her."

"And you definitely never met her?" Mike made some notes.

Laurent shook his head.

"Okay, Laurent. Now, we've had various accounts of Aline living here in London. But we haven't seen anything official to identify either of these two girls. Have you got anything that might help with identifying Eve?"

"No, not really. What things would you be looking for?"

"Driving licence, passport, national insurance card. Anything like that?"

It was at that point Laurent remembered he had something. He took out his wallet and opened it up. Inside was a carefully folded piece of glossy paper. He handed it to Andrea. "Will this do?"

Andrea raised her eyebrows; she could almost feel her heart stop as she looked at the photograph. She handed it over to DI Jeffordson who looked at it. In front of him was a handsome man with his arm around a petite lady in a black ball gown. He read the article...

***

LONDON EVENING STANDARD

6th August 1993

<u>CATEY AWARDS</u>

The prestigious catering award ceremony was held at The Ritz, London. Attended by some of the country's most outstanding restaurateurs.

The guests arrived to red-carpet treatment and a formal champagne reception. This had the makings of a Hollywood event, with guests arriving in luxury cars and ladies in long evening gowns.

WINNING CATEGORIES

RESTURANT MANAGER / MAITRE 'D - LAURENT ROSELLE - LONDON CADEAU HOTELS

Mr Laurent Roselle winner of restaurant manager of the year, accompanied by Miss Eve McDonnell.

***

"That's Eve and me at the Ritz last year. Look at the date. Look at her," he pointed angrily. "This is my Eve!"

"6th August 1993, it's the day before the IRA bomb. I was caught in the blast and none of us could find Eve. The last person we know she was with was Fabian. Don't you see? Have you asked him about her?"

Mike held up a hand. "She does bear a likeness to Aline," Mike commented.

Laurent was exhausted by the whole charade. "Fabian is at the bottom of all of this," he seethed.

"Ah yes, Fabian. Exactly what's your connection with him?"

"He was my best friend," he replied. "We worked together at The Cadeau Hotel; we came over from France and lived together in the flat in Kensington. But now I've discovered he's a liar and a cheat and he's mixed up in this somehow."

"This is Fabian Lambert you're referring to?" Mike questioned.

"Yes. I told you it is."

"Thank you, Mr Roselle. I'm inclined to think you may be telling the truth. I think we need to arrange for you to see our mystery young woman as soon as possible."

"Please can you tell me where she is?"

"She's safe. She's in a secure hospital ward at the Maudsley. We'll phone the hospital and see if we can go over there."

"What is the Maudsley?"

Mike looked at Laurent gravely. He touched Laurent's blazer. "It's a psychiatric hospital."

Laurent felt upset that she'd been admitted to a hospital for people with mental health problems. "Why is she there?"

"I'm afraid she's very ill. That's why this investigation has been so difficult." He took him by the shoulder.

"Please, drink your coffee and make yourself at home. We'll phone the ward and then one of us will take you over there. But be prepared. It might not be her."

"Thank you, thank you so much! I know it's her," he said.

Mike left the interview room and found a phone in the office next door.

"Hello there, Stuart. It's DI Jeffordson from Brixton Nick. Is Doctor Dhillon about at all? Can I have a quick word?"

"Aye, she's just with Aline."

"Brilliant, that's who I'd like to have a chat about."

"I thought you might. If you can hold the line, I'll go and get her."

Mike waited, and could hear the noise coming from the ward. He caught the sound of music and singing, then the footsteps of a woman in heels.

"Dr Dhillon, is it convenient to come to the ward for a visit?"

"Of course, DI Jeffordson, you only need to ask."

"I have some new information on the girl."

"Oh?"

"Yes, I have a gentleman here who needs to see Aline. He doesn't think that's her name. He says she's..."

But before he could reply she finished his answer.

"Eve McDonnell."

"You know?"

"I had my suspicions."

"You did?" Was he the only one who didn't see it?

"How did you find out?" she asked him.

"There is a young man here called Laurent Roselle, he says that she is Eve."

"Is he coming to see her?"

"Yes, he is very keen to see her as soon as possible."

"Okay, give us an hour, will you? Bring Mr Roselle straight in to see me first. I would hate it for him to be wrong. I wouldn't want to upset Aline unnecessarily."

"Not a problem, see you in one hour."

CHAPTER 57

RENDEZVOUS

Footsteps could be heard as they walked down the long cream corridor to Florence Green Ward, the heavy wooden doors swung opened as the two men entered the old nightingale ward. The taller man surveyed the area, frowning. He looked down at the older gentleman stroking his bushy moustache. Mike looked up and gave him a reassuring smile.

"It's gonna be alright, lad." He took his arm. Laurent grimaced.

"This way." Said Mike, directing him towards the office. A petite Asian woman sat at her desk typing up her notes in the large scruffy room. As soon as the men entered the room, she rose from her seat.

"This is doctor Dr Dhillon who has been looking after your friend" he indicated to the doctor. "Dr Dhillon, this is Laurent Roselle."

"Please take a seat Mr Roselle."

The small women sat back down, sweeping the sari over her shoulder. She smiled, extending her hand as she did so "Nice to meet you. How can I help"

"Dr Dhillon, this is the gentleman I was telling you about on the phone. Laurent Roselle. He came to the station this morning, to discuss the young lady who was found on the bench."

"Welcome Mr Roselle, I'm Dr Dhillon, the consultant psychiatrist looking after your friend." Dr Dhillon continued. "Detective Inspector Jeffordson has informed me that you can positively identify this lady, is that right?"

"For sure," Laurent replied. "This is Eve McDonnell. I can assure you; you've got it all wrong. This is not Aline."

"So, you are certain that this is not Aline Deniaud, the French midwife?" She challenged.

"This is definitely Eve. I have no doubt."

"Show her the photograph" Mike suggested.

"Photograph?" She frowned, looking from Mike to Laurent.

Laurent reached inside his blazer pocket and took out the photograph from his leather wallet. "Here" he said, as her passed the picture of Eve and himself across the table.

Dr Dhillon bought her hand to her chest "Oh my!" She raised her eyebrows, looking up at Laurent and Mike. "It truly is her, it's Eve McDonnell."

"Yes, that is what I have been trying to tell you!"

Dr Dhillon took a deep breath and smiled. "I've had my suspicions for quite some time that we had a mistaken identity. But it wasn't until I read through the notes from the counsellor in Reading that I truly believed that this was, in fact, Eve McDonnell." Dr Dhillon continued.

"You did?" Mike rubbed his forehead, "Why didn't you tell me?"

"I've been working on a strategy to help her realise her true identity, but now that you've arrived, I think we can progress quite swiftly. You see, I recognised one of the accounts of Eve and Aline in the counsellor's notes."

Laurent frowned. "Aline? Yes, I believe she had a friend called Aline in Reading, she made Eve's life a misery. She was always stressing about this Aline."

"Did you ever meet her?"

"No, I never met her. But I heard a lot about her, as I told the Inspector."

Mike Jeffordson nodded.

"What did Eve tell you about Aline?"

"Well, they met at school. They were friends at first and then it all went sour. Then Eve saw Aline again during her training and she turned up again in Reading where they worked as midwives."

"But you never met her?" asked Dr Dhillon. "Do you know where Aline trained or where she came from? Anything like that?"

"No," he said. "Why are you asking me so much about this Aline? This is Eve. She is who I care about."

Dr Dhillon adjusted her position and looked directly at Laurent. So, this was Laurent back from the dead.

"Laurent, Inspector..." she put her hands on her lap and paused. "There is no easy way of telling you this. I do believe you're right that this is indeed Eve. The evidence indicates that she has Dissociative Identity Disorder. This would have originated from a childhood trauma and then more recent triggers would have then made her become unwell."

"A trigger?" Laurent questioned.

"Yes Laurent, what could have been the trigger, do you think?"

"Apart from her believing that I was killed in a bomb?!" He exclaimed.

Dr Dhillon took a sharp intake of breath, "Yes that would do it." Her hands trembled very slightly. "Believing that your boyfriend had been killed would've certainly been enough to bring this on. She couldn't cope with her grief and mind shut off to Eve and became Aline."

"You mean Eve has a split personality?" asked Laurent, his face grew pale. "I don't understand this. I feel so upset that this has happened to her. I never expected any of this."

"No of course not," said the doctor. "Tell me, was Eve a happy person when you met her?"

"Yes. Okay, she was often stressed, but she had a difficult job. We had great times together...we were both very happy."

"How long were you together before you separated?"

"Separate? We didn't separate! You must understand. I was injured and taken back to France. I told Fabian to tell Eve, I wanted to her come to me. But he lied to her, to both of us!"

"I'm sorry. That didn't come out as I intended." said Dr Dhillon, apologetically.

"Let me rephrase the question. How long have you been apart?"

"About six months. I was in hospital in Lyon for four months, and then I went home to my family to recover. But we were together for over a year. We hoped to get married and go back to France together." Laurent paused and looked down. "I still hope that."

"You had no inkling she was unwell?"

"No, none at all. Obviously, she would get upset about stuff. But then who doesn't? We'd talk. It's what couples do."

"Did you know that Eve was seeing a counsellor?" Dr Dhillon.

"No, no I didn't."

Dr Dhillon looked at Mike Jeffordson and then back at Laurent. The psychiatrist looked nervous, biting her lip. She looked at them over her glasses, then took them off and placed them on her desk.

"Please forgive me DI Jeffordson, but I have something of a confession."

They all looked at her, waiting, confused.

"I'm sorry, but I don't understand," said Laurent.

"Go on, Dr Dhillon," said Mike.

"I thought Aline seemed familiar to me, the first day I met her..."

She paused, took a deep breath; pushing the papers around on the desk and looking incredibly awkward. "It wasn't until I saw Simon Thomas' notes that I remembered her name was really Eve."

"What!?" Mike looked at Dr Dhillon with complete shock.

He shook his head. "I didn't see that coming, that's for sure."

"I'm sorry," she said, holding up her hand, stopping DI Jeffordson going off into a rant.

Clearly trying to hold herself together., she continued.

"You see, Eve McDonnell and I were at school together. I thought I recognised her on the trauma ward, but I couldn't be sure. Then when I studied the accounts of Eve's therapy sessions with Simon Thomas, I was almost certain it must be the same girl. Eve and I studied French at primary school. She was given the name Aline as it meant "Little Eve". Eve had had a miserable childhood – she had a very dominant, bigoted father and her mother was emotionally abused by him. I didn't think he had hurt Eve until I read the notes. Eve was a very intelligent girl, but she'd nowhere to go with the emotional abuse she suffered back then. It wasn't long before I worked that out. From as far back as her schooldays, Eve has taken on the persona of Aline and dumped her pain into Aline's lap."

"So, I can see where the name Aline came from," said Mike. "But what about her surname?"

"It's quite simple. Deniaud is French for..."

"McDonnell" Laurent finished her sentence, looking from Mike to Dr Dhillion.

There was a pause. "So Daniels...is English for McDonnell" Mike took a deep breath "hence Mary Blooming Daniels...!" Mike scratched his head in frustration, "Oh my God, she's stitched us up like a kipper."

"Mary Daniels?" Laurent looked confused he rubbed his beard.

"Another name she used in the past Laurent, not another personality" Laurent looked relieved.

"So it's safe to conclude that Aline is Eve and Eve is Aline?" Mike questioned.

"Yes it is. Although Aline remembered some things, she didn't remember being Eve. I had no way of proving it until Laurent walked through the door, ready to testify that this was Eve," she told Laurent. "I hadn't had contact with Eve since I left primary school. We had both changed of course. I got married. Eve would have known me as Sunita Gill. But she didn't recognise me at all. With my change of name and the role her doctor is so far removed from our childhood friendship as it possibly could have been. It simply would have been too big a leap to make the connection. Particularly for someone who is unwell."

"So, when did Aline take over?" asked Mike.

"No one can know for sure but I would surmise that it would've been soon after the bombing. Aline was always lurking in her psyche. I suspect that when she received the news of Laurent's death, it would have been enough for Aline to totally suppress Eve. We also know that Eve took an overdose, but she was found in time."

Laurent hands went to his head, and he let out a groan of pain.

"From her mind's point of view," the doctor continued, "it was her way of killing Eve. With Eve gone, Aline took over completely and that's when she first appeared in London at Whipps Cross Hospital. She became Aline in her entirety, the dark hair, the French accent. The whole Aline persona. She had a whole new identity. But her life didn't improve. Things just went from bad to worse."

"So, just to clarify then, doc," Mike butted in. "Eve was unable to cope and her mental illness took over and she became Aline. Eve didn't exist anymore. She was suppressed and Aline became a walking, talking persona of someone who was previously just in her mind. No wonder we couldn't find any record of her!"

"Oh God, I had no idea this was going on!" Laurent was stunned.

"You wouldn't, Eve clearly loved you very much and was deeply traumatised by your death. She was unable to cope... so Aline took over. Eve herself would have been unaware that this was happening."

Laurent rocked in his chair back and forth holding onto himself. "This is so, so awful." His tears welled up. "I can't understand why it wasn't obvious when she was with me."

"Because Eve felt loved and secure with you, Laurent. So, you would never have seen Aline." This made his bottom lip quiver and a solitary tear rolled down his face.

Dr Dhillon got up from her chair and rested her hand on the Frenchman's shoulder and handed him a tissue. "She will get better, Laurent. With time and with your love and patience, she will get there."

"You think so?"

"I know so...it's a rare condition but she will be fine with the correct help. She's been through a lot. We know that there was trauma growing up, plus some pretty traumatic incidents at work. More recently, alcohol, drugs, and sexual abuse. Plus, we now know she was grieving the loss of her partner. You were the missing piece of the puzzle...we knew something major had happened but we didn't know what."

Laurent looked at Dr Dhillon, confused. "I'm sorry, what did you say? Alcohol, drugs and sexual abuse? Are you sure?"

"Yes, I'm sorry." said Mike Jeffordson. "She had high levels of drugs and alcohol in her system."

Laurent shook his head, blinking rapidly. "And sexual abuse?"

"Yes," said the doctor. "There were several bite marks and scars on her back."

"No! That's not possible. Why would she have marks on her? Who would do that to her?" he gulped. "I thought... it said in the newspaper that she had a head injury."

"That's right, she did. The other injuries were older," said Mike. "We think it was the dealer she knew."

"She's started giving accounts of the abuse she has suffered in our therapy sessions," said the doctor.

Heat rose within Laurent. With a sinking heart he realised he knew exactly who had done this to Eve. "Oh my God...this is simply awful."

"She has been through a lot."

Laurent took a deep breath, the anger inside him raging. He was so relieved to have found her. But to discover now that she'd been sexually abused made him feel sick! He could see now, how Fabian had completely manipulated the situation for his own gain. All the pieces of the puzzle were now falling into place. "This was Fabian. I know it's him who abused her! He told her I was dead. I couldn't work out why at first but now I understand." Mike looked from Dr Dhillion and then back to Laurent.

"Go on."

"He wanted her. He really wanted her. It was Fabian who watched her becoming ill Fabian was the only one that knew, Eve was becoming Aline as her illness progressed. It was him who took advantage of her vulnerability. The worse she was, the more he abused her. Oh my God, when I get my hands on him, I'll kill him!"

"Laurent, please calm yourself," the doctor said. "I think this is a matter for the police, you really don't want to sort this out yourself. Eve needs you here. Not in prison."

"Yes, Laurent," said Mike. "You don't have to worry. We're dealing with him as we speak. He's in custody and won't be getting out anytime soon. The charges against him are piling up by the day."

Laurent tried to calm down, but his whole body shook with rage. "Okay., okay. I know you're both right."

"Don't you worry about him. You need to concentrate on helping Eve get better. I'll keep you updated on what we're doing with Fabian," said Mike.

"So, what now ?" Laurent asked

***

Dr Dhillon closed her notes and folded her hands. All eyes were now on her. Dr Dhillon paused for a moment and smiled.

"It's time to go and see Eve, Laurent, what do you think?" Dr Dhillon got out of her chair, and held his shoulder "Come, come with me."

"What…. today…right now?" His eyes opened wide.

"Yes, now. But remember Laurent, initially you will be meeting Aline, and she's not aware that she's Eve. Does that sound too daunting?"

Laurent rose out of his seat tentatively. "That sounds fine. I'll be careful". He followed Dr Dhillon out of her office "Stuart" she called. A sandy haired man in a black t-shirt and stonewashed jeans got up from the sofa and walked over to where the three of them were standing.

"Stuart, Laurent is here to see Aline. Could you tell her that she has a visitor?"

"Goodness, her first visitor. How nice."

***

Stuart approached Aline. She was sitting with her CD player on. He could see that she was looking sad and wistful, her face pale. She was distant, her thoughts elsewhere.

Stuart touched her shoulder. "Aline, sorry to disturb you." She looked up and saw Stuart standing in front of her. She hadn't heard him approach.

"Aline, there's someone here to see you."

She couldn't hear him, so she took out her earphones.

"I'm sorry...?" She sniffed, wiping her nose with the back of her hand "I was a little distracted".

He smiled "It's okay Aline, was it a sad song?"

"Yes, yes it was. It gets me every time."

Stuart smiled. "There's someone here to see you."

She looked up.

"Who?"

"The Inspector has brought someone you might know," he said, nodding his head in the direction of a tall, handsome man with a well groomed beard and floppy dark hair.

She stared at the visitor for a moment then turned back to Stuart. "I don't know who he is, Stuart," she whispered behind her hand.

"He says he knows you, Aline," he said quietly.

"Does he?" Aline racked her brain...But it was as though it had been in a washing machine on a spin cycle and now everything was muddled and jumbled and she simply couldn't sort it out.

"Perhaps he knows what happened to me?" she suggested, feeling anxious, yet hopeful.

"Yes, perhaps he does."

Stuart gestured to Laurent to come over. He walked calmly to where they were sitting. He was graceful in the way he moved, his long legs striding out in dark jeans and expensive-looking ox-blood shoes. He quietly sat next to Aline and looked at her with his dark cognac eyes. When she showed no sign of recognising him, he looked down at the CD player in her hands.

"What are you listening to?"

"Oh, just some songs that I love. Lots of different ones, but this one is my favourite."

"What is it?"

"*Could it be Magic...*It reminds me of a happier time. But I don't know what or when it was." She looked up at his face and into his warm dark eyes. There was something special about him. She just knew it. Her face softened, the anxious lines relaxed, and her eyes danced as she looked him up and down.

"The original, or Take That?" His hand touched hers as he looked at the CD player.

"Take That...I think..." She looked again into his warm eyes. There was something about him.

"Aline, I'm Laurent Roselle, do you remember me?" he said, gently taking her hands.

She looked him up and down.

"No, no, no! Laurent Roselle is dead! It's not possible."

"No, I'm not dead."

"But you were killed by the bomb."

"No, I survived. I've been recovering in France."

"Why? How?"

"Do you remember? I was burnt. I've been in hospital; they have been looking after me."

"No! My Laurent died in hospital. His parents wouldn't let me see him after he had a cardiac arrest. I wasn't even allowed to go to his funeral." She grabbed her chest and took a sharp intake of breath, her eyes widened.

Laurent's expression changed as he saw her response. He took her hands appealing to her, "That's because there was no funeral! I'm so sorry, but Fabian lied to you."

She sat, stunned, her mind whirling. "Laurent, is it really you"

"Yes Eve, it is."

She took her hand, and touched his face, feeling the scars on his neck. Her fingers trembled.

"Is it really you? Are you really here? Or have I finally gone completely insane?"

He kissed her hand. "Yes, I'm really here, my petit chou."

As soon as he said this, tears surfaced, flooding her eyelashes. She knew it was him; no one had ever called her that before or since.

"Do you know why you are here?" he asked.

"No, I don't know. They said someone attacked me, but I can't remember who it was."

"Do you remember that you are called Eve, not Aline?"

She looked alarmed. "Am I really Eve? They said that I was Aline. I thought Eve was my enemy."

Stuart sat with them slightly apart, quietly looking from one to another; unable to hear what was going on. They were all anxious about this meeting between the two of them.

"So, you do know each other?" he asked.

"Yes," said Laurent. "We know each other very well. I'm Laurent Roselle, her boyfriend. She is Eve McDonnell." He brought her hands to his mouth and kissed them.

"Goodness!" Stuart sat in stunned silence. "So, this is not Aline."

"No, she most certainly is not," said Laurent, "this is my dearest Eve."

Mike and Dr Dhillon, who had been watching from the doorway, nodded to Stuart, who nodded back to them. "I think it's time for a tea, don't you?" DI Jeffordson and Dr Sunita Dhillon left the room. They entered the small staff kitchen. Dr Dhillon filled up the kettle from the cold water tap. Mike watched her, flummoxed by what had just happened.

"So, Aline is Eve," he muttered in disbelief. "You didn't think to tell me?"

"No, I'm sorry, but I couldn't. Not until I was absolutely sure. I was completely shocked seeing the references to me in Simon Thomas' notes. I just wasn't certain that it was really her and not this mysterious Aline. It's been a very long time since I last saw Eve," she replied, switching the kettle on and getting the coffee and cups out.

"I suppose so, but you could have told me."

"Yes, I could have." She looked up. "But I didn't think it would help my patient. So, I'm sorry, but..." She shrugged.

"So, do we know what happened to her on New Year's Eve?"

"Who knows? Aline thought Eve had attacked her. But her injuries weren't self-inflicted. Judging by what we know of her relationship with Fabian, we know that he is the likely culprit, but whether Eve will ever remember, I have no idea."

"Will we ever know?"

"I doubt it. People with DID or multiple personality disorder as you would know it, often lose a sense of time. They have periods of amnesia and aren't always able to recall events. I suspect she was operating as both Aline and Eve on the wards as a midwife, hence the confusion with the drugs. I don't believe Eve took them for personal use, but I believe that Eve was signing for them in both identities. It has been done before; it can happen again. The rest, we may never know."

"But surely the staff would have noticed."

"You would have thought so, but with the frequent use of agency and bank staff, it's very hard to keep up with the turnaround of personnel."

"But what about Whipps Cross, Sister Oliver was convinced she was a French Midwife."

Dr Dhillon sighed. "I know it's odd, but you know, it is not unheard of, to have bogus nurses." She paused. "Well she wasn't bogus, just had the wrong identity. Well it doesn't matter who she was at the time. All we know is that she was a poor young lady who has had an awful time. But who hopefully now, will be on the road to recovery. Helped in no small part, by the return of Laurent."

"None of us were expecting that!"

"No, I really thought that Laurent has been killed."

"Didn't we all...Well Doc, this has certainly turned out to be quite a twisted thread!"

"It has indeed, I am glad that we've unravelled it at last."

***

In the patients' lounge Eve had wrapped her herself around Laurent, her arm tucked in his black blazer. She snuggled her nose into his neck. The smell was so familiar; it triggered something inside, deep inside her memories. She opened her eyes and looked up into his face.

"Laurent!" she whispered.

"Yes... It's me."

"It really is you?"

"It is, mon petit chou." He stroked her hair softly, smoothing it from her heart shaped face.

"I can't believe that you're really here. You're alive!"

He smiled and his warm eyes twinkled, as he looked at her with so much love. Her expression suddenly changed, as though a black cloud had descended upon her. She gripped her chest and looked at him with great apologetic eyes.

"Oh Evie, my darling," he kissed her hair. "What is it?" He wiped away her tears with gentle fingers.

"I'm so, so sorry," she told him. "I've done so many bad things."

"What have you done?" he asked his expression gentle.

Her body shuddered as she looked at him. "I'm afraid you'll be angry with me when you know what I've done."

He shook his head. "No. I will never be angry with you. Not about this."

"I thought you were dead," she said, remembering her despair and becoming real again. "Aline made me do it, do you understand? The pain was so huge, I had to get rid of it, I couldn't bear it. Please, don't be angry with me, Laurent!"

She looked into his eyes longingly. He knew what she was going to tell him. But he couldn't feel angry with her, she'd been taken advantage of whilst she was vulnerable.

"It's okay, my love." He kissed her tenderly.

"But..." she pulled away from him. "I've been with Fabian," she blurted out. "Not once, many times!" She wailed in pain. "I swear, I've never been unfaithful in my life before, I would never have done that to you, but that's exactly what I did, isn't it? How could I do that? Laurent, you're my soul mate. What I've done is unforgiveable. How can you love me now in all this brokenness? I'm no better than a whore!"

"No Eve, don't torture yourself mon petit chou. It's okay, I know what happened now, Eve." He held her hands, looking her directly in the face. "I understand. Honestly, it wasn't your fault. I know that."

"Please forgive me."

"Eve, there's nothing to forgive."

"But..."

He put his finger onto her lips. "Shhhh," he soothed.

Eve dropped her eyes, feeling ashamed by all that had happened. How could this man still love her? She was unlovable.

Laurent sat with Eve in his arms and started to sing to her gently, a song he knew she'd remember. He sang softly and tentatively, his rich French voice slow and out of tune, encouraging her to look at him. He stopped singing and stroked her hair and ran his fingers over her face.

"Eve, do you remember when we went to The Ritz? You looked so beautiful in your dress." He curled his fingers in her hair, creating ringlets. "We danced together the whole evening. Do you remember?"

She frowned. "A little."

He put his hand inside his jacket pocket and pulled out his black leather wallet. He slipped his fingers in and took out a photograph he'd shown the police and Dr Dhillon.

Eve looked down and she saw the image of herself with this handsome man in his black tie.

"It's you and me," she smiled.

"Yes. It is you and me. Do you remember that night, when we danced at The Ritz?"

"We sat with your friends," she whispered.

"We did. And we drank wine and ate."

"We did?" she asked. "I can't remember it all."

Laurent lifted her to her feet. "You're a great dancer, you know," he smiled.

"I am?" She was surprised.

"Yes. Come with me," he said as he encircled her waist. She wrapped her arms around his neck and looked into his face as he started to sing to her again, this time very gently, like a mother singing a lullaby. It was the song they danced to at the Ritz, *Could It Be Magic*. The words struck a chord in him like never before.

Laurent could feel emotion rising inside and he held her closer. His body shuddered as he buried his face into her shoulder.

"Evie," he sobbed. "Oh, my petit Chou?"

It was the song she'd chosen on the CD. Eve hadn't understood why this song had resonated with her. Now she knew, it was their song. The tears started to pour down her face. They were running into her mouth, and Eve took huge gulps of air trying to surface from the pain. They clung onto each other, both weeping. It had been such an arduous journey for them both.

"Oh, Eve!"

"Laurent!" Her eyes widened and her face softened as she realised that he really wasn't angry with her. He loved her no matter what. "It's really you, isn't it?" She held his face in her hands, stroking his beard. "You didn't have this before." She chuckled through her tears; her hands touched his hair which was now longer than she remembered. "Or this... it suits you."

"No, no I didn't, it's true. I'm sorry; I didn't think to get rid of it," he laughed. "But it really is me, a bit scarred, but still me."

"I'm so glad you're back."

"I'm so glad I found you." Laurent leant forward and holding her tightly in his arms.

"Laurent, my Laurent," she said ignoring the tears still rolling down her face. "You're home. You've come to save me."

"I have, and I'm never going away again."

He wrapped her in his arms, singing quietly to her as they slowed danced in the dreary hospital lounge. But to them it could have been The Ritz as the joy in their hearts filled their souls. Love. There was no other word for it. It had won in the face of adversity. Love had conquered all.

LOVE

*Love is patient and kind; it is not
jealous or conceited or proud;*

*Love is not ill-mannered or selfish or irritable;
love does not keep a record of wrongs;*

*Love is not happy with evil, but
is happy with the truth.*

*Love never gives up; and its faith,
hope, and patience never fail.*

Love is eternal.

1 Corinthians 13